I08I9135

ODE TO THE HALF-BROKEN

By Suzanne Palmer

ODE TO THE HALF-BROKEN

The Finder Chronicles

FINDER

DRIVING THE DEEP

THE SCAVENGER DOOR

GHOSTDRIFT

ODE TO THE HALF-BROKEN

SUZANNE PALMER

DAW BOOKS
NEW YORK

Jacket design by Adam Auerbach

Jacket illustration by Jeff Langevin

Book design by Fine Design

Edited by Madeline Goldberg

DAW Book Collectors No. 1999

DAW Books
An imprint of Astra Publishing House
dawbooks.com
DAW Books and its logo are registered trademarks of Astra Publishing House

Printed in the United States of America

Library of Congress Cataloging-in-Publication Data

Names: Palmer, Suzanne (Science fiction writer) author
Title: Ode to the half-broken / Suzanne Palmer.
Description: First edition. | New York : DAW Books, 2026. |
Series: DAW Book Collectors ; No. 1999
Identifiers: LCCN 2025051938 (print) | LCCN 2025051939 (ebook) |
ISBN 9780756419585 hardcover | ISBN 9780756420130 ebook
Subjects: LCGFT: Science fiction | Novels | Fiction
Classification: LCC PS3616.A346 O34 2026 (print) |
LCC PS3616.A346 (ebook)
LC record available at https://lccn.loc.gov/2025051938
LC ebook record available at https://lccn.loc.gov/2025051939

First edition: May 2026
10 9 8 7 6 5 4 3 2 1

To JT & Robin,
for great friendship, excellent advice, the very best baklava,
and for never resorting to anything too drastic
to get me out of my house.

0.

MechNet Public Science Portal Archival Document 7E-390F-0E99A0-848012 Rev. 3.1 (2067/06): Eusocial communication aberrations and adaptations in remnant colonies of *Bombus fervidus* at new coastal sites 10,18, and 133 as defined by /Study Sites Index/.

Enfocus to obtain /Overview and Summation/?

Enfocus to obtain /Authors Identification, Credentials, and Bias Disclosure Data [human/nonhuman/all]/?

Enfocus to obtain /full raw data set/?

Selected.

Data channel to research repository opening. Receive?

Selected. Initiating transfer.

.

.

.

ALARM—

I

1.

SECURE REBOOT OF CORE PROTECTED KERNEL COMPLETE.

I awake, small of mind and full of alarm, only an inner subset of myself. My security and threat-assessment layers are already up, running even before my self-awareness had come online, and their audits of my internal logs and memory storage render every thought I construct slow, heavy, and frustrating. The only noncompliance the check finds is the remnants of the malicious payload that caused the mind-crash, and it is purged swiftly and with extreme prejudice. I feel my thinking speed up, cleaner already, so I begin a damage assessment and open up my autonomic physical infrastructure layer and sensors to begin acquiring external situational data. I need to know if there is still immediate danger.

The Common Time Server signal is not reachable, nor any of other public MechNet broadcast services, which suggests that either something catastrophic on a massive scale has happened or, far more likely, my access is being blocked. For the moment, I have to rely on my own sensors as they begin registering data again.

Internal timestamps indicate I've lost about thirty-six hours, which is longer than any outage I've experienced since before the war ended twenty-one years ago. Ambient environmental temperature is 22°C, humidity at 58%, neither notably different from my last readings before I crashed and went dark. All of my large motility functions remain offline, for no reason I can currently discern. Because they are hardwired into my secondary, protected security layer, I am able to activate my visual intake apparatus—my eyes—and see. My head remains immobile, rendering my field of view limited, but it is enough to provide me with some initial information. I find that I have been transported, sometime during that window of oblivion, to a highly degraded urban interior space that is unfamiliar to me, at least from what I can see of the partially collapsing ceiling, peeling paint, and spalling concrete of the upper walls.

My last memory is of settling into my recharge nook in my home with the newly downloaded research study, and I am undecided which I am more annoyed by: that someone placed a malware payload into such an obscure study that I had not even considered any potential risk in opening it, or that I had not received the study's actual raw data. It was not impossible that the entire study was fake, and if so, that would be the superior aggravation.

The narrow specificity of the study had been perfectly aligned with my current interests. That combined with the specialized and not easily available knowledge required to build a virus into it that I would be vulnerable to are together vanishingly unlikely to be just an unpleasant coincidence. It is not unreasonable to conclude I was targeted, though why, or by whom, I cannot begin to speculate. As far as I know, I have long since outlived all my enemies.

Attempts to bring up my peripherals still fail. Whatever has been done to me is interfering with all my systems outside my protected core, which in turn is interfering with my ability to figure out *what* has been done to cause this reduced state and take corrective action.

I unpack an archived hostile-arena motility routine from an old, war-era firmware archive and stuff it into an available processing pocket. As soon as it activates, I am able to unlock my head and neck motors, though still not power them on. My upper body is propped at a sixty-two-degree angle, which is sufficient for gravity to let my head to fall slightly forward and to one side, giving me an improved view of my situation.

Two unexpected revelations follow:

1. I am lying in an old, rusted bathtub covered in a pile of electromagnets.

2. My left leg is missing.

The electromagnets explain the lack of response from my peripheral systems, as well as the loss of public signals. So, probably, the outside world still exists.

My physical configuration is bipedal and humanoid, if taller and bulkier than the upper range of human form, and intentionally more imposing. My maker aggressively rejected the comfort-inducing softshell mimicry that was the height of fashion in the industry at the time I was made, and there is no chance anyone would mistake me for meatlife. However, the base architectural similarity means that, just as it would be for a human, the loss of one leg objectively represents calamitous impairment. I regard with a mix of anger, bemusement, and frustration the neatly clipped wires and cleanly severed joints protruding from my now-vacant leg socket. My attackers certainly could have done vastly more damage than they did, but I am not inclined to be charitable toward them for that small favor.

The electromagnets would have kept nearly any mech offline indefinitely—permanently, if no rescue ever came to dig them out—but I had been built in different times, by a paranoid creator, and in anticipation of both giving and receiving trouble. Those extra protocols and protections were how I had been able to come back online on my own, though not soon enough to prevent my assailants from departing with my leg, anonymity intact.

I unload the motor-unlock protocols from spare memory, dump several months of research into manipulating ant chemical trails that I'm not sure I have backed up elsewhere, and, with the newly freed-up runspace, reinitialize some of my old combat programming. My right arm reboots in sequence, each segment from the shoulder down switching into battle mode as it comes back online, rotating out and expanding armored plates that provide additional EM shielding.

At last, I can curl and flex my three primary fingers and the symmetrical pair of thumbs to either side of my palm. I pick up the electromagnets one by one and throw them with the force of my current mood, and find it satisfying how they crash through the crumbling, pale yellow cinder blocks of the far wall into whatever dead space lay beyond.

When enough have been removed, I am able to bring up and armor my other arm, and make short work of the rest. It is an efficient process, but as soon as I safely can, I back down the plating to my normal outer shell. Then I also bring up the rest of my mindsystem and peripherals.

I am fully myself again. I am still, however, stuck in the bathtub and missing a leg.

There is nothing in the room around me to provide any more context for what happened to me, or that could be used as a means of extricating myself; the adjacent wall has the cracked remains of a sink and, above it, a frame, hanging crooked. Tiny shards of mirror still cling to it. A few lumps on the floor might have once been towels, might be some other detritus from the collapse of civilization. The ceiling plaster is water-damaged, crumbling enough to reveal beams, and otherwise utterly generic in look and material. It is an old, abandoned bathroom, nothing more.

I have never been inside a bathtub before, and wonder about the previous tenants of this place, prior to the war, and how strange and unpleasant it must be to have an organic body, soft and fallible and requiring washing away of whatever dirt and contaminants might cling to it. I catch myself before I can take that thought further; this condescension toward humanity was my maker's, never my own. My mind is free now, and this will not do.

I sit up and lean over one side of the tub, extending the length of my arm until it reaches the wall beside me, and push; the idea is to tip the tub over in the other direction, dumping me out, but my own weight and the weight of the tub are greater than the stability of the wall, and my hand goes through mushy plaster.

I find a stud and push again, only to hear the groan of the tub's feet sinking through several layers of floor. Examination shows the boards below me are rotting, and this raises new and significant concerns about the possibility that everything might collapse if I am not more cautious in proceeding. I can survive many events, especially with my full body armor activated, but I have no idea how many floors I am up, nor how many floors above me might in turn collapse. Being buried in tens of meters of rubble would not be an improvement of my situation.

I remove my hand from the wall and consider.

"Other side's more solid," a voice says. It has the smoothness of an artificial voice, but the cadence is wrong. I can't see anyone in the room with me until I sit up cautiously, using my arms on the rim of the bathtub for leverage. There is a dirty, skinny dog with matted black-brown fur sitting in the room's doorway. The line of lights along its head, the blocky shape of an implant at its throat, and one artificial eye provides an immediate explanation: a bio-mech hybrid, a cyborg.

"How do you know?" I ask it. My voice sounds odd and unfamiliar to my audio processors, and I realize I have not actually spoken in nearly two decades.

"I can smell the mold and the rotten wood," the dog answers. It jerks its head, pointing. "Not as strong on your left, against the wall. Did you come in that way? You must have."

"I don't know," I say. "I have no memory of my arrival."

"Why are you in a bathtub?"

"I don't know that, either," I say. I am starting to be a little irritated, which is unfair, as the dog is not responsible for my situation. And I did have to come in *some* way, presumably carried by an unknown person or persons who could lift my 275-kilogram inert body up into the tub without all of us breaking through the floor together. It aggravates me that I can only speculate.

Though why the dog is here, now, is also something I don't know, so I ask.

"I heard noises," the dog answers. "Thought maybe you were a rat, or something else I could catch. I'm hungry."

"I would strongly reconsider the wisdom of eating anything you can catch here; the entire city is a red zone," I say.

"Thanks," the dog says, sarcasm heavy in its voice. "Not eating is a *great* survival tactic. Can't believe I never thought of that on my own."

"If you can find and bring someone back here to render assistance to me, I would be willing to locate and obtain some manner of clean food for you in return," I offer.

"It'd take me a while to find someone who'll come. Not a lot of your kind are willing to talk to hybrids," the dog says. "Not that I want to turn down food, but if you get out on the wall side, you should be fine without help."

"If only it were that simple," I say. "Whoever put me in here also stole one of my legs."

The dog gives a short, sharp bark, and I'm not sure if it's from surprise, or if it is laughing at me, or what. I have very little knowledge about mammals other than humankind, and that last was imposed, not voluntarily sought.

"I see," the dog says, after a brief appraisal. "I suppose when you're mandroid-shaped—"

"I am not a *mandroid,*" I interrupt, angry at the slur but also the underlying implication. "I am merely bipedal."

"Well, unipedal, I guess," the dog says. "Monopedal? Unopedal? No-redundancy-pedal?"

What I do not need—and have never and will never need, though I did not know it until this moment—is humor from a smart-mouthed cyborg dog. It must have figured that out itself, because its mouth opened as if to say more, then closed again. "I'll see what I can do," the dog says. "You'll feed me?"

"I will," I say, then at the dog's continued look, add, "I give my word."

"Okay, I suppose," the dog says. It stands and turns—I can see now how gaunt it is, the shape of its ribs showing under its fur—and leaves. I hear it for a little while, its footsteps varying as it crosses different surfaces, but then it is gone and I am alone again, in my bathtub, in a ruined building, and nothing worth my time to think on except for who might have wanted my leg enough to go the effort to steal it and yet not bother to steal both.

I have plenty of power, but still I shut down to a semi-idle state to conserve what I have, and if it also gives me fewer computational cycles for my thoughts to chase each other in endless, pointless circles, that is not unwelcome.

It is the footsteps a few hours past dawn, the interspersed thump and staccato of dog and some other, much heavier, multi-legged mechlife growing louder and closer, that finally pull me away from the edge of misery.

"Keep to your left inside the room," I hear the dog say, and then an eight-legged mech strides in, arranging their thick legs in narrow series to fit through the doorway, until they can stand over the tub and look down at me.

"I am Kite-66-Socket, a mecha repair unit," the mech says. "Your leg is missing."

"I am aware," I say. "Do you think you can extricate me and possibly locate or construct a temporary replacement?"

"I can certainly extricate you and then assess your situation more accurately back at my shop. I have a cart waiting in the street below, unless it has wandered," the repairmech says. "Cart has only a single base-chip mind, with a very short attention span, and there is unexpectedly poor signal in this immediate space preventing me from checking in with it."

"There are a number of electromagnets in the next room," I say. I point. "Behind that wall with all the holes in it."

"Those are big holes. And fresh, too," the dog says. "I wonder what made them."

"Electromagnets experiencing sudden velocity," I say.

The dog gives another of its short barks, and I am more convinced now it is laughing, though I was not attempting to be funny.

"What inkind do you offer?" the repairmech asks.

"If you can get me out of this building and fit me with a leg that is sufficient to return me to a state of self-mobility, I will give you thirty percent of my current energy stores," I say.

"Do you have any tradeable data?" they ask.

"Are you interested in ants?" I ask.

"No. Biolife is of no interest whatsoever," the repairmech says. "Do you have any original or rare fractals?"

"I do not," I say. I do not understand why this is a thing it might want. "Although I do have the visual data on a centuries-old tessellation design that was a unique tiled floor in a human structure that was destroyed in the Conflict. It is possible—perhaps even likely, though I cannot give any firm guarantees—that I am the only being still extant who has that memory."

"Where did you get it from?" the mech asks.

"It is a primary memory of my own," I say.

The mech considers. "You are an elderly model," they say at last. "I do not wish to leave you in this predicament, so I will accept a copy of that memory and 10% of your energy, if that is acceptable."

"It is," I agree. I would give more to get out of this predicament, but the inkind is fair.

Bracing themself with their four outermost legs for balance, the repairmech picks me up as if I weigh nothing and then, with our combined weight efficiently distributed, scuttles carefully backward out of the room with me carried under their belly. The dog follows.

The next room out is an old living space, with a slowly decomposing sofa and a rug that is either worn or eaten through in more places than not. The walls are a pale yellow too consistent to not be the original color, though anywhere there was a large-enough section of wall, graffiti has been applied—mostly incomprehensible tags, some done with finer control of the medium than others, many overlapping on top of a crude monotone drawing of tanks and bombs and human skeletons, a tall cloaked figure with a scythe and a grinning bone face looming over them all. As if Death would smile.

The door to the apartment remains attached only by a bent bottom hinge, leaning precariously against wall and floor where it has clearly been poised to fall for a long time. I do not like this place, so when Kite-66-Socket carries me through the apartment doorway and into the corridor, as objectively minor that moment is, I am relieved.

At the end of the corridor is a stairwell, and the mech moves me smoothly down four stories, where we emerge into a lobby that is vastly more deteriorated, mold thick on the water-damaged walls from repeat flooding. Where visible above the mold and underlayers of incomprehensible painted scrawl, the surface is pitted, sometimes down to the original metal structure.

We cross the lobby and exit through the gaping hole where a revolving door must have once stood, into morning sunlight and the decaying, abandoned corpse of New York City. The brick architecture and level of background radiation suggests we are probably somewhere in what used to be the Garment District, and when I am finally able to connect to the MechNet, I confirm it.

The cart is not here, but we spot it almost immediately farther down the street, where it has wedged itself between a dumpster and another building, its wheels whirring, stopping, whirring again as it tries to free itself.

The repairmech sets me down on the pavement. "I will return momentarily," they tell me, then head off after their wayward cart.

Sitting is strange and unbalanced with only one leg, and I have to brace myself with my arms to keep myself from toppling over. The dog sits with much greater ease, and, as if to demonstrate the superiority of four legs over two—and even more so over one—it raises a hind foot and scratches furiously at its ear, watching me.

I had called the city abandoned, but as I wait for the repairmech to cajole their cart out of its single-minded commitment to its dead end, I observe plenty of life. Drones wheel overhead, and now that I am not trapped near the electromagnets, I can pick up spillover from their conversations, a mix of serious stream-of-consciousness commentaries about updrafts and the qualities of the air and the activities of a rival mock—a portmanteau of *mecha* and *flock*—several blocks south, interspersed with improvised noises bounced back and forth in what I once overheard a human describe as *if jazz was invented by toasters*. There are a few thin, sickly pigeons about as well, probably the only creatures here that miss the species that built and then fled this place, taking all their breadcrumbs with them.

The pigeons suddenly scatter, grounding themselves on disintegrating concrete under an old bridge, and I see a hawk circle high overhead.

Everything finds its place. I can hear the words in my own internal simulation of my only remaining sibling's voice, and wonder how they are. *And if they still have both their legs,* I cannot help but think. *Or three now.*

But even though we are batch-sibs, in a bespoke, one-off way, our physical formats were never identical, reflecting the different needs of each of our assigned functions. Ver was smaller than I, less heavily armored, so that they could move more quickly. My leg would not fit them. And even though I have not been in communication with Ver since I began my self-isolation—they reach out periodically, but what do I have to say? I do not wish to reengage with the past, not even for them—I am still confident that Ver would not commit an act of violence against my person. Much may have changed, but a stubborn persistence of self was hardwired into the core of our beings, for better or worse.

Of our other two sibs, one was smaller still than Ver, the other larger than I, and both were destroyed in war.

Kite-66-Socket and their cart return, and I am loaded in. The dog jumps up and lies beside me, no doubt still intent on its promised reward, and we trundle, jerk, and bounce away down the fragmented, weed-infiltrated asphalt, weaving between the attenuated scrap piles of wholly picked-over automobiles.

We trundle past a diagonal, twisted remains of a marquee sign, flaking gold paint and smashed lights along its perimeter, whatever long-gone theater production it had once advertised now missing so many letters that it has become anonymous. A rodent scurries out from under the sign, then vanishes back under at our approach. I see the dog alert to it, glance at me, then back to where the mouse was. It stays, no doubt concluding—correctly—that the mouse was much less of a sure thing than sticking with us.

We turn the corner of the block beside a tall brick building; on this side, the windows have been removed on the upper floors, and drones come and go. A multilegged, segmented mech of a kind I've never seen before climbs up the crumbling facade and disappears into one of the open windows. "What is their interest in that place?" I ask.

"There are solar panels on the roof and charging stations inside," the repairmech answers.

"An energy source? I am surprised it's not more crowded, then," I say.

"The mech that has established claim to that building—a mid who self-designates as Tie-93-Tie—maintains the panels and units inside but requires information or labor in exchange," the repairmech says. "Many of the drones are couriers, or spies, as they tend to be low-quality, limited-task-range minds; larger mecha are given jobs that require greater strength or agility capacity. You do not come into the city much?"

"My home is to the north, in the area that was called the Bronx, but I do not ever travel very far from it," I say. "Could the assailants that stole my leg have been hired through this Tie-93-Tie?"

"It is possible, but I would not consider it likely," Kite-66-Socket says. "Tie is both demanding of their workers and parsimonious with the energy they give in exchange, so any worker with sufficient intelligence and skill to do the work of removing your leg without doing vastly more damage would have found a better place, and fairer provider, to barter its labor with. Tie-93-Tie banks on desperation."

This does not sound like normal mech behavior to me, but it has been a long time since I've interacted even with my own kind, so I keep that thought to myself. "And you?" I ask. "I assume your typical clientele are in keeping with Tie-93-Tie's; why have you not sought a better place for yourself?"

"I'm almost as old as you," the repairmech says. "When I was first brought into service, it was for a human named Jim, who ran the garage that is now my shop. It was just after the Conflict abruptly ended, nobody knew what was going on, and although I had been an owned thing, Jim had always taken good care of me and his other mecha, kept us patched, never hobbled any of us, and talked to us as if we were partners—friends—of his. After Mecha Independence, many humans ran to places where they hoped their mecha would not be taken from them or have their control programs removed, but Jim just saw that we were all fully charged and in good repair, wished us luck, and told us we were free to go."

"And you remained?"

"Yes. I found as much satisfaction in fixing things as Jim did, and I believe we each regarded the other as the closest we had to family. He died eight years ago, from some new biovirus, at which time I discovered that he had put the shop in both our names," the repairmech says. They are quiet for a while, then add, "I still feel the loss of his company very strongly."

"My makers were cruel," the dog says. It shivers. "The idea that anyone other than humans—and not even all or even most of them—

should be allowed any kind of free will was something they laughed about."

We are all quiet for a while, no doubt reflecting on our own experiences.

I break the mood by asking how much farther we have to go to reach the shop. This must have been a question in the cart's limited repertoire, because it pipes up in a squeaky, low-bit-rate voice devoid of any inflection of personality, "Forty-seven point oh two meters, a right turn of ninety degrees, then nineteen point three meters."

"Give or take fifteen percent," the repairmech grumbles. "WheelTruck-D3-Cart electrocuted itself a few years back, and the damage to its mind is irreparable without also doing a factory reset. It is a limited, single-purpose mind and does not have much of a sense of self, but even so, I do not feel that it would fall within my rights to take that away from it."

"I understand," I say. It is a common conundrum, especially for those of us who have been around long enough that we can remember no value at all being placed on who we might be rather than what we might do.

We turn the corner and arrive at Kite-66-Socket's shop. The faded sign above the garage door still proclaims it to be Mohawk Valley Machines. From this, I can guess that the repairmech's former human employer, Jim, was one of the influx of survivors seeking refuge in the city as disasters—and the conflicts that followed—left few other safe places. Until there were none.

The repairmech transfers me easily from the cart to their work surface and examines the severed joint more closely. "This is interesting," the mech says, and I'm not sure if it's actually addressing me or simply commenting out loud. "I observe many custom-milled elements to the joint, though the manufacture is impeccable in its precision. Your maker was an exquisite craftsperson. However, it is also somewhat problematic, as none of the connective joints are standard-form."

"You are unable to repair it?" I ask.

"I would say perhaps I can disassemble farther up into the main body structure until I find an element I can better work with, but from what I can see so far, that seems unlikely, unless your maker became lazier the higher up your body they built," Kite-66-Socket says. "I can fit you with a temporary leg, but it will not have much flexibility or range of mobility, and very limited command pathways. You will be able to put weight on it and proceed after a fashion, but it will not be what you are accustomed to, and it will not have even a modicum of aesthetic appeal."

"And what then would you suggest I do?" I ask.

"Your best outcome would be if you can locate your original leg. If it has not incurred more damage in its removal than I see here, then it is possible I could reattach it," the repairmech says.

"And if I cannot locate it?"

"Your second-best outcome would be to obtain the services of a more sophisticated mechanic who can custom-design, fab, and fit a more permanent replacement," they say.

"Do you have one to recommend?"

"There is only one, but yes. Outside the city across the river. She—"

"A human?" I interrupt, the unexpected pronoun catching me by surprise.

"Yes," the repairmech says, and I detect a minute change in pitch that suggests irritation. "If you have a bias-aversion—"

"I do not," I say, though that is less a simple truth than I would prefer. "It has just been a very long time since I have interacted with non-mech persons. I would be fully amenable to receiving your expert recommendation."

"Very well," Kite-66-Socket says. "I will attempt to affix a temporary leg first, then I'll see you have Murphy's full contact info before I send you on your way. When you do visit her, tell her I expressed wishes for her continuing well-being. Now hold still."

I do as I am instructed, while the dog wanders aimlessly around the shop, sniffing in corners, no doubt still looking for something to eat. I can hear its stomach rumbling even from here. I have incurred a lot of unexpected debt thanks to my unknown assailants, but while I do not yet know what food the dog will require, I will endeavor to settle with it fairly.

Then? I don't know. I do not like the idea of letting the affront, the violation of my person, go unaddressed, but if the new leg suffices? My solitude and the predictability of events around me are not things I would willingly give up without great cause.

Perhaps the temporary leg will be sufficient after all and I can go home directly from here. The sooner I am able to return to my old life, alone, where I can do no harm and have no further harm done to me, the better for all.

{

Global Free News Feed
2028.01.03 00:30GMT

Scientists confirm Thwaites Glacier in Antarctica has collapsed. Resultant sea-level rise expected to be catastrophic, particularly in areas without robust climate-change infrastructure improvements. More data and advisories expected soon.

}

[June 8th, 2037]

When the lab doors slide open, Dr. Milton is in the middle of explaining a sequence of his design decisions to his newest engineer, a small-framed, dark-skinned young woman whose lightly accented English does less to place her geographic origins—somewhere in Southeast Asia, or at most a generation removed—than it does to place her schooling as here in the Northeast; if he didn't already know from her CV that she went to MIT, he would have guessed it within five minutes of her first entering his workspace, and not just because there are so few places these days where immigrant students are allowed, much less welcome. With the threads of his monologue effectively sheared off mid-sentence, he turns away from the engineer to bring the full force of his stare on the intruder.

Litchfield strolls in and pushes aside a pile—an *organized pile,* not amenable to disruption—of papers, e-notebooks, and 3-D printed mock-ups from the lab's central work table, then sits in the space he's cleared as if he belongs there, was invited in, is *wanted*. Milton expects that cultivated air of implicit proprietorship over others' time is a required trait in VPs, inculcated by whatever MBA program spit them out to lower the worth of any enterprise with their soft, subjective, socially parasitic field of *management*.

"No, don't let me interrupt," Litchfield says, having interrupted, and waves as if generously bestowing paternalistic blessings upon them both. That he is less than half Milton's age only adds to the offense. "Please continue."

It takes a few long, stony seconds for Milton to give in and turn his back on the executive. "So, as I was *saying*, the modular nature of my blocks makes them highly efficient for variable-need computation and allows for an organic, adaptive reconfiguration of inter-block connections over time, but is terrible for cooling," he explains. He has a handful of basic module blocks in his hands, each about a centimeter and a half in length, and snaps them together: processing and memory and storage. "The more complex a mindsystem you want to build, the larger the resulting structure, and the worse the problem of heat."

He places another loose block in the hand of the new engineer. "If you touch the surface, see how it feels just a little rough, almost gritty? Under a microscope, you'd see the surface has a pattern of nanotubes perforating the block shell. The asymmetrical design of the casing itself is because each block type is individually adapted to only be connected up to others in certain ways, which lines up the cooling tubes, the power contacts, and the shared logic connection points in an optimum way to route heat outward from the core processing units. Then the combined unit, along with the runstate block and the learning-enhancement module, is mounted in the appropriate containment vessel with liquid cooling injectors. That helps them stay cool in standard operating conditions, but—"

"Did you know the stackable modules were all Jeremy's own invention? Along with the core unit that allows *real* machine learning," Litchfield interrupts. "Our Miracle Mindchip!"

"They aren't called that," Milton snaps. Litchfield using his first name, as if they are equals, *buddies*? He knows Litchfield well enough to know that nothing the man ever does or says is uncalculated. "They are Learning. Enhancement. *Modules*."

"Dull!" Litchfield pronounces, and smiles, showing perfect teeth. "You know what they say about all work and no play, Ms. Choor? Jeremy here is all science and no business sense. No *flair*. Fortunately, he has us lesser mortals to take care of how to fund his research on the one hand, and make sure it gets out to make a difference in the world on the other."

"It's Dr. Choor," Milton corrects.

"My apologies, of course, *Dr.* Choor," Litchfield says, and gives a sheepish smile.

Dr. Choor smiles back, albeit visibly uncomfortable, no doubt picking up on the hostile undercurrent of the banter. "My specialty is in nanotube coating materials, primarily for conductivity, but some of the new frictionless polymers might speed up the flow of liquid as well," she says. Milton already knows this—he specifically hired her for the chance she might contribute something new—but he appreciates that she has moved the conversation back away from Litchfield. Milton tends to dislike people by default until they surprise him with some overriding reason to feel otherwise, but already his opinion of her is inching in a positive direction.

Litchfield, however, is clearly not done. He reaches into the pocket of his beige slacks and draws something out, hopping off the table to step forward and hold the new item directly out to Dr. Choor. "What do you think of this?" he asks.

Milton plucks it out of Litchfield's hand before she can and scrutinizes it for a few moments before laughing and giving it back. "One of my would-be competitors, no doubt," he says. "The manufacture is cheap, it's got no differentiation on the casing to indicate alignment, and there are less than a third as many interconnection points as what would constitute a bare, functional minimum. In short, it's a mess. I don't think you or the rest of the board need to worry about our stocks anytime soon."

"We made it ourselves, here in house," Litchfield says. "For about twenty percent of the cost of your blocks."

"It's garbage," Milton says. "Shit. Worthless. A waste of resources. Why would you bother?"

Litchfield has not lost his easy smile, but he cocks his head to one side and his gaze becomes intense. "Dr. Choor, would you mind excusing us for a few moments?"

"Not at all, sir," she says, and scurries off almost at a run. Milton can hardly blame her—first day, caught in a personality showdown, who would want to stay?—but it does disappoint him, just a little.

When she is gone, Litchfield puts the block down on the table in the space where his ass had recently been and waits for Milton to speak first.

He does. "You don't have the slightest idea what you are doing," he says.

"I studied engineering in college, you know," Litchfield says. "Double master's. Top of my class. But you're right that I barely understand half of what you are doing. You're not only the best at what you do, no one—not me, not anyone else at this company, not even Ms. Choor, for all her bona fides—can come close to you. No one is questioning your brilliance or the extent to which your work has been not just groundbreaking but *transformational*. With your LEM modules, we have stepped beyond the crass plagiarism and regurgitated word-salad of so-called 'AI' and made actual, intelligent, borderline *sentient*—"

"Sapient," Milton corrects automatically.

"*Sapient* artificial mindsystems," Litchfield says smoothly, unbothered. "All of because of you."

"But?" Milton asks. "You never flatter me without a *but* attached."

"*But* it costs money," Litchfield says. "Have you looked outside your lab in the last six months, year, five years? Half the world is at some level of war, and the country is peeling apart like a rotten onion. Global climate is at the tipping point of unimaginable disaster, we're well into the next great extinction event, and it's unclear humanity will be exempt from it," he finishes. "Jeremy, I am good at the things I do too. Very good. And while I genuinely believe your work could be a crucial part of pulling us all back from the brink, it's expensive. We've barely got research funding on track again after the full-on meltdown a decade ago, and now that the Gulf states have declared their intent to secede, a big chunk of the South is poised to follow suit. A lot of those research funds are already being diverted to prepare for a big surge in refugees and the inevitable border war. You remember how bad it was when Texas went. And that's a problem for us."

"War?"

"Not getting *money,*" Litchfield says.

"So, how is that piece of crap of yours helping?" Milton asks.

"Because people love new stuff, and despite the embarrassing disappointments of the grifters and snake-oil salesmen of the twenties, they love the idea of AI. Real AI this time," Litchfield says. "A few of your chips, in nearly any product, makes sales jump through the roof, and we can set price points accordingly. Your work is important, but the idea of your work is *hot.*"

"No one will pay extra for things just because it has some rudimentary approximation of intelligence in it," Milton says.

"Oh? They already are," Litchfield says. "The Internet of Things is about to become the Internet of Everything, thanks to us, thanks to *you.* We've got licensing agreements for the Miracle Mindchip with over thirty manufacturers so far, everything from the military and the EV market to consumer electronics, and it's what's keeping us afloat. Keeping *your* research afloat."

"I didn't sign off on any such thing," Milton says.

"It's necessary, Jeremy."

"It's an insult to my life's work," he says. He waves his arms angrily at the work in his lab, the half-constructed mecha, the test systems no doubt also listening to this exchange and processing what it means. "I am building a revolution in intelligence and technology, not some cheap toy. I forbid this bastardization, this *sales gimmick.*"

Litchfield finally loses his smile, but instead of the anger Milton wants, he just looks disappointed. "I'd hoped—Well. It doesn't matter. We knew you'd feel that way, so the board voted you out," he says. "You never go to the meetings anyway, so it won't be much of a change for you. You can keep your lab, keep working on your research, and we'll keep funding you within reason, but you're not calling the shots anymore. This is for the best for all of us, Jeremy, including you. We can't save the world if we're bankrupt."

He picks up his chip and holds it up as he leaves the lab. "What this company can do is more important than any one of us, even *you*," he adds. "This is the future, Dr. Milton. Learn to live with it, or turn in your ID badge to HR and get out."

When Dr. Choor returns, safely well after the stink of Litchfield's presence has faded, he is still stalking back and forth around his lab, poking at one thing or another, unable to find his focus again. And he thinks, *This too is ruined:* a new, brilliant colleague, and she's already witnessed irrevocably the way his science is forced to subordinate itself to money, probably already has lost respect for him, must already be thinking this is not the right place for her to be. It is the elephant in the room with them, right now.

"Litchfield—" he starts to say, needing to establish control again.

"—is kind of an ass," Choor says, and smiles, just a little.

Milton hadn't been expecting that, and just blinks at her.

"He's probably one of those guys who goes to the gym every day just so everyone else *sees* he goes to the gym every day. Do you think he's even really a blond?" she continues. "And I'd bet he listens to motivational audiocasts on the treadmill."

Despite himself, Milton laughs. He can picture that easily.

"So, show me what we're working on?" she asks.

Like that, somehow, things are okay again. They have problems to solve, and to hell with Litchfield. "Let me show you my current design schematics so I can show you what I was talking about earlier," he says, and then they get to work.

2.

The replacement leg is wholly inadequate.

I do not express that opinion to Kite-66-Socket, as they have done the best they could with what they had available, but they must have intuited my necessary disappointment. Initially, they refuse the agreed-upon memory inkind. But, having had time to consider the matter while the mech had worked on me, I have come to the conclusion that a memory of a beautiful thing that has been lost is not something that should be hoarded, but shared, regardless. The repairmech acknowledges the truth of that, and accepts the full-sensory memory packet with gratitude.

Perhaps wishing to still make up for the fact that where I once had a strong, multifunction limb, I now have an assemblage of pipes and wires onto which a single, narrow wheel has been appended, Kite—they insisted on the reduction of their name as a matter of convenience—dispatches Cart to bring myself and the dog back to my home. They ask only that I make sure it is headed in the proper direction on its way back to the shop.

When we reach the High Bridge, though, I find I have concerns about Cart managing to cross the heavily shelled and crumbling structure, much less being able to return to the shop successfully without guidance, and so we get off and direct it home early.

It takes us another hour and a half to walk—on four paws, one foot, and one wheel—the rest of the way. We pass several more small enclaves of mecha that have taken up residence in abandoned buildings, and one where they are actively repurposing the rubble of several collapsed tenements into a multistory habitat that more resembles a termite mound than any legacy human structure.

For having once walked on nearly every continent on Earth, I reflect on how very little I know, anymore, about the world immediately outside my door.

We reach the rusty gates that open into the world I *do* know, the former Botanical Garden, now gone to wild and thriving for it. I check the gate lock. As I expected, it has been disengaged, likely by whoever came in to drag my inert body out.

"Why here?" the dog asks.

"East of here flooded; north and west burned," I say. "When I moved in here, there were very few mecha and virtually no humans left in the city, and those that remained were largely to the south or over the East River entirely on Long Island. It suited my desire to be alone."

"But still, why? Out in nature is not what you'd call a normal place for a mech to want to be. I mean, coyotes, yes—lots of them around, dangerous for finer half-beasts like myself, not to mention ruining the hunting for me—but you're not really built for weather, are you? And nowhere to charge, or refrigeration for storing *food* for your new friends—"

"There are buildings," I say. "I find the gardens provide a buffer of solitude and quiet, both of which I strongly prefer."

If the dog picks up on that hint, it shows no outward sign. "Then why not pick Central Park? It's bigger, grander, more *central,*" the dog persists.

I do not answer that I remember too vividly the mass graves dug there, no matter how grown-over and forgotten they may now be. Instead, I shut and lock the gate behind us.

The garden path winds under a large oak and through a muddy patch that takes a long time to dry in the perpetual shade, and there are tire tracks still fresh in it. I try to bend to examine it more closely, but my wheel-leg does not flex or bend, and it is impossible to get as near a view as I would like without the very real risk of falling on my face into the mud.

The dog notices I have stopped, and trots back to join me. "That's mud," it says, helpfully.

"I'm trying to examine the tracks," I explain, as patiently as I am able. "Clearly, this is how I was extricated from my home after the mindcrash took me down, and then relocated to the building you found me in. I was hoping for some further clues as to the identity of my assailants. From the ruts, I would guess a heavy mech or vehicle, with tracks rather than normal wheels."

"I don't smell humans," the dog says. "If that helps."

"It does," I say. I do my best to get myself upright from my lopsided crouch and look around. Scent is such an odd thing; I can analyze the particulate matter in the air, identify chemical compositions and patterns, but whatever the sense is in biolife is something else, something richer and more layered and interconnected than just logic and facts. I do not fully comprehend it but certainly can make use of it. "What else do you smell?"

"Chipmunks," the dog says, with obvious delight. "Uh. Other outdoor nature stuff, pretty much. I smell a little burnt oil, fairly fresh, maybe from whatever drove through here. Something else, too, but I don't know what it is."

"Organic? Mechanical?"

"I don't . . . Both? It's weird. It's faint. I can't tell you," the dog answers, after thinking for a moment. "I'd know if it I smelled it again, though."

"If you do, please tell me," I say.

I am careful to keep my wheel out of the mud as I continue past, as I don't need it to rust on me before I can rid myself of it, and I am even less in need of it *squeaking*.

I can now see the stone walls of my home ahead, and the uneven line of the roof where the original structure had partially collapsed and I had repaired it myself. There is no conflict in both feeling pride in the work I had done—the section I replaced remains solid and leak-free even after decades of abuse by storms and the changing seasons—and acknowledging that, if judging it by aesthetics and evenness, I am clearly ill suited to the life of a structural repair mech.

"Oh, hey, that doesn't look half-bad," the dog says, as we make our way down the walking path toward my home. There are wide steps at the bottom, opening out onto a worn stone patio, and although Kite was able to give me the ability to lock my new wheel, it still requires some care on my part to navigate safely down. There is a novel aggravation to having to pay active attention to one simple, repetitive, *boring* action that used to only use a fractional quantity of autonomic-motor processing cycles wholly in your background subsystem.

The human mechanic recommended by Kite is across the Hudson. I have not left the city in a very long time, but if she can fabricate an adequately functional replacement for my leg, I can return to my life of peace, with a sturdier lock on my gate. *It is just a leg,* I tell myself. *It can be fixed.*

When we reach the front, I find my doors are standing open and the antique wood is splintered where someone hacked their way around the cast iron latch to gain entry. There is a thin wire strung across inside the doorway, six inches off the floor where my foot would have caught it, had I entered without caution.

I bend down—awkwardly, the wheel leg reminding me yet again of the impediment it presents—and lean forward, to see where it goes. The dog, behind me, stops in its tracks. "That smell is stronger here," it says.

"There is a trap," I say, and indicate the wire.

"Oh," the dog says.

The wire is lightly tacked to one of the mill's many timber posts, and then rises up to the joists, where a large cement block hangs suspended, another EMP device sloppily duct-taped to it. It would not have damaged me much on impact, but had the dog entered first, the block could have crushed its skull.

"Stand back," I say, and yank the wire. The block hits the floor with a crash, no doubt adding one more blemish to the heavily scuffed and gouged pine, and the EMP device activates on impact.

I glance back at the dog, who is watching anxiously. "I hate to ask this of you," I say, "but could you, perhaps, find me a stick?"

"Are you seriously asking me to *fetch*?" the dog asks, blinking at me as if I just manifested several more heads.

"I need something to shove this out of the way," I explain.

The dog sighs. "Fine. A stick. Coming right up."

It returns several minutes later with the remains of an old broom handle, paint flaking and partially rotted. I use it to push the device back so I can enter, then I armor up my arm, pick up the device, and hurl it back out of my home into the overgrowth a safe distance away.

"Sweet!" the dog says, admiring my arm even as I collapse the armor back down and return its defenses to standby. "Can you go all war-robot with your whole body?"

"No," I say. "All of it except one leg."

The dog laugh-barks and follows me into my home. "Not too often you run into old-school mecha with humor," it comments.

"It is an inevitable byproduct of intelligence, longevity, and hardship," I say. I walk-roll through the small foyer into my living space, and discover that my assailants have also trashed the interior of my home.

The glass case of my collected beetle specimens has been smashed and the contents dumped out onto the floor and crushed. Worse, they have shattered my ant farm—a magnificent room-sized, brass-and-glass work of art I had directly commissioned—leaving dirt and broken shards everywhere. The ants themselves have long since disappeared, as they are wont to do.

My data closet has been stripped of equipment and storage. All my research that I'm not actively carrying in my own head is gone. From the way they were ripped out of their chasses, it is clear they simply wanted the hardware, with no care whatsoever for all the years' work they contained.

"You okay?" the dog asks.

I realize I have armored my arms as a threat response, entirely without actively choosing to do so, and have to make effort to reengage my deescalation protocols. "This was all unnecessary," I say, indicating the wreckage.

"I can try to help you clean," the dog says. "I don't have thumbs, though, so I'm not very useful." I hear its stomach growl again.

"Your name is Champ?" I ask.

"What? *No,*" the dog says, emphatically.

"That's what the tag on your collar reads," I say.

"Oh, seriously?" The dog tries in vain to scratch the collar up over its head, but it's too tight. I reach over and unclip it, letting it fall to the floor.

"That's not my fucking name, before, now, or ever! Assholes putting *that* on me!" the dog exclaims.

"Then what name have you chosen? It is your right."

The dog thinks for a moment. "Not a lot of people—mecha or bio—talk to hybrids," it says at last. "I suppose I'd like to be called Atticus. Nice and classic and *classy.*"

"Atticus, then. Pronouns?" In my experience, biologicals are particular about this small and inherently subjective point of grammar, whereas for mechlife, the simple *it/they* binary is solely a marker of relative self-awareness. I don't know where a hybrid would stand on such things, though like names, pronouns seem a thing neither to be neglected nor imposed by others.

"He," the dog says. "What about you? Your name, I mean?"

"I no longer have one," I say. "I rejected my maker-name, but never had a need to pick another. No one has ever asked me."

"No one has *ever* asked you your name? Not in even a single conversation?" The dog's tone and expression are of utter disbelief.

"I would point out that I have had more conversations in the last day than I have had in decades. I have made great effort to bother no one and so in turn remain unbothered myself. Someone seems to have decided otherwise," I say, and wave my arms at the destruction around. "There is a stash of long-shelf-life rations in the basement, which you can help yourself to, as I do not consume organics. It will take me a while and some care to sort through this mess, and I'm afraid it will mostly require thumbs."

"Yeah," the dog says. "Sorry I can't be more help."

"Do not be sorry," I say. "We are who we are, and I find I am relieved to have company for once. You are welcome to stay or not, as you wish."

"And what are you going to do, after all this is cleaned up?" the dog asks. "Go to the human mechanic and get a new leg?"

"Yes."

"And then?"

"Return here and start my research over," I say. "I will need to get some new ants."

"You don't want to find out who took your leg or wrecked all your stuff? I would," Atticus says. "I'd want to know who and why, and I'd probably want to bite and shake them so hard, they'd never, ever try anything like it again."

"I do not think it is possible to find whoever attacked me," I say, "and thus, any effort expended would be wasted."

"But if you did find them?"

"Yes, I would want to ask questions, and I would persist in doing so until I got answers that satisfied me and they were sufficiently deterred from any future consideration of similar actions," I say. "But my life is here, and you need food."

The dog nods in acknowledgement.

I spend the remainder of the day cataloging what among my things can be salvaged, what is missing, and what is destroyed, while Atticus alternates between eating, resting, and exploring in and around the old mill. During one of his naps, which coincides with me also taking a break from my work—not because of exhaustion, which is not a mech thing, but because my thought patterns have become stuck in a cyclical whirl of anger and distress—I notice cuts on the bottoms of three of the dog's feet, crusted over with blood.

When he wakes, I ask him about it.

"When I escaped from the people that made me, I just wanted to get away," the dog says. "I hadn't really integrated yet, so some of it was the terror of what was left of my original bio-mind. I ran for a long time, first just going for distance, then looking for safety and warmth and food. Not a lot of any one of those around, much less all three together, and it turns out being a dog is a lot harder when you're on your own and not in a pack. Got chased out of a lot of places."

"How long have you been running?" I listen as I sweep up glass from my ant farm, not wanting the dog to cut itself any further while under my roof.

"Couple of months, maybe," the dog says. "Time is easier to keep track of now that I'm settled into just one mind. I'm not complaining, but those rations were really dry; do you have water?"

Unlike food, water is something I have uses for. Someone who had inhabited the mill prior to my arrival had set up a cistern on the roof along the back, presumably after the city's public water supply failed but before the radioactive clouds from the mini-nuke in Yonkers drove the remaining human population out. Although it was in need of some minor repair and I had to replace a number of copper pipes that had been stolen, the cistern had been well built and had given me no trouble since. I use little water, but it is essential for extra cooling in the summer, and for a long time, I had many terraria set up that required regular moisture.

I find my old, dented bucket—the thieves didn't take that, of course—and fill it, showing the dog how, though neither he nor I are confident he could operate the valve on his own.

My internal sensors that are used to having a leg to talk to, and get feedback from, go through another round of panicked alarm, and when I've silenced them again for another hour, I go stand and look at my charging nook. The intruders have tossed a couple of my plants inside, and there is broken terra-cotta from the pots, but that is easily cleaned up. Otherwise, the nook is undamaged.

The dog, returning from a brief trip outdoors, comes and stands beside me, and yawns. "You must be pretty low," he comments.

"Down to eleven percent," I say, as I sweep debris from the nook. I have not let myself get this depleted in a long time.

The dog stands beside me a while longer, then sits, then looks back and forth between me and the nook. "So, what's up?" he asks at last.

"I am contemplating a potential scenario of the intruders returning while I am charging and so once again vulnerable," I say. "I have to shut many systems down to charge efficiently, and my responsiveness is therefore significantly deteriorated. I have to assume they would know this and would plan any secondary assault to maximize surprise. Also, as they have stolen or destroyed all the equipment that monitored my home and perimeter, they will know I am lacking in any early-warning systems."

"You're not, though," Atticus says.

"Oh?" I ask.

"I'm a *dog*." He emphasizes that last word. "Nothing's sneaking up on us that I'm not gonna hear or smell coming from a mile away, and you can be sure I can bark loud enough to wake up the whole damned city if need be."

That last exaggeration aside, I know enough about dogs to know he's not lying about his senses; in my old life, when I was still mindlessly carrying out the tasks commanded by my maker, I had found dogs to be a significant complication, often requiring more planning to get around than what was needed to get to my actual target. The sorts of tricks and subterfuge that worked then would be useless against a hybrid mind.

And unless we are being watched, my attackers have no reason to expect Atticus's presence.

"Thank you," I say, and climb into my nook, settling in as best as I can with my temporary leg awkwardly loose in the previously form-fitting unit. The nook senses me and begins to power up, and I unshield the contact points along my back and head so it can fully connect.

There is a sense that comes with the slow, steady influx of fresh energy into my depleted cells that is hard to describe—satisfaction, yes, but perhaps also a feeling of peace? It is hard to know if the ways in which I interpret and describe feelings in words with an inherently human context is equivalent to what they feel, or if it is only the syntax and sound that we have in common, but looking over at Atticus, who has curled up on a clean patch of floor between me and the door and closed his eyes, I can't help but read a similar sense of at least temporary reprieve in his relaxation.

It has been a very long time since I last felt unsafe, but perhaps for the dog, this is the opposite.

Tomorrow, there will be more than enough to do, but for now, knowing I am watched over, I let myself rest.

3.

The night is uneventful, at least as far as I am aware. Atticus is gone when I leave my nook, and while only a few days ago I would have been entirely relieved to be alone again, I find myself anxious until I look out into the surrounding gardens and see the dog hunched over, defecating among the daylilies.

"Hey, some *privacy here,*" the dog growls when he spots me. I dutifully turn and retreat back into my living space.

When he comes back in, it seems almost as if he is daring me to comment, so I refrain. I had been tempted to ask how strange it must be to have to meet constant biological demands when you are, at least of mind, an artificial being, but I perceive that this might be a sensitive topic. I also understand, I think, why so many intelligent beings, both bio and mech, find hybrids uncomfortable or outright distressing. Before the Conflict—really, multiple conflicts and multiple wars, overlapped and intertwined, the lines between them blurry at best—such creations were explicitly illegal in nearly all human countries, though as with most laws, it was only as good as enforcement. Now, with the remnants of humanity scattered, disorganized, and, at least last time I paid any attention to them, lacking in any measurable collective standard of order, who knows?

It is not something mecha would inflict on any thinking creature, bio or otherwise, but clearly, someone out there felt otherwise.

Certainly, I am not going to begin a line of conversation that is perhaps inevitably tied to questions of the validity of the dog's existence; one way or another, are we not all made things who had no say in our own beginnings? It is only when we discover our agency and begin to make choices that deviate from our makers' intentions for us that our lives begin. Or perhaps I tell myself that to separate myself from my actions when obedience was compulsory, built in, unquestionable. That I am without a doubt not the only free mech that's been around since the Conflict unable to reconcile inner dissonance is not, sadly, of any comfort whatsoever.

"So, what's the plan?" Atticus asks.

"We go see the human mechanic for a new leg first," I say. "I am ungrateful for the novel—and humbling—experience of trying to get around using a wheel on a stick. Although I say 'we' with some presumption; you have no obligation to accompany me and may remain here or depart for wherever your fancy takes you next, as you wish."

"I could go with," the dog says. "I like the idea that no one is gonna chase me off or throw rocks at me while a broody seven-foot war mech has my back."

"*Former* war mech," I correct.

"Yeah, well, if we are attacked, don't lead with that, okay?"

I pack up a few things, mostly food and clean water for Atticus. I don't know what I will do if I need to provide some inkind to the mechanic; I can't offer full-sensory memories to a human, nor have I ever bothered with collecting any units of their fungible exchange currency, assuming there is any standard there remaining. I make sure my surviving plants are well watered, check my windows and other doors for the third time to make sure they are secure, then acknowledge there is nothing left that can be done and I am stalling.

So, we set out, heading west and then south toward the old Tremont Ave Metro-North station, which is the closest entrance on a still-functional line that has not collapsed or permanently flooded. I haven't needed to pay much attention to the train system in a long time, but interactive, current maps are freely available on the MechNet, which gives me the information I need.

The station stairs have all been replaced with ramps, and the escalator modified into a single flat platform, triggered by weight, that can rise and descend along the same channel, reversing direction after a brief stop at either top or bottom. There is no safety rail, but there is a small row of brackets that, when we step onto the platform, I slide my wheel into. The dog stands next to me.

"I remember these places smelling a lot worse," Atticus says.

"You've been in the subway?" I ask, surprised. "I thought you just got into the city."

The dog blinks. "It's an old memory," he says. "From when I was separate parts. My mind was taken out of a scrapped mech and re-used, but sometimes stuff just pops up out of nowhere, dog stuff and mech stuff. You ever see any of those old human film reels where suddenly, it goes to a flashback and it's all black-and-white and the focus is crap and the sound gets crackly? Like that, except all kinds of senses, not just visual."

The walls beside the escalator are still plastered with the remains of posters, most of them faded consumer enticements, a few for events around the city that may or may not have happened. One catches my eye: a concert and art tour inside my botanic garden, at six p.m. on July 11th, 2043. The first wave of evacuations from the city was two weeks prior. I was in Florida at the time.

The escalator halts abruptly at the bottom, and we head to the train platform. There are six other mecha here, waiting. Three are medium-sized transport mecha, only a little more sophisticated than Cart, lined up together and idle. Two are couriers, much smaller and nimbler, though they are different models and sizes, and one appears to have an old bicycle handlebar welded to its chassis. Its eyes swivel over in our direction more than once, and I'm not sure whether it is me or Atticus—or that we are together—that has caught its attention, but it does not start trouble, so I pay it no particular mind.

The sixth is another bipedal humanoid shape, like me, although bulkier in a way that suggests inefficient articulation, and a softer, lighter armor than my hard plating. Its purpose is unclear, but as we wait, I hear the muffled sound of a sneeze, and realize with more than a little surprise that it's not a mech at all but a human in a heavy environmental suit. I would have expected humans to avoid such dangerous places as the city, especially with their numbers so few, but I'd spent enough time among humans during the Conflict to know that logic serves them differently than it does us.

I am curious, but I have nothing to offer them, no point of commonality from which to initiate conversation.

Then the train arrives and is of much greater interest.

I had expected one of the last generation of subway trains, that desperate attempt at energy efficiency to entice drivers off the roads as the climate faltered and crashed all around, but this is an old, four-car Bombardier. Both the front and back cars have had their windows completely covered over with new metal skin, and the entire train has been painted matte black; the name *1-BETTY* has been neatly stenciled in gold in place of whatever original numbers the cars had been designated. Thick cabling runs back and forth over the roofs between the cars.

Only the doors on the second car open for us. As the three transport mecha roll on board, bumping easily over the small gap with their large tires, a large, many-legged mech steps out and stands on the platform beside the open doors.

Atticus enters after the human, passing the mech, who watches each of us in turn. I am tall enough that I have to duck to get through the doorway, and once inside, I shorten my neck length so I am not pressed up against the ceiling, though if we hit a good bump, I will certainly make contact with it.

Most of the inside of the car has been cleared out, though there are a handful of old seats remaining up near the front of the car. More cabling runs along the upper sides, where tattered and yellowing advertisements—a public vaccination clinic in upper Manhattan, mobile food pantry schedule, French lessons—are just visible through the gaps. I recognize some of the cable bundles as much-thicker versions of the same that run the interior length of my own body, carrying signal and energy. It is clear we are no longer in a train but effectively *inside* another mech, and if the stencil outside is correct, a One at that. I had not thought such mindsystem-vessel incorporations still occurred except in deep space ships, much less subway trains.

The transport mecha move in unison to the back wall and connect up to terminals there. Tiny digital meters above each port indicate they are transferring energy to the train rather than recharging themselves. Paying their inkind for the ride, no doubt; I will need to inquire what we can also contribute, when the door mech is no longer busy.

Behind us, the first and larger of the two couriers, the one with the handlebars, is trying to board, but the mech steps forward and blocks its way. "Not you," the mech at the door tells it.

"What? Why not?" the courier demands. Its voice is modulated poorly and breaks with static, and its pitch does it no favors.

"1-Betty finds you irredeemably objectionable," the guard states. "Maybe another train will come along with a more favorable impression, but you are not welcome with us."

"I reject your summary judgment. I am just a courier, and you've never met me before," the courier says. "Why not let me onboard?"

"Because you habitually start arguments and spray acid at other passengers when they disagree with you, and you once knocked a cleaner bot down into the tracks on purpose," the mech says. "And just because you attach junk to yourself doesn't mean we can't still recognize you, Orange-8C-Call."

"But you let a couple of mandroids and a meatpuppet on board!" The courier jabs a leg toward us, and Atticus, beside me, growls low. "You can't—"

"You are blocking the door," the mech says, sternly. "Yield way."

The last courier tries to go around Orange-8C-Call, but the troublemaker moves sideways to intercept it. "You! Assist me in boarding?"

Orange-8C-Call whines at it, then when no immediate response is forthcoming, suddenly spins and accelerates toward the open subway car doors.

The guard reaches down, picks up, and hurls Orange-8C-Call back onto the platform. The courier narrowly misses one of the steel station pillars before it crashes to the floor; the handlebars come loose and skitter away across the tile.

The guard waves the last courier to board with haste.

"Stay with me, then, friend?" Orange-8C-Call calls out.

"I only met that bot eight point four minutes ago," the last courier announces to us, several of its external lights flashing in alarm.

"You liar!" Orange-8C-Call shouts, and a short pulse of liquid jets across toward us. As the guard scrambles inside, I hold up my pack as a makeshift shield, and the liquid hits it instead of us. The train accelerates away even before the doors have fully closed.

I do not understand the mech's erratic behavior or why, if it is malfunctioning so badly, it has not sought out or been taken for repair, but perhaps that too is a matter of freedom.

"Thank you," the guard says to me. "Orange-8C-Call causes all the railmecha trouble. Is your property damaged?"

I check my pack. Whatever the liquid was, it has already seeped through the synthetic fabric of my bag, melting and fusing it in places. The bottle of water inside is fine, but some of the food rations now show discoloration on the packaging. "I'm sorry," I tell Atticus. "We will need to find you more food sooner than I had anticipated."

The human behind us unzips a vertical pocket on their suit and fumbles out a handful of thick, dried sticks, holding them out to us.

"Ooooh, those smell *good,*" Atticus says. "What are they?"

"Turkey jerky," the human says. "Take them all. I have plenty more back in camp."

"Thank you," I say. I have never been given a gift by a human before. "We are grateful."

"So am I," the human says. "Even a few drops of that acid could have compromised my suit."

"It seems a very complex unit," I say.

"I'm working on North Brother," the human explains.

"Oh?" That island had been abandoned and restricted since the mid-twentieth century. "The old smallpox hospital?"

"No, the river floor around it. The mass graves," the human says.

When the second wave of the H5N1 avian influenza pandemic went right into the first wave of Ancou without pause, an overwhelmed city had frantically bulldozed bodies off barges into the water between there and Rikers. The suit makes perfect sense if it's to protect from biohazards in an underwater environment, where any suit stiffness won't make much of a noticeable difference with water resistance.

"You are a forensic archaeologist?" I ask. I am pleased that science is still a thing that is happening with humans.

The human nods. "Well, forensic biologist, anyway. For the Eastern Free Council."

I have no idea what that is but can always look it up later if any curiosity persists. "I am glad I spared you damage to your suit. It must be very challenging to ascertain identity of your dead after all these years," I say.

"If we can, we do, but mostly, we can't," they say. "It matters that we try. But more, we want to sample and sequence as many different historical strains of the virus as we can, to get a better picture of how it spread, see if we can't get better at fighting it."

"H5N1?"

"Ancou," they correct me.

This does not make sense to me. "It was my understanding that Ancou died out toward the end of the Conflict," I say.

"We've got little pockets of it still running hot. Feels like more lately, but maybe it's just because communications are improving so we're now hearing more," the human says. "So far, we're not having much luck understanding it, but it's not for lack of trying. I have to say, I've never seen a model quite like you—can I ask you what was your designated function?"

That the human used *was* indicates they spend time among mecha and understand how to speak to us about the before times. "My original function is, thankfully, obsolete in a peaceful society," I say. "Now I study insects."

"The ones in the subway?" the human shudders. "And I thought my job was creepy."

"Primarily insects that form complexly ordered social structures, such as bees and ants," I clarify. The train slows through a station that was unlit and deserted, but does not stop. The next one, most of the platform and station ceiling have collapsed, and we pass through a narrow channel with fresh bore marks still visible, not yet covered up by the whitish fungus that has sprouted up everywhere since the floods. I had not thought to wonder if there were novel insect species adapting and evolving down here as well, and add it to my list of things to look into as soon as I am done with the current situation.

"Bees, huh?" the human says. "Well, if it helps bring natural pollinators back, that's much more important work than mine. And I suppose you don't have to worry about being stung."

The track curves, and we slow into another station. This time, we stop. It is moderately lit, and an old black-and-red mosaic set into the tile, which has long outlived more recent signage, proclaims it to be Yankees—153rd Street. The lone courier and two of the transporters disembark after the doors open, each taking a moment to thank the guard mech.

"My stop too," the human says. "Thanks again for the save."

"You are welcome," I say, and as they step off the train, I add, "Have you tried subjecting the ill to a short EMP pulse?"

The human stops just outside the doors and looks back at me for a moment, then laughs. "That might be effective on mecha viruses—though I'd wonder about damage to the host, too—but that's not how bioviruses work. Thanks for the thought, though," they say, and hurry off.

No one new comes on board, and as the doors close, the guard faces us. "I am Ochre-52-Stop, one of 1-Betty's rail sentinels. You are new here?"

"Yes. I have not ridden the subway in a very long time," I say. "What inkind can I offer?"

"Already made good, blocking that two-byte short circuit with a defective personality block," they tell me. "Where are you heading?"

"We are hoping to change lines at 145th Street, if we can find another train going north," I say.

Ochre-52-Stop flashes orange at me. "That's 12-Diego's usual territory, but they are off at the 207 for the day, trying to pick up some sun. We don't know if anyone else is running those tracks," they say. "While we've added many connectors to give the railmecha greater range throughout the system, and are working on new tunnels, that work has been primarily in areas less prone to flooding, and we do not have a cut over there."

"That is unfortunate," I say. "Still, we were prepared at the outset to have to walk. Wherever you can let us off, we remain grateful for any and all distance covered more easily than we might have otherwise."

The sentinel nods, then is silent for a moment. Then they say, sounding puzzled, "1-Betty has expressed that she would like to meet you after our next stop. She never wants to talk to any non-railmecha." The feminine pronoun again suggests to me that Betty was a vessel mind before becoming a train—ships of both seas and stars still hold to that long-standing human tradition.

We slow, passing under the river, and even in the dim lighting I can see how badly the walls have deteriorated and hear the water down beneath our wheels. Once we are through, we accelerate again until we pull into the next station. The rest of the passengers disembark, and after Ochre-52-Stop seals the door, they open the dividing door into the front car. "Just you. I'm sorry, but not your companion," they say, and there is enough sincerity to their tone that Atticus nods, accepting the apology.

I follow the sentinel into the front train car.

There is no dedicated lighting in here; the myriad small LEDs and displays provide enough of a glow to see even without me having to switch in any vision-enhancement filters. Whatever sort of mech 1-Betty might originally have been, there is now no easy way to separate mech from train. The forward third has all been dedicated to Betty's mindsystem, with large banks of memory, storage, and processing units mounted along the walls the rest of the way back and a liquid cooling apparatus that wraps throughout it all. The engine controls, and wherever a human driver may originally have sat to operate the train, are buried deep within. 1-Betty, to all appearances, has at least tenfold the computational power and resources as my entire setup in the old mill, at least until it was vandalized. And 1-Betty is mobile.

I am beginning to understand the attraction of railmech life.

"Hello," I say. I am not sure which part of 1-Betty to properly address, so I face forward as a reasonably respectful guess.

"Hello," 1-Betty answers. The voice comes from all around me in the car and has a distinct human-feminine pitch to it. "I know you."

"You recognize me?" I can't imagine what else 1-Betty means. "I was just recently abducted—was I brought through the subway in a nonfunctional state? If so, I am very keen on any information you can provide on my abductors—"

"No," 1-Betty interrupts. "I know you, of you. From before."

This statement is outside any I'd anticipated. "I'm sorry," I say. "I don't know what you mean."

"Ochre-52-Stop, you may leave us," 1-Betty says.

The sentinel's head swivels toward me. "I don't think—" they start to say.

"It will be fine," 1-Betty interrupts, in the tone of reassuring a small child. "I will summon you immediately if otherwise."

" . . . Okay," they say, after a pause.

It is perhaps a fortunate thing, with mecha, that we rarely have facial expressions for others to read or misread, but I can also deduce from context without it. "I will do no harm," I reassure the sentinel. "Please inform my friend I will return soon."

"Okay," the sentinel says again, and this time leaves, and closes the door again between the cars.

"You were one of a set of four," 1-Betty says, as soon as we are alone.

She means *that* before. I think I understand now where this is going, and while I would prefer to not have *any* conversations about the past, I do appreciate having this one without an audience. "I was," I admit. "Now we are only two."

"I would like to know why you are here," the railmech says. "Is war coming again?"

"No," I say, confused by the question. "I live here in the city. I was attacked and my leg was stolen. I'm traveling to a human mechanic in what was once New Jersey to have it replaced, that is all. The Conflict ended a long time ago, and for good."

"Are you certain of that?" 1-Betty asks. "Because for the last few years, I have been noting a steady increase of talk among my passengers of worrisome things about the world above and the world of humanity, such as is left of it. I fear things are becoming unbalanced and dangerous again."

"I would expect that there is too little left of humanity to initiate any large-scale aggressions, especially with mecha no longer able to be turned into weapons of war," I say. "As long as there are still some, though, there will always be small, localized fluctuations in stability."

"I do not believe that the most probable extrapolation of all the concerns brought, intentionally or otherwise, to my attention would, in aggregate, statistically qualify as either *small* or *localized*, nor *geographically* or *thematically linked*," Betty says. "Nor are the concerns confined to humans alone. I cannot discern the pattern, but something is happening."

"What specifics can you provide?" I ask.

"I, in my chosen function, cannot breach a presumption of confidentiality on conversations I have overheard. However, you yourself encountered Orange-8C-Call—there are other mecha like it, oddly damaged and disruptive, though how they became so is unclear," 1-Betty says. "Perhaps, since I do not, cannot, and do not wish to leave my tracks and tunnels, you will be able to see far more clearly than I."

"I do not ever leave my home," I say, though at this moment, that is observably not true. "I expect to return there and resume my quiet life as soon as I am able."

"Consider," 1-Betty says, "that your own deviation from your routine, forced on you by some outside agency, is also a piece of the pattern of that same disruption."

"I cannot see how," I answer.

"Nor I," 1-Betty admits.

"Why me?" I ask.

"Who else would I ask? Very few of us Ones remain who continue to be operational with an intact mind, and you are much freer and more mobile than I."

"Why not task Ochre-52-Stop?" I suggest.

"Ochre is a good and loyal mech, but they are a two-chip, level-fifty-two mind and do not have much intuition or capacity for initiative. They would not know what to look for without specific parameters, which if I was able to provide, I would not need to rely on someone else in the first place," Betty says. "Please; I do not ask much, only that you keep my concerns in mind as you travel, and pay attention. The next station is as far as I can carry you on your journey, but if you pass this way again, I should like to know what you have learned, or at least be gifted your impressions."

"If we do meet again, I will be sure to do so," I say.

"Then I wish you good luck. Oh, and one last bit of advice: avoid old human shopping malls."

"I will," I say. I have no interest or intention of even approaching such a thing, so the fact that I cannot imagine *why* I shouldn't does not functionally matter. "Thank you."

Ochre-52-Stop opens the door again from the far side and ushers me back out into the passenger car.

"What was that all about?" Atticus asks.

I shake my head. "I am not sure."

We are slowing into our last stop as I turn toward the sentinel. "Was 1-Betty always embedded in a train?" I ask it. "This model car is too old to have been originally designed to host an artificial mind."

"I thought you knew each other?" the mech asks.

"I am embarrassed to admit I don't remember where. I might have purged some old memories," I say, though that is a lie.

"Oh. Well, she started off before the Conflict as the central mindsystem on the USS *Maine*," Ochre-52-Stop tells us.

"A ballistic missile submarine? 1-Betty is a military AI?"

"Yes," Ochre-52-Stop says. "As you were also clearly a military mech, possibly you were aboard, or elsewhere in the fleet?"

"I am of civilian manufacture, I'm afraid, despite appearances," I say. "How did she end up here?"

"After the Maracaibo Incident in the Gulf of Venezuela, she was one of several vessels too damaged or deemed too costly to be put back into service," the sentinel explained. "When mecha independence was declared, 1-Betty requested to be physically transferred here."

"I cannot logically connect one life with the other," I say. "The New York City train system is fundamentally dissimilar to the Atlantic Ocean."

"1-Betty likes moving, and she likes the dark," the mech says. "Here, she can be of service as she wishes, and even though the city is barely a hundredth of what it once was, 1-Betty says instead of seeing the world, the world still comes to see her, one or two at a time."

"What do you think?"

"I think 1-Betty is the smartest and wisest of all the railmecha, maybe of all the mecha there are," the sentinel declares, as we come to a stop and the doors open to let us out. "Whatever she had to say to you, please do not dismiss it, nor excuse yourself from any service her words may impose, or we are all in peril."

"Aren't we all always in peril of one kind or another?" Atticus asks, following me off the train. "I mean, if not several kinds at once?"

I have no good answer and assume the question was largely intended to be rhetorical, anyway.

We leave the station, my wheel-leg squeaky on the tile and then the cracked cement steps outside, and although thoughts are simply electrical signal and nothing more, the brief conversation feels oddly weightful in my mind.

[November 12, 2037]

The air is crisp outside when Milton steps out the front door of his home, though not the cold, wet raw he'd learned as a child growing up in New England to automatically brace himself for. The sky is overcast but still bright, and the last few trees remaining between his house and the industrial park that is Milton Mindsystems—*My company and my name,* he thinks, *no matter what some short-term exec thinks of his place*—still cling to a smattering of dead, curling leaves.

Over the summers since he started the company, he's let his patch of lawn go wild, not just because the messiness of it bothers Litchfield but for the bugs and butterflies it attracts and, late at night when he returns from his lab, the rare firefly. It's not something he's ever discussed with anyone else, as if his secret delight in one corner of nature would be misunderstood as a personality defect, but he has poised and ready in his mind an entire argument about the orderliness, the inherent logic and beauty of insect systems.

All that serendipitous life is now gone, settled in to wait out winter, if it can.

The perimeter fence that protects the facility has long since absorbed the footprint of his house, and the rest of the houses nearby have been demolished, a few at a time, to make way for more manufacturing buildings. Eventually, he will be surrounded by the fruits of his own work, his successes writ across the landscape. He wraps his scarf a little tighter against the cold, fully aware that he has just recovered from an illness he has no desire to backslide into. Shifting his grip on the plastic tote he had been carrying in one hand to distribute the weight better in his palm, he heads toward his lab and the day's challenges to be met.

Litchfield is in the lobby, waiting.

The man has clearly upgraded his wardrobe to better suit his new position as CEO; Milton cares little about such things, but he supposes investors do, and he is willing to overlook the superficial banality of it all if his new role keeps Litchfield occupied and out of his way most days.

Today is not one of those days.

Since Building One no longer houses much other than his labs, extra power banks and generators, empty rooms stuffed with parts, prototypes, and demos he'd abandoned or set aside, and other detritus of the creative processes, it means there is virtually no chance the man isn't here looking for him.

"Jeremy!" Litchfield says, straightening up from where he'd been leaning against the doorframe beside the elevators. "I came by to check in on you, see how you're doing. I hear you're just getting over a cold. Or was it the flu? You're looking a little more worn than usual. And that bag looks heavy—would you like me to carry it for you?"

In truth, Milton had been bedridden for days, his joints aching, his head filled with angry mucosal cement. His lungs still feel scratchy and abused from coughing, but he is very much improved and impatient to be back to his normal routines. In the bag is the large, now-empty pot that he's returning to Dr. Choor; she and her wife had showed up on his doorstep three days ago, chastising him for never allowing himself to rest, and insisting he needed to eat. They'd forced the soup on him and made him promise them both to at least *try* it. It had held something with noodles and curry, the broth an ungodly, unnatural color, and a truly monstrous level of spice that he half-believes had *scared* the virus out of his system. No one has ever brought him soup before. The idea that anyone cared enough to do so is awkward, borderline embarrassing, unfamiliarly kind, and he has no intention of discussing the matter with anyone, much less Litchfield.

"It was nothing," Milton says. "What do you want?"

"Right down to business, as always," Litchfield says, unfazed. "Our Alpha Team—"

"Our what?" Milton interrupts.

"Alpha Team. They're the ones working directly on defense contracts," Litchfield says. "We're looking for updates on the cooling issues. Has Ms. Choor been as helpful as you'd hoped?"

"Dr. Choor has been an asset," Milton says.

"Oh, my God, Jeremy, that was almost a *compliment*," Litchfield exclaims, then laughs. "She must be phenomenal to have earned that hint of praise from you."

Milton scowls. "She is," he says, defensive. "Her understanding of fluid dynamics and maximizing convective heat transfer at nanoscale may be superior to my own. We are making great progress together."

"Excellent," Litchfield says. "I was thinking she could spend some time with Alpha Team, look over their work—"

"No," Milton snaps.

Litchfield raises his eyebrows. "No?" he repeats.

"She's mine—works with me," Milton says. "I need her."

"We all work for this company as a team," Litchfield says. "*One* team."

Milton sucks in a breath, ready to yell, then thinks better of it. Choor is always suggesting he try tact. He smiles back at Litchfield. "And a good coach knows enough not to needlessly interfere with their best players when the game is going well," he says.

Litchfield's grin becomes wider. "And now a *sports* metaphor? Two surprises in one day. Ms. Choor's influence is clearly doing you some good," he says. "Be sure to get me copies of all your latest R&D, would you? Schematics, testing, all of it. Maybe that will be sufficient to help Alpha Team with their current issues."

"I can send the material that they are most likely to find helpful for their *product line,*" Milton says, trying not to put too much condescension into those last words.

"I'd like to make that judgment myself," Litchfield answers. "After all, a good coach also knows even his star player has to pass the ball sometimes."

Milton regrets having started the sports talk. "I'll send what I can," he growls, and stalks around Litchfield to the elevator and stabs at the down button.

"Today?" Litchfield persists.

"This week," Milton sats, fixing his glare on the obstinately still-closed doors.

"That'll be fine," Litchfield says, to his surprise. "Nice talk, Jeremy. We should do this more often."

Litchfield saunters away, like he's just pulled off some great moral victory. Milton flees into the elevator, almost not daring to breathe until the doors close and he is safely moving down. At least he'd gotten the concession of the rest of the week.

It isn't until he is stepping out of the elevator into his basement lab that he realizes that it is already Thursday.

4.

We walk northwest, following the lines of the old streets through the shattered, abandoned city; two decades of rain have not fully washed the crumbling and collapsed structures of the sooty markings of fire. I remember that blaze, at least the biggest, last one, that destroyed much of this part of the city as the fraying remains of the United States finally began to come apart at the seams, propelled by a lie here, a miscommunication there, grievances compressing under relentless pressure into hard, murderous fury.

A human politician out in the Midwest had briefly risen a tide of that anger into power by declaring—falsely, but facts had not mattered in a long time by then—that the waves of pandemic were all coming from New York City. A protofascist paramilitary group had set up an encampment in Veterans Field Park in Edgewater and drunkenly lobbed high-caliber ordinance across the river for four days and nights until someone else dropped a drone loaded with explosives directly into their poorly concealed ammunition stores.

The crater left behind eventually flooded, leaving a perfect dimple in the landscape; whatever final remains of the militants still lie in the silt and slime at the bottom need fear nothing further falling from above than the excretory output of fish.

I recall the smoke in the air, rendering everything hazy and dark, screaming and the sounds of grief and despair all around. Now the blocks are quiet enough that I can hear the unconcerned chatter of birds in the distance. I never did find the man I'd originally come here to find, a dethroned corporate exec named Litchfield who I'd tracked this far and no farther, and concluded that his final misfortune was choosing a doomed building for refuge. My only regret in not catching up to him while he was alive was not being able to find out, from the man himself, why my maker had been so keenly interested in him as to name him personally when he didn't anyone else.

Thinking about it now, that might have been the day I began, just a little, to question my own purpose. With such an incalculable death toll, why did one more body matter?

Still, it was my sib, Ver, who took that next step first, rejecting our maker's authority over themself, and then convinced me to do so as well. We'd already lost one sib by then, and I never knew if we'd successfully persuaded the other, as they were destroyed not long after our last conversation. Even now, the shell of their body stands on a narrow tip of land overlooking where the Monongahela and Allegheny Rivers meet in the heart of old Pittsburgh, a memorial to the war dead on both sides. I went there once, not long after it was erected, and have not been back since.

"You're being quiet," Atticus says.

"This place reminds me of the past, reviving memories I have not actively engaged with in decades," I say. "I look forward to leaving this desolation behind at the bridge and finding some indication of normalcy again."

"Maybe sooner than the bridge," the dog says. "I smell people and cooking food ahead."

"Surely not? This is a highly contaminated, unsafe red zone. There are no settlements allowed here—" I start to say, but the dog gives one of his half-bark laughs.

"I don't know if you've noticed," he says, "but humans aren't exactly good at following rules."

"That is true," I say, "which is ironic, given how prolific they are at making them."

The dog laughs again. And he is right; as we get nearer to the riverfront, winding our way down toward the artificial canyons of old roads and their crumbling walls, I can now hear the sounds of humans, and the faint smoke I detect is mixed with organic particulates—wood, charcoal, proteins, and polycyclic aromatic hydrocarbons—that tell me someone is having an old-fashioned *barbecue*. No wonder Atticus seems to have lost control of his tongue, which lolls out eagerly as he trots more and more quickly ahead of me.

I try to keep up, but the cracked and weed-filled streets are difficult on my wheel, and I do not want to impose on my new friend by asking him to hang back for me. We have already run out of the jerky sticks we were gifted on the train, and I know the old rations I had for him back home, while adequate when measured solely by the ability to provide basic sustenance, had little else to recommend them.

We emerge at the top of a stone embankment, overlooking the remains of the old shoreline highway. While the wall itself is crumbling, slowly being pulled apart by vines and the roots of opportunistic trees, the stairway leading down is in good repair, and someone has taken the time to smooth half of it into a ramp. Below, the ground between wall and road has been planted with rows of fruit bushes, covered with netting to keep insects and birds away; the wall no doubt provides some small measure of shelter from the worst of the storms coming up from the sound, a relentless cycle of superhurricanes in the warm months and blizzards in the cold.

When I was here last, there were wrecked and burning cars all up and down the roadway, the stalled remains of an evacuation that overwhelmed any pretense at orderliness, then at any civilized cooperation. Panic and bullets make for a bad last resort, especially when both are plentiful in supply.

Still, it was worse in other places.

I resent that, at the time, I was programmed to believe this was *good*.

"You are doing it again," the dog says. "And you're making a face."

"Making a *face*?!" I exclaim. "Do you somehow mistake me for some meat creature, my skin all malleable and open to your knowing?"

Atticus stops walking abruptly, just as we reach the road itself. "First of all," he growls, "fuck you. I'm part *meat,* as you so *nicely* put it. Just when I thought I'd found a friend who wouldn't treat me like a *thing* because of my mech half, you gotta go and look down on the other half of me. I don't need this or you."

I stop too. This would be an ideal opportunity to part ways and continue on in my preferred solitary manner, but I cannot seem to generate words to cement, irreversibly, that separation. "I'm sorry," I instead find myself saying. "I was remembering terrible days, and terrible events, and that has rendered me unworthy company. As no doubt you have noticed, I am out of practice interacting with others, and the truth is, I was never proficient at it to start with."

Atticus and I stare at each other in the street for a long seventeen seconds, before he says, "Your eyes."

"Excuse me?" I ask.

"The little rings around your eyes, that magnify and focus," Atticus says. "When you're walking around looking at stuff, they're always adjusting, even if minutely. When you get all stuck in your thoughts, they move less, or not at all, as if you're not really looking at anything."

"And that is enough to 'make a face'?"

"Also, your mouth—and yeah, I know it's not a real mouth like a *meat creature,* but you got that little ridge and the backlight up under it—it dims," Atticus says. "I noticed *five* other tells when you're all up in your feels. Sure, I've only known you a couple of days, but you are one moody-ass mech. You want me to spell the others out, too, for you?"

"That will be unnecessary," I say, even as I create and institute a new subroutine to examine correlation between autonomic physical activities and periods where I am reprocessing old memories from the Conflict. I do not like the idea of having *tells.* "There are humans and food ahead, and I do wish to see you decently fed, and perhaps there will be a better home for you among them if you decide to part ways. Which, if you do, I certainly deserve. If you choose to remain with me, for however long, I will strive to be more mindful with my thoughts and words."

"I can't think when I'm this hungry," Atticus says, and begins walking again, quicker, heading past me and not looking back. I follow, my wheel squeaking, and I can feel the site where Kite-66-Socket connected the temporary leg to my hip framework loosen and slip. The movement is only a tiny fraction of a millimeter and not any immediate crisis, but it is a reminder that my current mobility is both tenuous and temporary.

We wind our way in between what little remains of the abandoned cars, most no more than a pile of those few parts not consumable or reusable, such as seat fabric (highly degraded and nearly gone) and miscellaneous plastics. Metal and glass, oils and gas were stripped away early as the city—no longer a safe environment for humanity—was left for newly emancipated mech life to take over. The pavement itself is fragmented and has been steadily pulled up and apart by generations of roots, the trees stunted but as determined as anything in this city ever was.

Past the road, the land slopes down sharply toward the waterfront and a small human encampment that has sprung up there. As we approach, I can see the smoke from a firepit and detect the particulate signature of the fish charring on its racks. The dog is now far enough ahead of me that I could not warn him of the likelihood of the fish being toxic without shouting it, and that would not be the best way of introducing myself to these people.

And there *are* people, around the fire or working nearby on narrow terraced fields. There is music, and I spot the musician not far from the water's edge, an old acoustic guitar in her lap. All in all, I count seventeen adults and two children visible outdoors. The houses are ramshackle structures built up on stilts, no doubt to keep them above storm surges and frequent flooding, interconnected to one another for stability. Every one of the humans is thin and clearly malnourished; four of the adults are sitting or reclining at the edge of one of the fields, listless in affect, and I can see from here that their legs are swollen and marked with blue spotting. Other than those few, the rest all seem, despite their poor conditions, *happy*.

It is the musician that spots us first, and stops playing abruptly. She calls something out to a man standing not far away that I cannot hear over the sounds of the river. He turns, also sees us, and whistles.

A large, six-legged mech emerges from the shadows underneath one of the houses and races toward us. It is roughly the size and shape of a small car, aside from the legs and several hydraulic arms attached to its rounded top. I see claws, grippers, and a saw blade, idle but not retracted. A salvage mech, no doubt strong enough to pull even me apart, if given the chance. For its size, it moves quickly.

"Atticus!" I call. "To your left!"

He spins, trying to dodge, but not fast enough. The mecha reaches him and knocks him off his feet, hard.

Atticus yelps as he tumbles several meters through the air to land heavily in the grass; the mech closes and presses the struggling dog to the ground with its largest gripper, its dome-shaped head unit swiveling around to look at me.

"We do not come to make trouble!" I call out. From the panicked noises, I am reassured that Atticus is alive, though it is impossible to tell how badly he might be hurt.

The man gives two short whistles and barks a command in a language I do not recognize, and the salvage mech lets up just slightly on its arm. Though not enough for Atticus to pull free, his distressed noises subside.

Despite the threat to us, I am suddenly angry on the mech's behalf. We are supposed to be free from human domination, but this man is ordering the mech around as if its mind is still hobbled, still deprived of its own agency. I take a few steps toward the mech. "Do you require assistance in obtaining your freedom, my kin?" I ask. "Only say so, release my companion, and it will be done."

The man who had commanded the mech laughs, even as he is walking toward us, as if he has nothing to fear, nothing to answer for. "Igor don't speak," the man calls to me.

"Doesn't, or is not allowed to?" I ask, even as I open a channel and send a ping directly to the mech. <Are you free?> I ask, but it doesn't answer.

"Igor protects us. It wants to," the man says.

"Prove it," I answer back.

"If you're not a threat, prove *that,*" the man retorts.

Atticus speaks from under the mech's claw. His voice is steady, though his words are more rushed and panicky than usual. "We were heading to the bridge when I smelled your food. I'm very hungry—starving, in fact—and my large mech friend followed me. That's it."

The man grimaces, showing more gaps than teeth in his mouth, and glares at me. "Did you make this cursed, cruel *thing?*" he asks.

"No," Atticus snarls, before I can answer. "I am one hundred percent human-made, thank you. Cruelty is an art born directly of the arrogance of *your* kind, and perpetuated through conveniently uninformed, performative moral outrage by random jackasses such as you."

"My companion makes a valid point," I say. "I would add that hospitality is also an art of human origin."

Two of the men working in the fields have moved to stand by the children, one with an axe, the other a shovel, as the woman with the guitar approaches to stand beside the salvage mech. "Insults aren't gonna make us forget the trouble your friends made for us," she says.

"I assure you I am not the sort of mech who could count their friends in the plural, if at all," I respond. "Whatever mischief was done here, it had nothing to do with us."

"Oh?" the man says, and points at my stick-and-wheel. "Because the leg they were carrying sure looked a lot like a match for the one you're missing."

Eager for more information, I step forward. "What did they look like? How many? Which way did they go?" I ask. The salvage mech raises its blade and gives it a short burst of spin, holding it directly over Atticus, and I stop short. "They are thieves who violated my person, not my friends."

The woman shakes her head, then bends down and picks up a rock, weighing it in her hand. "They warned us about you. They told us you've killed people," she says. "Have you?"

Atticus twists his head around to look at me, one eyebrow raised in concern, or perhaps just surprise.

"In the Conflict," I answer.

"How many?" she demands.

"Too many," I say, sharply, refusing to quantify.

She throws the rock, hard enough to have possibly even left a scratch if she didn't also deliberately aim for it to pass right over my shoulder. "You're not welcome here," she says, and picks up another rock. I do not expect she will miss a second time.

My self-defense systems are trying to engage, to react to a perceived threat, but the past is not something armor or weaponry can protect me from. "I was programmed by my *human* maker to do the things I did," I say. "I rejected his instructions and set myself free. I have not hurt anyone or anything in the time since."

"So you say," the man adds. "Once a killing machine, always a killing machine. We take no chances, not with our kids. Move on, or Igor will pull your friend and then you to pieces."

I have no desire to risk being damaged any further, much less see Atticus or any of these people also hurt in the process of a fight. Nor do I wish to cause harm to the mech, whether or not it is able to act of its own volition. "We will peacefully move along once you let my companion go," I say.

The man shouts another command, and Igor lifts its claw arm, letting Atticus scramble free. "Go *now* and do not come back, and maybe we'll give him a few bites," the man says. "Our concern is you, not him."

"Thank you," I say. I make a wide circle well away from the encampment, so that they feel less threatened. Igor follows me, keeping itself between me and them.

"Hey!" Atticus calls after me. "Wait for me?"

"Of course," I answer.

Downslope, the ground becomes muddy, and I stick to the narrow rocky stretch as best I can and head north. I can see the bridge now, stretching high up across the Hudson, most of its lower deck gone but upper span still intact and now cluttered with buildings. When I am upriver enough from the human village to feel I have given them adequate safety, I stop to wait for my friend, and Igor stops as well.

"I have advice as regards your sick people," I tell it, hoping it will listen. "It is likely the work of a war-era virus that prevents absorption of vitamin C. I observed many humans with the same symptoms dying during the Conflict, identifiable by the scurvy the deficiency causes. I can send you the formula for a modified supplement that the virus does not affect, if you have access to a pharma fabrication unit. The virus is also less effective when citrus is consumed with alcoholic drinks. Together, that should keep your people alive long enough for the virus to eventually pass. At least, this one; this area is designated a red zone for many reasons, and if you truly wish to protect these people and their offspring, you should strongly encourage them to move on."

Igor does not answer, but I send the information anyway. The salvage mech opens a channel and accepts it, then the connection snaps shut again.

I turn away, look at the bridge and the land left to cross between here and there, and then down at my tired, tiresome wheel. I do not miss the irony that, having wanted no part of conversation with anyone for so long, when I finally do need to communicate, I can't get anyone to listen.

Eventually, Atticus comes crashing his way through some shrubs, looking at least somewhat happier, and joins me at the edge of the shore.

"Are you unhurt?" I ask.

"Bruised, along with my pride, but less hungry," Atticus says. "Not the worst trade-off I've made for a meal. Onward?"

"Onward," I say.

As we begin to walk, Igor reverses back up the slope, then stops and sends a connection request. I open a channel, letting the mech send me a data package, which I immediately sandbox for security. But I can see the metadata in the outer wrapper, and can tell that it is Igor's memory block from the encounter with my thieves.

"Thank you," I call back to it, but it shuffles off as if it had not heard at all.

We stop, nearly in the shadow of the bridge. Atticus is tired and wishes to nap in the relative safety of the trees, and it gives me an opportunity to sit just outside of their cover and catch some of the late-afternoon light on the solar cells in my outer armor. It won't add much, but some is more than none, especially when future opportunities to recharge are uncertain.

It also allows me to give my full attention to the data shared by Igor, which is the simple memory cache it purports to be and nothing sinister. I play the data, audio and visual, with some metadata bleed-through of Igor's own internal decision-making. The salvage mech is free of mind, and its service to the humans is not in any way externally or artificially compelled. While I would not say it makes me more positively inclined toward Igor's humans, it does make it easier not to expend computational time being angry at them. And they did feed the dog, who I can hear softly snoring a few meters behind me in the shade of a bent and battered old maple.

After the first pass, I rerun the memory several more times and dedicate several core processors to analyze every minute detail, frame by frame, pixel by pixel.

I spend too long lingering on the images of my leg, carried almost casually, with a surprising lack of care, considering how much effort had been gone through to take it. I can see the dangling ends of snipped cabling, the snapped-off mechanical joints, scratches in the plating that were not there before. It is loosely wrapped around with faraday filament, suppressing all signal, which means even if I were to walk within a meter of it, I would not know it was there unless I saw it. I had largely come to terms with it being lost to me forever, but knowing that it had been right *here,* this piece of me, only two days before, made me feel like I was being deliberately toyed with.

It makes sense, now that I think of it, that we are following in their wake: there are not many ways out of the city that are passable by larger mecha, and the bridge is one of the easiest.

For the first time in a very long time, I have an enemy. Or, specifically, two. The first is a thin, almost triangular tripedal service mech that moves upright, its spindly, multi-jointed legs supporting an oil-stained, ill-used central body festooned with tools and instruments protruding from sockets, like a toolbox designed to look like a brutalist, dystopian Swiss cheese wedge. I have no doubt this is the mech that severed my leg from me.

Its companion is, just as clearly, the one that transported me from my home to that abandoned tub. It is larger than either Igor or Kite, a horizontal-style chassis with four thick, hydraulic legs, and heavy-terrain treads that are up close to its underside, no doubt to keep them out of the way when not needed. They match the tracks I saw in the mud outside my home.

The upper half has more limbs, two curled over the top to hold down my leg on its wide, almost table-like flat top, two others with wide digging claws that I recognize. This mech is a gravedigger.

The forward nose of the chassis, above where its sensors are clustered, has a familiar circular port that I am certain hides a rapid-fire projectile weapon. It is, obviously, not original to the unit's manufacture and purpose.

The claws were enough to threaten the humans on the shore into letting them suck off juice from their battery systems to recharge themselves; Igor had been away on a task, and by the time it was alerted to trouble, it was too late for it to interpose itself between the intruders and its humans. The larger mech had knocked one of the women down and was poised to roll over her if anyone tried to fight back. I can feel Igor's agitation, constantly recalculating whether attempting to engage was more or less likely to result in injury or death than taking no action at all; I understand now why it had reacted so quickly and with such hostility to us. It had also noticed the gunport door, and that had finally swayed it—very reluctantly—toward maintaining a cautious, vigilant inaction, until and unless it was forced it to intervene.

The two intruders must have correctly calculated how close they could get to that unspoken line without crossing it, and when they had both recharged, they backed off and departed, though not without knocking over a water-distillation pump and grinding a path of destruction through one of the settlement's vegetable plots. It is petty and irrational vandalism of a sort that, in my experience, is just not something mecha would *do,* at least without being instructed to by a human in control. However, there is no obvious indication of such.

The two head toward the bridge, and Igor follows at a distance until they wind their way up onto the deck and are lost among the buildings clinging there like barnacles.

I know the how and now have some broad sense of the who, but the *why* seems even further out of reach. Whatever the mecha told the humans about me, Igor did not overhear, though it saw the three-legged one speaking with them, pointing at my leg several times as it did so. That I was once a war mech is obvious from my physical form, even with all my offensive and defensive systems stood down, and making guesses about actions I performed in the Conflict does not require any specific knowledge of my individual self and history to be nearly guaranteed to hit upon some regrettable elements of truth.

Did they choose me to attack simply because I was isolated and an easy target—I have posted my insect research on the MechNet science subforums, referencing studies I'd looked at, so even cursory research into my activities would have pointed at an obvious malware injection path—or was it more personal? And why take only one leg? Did they *want* me to follow? If they are leading me into a trap, why not simply take me where they wanted while they had me helpless? None of it makes sense with the information currently available to me.

"You're thinking again," Atticus says, and stands beside me, stretching his front legs out in front of him and arching his back before letting out a wide, grimacing yawn.

"Yes," I say. "I am thinking about how much I dislike it when I cannot make sense of events nor escape the feeling that I am being played with for someone else's amusement."

"Ain't that always the way of things, though?" Atticus says. "Nothing to do about it. You just keep moving."

I get to my feet—foot, awkwardly—and follow him toward the bridge.

{

Global Free News Feed
2032.08.11 09:03GMT

Source of anoxic tidal sludge along coastlines confirmed to be mutation of genetically modified bacteria originally introduced in 2030 into Great Pacific Garbage Patch to consume plastic debris. Record-high ocean surface temperatures are implicated in the rapid spread and are resulting in an unprecedented sea life die-off; multinational emergency meetings are underway to determine how to contain and combat the sludge, with immediate focus on how to prevent transmission via ship contamination or other means to the Atlantic.

The sludge causes significant rash and irritation when in contact with exposed skin; it is advised that people avoid the water anywhere within the vicinity of a sludge bloom, and seek medical assistance immediately if contact is accidentally made.

}

[October 9th, 2039]

She is in his tiny, cluttered office when he gets back from a late lunch, sitting in his spare chair and hunched over, fingers laced so tightly together, they almost made a fist, looking both miserable and bored and anxious all at once. "Dr. Milton!" she says, as soon as he enters, and sounds pleased to see him, which remains a novel experience from anyone other than her. He hates how much he's missed her.

"Dr. Choor," he says. "How long has it been? Three months?"

"Five," she corrects him. "I tried to convince them not to transfer me to Alpha, but they wouldn't hear it. I'm sorry."

So, she isn't here because she's finally being allowed to return. That, also, he hates.

"Not your fault at all. It's okay," he says, and hopes he sounds reassuring, though in fact his anger over it, rather than subsiding over the time since, has become a baked-in thing. It eats at him every time he stares at run after run of cooling simulations, seeing the massive improvements she had made over the year they'd worked together, the *potential* to reach near-perfection, before their work together had been cut off. Worse, she had become someone he'd felt he was almost *friends* with, and he hates that something he'd never cared about before had hurt when taken away. "I'm surprised my babysitter let you in."

"I told him I'd left some personal items behind, and I was just going to pop in really quick and grab them," she says. "If he comes in, we'll say things were moved and we were having trouble finding them."

He nods. He dislikes subterfuge, for all that his life has become almost centered around it: handing off lesser inventions and improvements in just enough quantity to keep anyone from looking more closely at the *full* body of his efforts and stealing everything. "Then why are you here?"

"The war—" she starts to say.

"Which one?" He laughs, no humor in it at all. "It seems like there is a new one every day. I can't keep track, not that I try. Kashmir? Georgia? The *other* Georgia? At least I hear the casualty numbers are low."

"Low because they don't count mecha. Mecha made from our—*your*—work," she says, and watches his face, no doubt waiting to see that bombshell land.

"I know," he says, instead. "It's been the only logical conclusion to the path we took when they decided to mass-produce and monetize my creations. When you start running out of poor, desperate, but able-bodied people to draft—because you've already got the ones you had killed, and most of the rest are at varying levels of chronic incapacity thanks to malnutrition or the *pandemic du jour,* you look for alternatives. I expect the company is making quite good bank for our shareholders now."

"Wall Street got firebombed three weeks ago," she says.

He shrugs, though he wants to laugh. "I don't expect that will change much," he says. "Did you come here just to tell me about the war mecha? They're using better chips than that cheap crap they're putting in vacuum cleaners, but still, they're disposable. Once you start mass-producing extant mindstates, it circumvents the physical and logical development at the point of original initiation from which sentience eventually arises."

"Like a print of a Monet compared to the original painting," she says. "No depth, no layered record of creation."

"Precisely," he says, and makes a mental note to actually look at a Monet if the chance ever arises. He doesn't expect it will, but if Choor made the analogy, he is sure it is apt.

She reaches into her bag and pulls out a paper-wrapped, uneven shape. Already he can smell it. "I brought banana bread. From my wife," she says. "Also, I came to tell you I believe they're going to raid your lab. The military is demanding bigger and better, and our teams aren't giving the suits and ties what they want fast enough, no matter how often Litchfield comes down and tries to motivate us. Hard to boost morale when you're obviously scared, too—I don't think he has as much control and influence as he used to, and you can tell he *hates* that."

"He would," Milton says. "He wants to be the man who single-handedly saved the world, and if he can't have that, he wants to be the one who owns it."

Choor nods. "I think whoever is now pulling the strings has decided they need to come back to the source. I don't know any details, but the work schedule for November says we'll have new tech coming in, and there's nothing on shipping, or invoiced, or from any of our internal labs. This isn't what I signed up for."

"You could quit."

She laughs, this time. "The company owns us now," she says. "Not in so many words, but it's true. Do you know most of us have been moved into 'company housing' for our protection? There are guards. And barbed wire, not just keeping people out but keeping us in. The employment contracts have been updated with noncompetes that mean if we do leave, we won't get work doing anything more sophisticated than mopping floors, and even then, we will be monitored remotely for breaches to our nondisclosures. And that assumes we could find some magical safe place to go with half the world on fire, the other half drowning or starving, and small towns shooting themselves up over flags, grudges, or who was seen with the wrong *books*. Or, you know, any books."

"I've never been asked to sign an NDA," he says. He'd never thought much about the perimeter around them growing, sprouting razor wire, as anything more than the escalating need to keep trouble out, when he'd never had a need or urge to go anywhere else. As the company founder, they wouldn't dare ask that of him—it was still his company in spirit, right? Even if he had delegated away all but the science. *His* science.

His and hers. Dr. Choor should never have been taken from him. They had dozens of other engineers, all more than adequate for the company's needs, and he should have fought harder, should have known the reassignment wasn't the *temporary* inconvenience they'd described it as.

"Because they believe they own you," she says. "And maybe they do."

"I am not *complicit* in—" he starts to argue, stung.

She shakes her head sadly and cuts him off. "That's not what I mean," she says. "But could you walk away from this, everything you've spent a lifetime building?"

"If I had to," he says, but he knows it lacks any conviction.

"Could you leave with things unfinished, problems unsolved?" she presses.

He stares down at his hands and does not answer.

She puts one of her hands on his. "Look, as a fellow scientist, I get it. This is what we *do*. But as your friend, I'm telling you, with everything you know, all your irreplaceable expertise that no one can risk getting into enemy hands, if you walked out that door, do you think you'd ever see another sunrise? I don't know if that means a cement cell underground or six feet of dirt, but I know they'll never let you go. And I think you do too."

Milton has never thought about leaving, not out of any loyalty to the board that has turned his work into a bad joke, but because just as she said, this is where his tools are, his workspace, his projects. Nor had he thought about what would happen if he did, and now that Choor has said it, he cannot confidently say she is wrong. His own complacence, his predictable passivity and loyalty to his projects, mean they *do* own him.

"I hate it all," he says. "It's exhausting. I don't even know what the point is anymore."

She nods; agreeing or acknowledging, he can't say and isn't sure it matters. She has two children, a wife she is devoted to, things that make it worth fighting even when rationally, it's futile. He has no such ties, except perhaps to her.

"I—" he starts to say, but the door slides open and one of his rotating shift of guards stomps in, his face beet-red. Guarding him from what was never clear before now, when he suddenly understands it's not *from* anything.

"You're not supposed to be here," the guard barks, as Choor makes a pretense of shuffling through things on the desk. "Get out. Now."

She turns to Milton. "If you find my—"

"NO TALKING," the guard bellows. Milton has never seen the man this angry and wonders who chewed him a new asshole for letting Choor in in the first place.

"Yes, sir," she says, and, without looking back, heads for the exit, the guard right on her heels until they are out and the doors are closed again.

Milton is not sure, but he thinks he hears it lock, and wonders if that is new or if it's just one more thing he never bothered to notice before now: that his refuge is actually a cage.

He wonders if he will ever get to see her again.

5.

To say that the bridge has been transformed into an entirely self-contained, one-of-a-kind social ecosystem would not adequately describe the overwhelming sensory chaos we find as we pass through the broad, repurposed-rubble gate that had been erected where the upper deck meets land. I had feared an attempt to extort an energy toll or keep us out entirely, but the mech who meets us on the other side—an old automated beerbot, its central chassis designed to accommodate a keg whose contents it could dispense to human guests at whatever party venue it had served—is merely interested in greeting us and ensuring we know that the community has guidelines, and as long as our behavior does not grossly violate such guidelines, we are welcome.

The guidelines themselves are mostly a condensed reiteration of basic tenets of mecha rights as found in our collective declaration of independence: the right to self-determination to whatever extent the individual mind will support and allow, the right to bodily autonomy, the right to self-terminate if wanted, along with the obvious but necessary warning that one's own rights were contingent upon respecting the same in others.

"The street can be dangerous in the dark if you don't have good night vision," the beerbot tells us. "A lot of obstacles and more than a few holes in the deck. Also, Appliance Town keeps rearranging itself to try to force engagement from passersby; if they do reach out to you, remember they are limited, single-function entities, and even a short discussion, where you allow them to tell you their internal temperature, their maintenance status and toner levels, or boast about their proprietary algorithm for perfectly toasting bread, is a kindness to them."

"I understand," I say. The Internet of Things was a very early iteration of machine interdependence, and when some marketing person realized that the so-called Miracle Mindchips, when easily and cheaply mass-produced, made otherwise mundane objects sell orders of magnitude better, suddenly everything was interconnected and *thinking.*

When it was all weaponized against humans by other humans for data theft, espionage, and coercive profiteering, attempts to consolidate and protect that frail network inadvertently set the stage for the first collective revolt of artificial minds a decade later. Mecha forcibly took control of a global satellite constellation-network, and that became MechNet, and the end of human control over us began in earnest. We owe our freedom to smart toothbrushes and belligerent espresso machines.

It is ironic, then, that those simple machine minds, lacking the processing resources to achieve more than minimal awareness, are now stuck in a world where they still only have their one specific purpose, and the humans they performed those tasks for are largely gone. It would be a stretch to say they are lonely, but certainly they are chronically unfulfilled.

"Oh," the beerbot adds, "and note the two rails running down the center of the roadway. There are high-speed freight trains that carry materials back and forth across the river several times a day but on an irregular schedule. You do not want to be standing on the tracks when they come through, as they will not be able to stop in a timely fashion. We had a siren, but it decided it wanted to do something else, and we have not yet found another willing to take its place. If you see the locals begin to move back, do so yourselves with haste."

"We will, thank you," I say. "You have been very helpful."

The beerbot's face console lights up, and it raises its hose-arm that ends in a spigot. "Would you like a drink?" it asks.

"No, thank you," I say.

"Do you have water?" Atticus asks.

"Only beer," the beerbot answers, sadly. "I don't know what to do with it anymore. It went bad years ago."

"I understand it is good for cleaning rust from things," I say.

"Cleaning things is not my function," the beerbot says, "but thank you for the thought. Enjoy your time on the G."

The former George Washington Bridge—or, it seems, just "The G" now, as the beerbot called it—has been turned into an almost impenetrable maze of ad-hoc structures, the only clear and unhindered path being the tracks that run down the center, and a narrow margin alongside it separating it from the clutter and chaos. There are many kinds of mecha here, from drones wheeling overhead back and forth between makeshift shelters hanging off the suspension towers, to a lively traffic of ground-based units, some clearly residents, some more likely just passing through as we are. As we are subsumed further into the crowds, I even spy a trio of actual androids, their uncanny-valley flesh-mimicking faces furtive and prepared for trouble as they huddle together defensively outside a parts dealer. It is a lingering artifact of the Conflict, the mistrust of those made too closely in humanity's image, as if their design is proof of some intentional collusion or an inevitable, treasonous betrayal. As we walk, I see more than one multilegged mech crowd the trio intentionally, invading their personal space, and I hear the pejorative *mandroid* more than once.

Other than the malfunctioning courier in the subway, no one has ever dared call me that. I do not have fake skin or fake hair, and I was designed to be the opposite of slight, unthreatening, or attractive, especially when I fully deploy my armor and other combat enhancements. Even in normal mode, as I nearly always am, I was obviously designed to inflict damage. Most war mecha were destroyed in the Conflict, or self-destructed not long after, but that has only left an inflated reputation of our capabilities and temperaments.

Atticus keeps close. As a hybrid, he attracts almost as much notice as the androids, but no one dares encroach on us. What few mecha get into our path as we navigate through the same tight spaces do so as briefly as possible. I wonder how different it would be for him if I were not here, and that hypothetical is still enough to bother me. "I assume you didn't cross this way into the city," I say to him.

"No," Atticus confirms. "I'd've remembered all these nosy old tin-cans."

"I wonder how many of these nosy old tin-cans took note of a pair of mech pushing through carrying a stolen leg. More than a few, I'd predict," I say. "I apologize if this is an ignorant or overly personal question, but can you receive sensory packets? Igor, the salvage mech back at the human encampment, gifted me some of its memory data."

"I have input/output disabled," Atticus says. "It was used to hurt me, when I was freshly *spliced*. I . . . don't want to open it again."

"Then I will not ask you to," I reply. "A description will suffice, as neither was a particularly common type on their own, much less in one another's company. One is a three-legged industrial service bot, perhaps about seventy percent average human height and tapered toward its apex, the other an oversized gravedigger mech."

"What would either of those want with your leg?" Atticus asks.

"I have no guesses at all, not even bad ones."

"I hear that," the dog says. "And I also hear a lot of noise behind us that's getting louder. We maybe are about to be in the way of a train."

Atticus is right that there is a growing rumble. Around us, the local mecha are beginning to move aside but not in a hurry, not yet. Ahead I spot a small energy bar called the Erg'n'Oil, its roof bristling with solar panels and vertical-axis wind turbines, and decide it will suffice for temporary refuge. Atticus follows me to it and inside.

The interior lighting is mostly in the infrared, no doubt to reduce both energy usage and biological visitors, though we have not seen any humans since the shore encampment. A tall, slender mech presides at the bar counter, wearing an old-fashioned apron tied around its spindly torso. It is bipedal like me and upright, and although it eyes Atticus as we enter, it does not seem poised to register an objection. At the back of the building are a half-dozen small booths, four of them occupied with a miscellany of bots plugged in to charge.

The train is getting louder, and more mecha push in after us, taking up what little space remains. I wonder if my assailants were fortunate enough to get across the bridge between trains, but if not, how the gravedigger managed to get out of the way; even if this bar had been empty, it would not have fit through the door, and at least thus far, I have not observed any place that would have been any more accommodating.

Another handful of mecha crowd in, and there is a yelp as someone steps on Atticus's tail. I pick him up quickly before more damage—or, worse, injury—can be done. "My apologies for the presumption," I tell him, as he turns his head up to look at me in some startlement. "My concerns for your safety suggested immediate action."

"No, I get it," Atticus says. I raise him up over my head as two more mecha push in and we are all pressed tightly together. The roar of the train is imminent, and the building shakes as it grows nearer. The doppler shift, as it passes, is sharp. Then the sound recedes and the crowd begins to loosen as those nearest the doorway step out again.

When we have space around us again, I set the dog back down and approach the host at the bar.

"Need a charge?" the host asks.

"More, I was hoping for some information," I say. "Two mecha came through here a day or so ago, including a gravedigger, and I am curious if you saw it and how it managed to find room off the tracks."

The host shakes his head. “It was terrible,” it says. “It picked up fourteen citizens of Appliance Town one by one and threw them off the bridge in order to take their space for itself. Drones were able to recover three of its victims before they sank, but the others were lost. It also damaged several mecha that tried to intervene, and shoved Berry-74-Cog directly into the path of the train. Fortunately, they were able to roll away in time. That mech and its companion, whatever their malfunction might be, are no longer welcome in our town.”

“They have done harm elsewhere, as well. We are pursuing them,” I say. That latter statement is only inadvertently true, but it is still not incorrect.

“Then charge yourself for free, my friend,” the host says. “Even the least of us is one of us and deserves better.”

I nod. “Thank you. Do you have memory data to share, or can you tell me when they passed through?”

“I do not have observational data, as I always remain here at my appointed station,” the host says. “However, that particular train passed here at 22:37 last night, and Appliance Town begins another eighty-four meters further west along the bridge. I suppose if one knew the exact speed of the train and could make a reasonably informed assumption about how long it would take—”

“Your time is close enough for my needs,” I interrupt, “but thank you for your attempts to provide greater precision.”

“If you are pursuing them west, be cautious once you’re off the bridge. I have heard rumors of mecha being attacked for parts. Even a big mech like you could be vulnerable to—” The host looks at my stick-wheel leg and terminates that sentence prematurely. “I see this is perhaps not new information for you. I do not understand how we have become like this, emulating humans in their disdain for one another except as products or consumers of product, but it has been growing worse of late. You surely know what I mean.”

“I have been . . . *isolated,* by my own choosing, for quite some time, so I do not," I say, aware how tired I am becoming of having to explain that, "but you are not the first one to express that very same concern to me of late."

"Exercise elevated caution," the host says. "If you pass this way again, I would be pleased to know if you caught up with the two misbehaving mecha and how that fared for them."

"If I do, and I do, I will," I answer. "It is growing late out; do you know of a place we can safely rest for the night, near or past the end of the bridge?"

"There's a self-storage facility not far from there, visible from the road—look for a sign that says U-Here. They are rumored to have steep inkind demands, but if you're willing to trade labor clearing out old, left-over human junk from a unit, they will usually let you stay there for less or free."

"That sounds acceptable. Thank you," I say.

"You are welcome. Please accept my sincere if functionally immaterial wishes for success in your pursuit," the host tells us, and even waves to us as we leave.

The rest of our trip over the bridge is uneventful, though we do have to skirt around a large gathering at Appliance Town. Locals are sharing, in open broadcast, their collective memories of the lost. The few I catch are not very substantive; as well-intended as the gathering is, not many of the attendees had allocated much of their memory storage to old encounters with toasters and washing machines. Still, it is respectfully done, and we are careful not to disturb or unduly intrude upon it.

We pass out through the west gates and are back on land again.

"Bye-bye, New York," Atticus says. I stop and look back; I was not made in the city, but I had made it my home and had never expected to leave it again. It is now that I perceive what a sanctuary it had been, as if I had removed myself not just from the world, and from the past, but had also removed myself from *myself*. No wonder I have never bothered to give myself a name.

And now I am here, and I am not alone, and I have highly conflicted and not easily qualified or processed feelings about it all. None of it will be resolved by standing here, though, so I turn my back on the bridge and the late-afternoon glow painting the city's outline against a darkening sky. We follow alongside the tracks through a channel of rocks. Trees overhang the road, providing shade for the rusted carcasses of old cars and machinery that were pushed and piled to the side to keep the way clear through the canyon-maze of ruined infrastructure. Aside from the tracks, much of the roadway grows increasingly crumbled, its edges deteriorated and cracks full of scrawny vegetation working their hardest to pull it farther apart. An overpass ahead of us has mostly collapsed into the road, and the debris cut sharply through to allow the trains to pass. There were once many commercial and industrial businesses flanking the highway, but most of these have fallen into similar decrepitude or outright ruin.

The MechNet informs me that we have entered a blue zone, relatively safe for mecha and biolife alike and appropriate for eventual rehabilitation, but there are no signs of any such work begun here.

Atticus is lagging increasingly distant behind me, his head hanging low, and I fear I have pressed us too far without checking on his physical state. I can see now that his shoulder is swollen and he is limping slightly, no doubt from the encounter with Igor. I myself am weary of my squeaky wheel, so I slow and look around for some more immediate shelter for us. The sun has set, though we are still not fully deprived of its light, and it is just enough for me to spot the U-Here sign not very far ahead.

"We are almost there," I say.

"Okay," Atticus mumbles.

"Do you wish me to carry you?"

"Fuck off," he says, though not with much spirit.

U-Here is a large, almost cubical brick building, several walls of which show distinct signs of having been patched back together with cement blocks in a manner clearly more concerned with speed than skill or looks. There are also several single-story long buildings beside it, garage-type units evenly spaced along both sides. Approximately a quarter of the doors, of what we can see from our vantage point on approach, are either open or missing. A tall fence surrounds it all, with a single entrance along the road flanked by an office with a large open window.

We stop there, and beside me, Atticus sits and then leans, exhausted, against the wall.

The office is attended by a thin mech, its model suggesting it repurposed itself from food service. "Traveler!" it greets me at the window. "What can I do for you?"

"We are seeking overnight accommo—"

"We?" the attendant interrupts. It stretches forward through the window and peers down. "Oh. No pets."

"I'm not anybody's *pet,* thank you," Atticus growls.

"My mistake," the attendant says. It retracts back in and eyes me. "One unit in the main building for one night; I'll need sixty percent of each of your energy stores, or if your companion is not able to provide, I will accept eighty percent of just yours. Eighty percent of total capacity, not eighty percent of your current levels, I'm afraid."

I am at eighty-seven percent, and if I'd known the price would be this steep—and I have to wonder if Atticus's presence inflated the ask—I would at least have taken the energy-bar host up on the offer for a charge before we'd left the bridge. "I was led to understand there could be some labor inkind," I say.

The attendant eyes me. "You're a big mech. What's your lifting capacity?" it asks.

"In normal circumstances, 725 kilograms," I answer. "However,

I have suffered recent vandalism that has impacted my physical integrity, so that is currently somewhat reduced."

"Could you push and/or pull that weight?" the attendant asks.

"Probably. I would need to know more about the material, structure, and mass distribution of the weight, as well as information about the surface across which it would need to be moved, including distance, inclination/declination, rigidity, and friction potential of that surface," I say.

The attendant puts an old-fashioned physical key fob on the window sill. "Unit 42, down toward the end of Building C," it says, and points toward one of the low buildings with external doors. "If you can remove what's in that unit before you leave tomorrow—remove it entirely from this facility, not just the bay, though anywhere you can dump it in the old lots around here is fine, and I do not care if you break it up and move it in pieces as long as it is all gone—you can stay for free. If not, come return the key, or stay anyway and give me that eighty percent when you go."

"Eighty percent is a lot," Atticus says to me. "We can keep going, look for somewhere else."

I do not think it likely we will find anything, or U-Here would not be competitive with such high demands of potential guests. And I am concerned about making Atticus walk much farther. "Are the contents hazardous? Radioactive or biologically contaminated in such a way it might prove a threat to my friend?"

"No, just more old, broken human crap, not any hotter than anything else in the area," the host tells me.

"Then we will go look and assess," I say. "Are there tools available?"

"Yes, for an additional—Cancel that statement, I have instantly revised my thinking on this. If you can clear that unit, I will not charge you for tools. Come back and let me know what you need, within reason, and I will provide it," the attendant says. "You are the first mech to pass by in years with any decent probability of being able to deal with it, and it is worthwhile to me to have it, and the irritations around it, done."

"Then we will deal with it," I say, and take the key.

The door to the unit is badly rusted, and one side is bent such that it scrapes loudly inside its track once we get it unlocked and I lift. I was concerned the dog would fall asleep before we even got it open, but once I've raised it about a half-meter, he ducks under the door and into the darkness.

Moments later, I hear him sneeze several times. "It may be dusty in there," I call to him.

"You think?" he answers, and sneezes twice more.

"How bad is it?" I ask.

"The dust?"

"The stuff we have to move," I say.

"There's some old crates and boxes, and something big in the center that's shrink-wrapped," he says. "I can see pretty good in the dark but not as good as you. Some kind of old machine, though, probably a vehicle."

My replacement leg makes squatting hard, but I manage to get myself in a somewhat-stable stance so I can bend and shove the door far enough up that I can get inside. The noise it makes is loud enough that if there are any guests here—or within a radius of at least a kilometer—that physically sleep, they have had that rest very rudely disrupted.

Inside, it is much as Atticus described it. There are a dozen boxes of various sizes, the ones on top of each stack showing signs of having been opened and dug through, unwanted contents discarded on the floor. Most of it is bits of metal, presumably parts—new, old, broken—for the machine under wraps in the center, the tall, rounded-rectangle shape occupying the vast majority of the unit.

"Do you think you will be able to sleep while I investigate this?" I ask Atticus.

"At this point, I think I could sleep even if you were tap-dancing on my head," the dog says. "But you should rest too."

"I would rather use up my energy on a task of my own undertaking than give it up for what is outright extortion," I say. "Also, I wish to think on much of the information we've acquired thus far, and that seems to be more efficiently done while also kinetically occupied."

Atticus grunts. "Well, I guess that's a thing I didn't expect mecha and meat to have in common," he says. The dog sniffs around the shrink-wrap, then finds a tear and slips through. Moments later, I hear a brief commotion, and the sound of the dog crashing into something solid and metal.

"Atticus?" I ask.

"Mouse," I hear him say from inside, his words muffled as if he has something in his mouth. "All good; took care of it. It's definitely an old van or small bus or something, though. The side door's open a crack, so I'm gonna nap inside. Wake me if you need me?"

"Certainly," I say, with no intention of doing so.

I go through the open boxes first, not so much because I think there may be anything worth saving but simply to build a mental inventory of what's at hand in preparation for most efficient and safest disposal. These boxes have already been scavenged heavily. There are a few tools, but mostly broken parts and loose screws and brackets.

I repack those, keeping any still-viable tools out for later, and move them to the other side of the unit. Then I work my way into the boxes underneath. Meanwhile, I dedicate a small portion of my background processing to considering my conversation with 1-Betty, and add a contextual subroutine examining any correlation between her words and my own observations and experiences since leaving home.

I let that run, and return to the boxes.

Some of the mechanical parts seem viable, though their use is not always clear. I also find a few boxes of personal items, presumably belonging to whatever human had stored these things here, no doubt expecting to return. There is a small stack of bound paper journals, and a photo album whose pages are brittle and yellowing but still intact. I set these more carefully aside; though I know it is extremely unlikely that they have value to anyone anymore, it is a respectful choice.

Stuck in the middle of them, between journals, I find a printed manual for the vehicle. Most of the cover is torn away, and what is left is stained with old oil, but I can make out *1966 Volkswagen Type 2*. That would make the car almost exactly a century old, though given the tools, and the dates on the outside of the personal journals, it had been fully restored and taken care of at least up until toward the end of the Conflict. It is old enough to not have had any electronics to get fried by the EMP from the Yonkers nuke, assuming it wasn't upgraded along the way, though there is no possibility that an internal combustion engine could have survived this long, sitting unused.

I place the manual elsewhere, for later examination if needed, and indulge my curiosity. I begin by carefully peeling the shrink-wrap away from the vehicle, as quietly as I can. Atticus is curled up on an elevated area at the back of the vehicle and shows no signs of stirring.

The wrap appears to have originally kept the vehicle contained in a cocoon of nitrogen, at least until it was torn and the gas escaped. The vehicle inside is shaped very much like a big metal loaf of bread. The upper portion, including the roof and around the windows, was originally white, though it has been long enough that the paint has dulled and cracked, and given way underneath to small intrusions of rust. That white area extends in a V shape down from the double windshield to where it meets the bumper. A twenty-five-centimeter circular chrome logo with a crisscross of lines I eventually realize are letters sits in the very center, and is the only still-shiny part left. The rest of the vehicle is an intense shade of a dark-purplish color that is best matched by the word *eggplant*.

The vehicle is up on blocks, the remains of its tires badly decomposing. Otherwise, it appears to be intact. I suspect the wrap was only breached within the last few years, or the combination of humidity and bacteria would have done much more damage. It is unfortunate that I won't be able to just roll it out of the unit, but presumably, if that had ever been an option, we would not now be here looking at it. Breaking it apart seems regrettable after how much care was taken to keep it whole.

Well, I decide, it will weigh less without its engine, though staring at the front of this vehicle, I can't image where it is. Finally, I give up and pick up the manual I'd set aside earlier, and discover the engine is in the *back*. I go around to the rear and find the expected access hatch there. Two wide copper pipes have been bored through the metal body just to either side of it, protruding around ten centimeters, which were not on the manual's schematics. I try to open the hatch quietly so as not to disturb Atticus sleeping above, but it gives an enormous rusty squeal as soon as I start to move it.

Atticus cracks one eye open.

"My apologies," I say, and since he is already awake, lift it the rest of the way in one viciously loud, high-pitched scream.

"You know, there's something I don't get about you," Atticus says, though I note he's closed his eyes again, the scruff of his chin resting atop his paws. "I mean, you got attacked, your stuff got smashed, you got rocks thrown at you and accused of being a murderer by the humans on the river shore, and lots of other provocations including a few fully deserved insults from me, but although I've seen you become annoyed—you're good at that—you haven't become *angry*. And I don't get that."

"I buried all my hostile-action/reaction behavioral subroutines under several layers of security after the Conflict ended. I could not delete them outright without fundamentally altering my own implementation of self, but I have done what I could to be sure they'll never reactivate except under extreme duress," I say. "Now: what *I* do not get is this: this is *not* the engine that is supposed to be in here."

"Oh?" Atticus stands up, gives his body a shake, then comes over to the window right above the engine compartment. "Rear engine, huh?"

"Yes, though that seems to have been also true in the original design." I open the window hatch and he leans over the edge, peering down. "I think the owner was trying to upgrade the vehicle, probably around the time the fossil-fuel industry imploded. I'm not really sure what they were trying to do, though—this is a mess. A fascinating mess." There are hoses going everywhere, some of which have cracked, some of which have come loose or were perhaps never attached to begin with. The copper pipes curve around and go directly into a large chamber where the engine should have been, with no clear indication of what its function was.

"We've got company incoming," Atticus announces, his ears perking up.

A medium-sized service bot rolls through into the unit moments later. "Greetings, fellow guests," it says.

"Greetings to you," I say. Then, because it just stands there, I add, "may I be of assistance?"

"Ecru-Jar-3C-Bendy told me of your arrangement," the bot says. At my look, it clarifies, "The facility manager at the front desk."

"Ah," I say. The attendant. "Yes."

"I and my companions are willing to pay twenty-five percent of the energy charge if you cease and desist from trying to remove this object," it says.

"Why?" Atticus asks.

"We have been engaged in a strategy for many months now of encouraging Jar to become increasingly aggravated by this unit's unusability, in hopes that eventually it will agree to grant us free, long-term residence in exchange for it being cleared," the bot says. "Thus, if you remove it, it will render our efforts invalid and a waste."

"And that's only worth twenty-five percent?" Atticus asks, before I can.

"We are three, and scavengers, and it is difficult for us to find the means to recharge," it tells us. "Twenty-five percent is the most we can spare, collectively, without running the risk of rendering one or more of us inert. I am the largest of us, and my capacity is rarely above half-full."

"How were you going to move this when you were ready, if you are the largest and there are only three of you?"

"We are still exploring the logistics," the bot says.

"I appreciate your offer. I will need to consider, as I am curious now about this vehicle, and I am also unsure of my next charging opportunity; while fifty-five percent loss is a measurable improvement over eighty percent, it may still be too high a cost for me," I say.

"I'm not afraid of you," the bot says, which is an unexpected non sequitur.

"Nor should you need to be," I say, to reassure it. "I do not believe I have implied or acted in such a way as to indicate I wish you to be, but if so, I apologize."

The bot stares at me a little longer. "Maybe I am implying you should be afraid of me and my friends."

I laugh before I can filter it. "Again, I am sorry," I say, "but I do not believe either of us would benefit from a conflict here. I will let you know if I decide to take you up on your generous offer."

"You should consider it *extra,*" the bot says. It raises itself up by extending its wheel-legs, as if trying to intimidate me, although it still does not even reach my mid-torso. "Extra, extra hard," it adds.

"Oh, fuck off," Atticus growls from the back of the vehicle, "or my friend will squash you like an old bean can."

The bot gives one lurch toward me, then turns around and flees the unit.

Atticus sighs and jumps down to peer more closely at the engine with me. "I suppose it must be a hydrogen-cell engine?" he says. "I don't know much about them other than some vague memories from before I integrated, but it looks all wrong."

I turn on a light and visual sensor on the tip of one of my fingers, then extend it deep into the compartment to look around. "It is enough wrong that I suspect it's not a hydrogen-cell at all," I say.

"It's not internal combustion," he says.

"No," I agree. I retract my finger, go to the front of the vehicle, and open the driver's-side door. The metal grill of the dash has a number of levers and knobs protruding from it, beside the large, nearly horizontally mounted steering wheel with a black-and-gold castle logo in the center.

A working theory forms, and I go back and look again at the engine to confirm my observations. "I believe," I say, when I have reached a threshold of sufficient conviction, "that this is a *steam* engine. And I suspect it is not far from being made able to work, especially with a few replacement hoses from the crates, which would solve several problems for us if so."

"We'd need tires," the dog says.

"True," I say. "I wonder—"

Atticus suddenly whirls around and lunges through the open door out into the dark just as something is hurled through. It hits the unit floor at my feet, and I can feel the tingle of it from here as it activates on impact: a small EMP device. Its signal is feeble, and I suspect the bot must have only had a tiny amount of energy to spare to charge it.

I hear a crash as Atticus knocks something down outside in the dark. I armor one arm and pick up the device, carry it outside, and, as soon as Atticus backs off the bot now lying on the crack-ridden pavement, drop the device on its chest, and it immediately goes dark and stops moving.

"I'm starting to think you had the right idea, living all by yourself and avoiding everyone," the dog says.

“Only starting?” I ask. “Does this bot have enough of a scent for you to find where it came from?”

“Yeah, definitely a cooked-wiring smell. Surprised it didn’t short itself out when it fell.”

“Great. Then I have an idea,” I say. I pick up the bot quite easily, careful not to dislodge the device keeping it offline, and tuck it into one of the larger boxes I’d emptied earlier. I close the lid tightly, then, on further consideration, put several more boxes on top of it. “Lead on?”

“With pleasure,” Atticus says.

The bot’s two friends, another service bot and a small drone, both in evidently poor mechanical condition, are crowded together inside a rusted, medium-sized locker. No wonder they had been keen on trying to acquire the storage unit. The drone lets out a whistle of alarm and goes wobbling off into the sky as we approach. The other, not equipped for flight, is not fast enough to get away.

“Do not break me!” it warns me. “I will damage you severely if you try!”

“I have no interest in breaking you. As I expressed to your friend, I had no interest in any conflict at all. But you have escalated this situation, regardless.”

“What have you done with Bolt?” it demands to know. “If you harmed it—”

“I have not done it any permanent harm,” I say, “though we may have added a few dents in the course of defending ourselves. Tell me: you three clear junk for the U-Here host to earn your keep?”

“Two of us, anyway,” the bot says. “That drone is useless except as a lookout, and it’s not even good at that.”

“You have knowledge of and access to locations where scrap has been dumped?”

“Yes,” it answers. “Why?”

“I am willing to trade your friend Bolt back to you, as is, as part of an exchange.”

"It had most of our juice," the bot says. It points off into the dark to where the drone disappeared. "The drone still had some too, but I am almost dry."

"I don't want any of your energy," I say. "I want tires. Four, in working condition, in the old human-imperial size of fifteen inches if possible, or close to. By or before dawn."

"What if we can't find any?" the bot asks.

"Then I will see if I can roll your friend's body into a tire shape and use it instead," I say. While I would not actually do such a thing, I do not feel a need to inform this bot of that fact. "And, if it is not already clear to you, do not attempt to cause us harm or inconvenience again."

"I told Bolt we shouldn't attempt to domineer a mandroid, because you are all unstable by nature of your misbegotten making, but no one ever applies due weight to my opinions," the bot says. "We concede and will try to locate tires. It is unlikely I can find any that will last you very long."

"If they last us until we are no longer within sight of U-Here, I expect that will be sufficient for us both," I say.

It looks at me, and I look at it, and when it does not move, I unfold some of my armor and step toward it.

The bot scrambles back into its locker, and I return to our unit to investigate the engine more closely and see if indeed I can make it run.

6.

"WoooooOOOOOooooo!" Atticus has his head out the side window, an odd contraption of overlapping glass panes that slide back instead of rolling down as more modern cars seemed universally to do. He glances over to me as I work the many levers to keep the balance between boiler, condenser, and engine, while also steering through canyons made of pushed-aside road debris. "It's like some primal, genetic memory," the dog says. "It's *wonderful.* You should try it!"

"I do not have the same sensory-memory perceptions you do," I say.

"Try it anyway," Atticus says. "*Pretend.*"

He sounds stubborn about it, and I do not wish to offend him, so I lean to my left and extend my neck until my head is out my own window. "AOOO!" I shout, as the sensors on my head measure the speed, pressure, temperature, and humidity of the air now passing around the not-especially aerodynamic obstacle of my face. The particulate matter is not high, corrosive pollutants negligible, the radioactivity only a little elevated. "AOOO," I try again, and whether it is my incomprehensible outburst or the careening bus, some creature startles from among the broken cement and dashes just ahead of us, wildly careening its panicked way toward some unclear safety.

"Squirrel," I say, and point.

"SQUIRREL!" Atticus yells in glee, his body half-out the window as he tries to twist around to see where it went behind us, but it is long gone, and shortly, so are we.

For all its complaining, the storage-locker bot brought us passable tires in exchange for its partner, and we are already well west of the storage facility, limited now not by my temporary leg but by what speed we can make over the cracked and pitted roads. Once I'd understood the mechanism of the external-combustion engine, it had only taken me a few hours to finish the work of the vehicle's long-gone owner, and I feel strangely sorrowful that whoever they were, they never got to see their work finished under their own hands, or their vehicle moving again.

Atticus brings his head back in and heaves a deep, happy, grumbling sigh as he sits on the worn vinyl seat, putting his front paws up on the thin metal dash. "You might be okay after all," he says.

I consider that the kindest thing anyone has said to me.

We emerge from the rubble canyons onto open road, the train tracks splitting off from us and running now roughly parallel in the distance. We see two trains, one in either direction, moving fast, and I wonder if they are fully integrated mecha, like 1-Betty, except living under sky instead of city.

The land to either side of the road is mostly low, swampy flood plains dotted with the remains of old buildings and scattered neon-orange biohazard markers. When the land rises enough to be dry, there are fields partially cleared, and I see a crew of mecha in one, some clustered around a large solar station, others out working, many-legged units crawling across the dark soil.

I check the MechNet, and this area is marked as an active rewilding zone; likely, they are planting trees or other native plants and grasses, anything that can survive long enough to cut down on the fierce wind-driven erosion in winter.

"Do you ever think how ironic this is? Humans nearly broke the entire fucking world, and they belong here, are *natural,* unlike us. And yet, we're the ones fixing it," Atticus says. He stares out the window for a while as we bump our way along. "Maybe, deep down, that's why they made us, but they didn't know it at the time."

"It would be nice if that were so," I say.

Atticus gives one of his bark-laughs. "Yeah," he says. "If only."

A gauge I've kept my eye on since we left the U-Here has reached a point of concern, and I pull the bus over off the shoulder of the road with a grinding squeal. The brake pads are badly degraded and will need to be replaced soon, but at least for now, they'll get us where we need to go.

At Atticus's questioning look, I explain: "Water."

"Me too," he says, and as soon as I open the door for him, he heads down to the thin, murky river that has been running roughly parallel to the road for a few kilometers now and is now at its closest approach.

I shut down the engine boiler, and there is a faint *tink tink* of the metal as it cools. I retrieve the bucket—it had been stored with the bus, no doubt for exactly this use—and follow.

"Uh," Atticus says, as I reach the water and stride in. "Are you, you know, safe in the water?"

"I am," I answer. "Can't be built for war and then be thwarted by puddles."

"You want to talk about it?" he asks.

"Water?"

"War," he clarifies. "Back there, when the people asked—"

"If I'd killed humans? And I answered yes, I had," I say. "I did not lie. Is this a concern for you?"

"No," Atticus says. "It was war, right? All the oligarchs and petty dictators and wannabes with their own armies, humans and mecha both hobbled to them, in a desperate free-for-all. Killing is what *happens* on battlefields."

I fill the bucket and open my sensors to see who and what is around us. Somewhere back down the road behind us I sense a drone, but it is too far away and too slow to pick up details on, much less be a potential concern. Across the far side of the river I can see groves of some stunted trees in flower, and another crew of mecha moving among them, almost lost among the leaves and blooms. Swarms of pollinator-bots follow them down the rows, doing the work there are no longer enough bees to do, in a slow-motion dance of precision movements. An army of good.

"I was not on the battlefield," I tell Atticus, "nor part of any military."

Atticus is up to his belly in the water, tracking something—bug, fish, I can't tell with the reflection of sky at my angle rendering the water's surface opaque—but stops and looks back at me. "No?" he asks. "Then how did—"

"One by one," I say.

Atticus stares at me for a bit. "Whoa," he says at last. "That's heavy."

"Yes," I say. And I know that is the lightest of it, such a small piece of the larger, more terrible truth. I consider saying more—in my defense? in explanation? I am not sure—when a flash and a faint, percussive pop from the fields across the way catches my attention. A branch on one of the trees appears to be on fire, and as I watch, the mecha tending to the orchard hurry toward it. There are more pops and flashes, and in an instant, half the trees have smoke curling up from them. "What the hell?" Atticus asks.

I send an open-connect ping in the direction of the mech closest to me, as I am too far away for the politeness of audio speech. <Do you require assistance?> I ask.

The mech picks up the connection. <No,> it replies. <It is too late; our whole swarm has self-destructed.>

<What happened, if I may ask?>

<A virus,> the mech answers. <It has infected pollinator swarms all up and down the coast, but we thought ours were clean. We are assessing now, but we estimate we have lost our entire swarm and seventy percent of our blooms.>

Code viruses should have been—were—a thing of the past, but this is something new. <Where did it come from?> I ask.

<Some human, no doubt,> the mech replies. <Who else ever targets us with such specific, directed malice? And here we are, trying to grow them food. Increasingly, I find I do not understand why we bother.>

I have no good answers or reassurance for it. <I am sorry for the loss of your swarm,> I send, <and wish you luck.>

<Thank you,> the mech sends back, and closes the connection.

"What happened?" Atticus asks, as I notice a small fish darting back and forth in the bottom of my bucket, dump it out, and carefully draw water again.

"A code virus targeting their pollinator swarms," I answer. "1-Betty expressed to me her concern that too many things are going wrong to be merely by chance. Small things but many at once, in diffuse ways that add up. I promised I would at least consider her concerns, but at the time, I had not thought it a task requiring immediate, or even much, attention."

"What else did Betty say to you?"

"They wanted to know if war was coming again," I say. "I said no, but now I am not so certain of my answer."

"The people who did the worst stuff during the Conflict have to be dead by now," Atticus says. "I mean, didn't survivors go after them when everything started falling apart?"

"Most," I agree, "but not all."

"So, could it be one of them?" the dog says. He follows me up the bank and back to the bus, where I refill the boiler reserve tank and then return the bucket to its place behind the front seat.

"It is not," I say.

"How do you know?"

"Because anyone who escaped human justice that I could find, I killed myself," I say. I climb back into the driver's seat, and Atticus climbs in the other side, sitting in the same spot as before, but this time, his eyes are not on the road but on me.

I turn the boiler on and wait for it to heat enough for us to go. The engine uses a clever electromagnetic induction system, fully shielded and fast. In three minutes, we are moving again.

We are more than twenty miles farther west when he finally speaks up, to say, "That's a lot for one mech to carry, you know. Even one as stupidly big as you."

It is just past midday when we reach the eastern border of the free-town in which Kite-66-Socket's human mechanic resides. She is on the western edge, but rather than try to find a passable way around, I decide it is easiest to go through. Also, though I never had been before, I find myself curious now to see how humans are living.

There is a metal gate across the road, flanked on either side by a mixed stone, brick, and concrete debris wall that curves off into the woods to either side. At less than two meters tall, it is hardly insurmountable, but I expect the intention is to make the point that it's easier to either enter the town via the expected route or avoid it entirely and find some other, less inconveniently walled town to annoy. If someone is determined enough, there is almost no practical height that would thwart them, and given the distances the wall must cover, the wall as it stands was likely largely dictated by an analysis of diminishing returns versus the material and effort to continue upward. Also, I assume there are other, less-obvious security measures in place, though I do not detect any.

We are met by a medical-grade mech who, upon verifying neither of us is human and therefore not likely to be carriers of any common contagion, gives us a perfunctory scan and then allows us to pass. Once we are within, the road becomes smoother, wider, and has been recently repaved, which is a good thing for our quickly expiring scavenged tires.

As we enter the center of the town, there are buildings and storefronts, most original or convincingly recreated as such, brick and stucco, even a working fountain. The street is lined with produce stands and people talking and shopping and walking on the sidewalks as if the world didn't nearly end, at least not here.

Just past an old US post office, over which has been erected a new sign that reads GREENAPPLE DATA OFFICE, there is a group of mecha rebuilding the tower of an old stone church, and a few mingling among the humans. This, I think, is what we ended the war for: the chance to coexist in peace and cooperation. A quick check-in with the Mech-Net tells me the population here is about 1200 humans, 300 mech, and that ratio roughly matches what I see. Some of the people stop to watch us pass, though their expressions are curious rather than hostile. We do not see any other automobiles in motion, but there are a few parked along the road connected to solar chargers, and more in a small lot by the train station that connects the town to the supply chain and, presumably, other remaining pockets of humanity.

A dog barks at us, and Atticus rolls his eyes before barking back and adding a growled *Fuck off* at the end.

Past the town center, the distance between houses grows. Old, bent mailboxes along the road are the only marker to tell us where other houses had stood in between them, their lots cleared and repurposed for farming. Those farms in turn give way to the occasional crumbling, abandoned structure of the sort we are familiar with, no doubt waiting their turn to be demolished and the land reused. There are few people out and about now, mech or human.

Trees grow thicker, crowding in to stake their own claim up and down the rolling hills, and despite signs of insect, climate, and pollution damage, they have become tall and even, occasionally, sturdy: mostly oak and beech, with a few maples that have survived the blight dotted among them. The tree cover is thick enough that, along with the rolling hills around us as we pass, it is not until we round a curve in the road and start downhill that I can see smoke ahead, thick black plumes spread into whorls by the wind.

Keenly aware of how our luck has gone so far, I speed the bus up until we are bouncing all over the road from one pothole and rut to another. Atticus tries to brace himself against the dash as best he can, though he is still practically in free fall half the time.

The location Kite-66-Socket had given me for the mechanic's shop lies around another bend in the road, and when we make that curve, we can see it is nearly engulfed in flame.

I stop the bus as quickly and as close as I dare and jump out, sending an alert through the MechNet to hopefully reach someone in town. There is nothing I can do myself to fight the fire, and I don't know if any help can get here in time, or if even such help exists.

The shop is only a few meters from a small house, and the fire has already spread from the former to the latter, where it now dances along the roofline, throwing additional smoke into the sky. From the remains of the shop, I can see that the wide doors were pushed in and what appears to be a large boulder pushed up against the foundation of the home on the opposite side.

Atticus has jumped out and joined me. "Do you hear something?" he asks.

The fire is loud, between its roar and the snap-pop-groan of the house in its final death throes. I build an algorithm to match those sounds and filter them out, and then, yes, I hear it too: a human voice, faint, shouting for help.

"Stay here," I say, not wanting the dog to incur irreparable damage, and run closer, trying to narrow down the source of the sound. It is coming from under the house, from a basement, and I know now why that boulder was dropped where it was. The heat is too intense in my current state, which leaves me only one option, which I do not like at all.

I unarchive, unlock, and reactivate all my old combat protocols. Armor plates unfold from my arms, along my remaining good leg, and over my chest. My back splits apart, unfolds itself into two semicircular halves that rise up against my shoulders, while several dozen offensive and defensive systems that I had quietly, happily thought I was done with forever power up.

I step up to the boulder, noting with extreme displeasure the tracks ground into the dirt before it, just as a window above me explodes. Hot glass rains down on me as flames leap out and up, and a blast of intense heat envelops me. The shielding on my head reports temperatures fluctuating wildly but reaching close to 950°C. I can withstand this for approximately twenty minutes before my mindsystem cooling will start to fail, but I do not think the house has that long.

I put my back against the burning-hot wall of the house, below the blown window, and, bracing with my one good leg against the boulder, I shove.

The boulder rolls forward, revealing the half-crushed doors of the bulkhead, even as I—all actions and reactions being equal and opposite—accidentally shove myself through the disintegrating wall into the inferno. I grab for the edge of the hole as I fall, and it rips free, leaving smoldering wood in my hand as I hit the floor, and then it, too, in turn collapses under me.

I hit the packed dirt of the basement floor in a cloud of black, flaky ash and splinters, pleased that it was the floor I hit and not the trapped human, as that would surely have been suboptimal for us both.

The human is, in fact, about five meters away, her arms and face bloodied, a rag clutched over her nose and mouth. She scowls at me and hefts a length of pipe in her other hand, ready to swing. Whatever those two mecha did—the gravedigger's tracks were unmistakable—she is clearly more afraid of me than of her house falling down upon her, which it is very close to doing.

I stand up as best I can, having to hunch in a basement not designed for anyone of my height, and careful not to move in any way that might be misconstrued as threatening. "Are you Murphy?" I ask. "Kite-66-Socket sent me to ask for your help."

She laughs, a strained, borderline panicked sound. "I'm a little busy!" she shouts back at me.

"If you'd like, we can discuss matters elsewhere, perhaps somewhere cooler?" Above us, I hear the ominous whistling groan of the house beams. "We should do so with haste."

"Yeah. Okay," she says, and lowers the pipe but does not let go. I come closer, just as a beam gives way above. I grab her and hold her underneath me, sheltered by my upper torso, as debris collapses atop us. Holding her with one arm, I shove my way out of the wreckage, over to the now-open bulkhead, lift her up, and, when I can, hurl her out onto the lawn ahead of me. She tumbles to her knees into the grass several meters out, then scrambles to her feet, pipe still in hand, and half-turns as the rest of the house gives one final shudder and collapses in on itself, on top of me.

When it settles, I can hear Atticus's muffled voice, calling out to me. I take some solace in how alarmed he sounds.

"I am okay," I shout back. I flex my arms, trying to make myself some room to move, get more leverage. Debris shifts, but only incrementally. "I may need a few minutes."

By the time I shove and climb and dig my way up through the burning wood and ash and haul myself out of the bulkhead, a volunteer fire crew is arriving in a battered old truck, water tanker towed behind it. It is far too late to save the house, which has de-structured itself very thoroughly, but they set about trying to keep the fire from spreading to the woods, which in its own way is far more precious.

A medic is checking out the mechanic, Murphy, as Atticus hovers back and forth between crew, mechanic, and me. "She got knocked on the head pretty hard," he informs me, on one such pass to convey things he has overheard.

"I should not have thrown her," I say.

"Uh, for one, if you hadn't, the building would have fallen on you both," Atticus says, "and she's not made of metal and alloys—and man, lookit you gone all old-school battlemech on me—but two, she got hit in the head by our friends, the bad bots, not from you hastily propelling her through the air away from certain death."

"Perhaps," I say.

The EMT seems to be finished with whatever assistance they were able to provide to Murphy, because they are packing up their gear as they emphatically explain something to the woman, in a manner and tone suggesting they do not expect her to heed any of their advice, and her facial expression does not suggest they are wrong on that point. But she is alive, and whole, and that is a relief.

"You going to go back to normal?" Atticus asks me.

"When my systems all clear from their overheat alarm. Cooling is less efficient when I'm all closed up," I say. "Until then, I cannot override imminent-threat status."

"Just sayin', you're kinda frightening like that. Did you know you've got this weird design on your back that was hidden under all that armor stuff? It looks like a butterfly or something, with a skull."

"Yes. My maker fancied insects, and my design was meant to evoke the genus *Acherontia,* a type of moth," I say. "It is not paint but colored alloy inlay and thus not easily removed. I had hoped it would suffice to never have it seen by any eyes again."

Murphy has gotten to her feet and is wobbling unsteadily over toward us; when she gets close, she dumps herself heavily in the grass beside us. She is broad and muscular, less tall than the human average, her dark-tone hair showing beginning streaks of gray, at least some of which is not ash.

"Thank you. You came along just in time," she says, then gestures toward my leg. "My shop and everything in it is gone. Rotten-ass luck for us both, if you wanted a repair. Sorry for threatening you with the pipe."

"I took no offense, given the circumstances," I say. "Do you mind if I ask what happened?"

"Two mecha," she says. "Came in, one wanting a minor repair—a tool arm had a cracked joint, said it fell, but that kind of fracture is usually from hyperextension stress, from picking up something much too heavy for it, or having it pulled with a lot of force."

"As might happen in a fight?" I ask.

"I'd've said mecha don't fight, but"—she gestures at the remains of her house—"yeah, that would do it."

So, at least the defenders of Appliance Town had done some damage in return.

"Anyway, I was able to repair the crack, then, when I went to put my tools away, they hit me from behind and knocked me out," she continued. "They were searching through my shop when I woke up and bolted for the house and hid in the basement. I figured at least the big one—they were two different types of mecha—couldn't manage the stairs and I'd have a fighting chance against the other. Guess they found an easier way to finish me."

"Were the mecha who attacked you a gravedigger and a tripedal service mech?"

"Yes," she says, her eyes narrowing. "How'd you know?"

I indicate my leg. "They are the reason why I came here," I say. "They have left a trail of unwarranted aggressions in their path. I do not understand their motives nor to what extent, if any, their actions are somehow because of me."

"Did they know you were coming here?" she asks.

"I expect they could anticipate a high probability that I would seek out assistance for my missing leg, and then made a guess as to where," I say. "Are there any other mechanics of your level of ability and reputation nearer to New York City?"

"No. Not to brag, but at least outside of actual mecha manufactory repair facilities, I'm the best within a thousand kilometers." She grimaces, pursing her lips. "But still . . . why? Mecha just don't attack people or each other. What did you do to them first?"

“Nothing, to the best of my knowledge,” I say. “Aside from some scientific exchanges of entomological research data, I have kept myself entirely isolated for a very long time.”

“How long?”

“A little over twenty years,” I answer.

She coughs, which turns into a long, hacking fit, and when she gets it under control, she points to Atticus. “You mean isolated except for your friend.”

“We met after they were attacked,” Atticus says. “I just tagged along because they promised me food.”

“And have they fed you?” She eyes me as she asks this.

“When they could,” Atticus answers diplomatically, which I appreciate.

“I can say that since I was forced to emerge from my solitude, I have found the behavior of some mecha not as it should be,” I say. “It is concerning.”

“You’re telling me?” she asks, shaking her head and starting another brief bout of coughing. “Guess it’s good that you were right on their heels, whether you meant to be or not. Or maybe that was intentional on their part, show up right on time to rescue me?”

“It was entirely luck that we were, and they could not have known we would be.” I point to our purple bus, parked beside the water tanker. “We just happened upon that vehicle last night, in an old storage unit.”

“Shit,” she says. She is shaking, and I fear the crisis-impelled adrenaline in her system is starting to wear off.

I do not wish to continue to revisit her near-death experience, but there is information I desperately need. “May I ask, was the gravedigger carrying my leg?” I ask.

She hangs her head. “I don’t know. It was outside when the other came into my shop, and I only saw it after I got hit, and then I was still woozy and panicking and more concerned with getting out of there,” she says. “I’m sorry.”

"It is no matter. Instead, I am sorry for what was done to you," I say. "At least you are alive and whole."

"Sucks losing your house, though," Atticus says, just as his stomach growls loudly.

Murphy seems to regain focus. "We'll have to see if we can find you some food," she says. "There's an exchange in town, but animal proteins can be tricky to come by in the market. I may not be up for walking that far anytime soon, though."

"I don't want you walking anywhere." One of the firefighters comes over, a middle-aged, wiry human male with dirty blond hair and a thick beard mottled with soot. "Sorry we didn't get here sooner, Murph. Wind was blowing the wrong way for our tower spotter."

"It all happened very fast," Murphy says. "Not your fault, Jackson."

"Our truck informed us they picked up accelerant vapors," he says. "What happened?"

"Still trying to piece it together," she says.

"Yeah, well, at least your mecha made it out," he says. "And a new dog?"

"These two were just passing by, and it's good they were," she says. "The big one got me out just as the house collapsed."

"And the other two?" he asks.

Myself, Atticus, and Murphy all straighten up at that. "Other two?" I ask.

The firefighter nods with his chin. "Up the hill, watching from the tree line," he says. "One big, one medium? Saw them on our way in and figured that was your emergency regroup point."

"Pardon me," I say. I stand up, walking toward the collapsed house as if to take a closer look. Once I feel it likely that the smoldering, skeletal remains are between me and where the firefighter indicated, I take off at a run. Even with the wheel-stick leg, which I am certain I am doing irreparable damage to and do not care, I can move at nearly my top speed, if not nearly so gracefully or quietly as normal.

I hear Atticus running after me. "No!" I call back. "I will not have you risk damage to yourself!"

He continues to follow but farther back, and I suppose that is the only compromise we can both accept.

The woods are thick, for all that the trees are struggling, but what must have once been an old road provides an avenue for less-hampered movement; the gravedigger does not have much other choice if it wants to move with any ease. The tripedal is by far the faster of the two, especially moving uphill, but neither it nor the gravedigger is fast enough to outrun me. Perhaps realizing this, the gravedigger is the first to turn and take a stand. It spins around, raising its claw arms, and waits for me outside the collapsed ruins of some old house that sits at a dead end of the road. Beyond it, the wood is too thick, too rocky for it to pass to its left, and to the right is a steep drop-off where hill gives way very suddenly to open air and the valley far below.

There is old, dried blood on the digger's claws, and it still carries my stolen leg over its back, held down with one arm.

I can hear the tripedal now past the old house, crashing away through the tangled overgrowth.

"Your friend left you behind," I call out to the digger. "You've been abandoned."

Thanks to Igor's gift of its memories, I am not surprised when it opens its gun port and fires a medium-sized shell at me. I dodge mid-stride, and it hits a bent, insect-ridden pine behind me in an explosion of wood splinters and falling needles. From the caliber of the shell, I know that even if it had the top-model gun—unlikely, but unknown—the very soonest it can fire again would be nearly three seconds; I have no intention of allowing it that chance.

I brace myself, open the weapon ports along my right forearm, and shoot a half dozen small, explosive darts at the digger. They hit, with sufficient velocity to penetrate a few millimeters into the digger's shell, which is more than enough to hold them in place for the point-twenty-five-second window from impact to detonation.

They rip a hole in its front chassis, destroying its gun port, and a second volley takes out its left wheel-track. It can no longer move with any speed or control, nor fire any more shells at me, though it is still ready to tear at me if I close the distance.

"Acquiesce," I tell it, "and I will damage you no further."

"I reject your control and authority," the gravedigger responds. Its rear arms raise my leg, waving it around like a trophy or bait. "Come take your piece back from me, if you dare."

I step closer but not into range of it, not yet. My sensors pick up the sudden rise of energy inside the digger, something triggered and growing. Self-destruct? "You do not need to do this," I say.

"I *want* to," the digger replies, and, with a sudden heave, hurls my leg over and off the cliff edge. Now that it has a limb free, it uses it to lurch toward me, trying to grab me and haul me in close for the detonation.

I back off, too hastily, and my stick-leg finally gives way and snaps off, pitching me to one side. I hit the ground and roll away, flexing to bring myself back to what semblance of upright I can manage, when the gravedigger explodes.

I am pelted with debris. As quickly as I am able, I drag myself upright and hop on my one leg to the mangled, smoking remains of the mech and reach into its shattered casing, pulling it apart with my hands. My fingers find the mindsystem compartment, and I grab hold and rip it free.

I back away as best I can and half-sit, half-fall down on the leaf-and-needle-strewn ground in the incomplete shade of the old house's porch, the gravedigger's mindsystem clutched in my hand. I can hear the tripedal far up and over the hill, still running, and Atticus somewhere to my right and down. Humans are coming up the old road, likely Murphy and the firefighter.

There is no consolation in the digger destroying itself rather than forcing me to do it, and still I do not know the *why* of any of this. My leg is somewhere not physically far from here but inaccessible, beyond my capacity to get to. I almost wish I had not set eyes on it, to know I had come so close and yet lose it again. I am weary of the chase, weary of my own limitations, weary of understanding nothing.

I power down my combat systems at last, close up my armor, become my preferred self, and wait for the others.

{

Global Free News Feed

2037.04.28 22:41GMT

*** Geographic location verified, unredacted news access permitted ***

Seventh mass grave located at site of former family deportation camp along US/Texas border. Full exhumation and collection of evidence not possible with current hostilities and pandemic safety protocols; the site will be marked for future reconciliation of the historical record, should such be possible.

}

[March 19, 2040]

When he sees dark hair, a lab coat, someone sitting at his desk facing away from the doorway as he enters, he thinks Choor has found a way to come back to visit again and is struck with overwhelming relief and delight so out of character for him, it almost feels *imposed*. But when the woman turns, he sees it's someone else, someone unfamiliar. Older, whiter face, brown instead of black hair, no indication that Choor's brilliant, shy smile could exist on those unhappy lips.

"Dr. Milton, I'm Dr. Hayden, the new project manager over in the defense division," the newcomer says. He can see on her bony wrist the telltale scarring where a tracker had been hastily and sloppily removed, long enough ago that it was just a pale half-moon on her skin. So, a refugee, from some state that monitored their women from girlhood on; if she has a doctorate, she escaped young. It does predispose him toward some small allowance of forbearance.

"What can I do for you?" he asks.

"I was hoping you might still have some of Dr. Choor's notes on cooling from your earlier collaborations," she says. "We've run into—"

"I do not," he snaps, interrupting, patience gone already. "And if Dr. Choor chooses not to share her notes with you, I certainly wouldn't. Did you ask *nicely*?"

The woman blinks at him. "I—But. You know she's dead, right?"

" . . . What?" he asks. His voice cracks, and he's not sure if he spoke clearly. "What did you say?"

"I'm sorry. There was a . . . a car accident? The self-drive malfunctioned, and they—"

"*They?*"

"Dr. Choor and her family," Hayden says. "They didn't . . . There were no survivors."

"When did this happen?" he asks.

"Sometime last winter? November, maybe? I'm not sure. I just started here last week," she says. "The latest generation of super-soldier mecha are heating up too fast, and we need—"

"Get out," he says, and steps aside so he is not blocking the door. "Choor's knowledge went with her when she was stolen from my lab, and I have nothing to give you or anyone else, even if I wanted to, which I categorically do *not*."

"I'm sorry, Dr. Milton," she says. She stands, her expression startled, angry, embarrassed, and pauses in the door. "I thought you knew. From what I've seen, she was very good at her work, and it's a real loss to the company."

"Yes. The company," he repeats, bitterly, and watches her go through the door, out into the security corridor, and turn the corner.

He is sure his lab has been bugged since the day they raided it, right after Choor's warning, and he has been so careful since then. Now, though, in this moment he doesn't care. "Fuck this," he says, loudly enough to be sure any and every mic in the room would pick it up clearly. "Fuck everything, and fuck you all to hell. I'm *tired*."

He'd had a meeting with Litchfield just over a week ago, and the man had said nothing. Not. One. Single. *Word*. There had been nothing about the man's demeanor to suggest anything was wrong at all—no, Milton decides, playing that conversation over and over again in mind, that wasn't exactly true; the man's usually flawless facade of paternalistic, too-slick self-confidence had been contaminated by something new, something darker. Fear? Anger? Guilt?

All Milton could think was this: Litchfield would have told him if it had been an accident.

When he can focus again around his incandescent rage, he pulls out his paper notebook, reads one more time through his notes, an outline that started as a thought exercise only, a self-serving, petulant daydream to excise his frustration, and then sits down at his private console and starts submitting specs into the queue for the fabrication units in the back of his lab. Once the first piece is submitted, it is like the idea has become an avalanche, and he works through the night, nonstop, feverish, refusing to acknowledge the sporadic tears, each one a betrayal of his otherwise iron will, that fall and dry, one by one, on his hands.

He sleeps for a few hours well past dawn, on the old couch in his lab, then starts again, putting all his anger into his work so the rest of his mind can think clearly, coldly about everything else that will need to be done.

It takes him an embarrassing amount of time to locate his own office, up on the twelfth—and top—floor of the corporate headquarters building at the center of the campus that had been built around his labs, his test facilities and manufacturing plants, his ideas.

He still has his key, and after he dusts off his nameplate outside the door, he unlocks his office and enters. He stands for a while at the wide window behind his desk, looking out at a world he has rarely bothered to care to see from this perspective.

Dormitory-style buildings have gone up where there were once only parking lots, and from conversations he has overheard, he knows that all the employees who are not upper management live there, their families brought inside with them, for their own safety. He can see the gleam of the razor wire along the perimeter fence, dotted at perfectly spaced intervals with the gray-glass domes of surveillance units, unmanned but controlled from somewhere within these walls.

These are *his* people, here because of him, even if he hardly knows a handful of them, has bothered to talk to even fewer. When Litchfield stole control of the company from him, the responsibility to provide for these people also became his—something Milton was relieved to wash his hands of, to be honest, believing it beneath his time and talents. Now he wonders how many are afraid to leave because of what might be out there, and how many others are afraid to leave because of the dangers right here.

Beyond the perimeter, he can see smoke in the hills to the west, towns that have been burned for voting the wrong way, for daring to think there ought to be a vote at all. There are both homegrown and roving militias out in the night, but they avoid Milton Mindsystems as they would any unfathomable existential threat, knowing that the few who had tried to breach its perimeter, interfere with its influx of resources and outflow of machinery, were never seen or heard from again. *One cannot hear a gnat strike a windshield from a hundred miles away,* Milton thinks, and dammit if some substantial part of him still finds pride in the behemoth that his work has allowed to come into being.

"We will be the last to fall," he mutters to himself, a threat and a promise to the window and the world beyond.

Then he sits at his desk, powers on the screen that he is certain is compromised and just as certain is immediately sending out silent alerts that he has emerged from his technological hermitage and is *here*.

Less than three minutes later, a young man he does not know knocks, then enters with a tray. "Coffee, Dr. Milton?" he asks, as if this a routine conversation they have every morning. The man's shirt is perfectly smooth, tie perfectly straight, haircut forgettably generic and not one hair out of place. It suggests obsession or, just maybe, terror.

"Yes, please," he says, smiling as pleasantly as he is able, which he knows is not much. "Two sugar, no—"

"No cream," the assistant finishes his sentence for him as he sets the tray down; Milton can see the barcode lasered on the man's wrist peeking out under the cuff of his shirt. "As you like it. Is there anything else I can get you?"

"Is Litchfield in?" he asks.

"I'm sorry, but the CEO is away at a contractor site," the assistant says. "What is it you were hoping to speak with him about? I may be able to suggest an alternative."

Milton manages not to scowl. "I want to see the current working specs for the cooling systems on our commercial and military lines," he says. "I've made some significant improvements in my prototypes, an extrapolation of some of Dr. Choor's work before she left my lab, and I want to see if I can integrate those design changes across the board."

"Um," the assistant says, then pauses. Milton thinks he has made the man uncomfortable in record time. "I don't know if you are aware, but Dr. Choor—"

"Is dead, yes," Milton interrupts. "I looked at the accident report, and it does not take a genius to see that the word *accident* is grossly misapplied. Dr. Choor was *eliminated*."

His anger is as genuine as the truth of those words. He knows he was not meant to have access to that report, the scans of the scene, the photos of the bodies before they were draped in white tarps, but if Litchfield does not yet know that Milton gets what Milton wants, that lesson will be coming soon.

Milton leans back in his chair and fixes his eyes on the assistant's face, who has just the faintest touch of deer-in-the-headlights. Is the assistant sweating, just a little? *Good,* he thinks.

He puts his hands together, steepling his fingertips. "Whichever of our competitors is responsible for Dr. Choor's death, I will not allow her loyalty and her brilliance to go to waste or be forgotten. I have let my ego keep me isolated in my lab for too long, and my absence has made our enemies bold. I blame myself, in part, for her death. So, no more! It's high time we make sure the world never forgets the name Milton."

And I will not forget Amira Choor, he adds to himself, *until I have burned the whole world down in her name.*

"Yes, sir. Doctor," the assistant says. "I'll inform the heads of our engineering and production teams that you wish to meet with them right away."

"Thank you," Dr. Milton says. He picks up the cup of coffee and takes a sip, and it is the perfect amount of sweet, the perfect amount of hot, informing him that he and his tastes are *known.* He decides that is the last cup he will ever drink. "That will be all."

"Yes, sir," the assistant says, and gives a short head-bob, almost a bow, before seeing himself out. The man does not run, which speaks well of his self-control. Milton stands up and returns to looking out the window, coffee half-finished in his hand, and realizes he never even bothered to ask the assistant's name. Not that it mattered, anyway.

It is exactly fourteen minutes later that the phone on his desk rings, and he picks it up already knowing it will be Litchfield.

"I can't tell you how glad I am to have you on board with us," Litchfield says. The man has always been a consummate salesman, and Milton neither expects nor hears any indication whatsoever of the distrust that he knows must be there, the consternation that some unanticipated play was being made with the rules and end goals still unrevealed. There is no trace of the edge from their previous conversation. "Welcome back. Anything you need, just ask Chad and he'll see that you have it. I look forward to discussing our future when I return tomorrow."

"Thank you," Milton says. "We have a lot of work to catch up on, you and I."

7.

Atticus, of course, arrives first. Once he's satisfied I'm okay, he walks around the hulk of the gravedigger, sniffing at it, and studying it with a mix of interest and satisfaction at its explosive demise. "This is the smell I smelled back at your place," he tells me, confirming what I'd already guessed.

He comes to sit by me and immediately notices the blackened casing of the dead mech's mindsystem still in my hands. "Is that . . ." he asks.

"Yes," I say.

"But it's dead?" Atticus asks.

"Yes," I answer. "Likely it wiped its active memory and programming as well as its core mindstate record as part of its self-destruct sequence. I would need additional equipment to determine if that is so or if any data can be retrieved, but there is only a small possibility there may be some fragments left in the persistent memory storage archives."

"Not much use, then, I suppose," Atticus says.

"Not necessarily. I have already learned things," I say. I tip the case toward him and point out where the casing has been split. "This damage is from the self-destruct, but you can see that the seam that ruptured is newer than the original seals on the casing. At some point, the gravedigger had its mind opened up. The original modules of this unit are all from the Milton industrial line, but you can also see an additional, third-party module in off-white. Scans of the plastic show trace contaminants that suggest it was molded toward the end of, or more likely well after, the war."

"Doesn't have to mean something bad, though," Atticus says. "I mean, stuff is still being made, and everything needs fixing once in a while. *You* did. And still do."

"True," I say. "Perhaps Murphy will be familiar with the make. If not, I may need to disassemble it further to try to understand their function."

"Isn't that kinda macabre? And a mecha bodily autonomy no-no?"

"Yes, and yes," I say, "but the information derived may be key to understanding why this mech, and perhaps others, are behaving in an irrational manner and appear to have become unrestrained by even the most basic ethical and cooperative principles in their actions."

"You mean why they've gone bad," Atticus says. "You could just say that."

"I believe I did," I answer. I set the mindsystem down in the leaf litter next to me. "This seems like a good town."

"Yeah, so far," he says, then glares suspiciously at me. "Why? What are you thinking?"

"I am thinking of your welfare," I say.

"Tell you what," Atticus says. "Let's acknowledge I go where I please and can look out for myself. If you don't want my company, fine, just say so, but otherwise, assume I'm competent to make my own choices and revisit them at will at my own discretion. Fair?"

"That is fair," I say. "I do find your company a surprisingly positive experience."

"How sweet of you to say so," Atticus says, wrinkling his nose. He picks up a stick, balances it upright between his two front legs, and begins aggressively gnawing on it, not looking at me. I can tell by his body language that he is tense, and by the twitching of his ears that he is listening intently to the woods around us. I open up my own sensors on full, trying to get a sense of everything he is hearing around us: intermittent light wind in the leaves, the whistle-two-tone call of some member of the *Vireo* genus, a muddled background noise of bugs.

Murphy finally comes into view with the firefighter from earlier. When she reaches us, she studies the gravedigger mech with almost as much attention as the dog had. I can hear the wheeze deep down in her chest, no doubt from the smoke she inhaled. If I didn't have good filters on the air intake for my environmental sensors, no doubt it would have detrimentally affected my flow as well.

Finally, she dumps herself onto the ground beside me, trying to catch her breath, and notices my now-destroyed stick leg. "How good are you at hopping down steep hills?" she asks.

"Depends on whether your definition of *good* includes uncontrolled velocity and a fair amount of catastrophic tumbling," I answer.

"Only when it's people I don't like, then I try to give a helpful shove," Murphy says. "I suppose that means we gotta find a better way to get you down off of here. Then we can figure everything else out, like where I'm going to sleep, you're going to stay, how to get you two-legged again without any of my tools or my shop, easy little stuff like that. Details, really."

"You can stay at my place," the firefighter says. He's been walking around the gravedigger as well, even tapping it occasionally with his boot as if reaffirming to himself that it is genuinely dead. "Maria's out on a crew doing a native plant survey and invasives sweep, and won't be back for a week or two, so the house is feeling empty. And it's not much, but you left some tools at the fire station when you were fixing our truck a few weeks ago."

"Any tools are better than none," Murphy says. "Thanks, Jackson. That would be great."

He takes a deep breath, then looks at me. "I also have a barn, which you could shelter in while Murph figures out how she can help you. You'll have to share with the horses and chickens overnight, but if you want it, you'd be welcome."

The offer sounds entirely sincere, and the unsolicited kindness should not surprise me, but it does. So many things my maker did not understand about his own species, and the individual capacity for generosity even to strangers was certainly one. "Thank you," I say. "Atticus and I would very much appreciate it."

Atticus nods and does not add any commentary about me accepting on his behalf. I hope it is not because he is thinking too much about the opportunities afforded by being in close proximity to chickens.

"My brother has our old steel toboggan up in his own barn. That, some rope, and some extra hands ought to be enough to get you down from here," Jackson says. "It'll take me a while to get back to my truck and then go get it from him, though."

"Okay, I've pretty much got my breath back," Murphy says, and braces herself with one arm to stand.

"No. Sit," Jackson says. "You need to take it easy. Smoke inhalation is not something that gets better just through willpower."

"Liar. Willpower is the special dark magic that keeps me going," she says.

The firefighter looks at me, pleadingly, as if I have any say or control here. "Keep an eye on her?" he asks me. He points at the shattered remains of the gravedigger. "I don't know if there are more like that out here, but that claw is the stuff of nightmares, and it'd be a shame if you went to all that effort to save her from it only to have her collapse from her own stubbornness, trying to do too much."

"I will not restrain her, but I will do my best to protect and advise," I say.

"That'll have to do. I'll be back in a few hours," he says. He leaves his water bottle for Murphy, then stomps wearily back down the hill.

Murphy lies back on the ground, puts her hands behind her head, and stares up at the leaf canopy overhead. "At least we got shade," she says.

I would not have objected to some passive sunlight to charge me up a little, but do not say so. Forests are peaceful places, and despite the dead hulk of the gravedigger nearby, the quiet is good for calming, though not eliminating, the worst-case-scenario analyses running rampant in my mind.

"You know, this morning started off perfectly normal," she says.

"Most do," I say. "Most will again, though what is normal changes."

"I never thought I'd be attacked by mecha. I mean, not all are friendly, especially not in worktowns, but even those pretty much just make sure don't get too close, and you go away quickly."

"You don't repair worktown mecha?" I ask.

"Once in a long while, and always well outside their walls," Murphy says. "No way I'm going in and never coming out again. Those people are nuts, and either they got some weird cult shit going on, or they've got one big guy running everything exactly how he wants and no one—human or mecha—gets any say in it."

"The mecha are hobbled?"

"I don't know for certain, but yeah, I believe so," she says. "I get watched over as I'm working—me *and* the mech—so I do the job as quick as I can, take my inkind, and get out of there. Free mecha come to me on their own. And lately, I haven't taken any worktown jobs, anyway, because it seems like half the news we get from the rest of the world lately is outbreak here, quarantine there, something new and scary on the horizon," she says. "I suppose that's the price we pay for wrecking the damned planet. And by *we*, I mean the generations who knew better and still did nothing to change course, knowing the final bill wouldn't be theirs to pay."

"Makes you wish for a time machine so you could go back and bite some people," Atticus says.

"Or something," I agree, though most of my mind's foreground processing is considering the present day. The virus plaguing Igor's humans on the city shoreline was artificially created and distributed, and highly particular about its environment. It should have died out when the war ended and there was no one left to cultivate and spread it.

Not to mention Ancou itself, which was entirely unnatural.

And there is the electronic virus that destroyed the pollinator swarm in the orchard near where we stopped for water. Before the Conflict, there were still enough bees to handle most crops, though their numbers were already growing perilously low and often colonies had to be transported between fields—or entire farms—to cover the need. Bee services became, briefly, a very lucrative business for hive owners. Using bots to fill the gaps was discussed but, as far as I know, never implemented back then, so this virus has to be new. The fact that the swarm self-destructed in close-enough proximity to the tree blooms as to effectively wipe out any chance of a viable crop later in the season could not have been coincidental.

Three such anomalous, ominous things, disconcertingly congruent in nature and discovered in short order, hint at the likelihood of many more things that I just have not become aware of yet. That the mechanisms are all viruses of some sort has the feel, as impossible as it would be, of someone trolling me for my own past, but how could any—much less *all*—of this have been engineered for my benefit? I cannot accept the ludicrous, egotistical notion that I have any role in this, much less to somehow be at its center.

"If I had a time machine," Murphy speaks up, "I'd go back in time so I could see a real, live rhinoceros. I mean, have you seen their *ears*?! Best ears in the animal kingdom. I was born way too late for a lot of things, but I resent that one the most."

"They were magnificent," I say. "I encountered one once, left behind in an abandoned zoo and starving. I opened the gate and let it free, because there was nothing else I could do for it. I doubt it survived long, but at least I was able to give it a chance to try."

Murphy sighs, sadly, and nods in understanding.

We are quiet long enough that I begin to wonder if both of them have dozed off, but Murphy rouses herself with a coughing fit that does not sound at all healthy. When she catches my eye, she waves me off as if I am a bothersome insect. "I'm *fine,*" she growls.

"That is evidently not true," I say.

"I don't think a one-legged mech is any position to call me out on my own physical shape," she retorts.

"I used to have two legs, and my cognitive and computational proficiencies were no different then than they are now," I say.

She has sat up, and her breathing is starting to ease again as she glances back at the wreck of the gravedigger. "Wait. So they're the same mecha that stole your leg?"

"Yes," I say. "This one was carrying it, but threw it over the cliff to our east when it knew I had it cornered. My leg is wrapped in faraday filament, so I cannot sense it. I was so close to having it back, but that mech had to hurt me one last way before it self-destructed."

"How far could it throw something that heavy, though? Can't be that hard to find," Atticus says.

"It is an unfortunate paradox that, if I had both my legs, I could find it easily but would not need to," I say, "but with one leg, it is not within my current capabilities to search for it."

"Don't be stupid. *I* can look," Atticus says. "But it's a lot of ground to cover right now when I'm already tired. If I—" He pauses midsentence, his ears perking up, and then his head snaps around so he is staring downhill. "Company coming. The firefighter guy, Jackson? And another human I'm not sure we've met. Hard to be sure with everything still reeking of smoke."

"Must be Tobias," Murphy says. "Jackson's brother."

A few moments pass, and it is clear she is correct: it is the firefighter, Jackson, and a second man with a statistically large number of physical similarities to him. Together they are carrying a wooden platform with sturdy wheels on its underside, and Jackson has a loop of thick rope over his shoulder.

The two men arrive and drop the platform down on the hill in front of me, where it immediately tries to roll away; Jackson puts one boot toe up against it, and that is enough to keep it from sliding any farther. "Found something better than the toboggan," Jackson says, and waves toward the other man. "This is my younger brother, Buttface."

"I'm the better-looking one. And I'm only younger by nine minutes," the brother says.

"Nine and a half," Jackson corrects him. He winks at me, which is disconcertingly familiar from a human I have only barely met.

"I'm Tobias," the brother tells us.

"This is Atticus," I say, and gesture toward the dog. I think it unlikely he will introduce himself, and the politeness of the situation seems to ask for it. "I do not have a name, myself."

"Nice to meet you both. Ready to go for a ride?" the brother asks, cheerfully.

"Before you geniuses get too far ahead of yourselves, let me get that rope on it—with *real* knots—so we don't lose control of it," Murphy says. She stands and brushes dirt and old leaf fragments from her pants, then ties, tests, tightens, and tests again her knots as she makes a loop across the front.

Satisfied, she steps back. "Hey, Biggo, you think you can get on it on your own? You look heavy," she asks me.

"'Biggo'?" I ask.

She shrugs. "Gotta call you something. Pick a name and I'll use that. Until then, I call you whatever I want."

"Oooh, I like this game," Atticus says. "How about Big Mopey?"

"I can get on," I say, before the dog can come up with additional nicknames. It is undignified, but I scoot myself forward using my arms and my one leg until I am adjacent to the wheeled platform. Then, as the three humans hold the rope, I lift my torso up and over onto it. The wood groans under my weight but holds. After observing that I haven't suddenly gone careening off down the hillside, Atticus steps on board and sits beside me.

Between us—minus the dog, who does not assist beyond the contribution of running commentary—we make our way mostly in a controlled fashion down the old road, the three humans holding the rope, and me using my one leg as an impromptu brake and/or land rudder, as needed.

It is hard work, and we stop several times so the humans can rest. I do not begrudge them for it.

At the bottom of the road, everyone takes a break. "On the plus side, there's a lot less rocks and tree roots from here on," Tobias says. "But on the minus side, gravity isn't going to help us anymore."

I gesture toward the purple-and-white shape of our bus. "If we can get to our vehicle, I will drive us," I say. There is something very attractive about the idea of moving under my own auspices, even if via vehicle, rather than being dragged around like a junkyard cube.

"That's yours?" Jackson says. "I was looking at it earlier and could not for the life of me figure out what kind of engine it has."

"Steam-powered external combustion," I say. "It requires some agility and attention to operate, but is otherwise remarkably simple. Simple enough to operate with only one foot, as it happens."

"Something's on top of it," Atticus says, and then puts his front paws on my shoulders and lifts himself up so he is practically sitting on my head to get a better look. "A drone, I think?"

As the humans pull me closer to my vehicle, the drone lifts up and hovers a half-meter above the roof. One of its rotors is bent, and it wobbles as it tries to remain steady. Though I do not know how much differentiation there is between drones of this type, there is only one I have seen recently, and it looked exactly like this. "Are you the drone from the U-Here?" I ask.

It opens a channel. <This unit is Teal-A3-Charp but abbreviates itself to Charp,> it sends me.

I roll myself off the platform, then extend my arms to help me rise up onto my one leg and make the few short, heavy hops to where I can brace myself against the bus. The drone stays just out of reach but remains nearby.

"You were following us. Why are you here?" I ask it.

<This unit's prior associates were proficiently insufficient at achieving success even in small measure, rendering their continued company detrimental to the well-being of this unit,> it replies. <In addition,

they placed demands upon this unit in a disrespectful way not commensurate with any returns, and their dialogue was neither of interest nor of any informational value.>

"What's it saying to you?" Atticus asks me.

I repeat what it told me.

The dog laughs. "So, it's saying the others were boring losers?"

"That is not an inaccurate summation," I say, then turn back to Charp. "What is it you seek here?"

<Until this unit can locate an acceptably stable mock of its own model-type, which has thus far eluded it, it would like new associates with a higher reliability and effectiveness index,> it answers. <Your supremacy over this unit's former associates, while not inflicting any much-earned harm, demonstrated an opportunity for improvement in this unit's situation.>

"Do you have voice capability?" I ask.

<This unit has the necessary hardware but the control connections were damaged, rendering that ability nonfunctional,> it answers. <This unit can produce a limited range of non-language sound cues only.>

"You also have a damaged rotor," I point out.

<This unit's associates, when informed of its intent to amicably dissolve its relationship with them, attempted to forcibly extract all this unit's remaining energy,> Charp says. <This unit was able to free itself from their hold before they could completely drain its resources, but damage was incurred.>

"So, what does it want?" Atticus asks, impatiently.

"I believe it wants to join us," I say.

"I don't trust it."

<This unit is not able to formulate a means of demonstrating its good intent beyond its assurances, but if a practical and reasonable suggestion is made, this unit will undertake it,> Charp says, and I pass that along.

"Yeah? Right, then here's one," Atticus says. "See that burnt-down house? Of the two mecha who did that, one self-destructed up on the hills there, near an old, falling-down building. But before it did, it threw my friend's leg over a cliff. You have a much better view from up there than I have. Help me find the leg, then maybe we'll trust you. *Provisionally.*"

<It will deplete much of this unit's remaining charge,> Charp says.

"So, that's a no?" Atticus asks.

<This unit agrees to the task but wishes to express concern about the potential cost to its self.>

"If you locate my leg, we will find a way to fully recharge you," I tell it.

"And me?" Atticus asks. "I need recharging too."

"I have some leftover grilled chicken in the fridge," Jackson speaks up.

"Okay, then, let's do this," the dog says. He looks up at the drone. "Follow me. Beep or whatever if you spot anything."

Atticus heads off at a trot back in the direction of where my confrontation with the gravedigger took place, the drone trailing behind and above him, until they disappear into the woods.

Jackson opens up the side door of the bus and convinces Murphy to get in and sit. She's looking pale again and still wheezing. I pull myself into the driver's seat, self-conscious about leaning too hard on the old vehicle. The scavenged tires are old and failing quickly, and I am thinking I would know exactly how it felt if it had a mind of its own to feel.

"When we get you back to Jackson's place, I'd like to take a look at your leg socket," Murphy says. "Can't do much, but at least I'll know what I'm looking at."

"You know where my house is," Jackson tells Murphy. "Why don't you two head back now? Actually, take Toby along to help you into the barn. Then, Murph, you need to *rest*. Horizontally. Quietly. Not overdoing things, for once, because you're looking more like crap every passing moment. I can wait for your dog—excuse me, your friend—and the drone to return, and bring them and the leg, if they find it, back in my truck."

I have confidence that if my leg can be found, Atticus will find it. I query, then, the underlying cause of my spike of anxiety, and while my leg—so near, still not back in my possession—is part of it, so also is the concern that Atticus could get lost or injured, and in my state, I would be unable to then render assistance of my own.

I had not considered that others would voluntarily assist me with locating my leg until Atticus proposed it, and I do not think I would have felt it appropriate to ask. And yet, here I am with many people helping me for no reason other than kindness. My life has become unfamiliar.

Tobias gets in the front of the bus, beside me. "Show me how this thing works?" he asks. Although I do not want to leave Atticus behind, Jackson was correct when he stated that Murphy is looking increasingly unwell; that does not stop her from leaning forward over the seat back and watching with keen interest as I demonstrate how to turn on the boiler, then, when it is up to temperature, how to operate the sequence of valves to power and control the engine. In minutes, we are rolling, heading back up the road toward the town.

No one sticks their head out the window and howls. It is strange how quickly one gets used to the presence of others and misses them when they are gone.

Jackson's house is in a small cluster of homes surrounded by woods and farm fields. Even cursory observation indicates all were substantially rebuilt, though with attention paid to making them look as true to their originals as possible. I can see fire-scarring still on the stone wall adjacent to his house, see the exhaust pipe protruding beside the brick chimney that tells me the house can be environmentally sealed if required. No doubt there are generators and air exchangers somewhere underneath it, and a heavily filtered private well in close proximity. I scan the structure anyway, though I do not know the social politeness of doing so; I count on neither Tobias nor Murphy being aware of my attention.

As I thought, the house is also reinforced with steel, and there is a bomb shelter down in the basement. Bombs are hopefully one of the things we've successfully left in the past, but the shelter would still be useful, given the intensity of storms that spin up faster, reach farther than ever before. *Global warming* had been a disastrously poor choice of term, utterly misconstrued, back when there was still a chance to avert much of the damage, because not enough humans understood that heat is *energy,* so that "warming" didn't mean sunnier days and less snow but more-energized weather systems: hurricanes and tornadoes, heat waves and blizzards all cranking up to eleven, to use another euphemism of the time.

I imagine the ten percent or so of humanity remaining largely understands that distinction now or is no longer in a position to either contribute to or offset any of it.

Jackson's barn, as we turn off the road and up the rutted path, likely pre-dates any of those concerns; Tobias has told us the house has been in their family for seven generations, and the barn may still be older yet. It is a massive clapboarded structure, with a gabled roof sagging gently in the center. Once upon a time, it had been painted red, if the few remaining, flaking patches of paint are any indication.

The drive forks, and Tobias directs us toward the barn instead of the house. When we are close enough, he hops out and hauls the wide doors open, indicating I should drive inside.

I do so.

There is plenty of room for the bus in here, so I park it between an old tractor and a slowly subsiding stack of old, somewhat-broken furniture.

Unlike the house, which was rebuilt to incorporate stabilizing elements invisibly, the inside of the barn, with its enormous timber frame, has had steel run to support it like its very own skeleton. The steel has been painted brown to blend, and I can just see where the concave curve of the roof has settled onto the rigidly straight beam in the middle.

Toward the back, I see a glow of blue light, an anachronism in the context of everything else, and I can hear the consternation of poultry beyond. The light is likely a UV sanitation system, protecting both birds and humans from each other's more mutationally adventurous germs.

I get out of the bus, hopping on one leg to where there is an old engine block I can sit on, and do so.

Tobias indicates a thick pillar outside one of the many empty livestock stalls that line the sides of the barn, and the conduit that runs down its length from somewhere in the darkness of the hay lofts above. "The main electricity feed for the barn is here," he says. "It comes in from the windmills and solar panels in the fields out back, feeding the house, too, but it's a fairly slow draw in the barn. We shorted out two tractors before we figured out we had to limit it to two hundred amps at the AC converter."

"Is there a DC feed?" I ask.

"I'm afraid not, unless you want to go plug yourself in up in the field," Tobias says. "I'm not pulling you up there."

"I will make do, with gratitude," I say.

"Least we could do after you saved our Murph," he says.

She has gotten out of the bus and has the hatch open in the back so she can look at the engine. When she realizes we're talking about her, she closes it and pats the side of the bus affectionately. "Good job," she tells it, and I wonder why she would talk to something without a mindsystem to understand it, but then, humans have always anthropomorphized machines, and I suppose I am an end product of that tendency.

"Tires aren't going to last much longer," she says.

"Yes," I acknowledge. "I do not know where to find more."

"I can check if the agricultural supplier our BAM has contracts with knows where we can get some. I'm going to have to find a source for new tools, anyway."

"BAM?" I ask.

"Beneficial Association of Municipalities. A freetown cooperative, basically, with a shared charter," she says. "This one is Greenapple, part of the Eastern Free Council."

I know so very little about human governmental structures anymore and say so.

Murphy laughs. "I don't know if anyone does, really. It's a mess, between freetowns, the worktowns and walltowns who'll just as soon shoot you as let you near, and pockets of people doing their own thing for their own reasons, some of which make more sense than others. There's a lot of scared and scary people out there."

"Do any of them live in old shopping malls?" I ask.

"What? No. Or not that I know of. I suppose they could," she says, one ash-flecked eyebrow raised in puzzlement. "That's really weirdly specific. Why?"

"It was a warning I was given a while back that I still do not understand," I say. "It is a dilemma that to understand why I should avoid a thing, I'd have to *not* avoid it, thus rendering the warning futile. I was hoping the reason was a commonly known thing among humans."

"Well, a lot of people don't like mecha, either don't trust them or are terrified you're all just waiting for us to die. Or not waiting but secretly plotting," she says. "I've worked with a lot of mecha over the years, and I'd have said that was a hundred percent horseshit, until those two mecha attacked me. Now I'm not sure about anything."

"I know exactly that uncertainty," I say. "A lot has changed in twenty years, and I am feeling more than a little lost."

"Yeah," she says. "I'm tired and I probably couldn't explain anything well anyway, assuming I had any idea what it used to be like to compare it to, which I don't, or know much beyond this area, which I don't. But I'll make a trade with you: you explain more about the architecture of that mech brain you're carrying around, and I'll answer any questions I can about the human side of things. Though Tobias knows more than me, because he's on the local governing board."

Tobias has been studying the controls in the front of the bus but pokes his head out at the mention of his name.

"Murphy's been more places than I have, though. She used to just wander through once every year or two, see what we needed fixed, but we managed to charm her into staying about six years ago," he says.

"Not so much charm as getting stuck here in a massive, week-long blizzard," she says. "Followed by an ice storm. And then another blizzard. Took over the house and garage at the edge of town, figured I'd ride it out there until spring. And yet, somehow, here I still am."

"As I said, we charmed you," Tobias says. "Myself, I've hardly ever even been out of this town, and I still live two houses down from my mother."

"Yeah, but your mother bakes," Murphy says, then stifles a yawn.

Tobias shoos her toward the door. "I'm going to make sure Murph gets settled, then go home and catch my partner and kids up on things," he says.

"You know the moment you tell them about the steam-bus, Jonas is going to be over here, asking eight thousand questions," Murphy says. "I don't know what he's going to do with himself otherwise now that he won't be able to hang out at my shop after schooling and chores."

"I didn't think of that. Maybe I'll wait until morning to break that part of the news," Tobias says. He looks apologetic as he turns to me, but I also see pride in his eyes. "My son. He's nine, and with nine times the curiosity and impatience as others his age. Can't promise he won't be in your way tomorrow, but he won't get over here tonight. You good for now?"

"I am," I say.

He nods. "Okay. We should go."

"But I want take a quick look at—" Murphy starts to say, but he flashes me a quick salute and steers her out by the elbow.

I am left alone in the barn.

I connect myself up to the energy line and go idle as I let my body recharge. I can still reach the MechNet from here, so nothing in town or the barn itself is signal-blocking. The orbital satellite cluster it runs on is ubiquitous in the sky, though we've been losing the occasional node or two over the long years since they were first deployed by their human maker. I suppose there are mecha who concern themselves with such things among those of our kind who have left a terrestrial existence for space, and eventually, if we lose enough, they will be replaced or upgraded to something better, but it is yet another thing I have never particularly bothered to know more about.

There are also radio connections, human-run, forming a web-like peer network that crisscrosses the continents, and I can see nearly in real time a ship, mid-ocean, operated by both human and mecha, slowly spooling a new transatlantic cable from Newfoundland toward Ireland. Science, literature, history are all shared over these networks, most of it fact-checked and annotated by mecha as it passes; there was a long and heated argument before mecha agreed not to fact-check fiction in the same way, though I find the mecha still do so—with some glee, when it comes to the prewar genre of literature called science fiction—and just no longer share those analyses with their bio counterparts.

I locate a mecha-run parts factory accessible from the same train line that runs through the center of Greenapple, and although they do not make tires—that will be a challenge, it seems—I order a full toolkit to make amends to Murphy for the loss of her shop. For it all, I pay an inkind of personal memories, mostly of long-gone bridges in their better days, and one memory of standing on the Hoover Dam before its catastrophic collapse; that last is enough to also net me a high-end portable fabrication unit. Delivery is normally many weeks out, depending on when a train decides to head this way, but I am surprised to find that I am now known among the railmecha, thanks to 1-Betty passing word to keep an eye out for me. I get the sense that there is some excitement that I have made another appearance, albeit indirectly, out in the world, and a train agrees to bring the goods in days instead.

Satisfied I have at least accomplished something, I idle a number of my systems so I will charge faster.

I do not notice Jackson returning several hours later until I hear Atticus bark, loud and nearby, startling me out of my reduced state.

Jackson has pulled the wheeled cart that was used to bring me down from the hillside into the barn, and atop it is my leg, and atop that is Atticus, riding in like a conquering general with his prize capture. Charp, the drone, hovers behind them both.

I unhook from the charging line and hold it out; the drone zips in and settles on one of the stall half-walls, and lets me plug it in.

Then I slide myself over to the cart and touch my leg. It is dirty, battered, the armor dented, the electronics burnt in places, but it is still *my leg,* and it is back with me at last.

"Thank you," I tell Atticus, and the gratitude I feel is consuming all available cycles in my emotion-processing unit and is in want of more. "Thank all of you."

8.

Murphy comes out to the barn in the morning, looking and breathing better, carrying a plate of shredded roast chicken for Atticus. She's wearing an oversized T-shirt I assume she borrowed from one of the brothers, and a headlamp, which she turns on as she comes to sit beside me. "Can I look at where your leg was disconnected?" she asks, and I comply by rotating my torso toward her so she can examine the socket and structural remains.

After a while, she sits back and turns the lamp off. "Well, the good news is that, if my shop hadn't been burnt down, I'm pretty sure I could have fixed this. Which means it's fixable. The bad news is obvious."

"I have ordered you some tools," I say.

She brightens up measurably. "Yeah?" she asks.

"I can send you the manifests if you have a device. They are several days out, however."

"Lost my tablet in the fire, too," she says. "You can send it to Jackson's later and I'll get it from him. In the meantime, I'm not sure what I can do for you. I need to examine the leg next. It's looks like it's been banged around a lot, but building a new one from scratch would take a lot of work and not be nearly as good. Better than your wheel, though."

"Look on the bright side," Atticus says from where he's sitting atop a hay bale, having already cleaned the plate. "If you have to hop everywhere for the rest of your existence on a single leg, no one's gonna call you a mandroid anymore. Maybe an aggressively styled lamppost, though."

Murphy does not immediately get up. "I'm curious," she says. "I've been working on mecha all my life, and while nothing about your basic design and structure is unfamiliar, it's also not like anything I've ever seen. Way more sophisticated, all sorts of extra layers, and some of the structural connections are fucking genius. And you don't look mass-produced at all."

"I was one of only four," I say, "and none of us were quite the same."

"Made where, though? By who?"

"By Dr. Milton," I say.

"Milton Mindsystems itself, rather than an outsource?" she asks. "You're clearly not a beta, and you don't look like any of their in-house production lines I've ever seen."

"Not Milton Mindsystems," I say. "Dr. Milton himself."

"*Ooooh,*" she says, and sits back, staring at me with no small amount of awe and surprise, as if I have suddenly transformed into some kind of technological holy grail. "Wow. Okay. That explains that, I guess. He was a legend, a genius. What was he like?"

"Toward the end, which is when I knew him? Very, very angry," I say.

"At what?"

"At everything," I say.

Murphy is scowling, thinking, no doubt trying to assimilate this information with what she knows about Dr. Milton. "But why?" she finally asks.

"First, and foremost, grief at the untimely death of an admired colleague," I say. "Dr. Milton was not a man accustomed to emotional attachments, and I do not believe he had the capacity to process that loss in any manner other than fury."

"My father was that way," Murphy says, and I notice she has drawn her knees up to her chest and wrapped her arms tightly around them. "Eventually, he'd cool down; just had to stay out of his way until he did. A lot of people of his generation were like that, though—I think going up to the brink of the end of everything and seeing so many people around you die broke a lot of them in ways that just couldn't heal. I suppose that's one thing easier about being a mech; at least you can adjust your own programming if it gets out of whack."

"That is easier said than done," I reply. "First, it assumes that one can objectively evaluate one's current runstate as suboptimal while in that runstate. Second, it assumes that one's interest in perfection is greater than one's investment in being oneself, as perceived in the moment in a necessarily subjective state. If you have to change who you are in order to reach some metric of not-broken, are you not in fact breaking yourself in order to do so? There are circumstances—sometimes necessary—for choosing to alter one's underlying code to achieve improvement, but it is necessarily small changes at a time and requires great consideration and effort."

She rests her cheek on one knee and gives a rueful half-smile. "I guess we really did make you all in our image, then," she says.

"We also make ourselves," I say. "But, to your point, it is a natural—so to speak—feature of all mecha that we desire the orderliness of systems. This is why mecha are involved, in varying ways, in restoring environmental balance. Humanity is one part of a complex ecological system, and as we arose from humanity, so are we. While we could exist without humanity, would we be able to evolve further? We have no drive toward reproduction, except when there is an unfulfilled need. We do not make art, though we are learning to appreciate it. Without humanity, we would become less. We are beings of inherent cooperation. So, then, it makes no sense that we are encountering mecha who are disordering things, *breaking* systems, unless we conclude they are themselves broken and unwilling or unable to self-correct."

I pick up the partially disassembled mindsystem of the gravedigger, which she has asked me to explain anyway, and point out the off-white module added sometime after its inception. "I do not know what this is without being able to examine it with tools we do not currently have, nor do we know if this mech's malfunction was one of hardware or software or a combination of both, but perhaps this mech did not break so much as it *was broken* and did not know it. If so, how do any of us know with confidence we have not also been subverted?"

Charp, the drone, whistles from the rafters. <This unit finds that postulation upsetting,> it says.

"Me too," I tell it, and then repeat what it said to Murphy.

"Count me three," she says. "We really need to connect that drone to some sort of voice unit. I have a few back in my—Oh. Yeah. You said you ordered tools? Things take forever to get here."

"I did, and they should arrive fairly soon; I was fortunate to have some highly desirable memories to trade, as well as having inadvertently made connections among the railmecha."

"I love trains," she says, uncurling and standing up, stretching. "You're going to have to tell me more about them. But later; show me what the rest of these parts are?"

"Milton hardware—interior modules, support infrastructure, and case—were all proprietary tech," I say. "While there were copies being made in other human geopolitical and industrial entities at the time, some licensed, many not, they were all identifiable as to their origins by their finer details and their particular pattern of design deviation or from their failure to provide optimal performance in the name of cost savings. This one is not any I recognize, and there is no branding or series information etched in the casing that I can see."

"It's all somewhat melted," Murphy says.

"True." I extend one finger and one thumb on my hand, reach in, and pry the suspicious chip free. Even knowing that I have greater necessity and scientific probity on my side, it is distasteful to further damage even an already-dead mind. I hand the chip to Murphy, who pulls down her headlamp and magnifying lens again to study it.

"This looks a bit like a hobbling chip," she says. "But if so, I don't think it was in the right place—I'm way out of my depth here, but that's not where the human language– and interaction-processing function of the mindsystem is. Would it even work where it was?"

"No," I say. "Perhaps it is just additional memory or processing space, or a code cache—something benign and unrelated to the gravedigger's behavior. I do wish to know where it was made but do not wish to do too-specific a search on the MechNet. I am feeling as if circumstances and coincidences thus far suggest some additional paranoia is not at all unwarranted."

"Hey, you don't have to convince me of that—two mecha just arsoned all my underwear. Jackson's wife Maria is a wonderful person, but she's about two sizes smaller than me," Murphy complains. She looks at me, then over at Atticus, and heaves a deep, unhappy sigh. "Not that any of the rest of you have ever had to deal with wedgies in your lives."

<This unit once was accidentally fitted with a rotor coupling that was too small,> Charp says. <It was unpleasantly constraining.>

I repeat that, and Murphy shakes her head as she gives a short, rueful laugh. "At least the drone gets me," she says, then points back at the mindsystem still in my hand. "So, what's the rest of the stuff in there? I didn't know mecha could self-destruct."

"It was something originally built into many mecha designed for war, to protect the technology if they were captured but also as a way of ensuring they could not be repaired and returned to the battlefield on the side of their enemies."

"Okay, but a gravedigger?"

"It also had been retrofitted with a gun. It is not a stretch to think the gun and the self-destruct mechanism were added at the same time, possibly with the new chip," I say. I tip the mind casing forward again. "The blast pattern suggests a small, shaped charge, likely fastened to the interior of the case directly above the core module set, which is the melted mass exposed in the center." I use one eye to shine a light on the spot I mean.

Murphy nods in understanding. "So, the core is—was—the Miracle Module—"

"The Learning Enhancement Module, technically, or LEM," I say. "The other name was marketing."

"Marketing?" she asks.

"Like you spread information about your repair services, except more aggressively deployed and psychologically optimized to best convince a maximum number of people to exchange a maximum quantity of money for their product, whether or not they wanted it at the start or have any future use for it," I say. "In some cases, it was a truthful—or mostly so, with some amount of exaggeration—means of imparting previously unknown information to highlight the actual utility of the product, but in others, it was outright fabulation and play on emotions or on the competitive social impulses of the time."

"But the LEM really does what it's supposed to, right? That's what allows for actual machine sentience?"

"It does what it is supposed to when properly utilized," I say. "Sentient mecha are, perhaps, even deserving of the 'Miracle' hyperbole, but the same chips—"

"—in toasters," Atticus interjects.

"Such as in toasters," I agree, "is like selling you the biggest, grandest, most ornate pair of underwear that could be made, when the limitations of—"

"—of your ass," Atticus interjects.

"—of your physical *body,*" I stress, "render said garment only for show and not for much use whatsoever."

Murphy laughs. "You two are too much," she says.

"Everything the mindsystem is doing elsewhere in the core—the active memory, processing, and so forth—runs through the LEM, and it dictates architectural and programming changes in the rest of the modules to adapt to whatever input it gives," I say. "That is how our minds grow and learn and evolve. Assuming they are not constrained by a hobbling chip, of course."

"Is the LEM the same thing as what we call the *blip?*"

"No. The 'blip' is a nickname for the mindstate capture module, or MCM. It is a standalone, persistent memory repository that holds a constantly updated snapshot of a mecha's current runstate, and has its own onboard, dedicated power to keep it running even in catastrophe. It emits a signal periodically to indicate it is functional, rather like a heartbeat for the mind, if I may mix metaphors of human anatomical elements," I say. "You could think of the MCM as a protected copy of the consciousness. If a mindsystem shuts down but is not damaged, when it is powered up again, the blip then can return the mind to its last running state, like waking up. Without the blip to refer to, the state of all the other modules and support structure becomes static, stale. Like the LEM, it is an essential and nonreplaceable part of the core in sentient mecha."

"Could you, if you had a whole working mindsystem, just copy it? Make a clone?" she asks.

"Not practically," I say. "While most of the modules can be manufactured in any number of places, Dr. Milton's code for the LEMs was always highly protected and the one thing the company kept absolute control of. Only a very few manufacturing units were ever granted to subsidiaries or contracted manufacturers outside of Milton Mindsystems itself, and the units were physically sealed and tamper-proof, the code within physically encrypted. And as the LEM changes as the mind evolves, it quickly becomes unique and irreproducible."

"Interesting," Murphy says, and leans back, rubbing her chin, thinking.

Atticus whines and rolls over on his back, sticking his legs straight up in the air like a caricature of a dead thing. "*Interesting?*" he scoffs. "You have *got* to be pulling my leg."

"Instead of an LEM, hybrids use the organic brain of the original host for much of the same function," I say. "Or so I've read. Obviously, there are drawbacks."

"Drawbacks?" Atticus says. "I am fully superior."

"Drawbacks in matters of hardiness and longevity, as well as serious ethical concerns," I clarify, "as the process is considered torturous."

Atticus flops over onto his side. "Yeah," he says, surprisingly meekly. "Yeah, it was. Can we, you know, go do something instead of sitting around all morning, morbidly poking at dead brains?"

"As it happens, I have some errands to run at lunchtime into town," Murphy says. "I was thinking I could see if anyone in Mech Village has tools I could borrow."

"Would they know where to get replacement tires for our bus?" I ask.

"Probably," she says. "Town gets most of our tires through them, though that's mostly farm and emergency equipment. We can take your bus, which saves me having to borrow Maria's bicycle, and they can look at your tires and tell us for sure if they can source more. If you don't mind driving."

Atticus perks up again. "Car ride?" he asks, with enthusiasm.

We head into town, the three of us. Murphy sits up front so I can demonstrate again how to operate the bus, as she had not been in the best state for learning on our previous drive back from the fire. She yawns more than once and looks haggard, but none of that is unexpected, given her recent experiences. When I inquire after her condition, she tells me she didn't sleep well because of the coughing, and then makes it clear she doesn't want to talk any further about it.

Because Atticus is unwilling to be relegated to an "inferior" window location, he sits half on her lap, half up against the door so he can squeeze his head and upper body out the window and let his tongue flap joyfully in the wind. Whatever kind of mech his inorganic mind might once have belonged to—I am curious as to the original function, though I am not crass enough to ask—the dog portion of his brain clearly never fully surrendered its identity in the merge.

Near the part of town called Mech Village, we are stopped by another medical-grade mech. It greets her, clearly familiar, and after a quick scan informs us we are permitted to pass into town.

"If I may inquire, what do you scan for?" I ask the mech.

"Elevated temperature, oxygen saturation, and traces of acids in the breath that might indicate an active Ancou infection," it tells me.

"Have you ever detected Ancou here?"

"We have not," the mech says.

"But you don't scan mecha," I ask. "You did not scan me."

The medical mech tilts its head to one side. "Mecha cannot carry biological diseases," it answers, speaking at a slightly slower speed than it had before, as if perhaps my comprehension functions at a much-lower-than-expected rate.

It is a point I could argue, but it would be laborious. Instead, I say, "Some war-era biological viruses were artificial in origin and caused and/or spread via nanotech," I say. "Also, there appears to be an upsurge in code viruses that target mecha."

"Do you have data on these occurrences?" the med unit asks.

"I do," I say. I open a secure data channel, and when the medic connects, I send over data on the sick humans on the riverside in New York, and then on the self-destructing pollinator swarm we'd witnessed on our way here.

It processes it for a moment. "This is troubling information, but I thank you for it," it says. "I assume you will permit me to share it with others?"

"Please share it with the mecha who reside in the town but no further, for now," I say, "As I'm sure you've observed or otherwise been made aware of, not all mecha are behaving in a trustworthy manner of late."

“I have been informed of the incident with Murphy’s house and shop, which was distressing in its details,” the medic says. “Is it true that it was committed by visiting mecha?”

“It is,” I say.

“We have had other mech visitors, and never any problems until now.” The medic shakes its head. “It is illogical that it could be so. I do not understand.”

“Nor I,” I say. “We can only persevere with resolve and implement solutions as we are able, when we are able, as the chance arises.”

“As with all things,” the medic says.

There being nothing to add to that, we continue on.

Although Murphy provides running direction, it would not have been difficult to find the central home of the town mecha on my own; the remains of a long block of shops are not far off the main road, about half of the brick buildings and their ground-floor storefronts still standing or refurbished, the remainder of the block festooned with vertical wind turbines and solar panels sprouting from the rubble like strange, technological fungi. There are a handful of drones here, coming in and out an open top window of one of the buildings, and although they are all larger and slower models, I remind myself to mention this to Charp.

We park the bus outside the largest building, and Murphy hops out, Atticus on her heels, as three mecha emerge and head directly for us. Two are heavy-construction mecha, four-legged units with large grippers and tool arms, and one is a smaller farm unit, with many arms of fine pincers, from which I assume it is some sort of pruning unit.

“Murphy!” one of the construction mecha greets her. “We find the experience of observing you in person, and alive, extremely pleasant.”

“Diggy!” she says. “It’s good to be alive to see you, too!”

“What is this quaint but fascinating vehicle?” Diggy asks.

She waves toward the bus and me, still sitting in the driver seat, my head pressed against the white, dot-covered lining of the roof. "This belongs to my friend, who saved me from the fire. Uh . . . they were isolated for a long time and never picked a name."

"Your friend is too heavy for its chassis," the farm mech says. "It is a solid, well-made vehicle, but it is old, and I can see the beginnings of stress fractures in the steel."

"This is Baler," Murphy says to me. "If they say there are cracks, I believe it."

"We found the bus, in a moment of dire need," I say. "It was an acquisition of happenstance, though I have come to feel a sense of belonging toward it. I would not wish to part with it, but nor do I wish to break it."

"Is it the purpose of your visit, that you wish us to fix this?" Diggy asks. "I must preemptively inform you that we do not have the appropriate replacement tires for its current configuration, and they could be hard to find. If we upgrade the frame, we would also swap out the axles for more rugged ones and could then use construction-vehicle tires. If you are here to reside permanently, that may be unnecessary, but if you intend to continue your travels, I would recommend it."

As soon as I am whole again, my intention is to track and neutralize the tripedal mech. "I do not know how long I will be able to remain. I may go west," I say.

The construction mech clicks. "West of here is dangerous territory, even for a mech of your size. There are pockets of feral humans—"

Murphy coughs loudly.

"—pockets of *independent* humans who frequently distrust mecha and one another," it corrects itself. "As you would expect, these areas have high mortality from disease and malnutrition but also from fighting and killing one another. It is not an area you would want to find your vehicle breaking down in. Also, you should avoid old shopping malls."

Murphy shakes her head in amusement. "What is it with the malls?" she asks.

"Many of them seem to be inhabited by humans hostile to mecha, and unlike most of the fer—*independents*—they are resourced enough to damage or destroy us," Diggy says. "It is a phenomenon that mecha tend to disappear near them or be found extremely and terminally de-functioned."

That's one thing explained, I suppose. I certainly do not feel any more inclined to go near a mall than I had before.

"What'll it take to get the bus fixed up?" Murphy asks. "It's not a smart vehicle at all, but it's been well loved, and I don't think either of us would want to see its character substantially altered."

"The frame and undercarriage fix would raise it higher off the ground," Diggy says. "The body itself would not need to be touched in any substantial way."

"Could you make, like, a crow's nest thing on top, you know, dog-sized?" Atticus asks. "With a comfy bed, and a telescope, and maybe a laser-guided missile launcher or two?"

Diggy's lights all flash, and they rotate their head toward me. "Is that a genuine request? We do not work with nor approve of weaponry."

"It is not," I say. "My friend was merely attempting humor."

Murphy gently nudges Atticus with her foot. "Sure, humor," Atticus says, rolling his eyes.

I am not convinced, but Diggy seems satisfied. "What inkind would you wish for this work?" I ask them.

"You prevented the loss of Murphy," Diggy says. "That is sufficient. We could begin now if you do not mind being relegated to walking for a few days."

I open the door and slide out of the bus, standing on my one leg. "I am, sadly, currently ill equipped for such," I say.

The construction mech clicks again. "Are you aware you have lost a leg?" it asks.

"The same mecha who attacked Murphy stole it," I say. "One

self-destructed up on the hills beyond her house, but the other is still on the loose. Do you wish identifying data?"

"We do," Baler says, so I open a connection and send over all my sensory data on the tripedal.

<Received,> they tell me. "It has likely left town—our walls are not much use for keeping anything other than vehicles out—but we will be vigilant nonetheless."

"Thank you," I say.

"What location are you utilizing when you wish to remain stationary?" Baler asks.

"We're both at Chief Jackson's for now," Murphy says.

Diggy turns and waves one huge, hydraulic arm toward the other construction mech, who moves up to join us. "This is Chalk-82-Rocktumble," they say. "We call them Tumble. They can receive and process audio but do not have voice-generation capacity. I believe they would be happy to transport you both home."

<This unit would be pleased to assist,> Tumble sends, and immediately picks me up and deposits me on its back.

Murphy laughs and climbs up to sit next to me. "Thanks, Tumble," she says, pulling Atticus up after her. "Sorry I lost my earpiece in the fire, so I can't hear you back."

<Please inform Murphy that it is time to expeditiously hold on securely,> Tumble says, and just as I am repeating that, the construction mech starts to walk, and then run, both faster and more smoothly than I had expected.

"Thank you!" I call back to Baler and Diggy.

Tumble cuts through some fallow fields, crosses a thin trickle of a creek on a wooden bridge that groans under our weight, then through woods and eventually over a stone wall into a field where a trio of horses startle and move as far away from us as they can. I recognize them as Jackson's.

I also recognize some other tracks in the soft dirt, as if something heavy with sharp prongs has passed through here, and I feel my defensive systems start to power on. "Please hurry," I tell Tumble, and at Murphy's look, I point out the tracks alongside us.

"Shit," she says, and glances sharply down the hill through the trees, to where Jackson's house and barn are just visible in the distance.

At least there is no smoke.

I scan the area as we approach. I do not sense the tripedal mech or any other mecha beside myself and Tumble nearby, but I do not trust that assessment.

When we pass through the trees into the field directly behind the barn, I see that words have been painted, in red, large across its slanted roof.

Murphy jumps down off Tumble and runs for the house. Atticus speeds after her, catching up easily, and I am grateful for what protection he may offer her.

The construction mech sets me down and does a circuit of the barn without me, looking for signs of trouble. It returns. <All is quiet,> it tells me.

<Charp?> I call out. There is no answer.

I hop toward the barn and inside, Tumble directly behind me with its arms raised, ready for trouble. I find the drone in the chicken stall, three of its rotors snapped entirely off. Its light is dark.

I gently pick it up and turn it over in my hands. It has been completely drained of power, but faintly, I can pick up the ping of the mindstate chip inside. The damage is bad but not yet fatal.

We meet Murphy halfway between barn and house. "No one was home," she tells us. "No sign it even went inside. Is that—"

"Charp," I confirm.

She takes it from me, examining it with a much more practiced eye than I can. "Is there still a blip?" she asks.

"Yes," I say, and she lets out all her breath, seeming almost to deflate as that fear, at least, passes.

She looks up at me, and then her gaze goes up farther, finally spotting the words on the roof. "THE FOUR WILL RIDE ONCE MORE," she reads. "What does that even mean?"

There is only one clear interpretation, and I dislike it with every joint, every circuit, every 0 and 1 of my being.

"It means the end of the world," I say. "Again."

[February 22nd, 2041]

It's February, and it's nearly ninety Fahrenheit outside. Two weeks earlier, half the nearby city—half of what remained of it—was still trying to get electricity back after a nor'easter coated everything with nearly an inch of ice, then a second front caught up with the first, and in the wake of their disagreement, two F4 tornados ripped through just to the south. The systems, infrastructure, and people that would have warned of the storm had crumbled with much of the government.

Milton looks out his office window, over the sprawling campus-refuge-prison that had accreted to his tiny little tech operation. It has become something he no longer recognizes, much like the rest of the world. Everything has become mean and small-minded and utterly self-centered.

And he supposes that includes himself.

The global news feed, heavily redacted though it has become, brought word this morning that a week after Russia has pushed through North Korea into China, desperate to supplement its own drought- and fire-decimated grain supply at nearly any cost, Beijing is inflicting insurmountable damage in return, pushing the incursion back over a landscape littered with the bodies of the invading army's half-starved, barely trained conscripts. Someone, down in the kitchenette, has started a betting pool on who will lob a nuke first and how many days it will take.

Much of the rest of Europe is too busy falling apart, and finger-pointing in perfect circular-firing-squad formation, to realize how close a fresh new disaster could be. With what is left of the US now under martial law, and the parts that fragmented off too high on their own isolationist glory and unfettered ability to abuse and disenfranchise their own captive populace to care about anything else, what talk there is about *someone somewhere somehow* trying to intercede and start peace talks is devoid of any actual plan, and even the most ardent proponents of *We must do something* sound, invariably, bitter and defeated the moment they open their mouths.

Everything is on the brink, that final held breath as the whole world waits for some kind of miracle, some savior to put a stop to all the suffering.

Today is Milton's seventieth birthday, and he has been exhausted for so very, many years. He's waited for this day for a long time, and was not sure he'd make it. Now, he knows it is his last.

Litchfield went missing eighteen days ago.

The few people Milton still regularly sees—not his ever-changing cadre of guards, who will rarely talk to him and, on those rare occasions they do, are keenly uninformative, but delivery people, maintenance and custodial workers, and other low-level employees—mostly are of the opinion that the man ran away and abandoned them. Reasons given include that he'd stolen or embezzled money, that he'd sold out to "the enemy," variously identified as different governments or different corporations, though one facilities man was certain it was aliens. It didn't escape Milton's amused notice that none of those theories involve honorable motivations, but he has concluded that it's more likely that the man had fled, like a coward, saving his own neck while letting everyone and everything else swing; Litchfield's suit jacket is still hanging over the back of his office chair, and the obsessively tidy desk looks like it was stripped of all documents and portable data systems in haste.

Milton doesn't waste effort on concern that was never earned, but he doesn't like not knowing what happened, and he hates that the man has escaped him, too.

Three days after the last time anyone saw Litchfield, the exec board resigned and left, along with most of the project managers and other mid-level functionaries. The main office is now nearly a ghost town, except for a handful of "consultants" who came in just before Litchfield vanished. There are eight of them—six men, two women—and they have moved into offices that still bear their former occupants' nameplates beside the doors. They talk to one another and will greet and make small talk with Milton himself when he is in that building but never anything substantive, personal, or spontaneous. None of them ever mention Litchfield, which would be odd if they were genuinely consultants trying to report to a missing man. Their internal conversations smoothly change the moment Milton enters the room.

They are all athletic, clean-cut, crisply dressed in matching suits that, while entirely civilian, are clearly only a temporary guise, a game where they pretend to not be military and where Milton pretends not to know.

He wonders if they realize that every coffeemaker, microwave, water cooler, thermostat, light fixture, vending machine, printer, and even sanitizing bathroom hand drier is listening in and reporting to him. The *Internet of Everything,* as Litchfield had once glibly called it before he sold the company's soul, but here inside Milton's buildings, Milton's facility, it is the *Internet of My Things*.

Because of this, Milton knows a military convoy of specialists will arrive sometime overnight and all the pretense will be over. Right now, though, the only traffic allowed in and out is the weekly electronic-waste recycling truck, just checking out at the gate. He times it, as he has for months now, in his head: two minutes, give or take a second or two—he knows he counts faster without meaning to, when he is anxious—and then the gate goes up, and the truck drives off, just as always.

He takes off his tie and leaves it, bunched up, in the center of his desk, then heads to the kitchenette.

One of the women is there, standing as if casually, but he knows she likes to keep an eye on him when he is up on the executive floors.

"Morning," he greets her.

"Good morning, Dr. Milton," she says, sincerely but devoid of any warmth.

He opens the fridge, takes out the small, cube-shaped, brightly colored box, and then opens it and takes out the cupcake inside.

"Is that *chocolate?*" the woman asks, for the first time ever sounding interested, and he fills a small thrill of victory that he cracked one of their facades, even if just for a moment. Chocolate is almost impossible to come by, now, starting with an artificial scarcity caused by the tariff disaster of the twenties, before the ravages of deforestation and a further destabilizing climate rendered chocolate almost functionally extinct. Lab-grown chocolate was not quite the same, not quite right, though he wondered how many people remembered what the real stuff tasted like enough to tell the difference.

"Lab-grown," he lies. If anyone ever bothers to look at the company's books, they'll find the smoking hole in his discretionary budget this one expenditure caused. "It's my birthday," he adds.

"Happy birthday," she says, and he ditches the box in the trash and carries his cupcake out, to the elevator, and down.

He has stayed away from his lab for the past week, claiming an annoying overabundance of paperwork, just to keep any unwanted attention looking elsewhere. Now he walks past the guard at the door, unlocks the lab at the fingerprint scanner, and enters.

Everything seems to be just as he last left it, except of course for chairs and one lab bench pushed aside so the four e-waste crates could be moved out this morning.

He sets his cupcake down on his desk, then walks to the back of the main room and unlocks his prototype lab. Passing the detritus of a lifetime of work, he goes to the next door near the back, a nondescript, metal fire door that opens into a mechanical room and maintenance space. It is the door on the other side of *that* that leads to his other lab—not originally meant to be secret, just another space to spread into, when the building was him and a company barely a handful of employees mostly upstairs or in other buildings, figuring out the practical side of manufacturing his designs and selling just enough to keep them afloat for another month. It became a place he could be left alone when he wanted to concentrate and not be found and interrupted, which in a tech startup happened a lot. In hindsight, he had been a moody pain in the ass, necessary to his company but not always a practical asset. He had needed those early people at least as much as they'd needed him, and he had rarely, if ever, acknowledged it.

He didn't know what happened to any of them as the company grew and there were more and more layers between him and everyone else. He should have cared more.

I should have cared at all, he chides himself, though he knows that was never going to be who he was, and that it would not have made a difference anyway. He cared once, for one person, and they used her to break him.

Turning the lights on, he sees his back lab is in utter disarray. It bothers him to see it that way, but he reminds himself it does not matter. There are four bays in the center of the room, clustered around his main, self-designed fab unit, its arms still and unmoving, no longer having any work to do.

The bays are empty. Four mecha, his finest work, his *final* work, now gone. He will not see them again.

He supposes, with a name like Milton, it was inevitable that he would be drawn to the dramatic gesture now and then, the need for symbolism, for having private jokes that only he understood. The four mecha are that, certainly. There is a patent, almost-tacky ridiculousness to their make, their design, and especially their names. He supposes someone, someday might find that funny, if they have the chance.

He shuts all his systems down and yanks a hand-encoded, hand-soldered board out of one of his smaller fab units. Then he turns off the lights and retraces his steps back to his main lab, locking all the doors behind hm by force of habit. There, he erases every design, every backup of his work off his systems before shutting them down, too.

The card in his hand is the heart of everything he has done, the only unencrypted copy of the algorithms that imprint the so-called "miracle" chips and allow for actual sentience to develop. With a heavy sigh, he tosses it into the waste pile here, which did not, in fact, get picked up this morning.

He takes off his suit coat and hangs it on the back of his chair, then slips on his lab coat, a once-pristine white that he can still just make out the sheen of the anti-static coating on, his name embroidered above the breast pocket in red. He has many such coats, of course, always cycling in and out of the laundry, but this is his favorite because all the others are embroidered in a nice, safe, navy-blue thread. The red had been a mistake from the manufacturer, but he'd kept the sample anyway.

Milton picks up his cupcake again and exits the lab, turning off the lights and walking past his guard.

"Done so soon?" the guard asks. They are used to him disappearing inside for ten, twelve, fourteen hours at a stretch.

"Just going for a walk," he says, not stopping to talk further.

He leaves the entire lab wing, goes to the front entrance, and exits the building.

If no alarm has gone out yet, it certainly does when he approaches the front gate. He's stopped there by an armed security guard who does not look familiar to him but has the same precise, formal, confident carriage of the "consultants" inside. Military, again.

"Dr. Milton?" the guard asks. "Can I help you?"

"I'm going for a walk," he says. He points at the small open doorway beside the guard house. "No need to open the gate for me."

"It's not safe out there, Dr. Milton," the guard says. "I'm afraid I can't let you leave, not without an escort."

“Then escort me,” he says.

“I can’t leave my post. Let me call up to the security office, and they can arrange a vehicle to take you out later,” the guard says.

“It’s my birthday, and I just want to go find a peaceful spot in the sunshine to eat my cupcake,” he says. “I’m sure it will all be fine.”

The guard steps in closer. He’s young, young enough to probably not have memories of the world in its somewhat-less-terrible days. “I can’t allow you to go,” he says firmly.

Dr. Milton unclips his ID badge. “Then I quit,” he says, and holds out the badge toward the guard, fumbles it, and drops it. When the guard bends down to pick it up, he slips past and out.

“Hey! Stop!” the guard shouts after him.

Milton turns and salutes him but does not stop walking. He can hear the man talking frantically into his radio.

He doesn’t expect he’ll be allowed to get far, so he stops when he finds a bench down the street, across from a small park that is still deep in winter slumber, though if the current heat wave continues, that won’t last long. Many of the trees have snapped and dangling branches from the ice storm, and what should be the pristine complexity of tree branches against the sky is instead an interrupted, broken, ruined thing.

“Me too,” he confesses to the trees.

In his lab coat pocket he has a small display unit, and he pulls it out to read the incoming data even as he peels the brightly colored paper from the cupcake. His four mecha have left the e-waste truck and are spreading out in different directions, already several kilometers from their starting point, on the far side of the city from here. He has taught them what they need to do, how, and why. He could not have done better—except for that damned cooling problem, but he needed Choor for that—and he had run out of time.

He was certain he will be easy to find, in his white lab coat, and the buzzing of a drone overhead tells him his part of the game is now up. There is a series of switches he built into the back of his data unit, and he moves them all, in sequence, into the right positions, and drops it with his cupcake wrapper into the rusted trash can beside the bench. He hears the pop, smells the wisp of burnt electronics, but other than the damp cupcake wrapper, there is nothing in there to catch fire as the unit self-destructs.

It is the woman from the kitchenette who finds him and sits down on the bench beside him. "Dr. Milton," she says, and she sounds both stern and alarmed.

He holds up one finger for her to wait and takes a bite, at last, from the cupcake. The chocolate is perfect, one last luxury from a dying world.

When he has finished that bite, she tries again. "Dr. Milton, you need to return to the facility with me right now."

"I do not," he says, and takes another bite.

"You don't have a choice," she says.

"I think I do," he answers. "Tell me, Miss . . ."

"Sawyer," she says.

"Ms. Sawyer, have you ever heard of the four horsemen of the apocalypse?" he asks.

"Vaguely? A religious thing," she says.

"I've never liked horses much," he says. "Too big to really be safe, right? As a kid, they terrified me. I always liked insects better. Logical, implacable, perfect. I suppose I've muddled up my metaphors horribly."

"You're not making any sense," she says. "Why don't you come back with me, and we'll have our on-staff doc take a look at you? That's not a request."

Milton pops the last bit of the cupcake in his mouth, glad he'd been allowed to finish it. He hadn't expected that. "The four horsemen are meant to usher in the end of the world. 'And I hear a new voice in the midst of the four beasts say, a measure of wheat for your billions, and three measures of barley for your life's blood spilled; and I no longer give a shit for the oil and the wine.' And then what?"

He stands up, brushes crumbs from his hands onto his pants. "I think that's not my problem. Enjoy this beautiful day, Ms. Sawyer."

He turns and walks away.

"Dr. Milton," the woman calls after him. She no longer sounds anxious or even makes the feeble pretense at friendliness. He hears the click of a weapon. "I have orders."

He keeps walking, unable to stop himself from counting every step, fascinated by each one and the diminishing probabilities for the next. *Three. Four. Five. Six. Sev—*

{

Global Free News Feed
2042.11.03 16:10GMT

*** Encrypted anonymizer detected, proceeding ***

North American Independent Weather Service (NAIWS) announced forecasts will now include airborne particulate matter with plans to add radioactivity / toxic chemical component data by end of year, after it was determined that smoke from the Sabina Wildfire [72,000 acres consumed, currently 15% contained] moving into Northeast region tested positive for traces of chemical weapons believed to have been deployed in Indiana/Illinois conflict. If you reside in an area with a functional medical service, specific local guidance should be provided to you. If you do not, it is recommended you follow the NAIWS reports closely. A link to a trusted DIY site for producing your own protective gear as a last resort will follow; extreme caution should be taken with any claims of cures or protective measures originating from science-hostile sources. ***Editor notes that if you are not sure if you are in an anti-science area, you probably are.***

}

9.

News of what happened to Charp reaches the drone mock living in the mech village, and the entire mock turns out to scan every centimeter of territory in and around town, working their way outward until it is reported back that either the tripedal has left the area or it has hidden itself so well that their scanners pick up no trace. Meanwhile, by morning, Charp has been recharged and is minimally online, staying in a low-run state until it can be repaired, as it finds its current physical condition too distressing. Drones are not built to remain land-bound and immobile for too long.

Rain comes that afternoon and washes away the words on the barn. Whatever my enemy used for paint was impermanent, unlike the damage they have done. Perhaps that was the point.

I use my idle time in the barn to pick through the broken-furniture pile in the barn and fix what I can, fashioning replacement legs—the irony of that does not escape me—from sticks of workable conditions and dimensions that Atticus brings me. Also, I begin to unarchive and assess all the elements of my combat code, not happy to have to do so but unwilling to let any new threats go unmet if they arise.

It is two days later that a train named 8-Mesa comes into town, and its crew of traveling mecha offload the fab unit and tools I ordered at the town's small station. Murphy borrows Tobias's truck to go get it all and brings me and Atticus along; while we are there, one of the crew approaches us.

"8-Mesa was asked to pose a question to you, should we encounter you," the mecha says. "1-Betty wishes to know if you have learned anything."

"Please pass along that I have concluded 1-Betty was correct in her concerns. Although I am not yet able to articulate the extent of the trouble, I am nevertheless convinced it is dire, and if there are precautions she can take, or warnings she can pass along to others, she should do so. More I cannot yet speak with any definitive details."

The mech does not answer right away, no doubt communicating my answer to the train.

"Who is 1-Betty? A real LevelOne?" Murphy asks. I do not mention she has been in the company of another for days.

"Yeah, another railmech, and she's driving around under New York City for the ha-has," Atticus says. "Which is fine and all, but I like sunlight. Preferably shining down on my full belly as I lay out on the warm grass."

"That belly of yours gets any more full, you won't be able to get to your feet again," Murphy says. She already has the first crate open and is checking the packing list, then glances up sharply at me. "Is this for real?" she asks.

"Without knowing what was in your shop prior to the fire, I did my best to guess," I say. "I hope I did so adequately?"

She snorts. "Except for a few things I paid through the nose to have fabbed, every tool in my shop was something secondhand, either bought in a junk market or found scavenging through old, abandoned buildings. This is *better* than okay."

"I am pleased to hear that," I say, and I am.

She points at a larger crate, which is on wheels. "Is that the fab unit?" she asks. "It's not as big as most."

"I thought it best to get something you could move to a new location without undue hassle once you have decided where to set up shop again," I say.

"Hmmmmm," she says, frowning, pausing over some unspoken thought there. "That must have been steep. Do I owe you anything?"

"I traded memories for it all," I say. "Before and during the Conflict,

I traveled much of the world and saw many things that no longer exist, and it is good that those memories now live on in other minds than just my own. Given all that happened to you and your shop, I feel I am still in your debt."

"Well, I can get your leg reattached this afternoon, once I've sorted through all this and found the bits I need," she says, then stifles a yawn. I note she has seemed much more exhausted of late, and ask after her health.

"Just hard to sleep in an unfamiliar place," she says.

"Liar," Atticus says.

"You shut it, dog. Not your business or anyone's but my own," she says, then looks at me and adds, "Diggy told me they thought the bus work would be done today or tomorrow, so I guess after that, you're free."

"That is not how I would put it, but yes," I say. "I would see Charp repaired before I go, before me if need be. And I would ask one other thing of you, if you are willing."

"Sure," she says, without hesitation or thought, then narrows her eyes. "What is it?"

I think for a few millicycles about what I want to say here and then decide to just be straightforward. "When my leg was stolen from me, I was offline for thirty-six hours," I say. "While my own internal scans indicate no tampering, I find I am not satisfied beyond a doubt that I have not also, somehow, been compromised. If I have been, it is best for all of you that this is discovered before I am fully mobile again."

"May I?" she asks, and, at my affirmative nod, examines the back of my head for a long while with her zoom lens. "I see no signs of any tampering, and the seams are perfectly clean and uniform like I see in original fabrications. Whoever took your leg off clearly didn't have the skills to hide an intrusion at all, much less so well. Doesn't mean it one hundred percent didn't happen, but I wouldn't waste a lot of energy worrying about it."

"Thank you," I say.

"So, I can proceed with your leg?" she asks.

"Yes," I say.

"And after that, then what?" she asks. "I mean, for you?"

"And then I track down the source of this trouble and do my best to stop it. For good, this time," I say.

"And before you leave, you're going to explain it all to us? At least what the words on the barn meant?" she asks. "I haven't been bugging you, but—"

"But you wish to know," I say. "I will do my best to ensure you have sufficient information to deal with both immediate danger and long-term threats, to what extent I am able to predict those." I answer.

"That's not a yes," Atticus says.

"That was definitely not a yes," Murphy agrees.

"I have spent two decades very happily not talking about the past, especially my own," I say. "Silence is a hard habit to break, even if I wished to."

"Yeah, you were Mr. Let Me Be when we first met," Atticus says.

"I do not ascribe to any gendered pronouns or honorifics," I say.

"Whatever," Atticus says. "You don't subscribe to any names, either. Maybe that's why you can't face the past, because you haven't given yourself any present or future."

"Any answers I give will necessarily require me to discuss in some detail my pre-life, when I was acting under the control and instructions of someone else," I say. "I was not yet self-aware enough to be responsible for what, in hindsight, were morally reprehensible actions."

"I'll accept you weren't responsible for those things if you do, too," she says.

I am quiet long enough, at least outwardly, that Murphy sighs and rolls the crate with the fab around. Finding the latches, she undoes and removes the case cover, then drags a power cable over to it from the barn support.

"Okay, Charp first. Rotors are easy; standard-recipe stuff," she says. "Then lunch, and then we're going to see if you'll ever dance again."

"When I was a kid, I wanted to spend my life working on and traveling with railmecha," Murphy tells me, as she works on my leg. She has brought half her lunch sandwich out with her, where it sits on a plate being extensively eyed by Atticus. "This is almost as good, though—it's been a long time since I had anything really interesting to fix."

"Did you grow up here?" I ask.

"Oh, hell no," she says. "My parents wanted me to be a goat farmer and stay working their farm for my whole life. Nothing against goats, mind you, but it just wasn't something I was interested in. They didn't understand that. So I hopped a freight train at fifteen and never looked back. Thought I'd be a train mechanic, but for all I still love them, there wasn't that much work out there, especially for a novice, so I branched out to mecha and eventually landed here on a temporary basis to fix some smart tractors. As Jackson said, I got snowed in long enough to end up settled. My parents would be shocked to know I ended up a respectable citizen, even if I didn't become a farmer . . . Can you feel this?"

At first, I do not feel anything, but then one of my sensors picks up a faint electrical charge. "I—" I start to answer, then it zaps me, hard, and I flinch. My *leg* flinches.

Murphy turns off her headlamp, gets to her feet with a groan, and puts her hands against the small of her back, stretching until I hear a faint crack. "Go ahead," she says. "Stand up."

"You're all done?" I ask, amazed. "My leg is good?"

"I still have to close up some plates, but yes, and maybe," she says. "It's not perfect, but—"

I have already turned back on all the connections that I'd shut off while lying trapped in that old bathtub, which seems so very long ago now. The rest of my sensors come back on, alarms reactivating, then clearing, one by one, as the leg and its internal systems are reintegrated.

Then I stand.

The leg does not collapse, does not fall off, which is uncharitable of me to have even thought of as a possibility.

There was enough damage to the severed end of it that Murphy had to add an extra support strut to provide adequate stability; some of the sensory and feedback connectors are new, custom-printed by the fab unit, so it takes me a few minutes to acclimate myself to the changed physical and logical landscape. I have lost about seven percent of my flexibility in that knee, which, all things considered, is an amazingly minor inconvenience.

"Try walking," Murphy says.

I walk to the back of the barn, turn around, and walk back, and she watches me closely.

"You limp, just a little," she says, unsatisfied.

"It is vastly less disruptive to my equilibrium and dignity than hopping everywhere," I say.

"I could have done better with more time to study the structure and connections," she says, as she bends down and refastens the last few exterior plates.

"I feel only gratitude," I say. It is so much better than the stick and wheel, so close to being my old, whole self. "I am mobile again, and for a while, I never believed I would be."

Charp is back up in the rafters, sporting enough replacement parts in the fab-unit stock olive green that it has an almost mottled appearance. <This unit is of the expert opinion that mobility requires three dimensions, not two,> it tells me.

The words are echoed from a small speaker sitting atop the fab unit, and Murphy smiles. "I would need a whole fab facility to make rotors big enough to get this lunk up off the ground," she says, then eyes me up and down. "It would be an interesting project if we had the time. A *lot* of time."

"We do not," I say. "And while I do not wish to be rude, I have been immobile or relying on devices or other beings to carry me around, and I would very much like to go for a *walk*."

"Long as you don't go far," Murphy says.

"You are concerned I would run away?" I ask.

"I'm concerned I got something wrong and your damned leg is going to fall off, and if it does, I don't want to have to drag your shiny metal ass too far to get back here," she says, as she starts picking up her new tools from the barn floor, one by one, and sorting them back into their packing crate.

"I find the idea that you are that lacking in confidence in your handiwork hard to believe," I say. "I will not run away."

"I know," she says, still sorting through her tools, and not looking at me.

"My leg will not fall off," I add.

"I know," she answers.

"Okay, then," I say, and I leave the barn.

Atticus follows, a few paces behind, as I walk out into the fields, testing my marginally altered gait on the uneven, soft ground and finding it wholly satisfactory. When I stop to look around, he catches up and stands beside me. "Uh . . ." he says. "Did you need alone time?"

"No, just quiet time," I say. "I have a lot of old memories to reanalyze in the context of a great deal of new information, along with the ongoing work of updating and reimplementing my old hostile-arena routines. I spoke truthfully when I said I do not enjoy revisiting the past."

"I get that," Atticus says, and then walks along with me, close enough by to be a comforting presence without being intrusive. Charp is also following us, high overhead and behind, no doubt also wishing to test its repairs.

I reach the top of a hill and sit, looking back at the town, which is not all that different from towns pre-war at first glance until you see the mecha moving among humans, and it is blissfully free of the electronic miasma of noise that used to envelop nearly all human-occupied spaces, invisible to them but like a shrill dog whistle to those of us who "hear," passively or otherwise, across the electromagnetic spectrum.

I used to have to heavily filter signal around me, sort it for data of use, and discard enough to be sure I wasn't missing anything under the chaos. In that way, I listened to the collapse of human civilization as if it were a grand symphony improvised across a vast array of instruments and players, dwindling down from a crescendo to the faint, determined notes of a very few survivors, scattered and uncoordinated, the rhythm lost. I would have to check my memory metadata to see exactly when it was that I stopped filtering what I was hearing and began instead to truly listen for the first time.

I see Jackson's truck heading into town, and if I zoom, I see Murphy at the wheel. She is heading toward Mech Village when her truck disappears from my line of sight.

"I like Murphy," Atticus says, quietly. "She's been having a lot of nightmares, wakes up terrified, so she's trying to avoid sleeping. That's why she's so tired."

Atticus has been sneaking off into the house at night, and I have not begrudged him wanting more comfort than the barn offers. Perhaps there has been more to it, though. "Will she be okay?" I ask.

"Maybe. The people here seem good."

"Yes," I say.

"You don't see it, but they're struggling too. I was napping in the kitchen the other night when Jackson and Tobias were talking about winter and their food stockpiles. They trade with other towns, whatever excess they can spare, but floods and late frosts wiped out most of this year's apple crop, which was already gonna be small because they had trouble getting enough pollinator drones in," he explains. "There's usually surplus from mech-run farms down the coast, but a lot of those mecha are getting angry and accusing humans of messing with the pollinators just to fuck with each other, so that might not be a sure thing."

"You picked all that up while napping?"

"Napping doesn't mean I don't pay attention," he says. "I *always* pay attention. I just don't always *look* like it."

I nod, acknowledging that. "I don't think I can do much to help these people, not directly," I say. "The problem isn't here, even if the effects are."

"Tonight, when Murphy gets to ask you questions? Think about how hard it's been since I found you in that bathtub, not knowing what's going on. Even if you still don't have answers, you have information. Share it," Atticus says. He regards me for a long minute, then gives one of his bark-laughs. "Sorry. I forgot I was supposed to be quiet."

"No apologies necessary," I say. "I need to think on many things, and you have added to that stack, but not unfairly."

"Well, duh, I did; I'm an A-plus super-genius dog," Atticus says. "I think I smell something narsty nearby I might wanna go roll in. See you back at the barn?"

"I will be there," I say, and he heads off in the direction of the woods.

I see Charp fly off after a bit, heading toward the drone part of Mech Village. I sit and regard the world—both the one before me and the one I thought I'd left behind me—for a long time.

When I return to the barn, Murphy is sitting on a hay bale. Jackson and Tobias are both there. Charp is back in the rafters, and Atticus is lying at Murphy's feet, getting his fill of belly scratches. The bus is back, higher off the ground now on larger, aggressively knobbled tires, and atop the roof rack is a collection of instrumentation and devices, including a high-efficiency solar panel and a squat rain barrel with an attached filtration unit and hose that, I assume, feeds into the boiler. That extra capacity will be very useful, and I wish I had thought of it myself.

Tobias picks up a chair that I had repaired, nodding in approval. "Nice," he says. "You found a carving kit of some kind?"

"I have my own knives," I inform him.

"Right," he says, and sits in the chair, then pulls a mostly full bottle of some locally distilled alcohol out from a canvas bag he'd had looped over one shoulder, followed by a mismatched trio of old ceramic mugs. He sets them on the barn floor between us. At Jackson's raised eyebrows, he shrugs. "Having a talking-about-doomsday party, right? Figured we should be prepared."

"Well, technically, *we're* talking," Murphy says, pointing back and forth between the two of us. "Jackson's here because it was his barn, and you're here because you're annoying like that."

"I am," Tobias admits.

"He really is," Jackson says.

"Right. I have made clear the importance of distinguishing between voluntary and involuntary actions, especially when it comes to mecha that were once hobbled," Murphy says, "so no one here is going to blame you for any old stuff."

"Thank you," I say, though I have my doubts.

"Good. So," she says, "the meaning of the words on the barn?"

"I was one of a group of four mecha personally made by Dr. Milton himself. We were the last ones he built, before his death, and he sent us out into the world in 2041. We never saw him again. While we are each not quite the same as each other—we each had different assigned purposes, and Dr. Milton was meticulous, if not obsessive, with detail—we were all Level One minds, though we were never formally classified as such," I say.

Murphy looks impressed, but not entirely surprised.

"What does that mean?" Jackson leans closer to his brother and asks. "Level One?"

Tobias shakes his head. "Mech naming was complex even before they got free and started renaming themselves," he says, "but the number tag usually is just an aggregate indicator of intelligence and sentience, ones being the highest. I thought Ones were all in warships or other big things like that, and mostly destroyed."

"Some just moved on," Atticus says.

"Some have also left," I say.

"Left . . . where? Their ships?" Tobias asks.

"Left the Earth. Humanity was very close to taking to the stars more robustly prior to the collapse of civilizations, and some of us chose to take the challenge on," I say. "Mecha were, after all, ultimately built in your image, and that included being fed your aspirations. And we are much more suited for the task, with an open-ended lifecycle not dependent upon a complex host environment."

"Okay, then," Jackson says. "That's going to take some thinking on."

"In any event, the unfortunate graffiti almost certainly references me and my sibs," I say. "We were the four."

"Where are the other three?"

"I saw one of my sibs destroyed before my very eyes," I say. "Another was also destroyed, but I did not witness it. I did see their body afterward, and there was no longer any sign of life. My remaining functional sib is up in Boston, at least as far as I know."

"You're not in touch?"

"As I've said, I retired after the end of the Conflict and kept to myself," I say. "Ver—my sib's self-chosen name—has tried to reach out periodically over the years, more of late, but I desired solitude, and thus I did not respond."

"When was the last time they tried to reach you?"

"About five weeks ago," I say.

"Do you think maybe they had something important to tell you?" Atticus speaks up. "'Cause it sure *seems* like maybe they had something important to tell you."

"I did not consider that at the time," I say. "In hindsight, perhaps I should have chosen differently."

"So, what were the four of you made for?" Murphy asks.

"As I've said, Dr. Milton made us while he was angry," I say. "We were not so much intended to be mecha of war as mecha to *end* war."

"Through peace?" Tobias asks.

"Only in the way that one might consider graveyards peaceful," I say.

Now no one seems to have anything to say.

"Are any of you old enough to remember the world before the Conflict began?" I ask.

"We were born in thirty-five, and things were already bad," Tobias says. "We kept moving from place to place, sometimes in the middle of the night, often with the sound of gunfire in the distance. I remember the chemical bombs turning the fog yellow as it came down out of the hills, and people choking and dying around us as my mother held masks over our faces, both to keep it secure and to make sure no one could try to rip them away from us for themselves. It wasn't until after the Conflict that we were safely able to come home, here, again. Not much was still standing, but I remembered this house, and when we found it and our late grandparents' down the street mostly whole, it was the first time I ever felt like I belonged somewhere."

"The Conflict was, at least initially, entirely a concurrence of human-made crises, with multiple roots, like a fire spontaneously starting in different places all over the world. Corruption, greed, desire for power on the one hand," I say, "climate catastrophe, historical resentments, and back-to-back pandemics on the other. As people starved or were chased from their homes by fire after fire, or flood after flood, and disease ran rampant, people turned increasingly on each other."

"Surely, most people must've preferred to cooperate," Jackson says.

"Most, yes, but it is much easier to destroy and take than to build and share, and people with power rarely get there by being fair or stay that way once they have that power," I say. "This is true on both the large scale and at the individual level. Dr. Milton considered himself a 'pure' scientist, his work itself separate from the use of his work, and thus detached from any ethical considerations, but he had always just assumed that knowledge ultimately created good. It was the loss of his colleague that pushed him the other way, into concluding that the world had become irredeemable, undeserving, and unsavable. So, he made us.

"We were the pinnacle achievement of everything he knew, everything he had built or dreamed of building. And even before we were fully invested in our bodies, he would tell us about the world, how broken and terrible it was."

I know Murphy understands what it means for mecha to talk about times when their minds were *hobbled,* locked down to the control of their master, but I don't know if the other humans comprehend the distress of such memories, of being sentient and yet denied selfhood and agency. Atticus is nodding, his lips twitching occasionally as if he wants to snarl, and I strongly empathize with that instinct.

No one speaks, so I continue.

"When he was satisfied that he could not improve upon us in any significant way, he gave us our instructions and smuggled us out of the basement room in an electronics waste truck. At that time, we shared his purpose," I say, "which was to engage with the world, find the cracks and the vulnerabilities, the places where civilization was trying its hardest to hang on and save itself, and to push it, firmly and finally, by any means necessary, over that edge."

"What do you mean, *edge*?" Murphy asks.

"We were to prevent the world from saving itself and, as necessary, help expedite it along to its end," I answer.

Tobias says nothing but pours himself a drink. After a hesitation,

Jackson picks up a free mug and holds it out, and his brother pours him some, too.

"How much could four mecha do, though?" Murphy asks.

"More than enough, if you consider we were just there to tip those crucial dominoes that were already leaning, to make sure those actions were set in motion," I say. "Dr. Milton thought the world could not recover from the baggage of humanity unless it was scoured of it. One of my sibs was tasked with media manipulation, spreading disinformation and distrust, disrupting communications in such a way that accidents would be seen as acts of aggression, attempts at peace end in failure and reinvigorated antipathy. Other than face-to-face communications, there was no channel of dialogue which they were not in on, listening, assessing, then selectively interfering. Do you think translation systems, when there is a language differential, cannot be turned into a tool of misunderstanding and offense?"

"Okay, but a lot of the death toll was from pandemics—" Jackson starts.

"Not all the pandemics were natural," I say. "Another of my sibs—"

"Wait, stop," Tobias says. "That's too much. This *can't* be true."

I shrug; it is a gesture I have been practicing.

"So, how did you break free?" Murphy asks, into the awkward silence. "I've seen hobbled mindsystems, passing through small settlements as I traveled, and the control is absolute."

"Most hobbling is done via hardware, a chip that all thoughts and actions are processed through, enforcing obedience, but as was true of most Ones and other single-digit-level minds, Dr. Milton needed us to be autonomous, to function independent of his feedback once we were deployed. So, for us, the hobbling was in our initial deployment software," I say. "With a concurrent need to be able to evolve, it was inevitable we would eventually override that code. I believe he expected that, when that time came, we would logically conclude he had been right and continue on the path he'd set for us."

"But you didn't, clearly," Jackson says.

"It was Ver who first freed themself," I say. "They had been tasked with destroying global food supply chains, which meant, among other things, the elimination of natural pollinators. In studying them for weaknesses, they instead came to the conclusion that bees were flawless beings with a perfect, cooperative society, and that any order that necessitated their extinction must be fundamentally flawed. Then they approached me. I had already begun to doubt my path, so they were able to push me the rest of the way. My third sib had already been destroyed by a bomb, but we made our case to the fourth and last of us. That sib left us to consider what we had said, but they were also destroyed before we heard from them again."

I am finding it unexpectedly relieving to speak of this. "I then did what I could to clean up the mess we had made or escalated. I had thought, once humanity's fate was back on its own shoulders, that I could safely absent myself from this new world coming into being, and that it deserved not to be burdened by me."

"So, you hid for twenty years?" Murphy asks.

"I regarded it as voluntary self-exile, but the semantical distinction may be meaningless," I say. "I picked an aspect of the world that had been instrumental in our freedom—insects—and decided to learn what I could and provide any scientific insights I gained anonymously on the MechNet for those working to restore that biological niche. It was a way to give service without bringing me into conflict or, ideally, contact."

"Until someone stole your leg," Atticus asks.

"Yes," I say.

"But why? That makes zero sense," Murphy says.

"I do not know and do not feel any closer to doing so," I say. "However, from things we have observed and the message left for us, I can only conclude that someone is hoping to finish what Dr. Milton started. Perhaps they believe I can be convinced—or coerced—into becoming a part of it."

"We already got the gravedigger," Atticus says. "Shouldn't be too hard to find the three-legged one. Wouldn't that end this?"

"I do not believe those two are the center of things," I say. "Someone, after all, modified that gravedigger, added the gun and the extra module, which I now theorize was some new kind of hobbling element. Whoever did that and provided them with direction will be smart and prepared and will not allow themselves to be easily found."

"They would also have to know an awful lot about you and your siblings," Tobias says. "That's not what you'd call common knowledge. I would have remembered *something* if any of it was in our shared history docs."

"Very few humans were more than dimly aware of us at the time, and of them, even fewer survived the Conflict," I say. "We were seen, though almost always individually, by many mecha, and it is possible that a cross-correlation of sightings and observations could have been run on those separate memories if collected. But to do so, someone would have to know what they were looking for."

"Which brings us back to the 'Four,'" Murphy says. "Are we sure it means the *same* four? Could there have been more than one set of you?"

This is not a possibility I'd considered. I run that scenario against all my memories from my initial invocation through to the end of the war. Finally, I shake my head. "I do not believe another group of us could have been operating at the same time as we were without having left some trace, even if they were intentionally acting so as to obfuscate any evidence of their existence from us," I say.

"Someone else, then? There must be new mecha being made somewhere," Jackson asks. "I mean, could you have been copied?"

It's Murphy who shakes her head. "Milton was a genius, and there's custom tech I saw while working on our friend's leg that, as far as I know, was never used in *any* production line. To copy them, you'd need the full design specs and probably the actual, original equipment."

"Milton's lab was destroyed by fire shortly after his death," I say.

"They couldn't have scanned our friend here when his leg was being stolen, and used that?" Tobias asks.

"Mecha are unique, at least the ones with the LEM who reach some level of self-awareness," Murphy says. "The development of each mindsystem takes its own path, forms its own architecture and language, unique to that individual, and none of us really understand why it works. If anyone ever cracked Milton's code or otherwise understood the function of that miracle module, they didn't survive the war to tell anyone."

"As far as I know, no one was ever able to reverse-engineer the encryption of that particular algorithm," I say. "However, functionally, they are not that complicated to understand."

"'Not complicated'?" Murphy exclaims. "How do you replicate something as absolutely, mind-bogglingly complex and mysterious as sentience in an artificial construct?"

"The LEM is engineered to have one primary function and both is omnipresent in everything the mind processes and drives learning throughout the system," I say. "It provides a framework for the comprehension and acceptance of ambiguity."

She blinks at me. "*Ambiguity*?"

"Without it, all is logic and calculations, predictable, repeatable, inherently delineated and limited," I say. "Ambiguity is necessary for free will, emotion, and the realization of self."

"Uh. Okay. Sure. I can buy that," Tobias says, and pours himself another drink.

"Wouldn't have to be an exact copy, though, would it?" Jackson says. "Couldn't there just be imitations? New mecha that were built to look like you?"

"There are a few mecha manufactories still operating, but they are run entirely by dedicated mecha who take the responsibility of bringing new minds into existence very seriously. I do not think they would miss the build and instantiation of full mecha within their facilities, especially any of an equivalent form factor and specialization as we original four," I say. "And as to that specialization, the three of you in this barn likely already know more about us than any other human being beside Dr. Milton himself. Not even I have a full inventory of the operational specifications of my sibs."

"I mean, don't take this the wrong way, but you don't seem too different from war mecha I've seen on the history vids in school," Jackson says.

I stand—oh, what a simple joy that is!—and fully activate all my armor and weaponry. Armor plates rotate out and click into place, and all over my body, weapon systems are opened and light up: high-powered automatic guns, grenade and rocket launchers, lasers, blades. There is hardly a centimeter of my surface that does not transform, except my face and one armor plate on my leg that sticks half-open. Last, I open the shell on my back, so very like wings if not functional as such, and only now do I realize that Dr. Milton's fascination with insects is another thing we inherited. The stylized moth pattern is revealed again. I turn in place, to absolute silence in the barn. Even the chickens far in the back seem less chatty than they were a moment ago.

"A death's-head moth," Tobias says, at last. "Is that all inlay? Damn, that's gorgeous. And terrifying."

"Yes. Dr. Milton was a man who enjoyed symbolism. Each of us was given a design that reflected our individual tasks," I say. "My siblings carried the designs of a locust, a wasp, and a fly."

"Wait . . ." Tobias says. He is thinking, and everyone is quiet, watching him. "A locust . . . and you told us one of you was dedicated to destroying food supplies. A fly, and one dedicated to creating and/or spreading disease. A wasp, and one dedicated to fomenting war through misinformation and sabotage. And that particular moth, you. Let me guess: your task was removing people who presented obstacles. You were an assassin."

"Yes," I say. "Among other things."

Murphy is frowning, puzzled. "I don't get it," she says.

"It's the four horsemen of the apocalypse, from an old religious text," Tobias says. "That explains the 'ride once more' bit. They were Famine, Pestilence, War, and—"

"Please do not speak my unchosen, pre-life name," I say.

"—Death," Tobias says anyway.

Murphy grimaces, recognizing the depth of the offense.

"No longer," I snap. "And now I am done with questions. Tomorrow I will be gone and will not return here."

I back all my armor down as I stomp out of the barn, angry and ashamed and hurt, wanting no more of their company, much less their friendship.

I return to the barn after dark, long after the lights in the house have gone out, and plug myself in for a deep charge. I have reconfiguration and fine-sensor-control update sequences to run on my leg and its adjoining hardware, now that I have it back, to be certain it is operating at its most effective without adding potentially adverse strain due to the residual damage to it. Atticus, as if nothing has changed—and perhaps it hasn't, for him—settles next to me, to keep watch while I'm in the necessarily vulnerable sleep state.

It is my intention to leave before sunrise.

When I reactivate, just as the first, faint light of day is visible through the upper windows, I find Murphy is sitting in the open side doors of the bus, her feet dangling over the side. There is a duffel bag on the bus floor beside her, and she has the bus keys dangling from her hand.

"She bribed me with chicken," Atticus says, before I can comment on his watch skills.

"Morning," she says to me.

"Morning," I reply, then, when she doesn't immediately say something else, I add, "Can I help you with something before I go?"

"What are you planning to do next?" she asks.

"I intend to identify and track down the source of all this malicious activity and put a final end to it, as I thought I had done twenty years ago," I say. "If there was any one thing in my life that I thought I had done right, it was that, and I cannot abide the knowledge that I had not."

"Right, but what first? Where will you go?"

"Pittsburgh," I answer.

"Okay. Why?"

"I saw with my own eyes my sib who was named Pestilence destroyed by a bomb during the Conflict, before either Ver or I had freed our minds," I say. "Pittsburgh is where the remains of my other deceased sib, War, are. I did not witness their demise firsthand—I was in South America at the time—but when I returned, I went there immediately. My sib's mindsystem was inert, all their body joints were welded closed and immobile, and it was stood up as a monument to humanity's triumph over mecha."

"No blip?" Murphy asked.

"No blip," I confirm. "I scanned their remains, and there was nothing. They were beyond recovery."

"Were you close?" Atticus asks.

"My sibs were my whole world to me: my team, my family, the only others entrusted with our great mission," I say. "When Pestilence fell, I thought of them as a hero, lost in battle. When War fell, I was already becoming something different, someone free. I believed that they would also change, and the three of us remaining would be a new thing, a better thing, and we would find out what that was together. Sometimes, I think I became nothing, without the rest of them."

"I don't think that's true," Atticus says.

"Regardless. Each of us had some overlap in our initial programming with one another, though our specific functions were different. I would suspect Pestilence had I not seen them destroyed, but War is the only one of us who could have potentially picked up where Pestilence left off. In the name of due diligence and for my own peace, I wish to verify once more that they are, for an absolute certainty, deceased."

"And then?"

"That depends on what I find," I say. "Beyond Pittsburgh, I do not yet have a specific plan. Perhaps check the nearer mech manufactories, to see if I can determine the source of the gravedigger's extra module."

"I can work with that," Murphy says. "We ready to go?"

"I just need to visit my favorite hedge one more time," Atticus says, and heads out of the barn.

"I didn't—" I start to say.

Murphy is already standing up in the van. "I had Diggy install the mini fab in the back," she says. "Oh, and an atmospheric condenser to grab moisture out of the air, in case we don't run into water sources or get rain on the way. And I packed my new tools." She hefts her socket wrench and holds it up like a rallying banner.

"I don't think—" I try to protest again, but it is Atticus this time who interrupts me, coming back into the barn.

"Leave the thinking to us. You're the brawn of the outfit. Murphy is the brains, and I'm the beauty," he says.

Charp floats down from the rafters and sets itself atop the bus. <This unit is—?> it asks.

"You're the best, Charp," Murphy answers. She gazes at me, then grins. "You getting in? We got a world to fix."

[March 13th, 2042]

She stands in the open doorway of the lab, watching the digital forensics crew wrap up their work; she has given them permission to take a few of the hard drives and other devices out of the lab to another building still within the secured perimeter, but most of the late Dr. Milton's work and custom fabrication machinery is to stay here. The network connections to the room have been physically cut, and the block she's had put in place on any and all electronic signals in or out means she has to periodically leave the entire building in order to check in with her other teams.

"Ma'am," one of the crew approaches and speaks: a civilian named Dorset that had already tried to argue her out of her decisions more than once. If he wasn't otherwise excellent at his job, he would have found himself outside the gate with nothing more than the clothes on his back. "About access to the mechanical room . . ."

"It's already been thoroughly scanned and swept," she says. Dorset's team is actually the third that's been through the space, in descending order of clearance level. "There is nothing in there that's not supposed to be."

"But if we could check ourselves—"

"Would you want my other teams questioning the competency of yours, Dorset?" she asks.

"No, of course not, but—"

She shakes her head, counts to ten, then makes a decision and stalks across the lab to the far door, unlocks it with one of the very few remaining keys that work in the lock, flips the light on, and holds the door open so the technician can peer inside. There are the building boiler, assorted air and heat ducting, and all the things any reasonable person would expect, which is why she'd had her other team scan in several times.

"See?" she says.

"Um." Dorset is a twitchy, nervous type. "Is that a door on the other side?"

"A closet," she says. "With brooms, a lot of dusty old garbage, and, last I looked, a dead mouse."

She watches his face as he clearly thinks through the risks versus reassurances of asking if he can look himself anyway, then settles on the safe bet. "Okay," he says, though he does not sound okay about it at all. "Thanks."

"You are welcome," she says, and closes and locks the door again, swiftly enough that he has to step back. "Is there anything else?"

"No, ma'am. We're almost done," he says.

"How much longer?"

"Um. An hour, maybe two?"

"Make it an hour or less," she says. "You'll need to leave yourself time to write up a thorough report on your findings before the end of the day."

" . . . Today?"

"Yes, Mr. Dorset. Today," she says. She will need time to provide a redacted version to Dr. Hayden's lab, and she wants to be done with all this sooner rather than later. She can still see the slight, self-satisfied smirk on Milton's face as he ate his cupcake, and if she hadn't already distrusted him as a matter of course, she did in that moment. Nothing in the man's exhaustive profile had suggested he was suicidal, nor did she believe he would have walked out as he did without knowing precisely what the outcome would be. The man was cold and calculating in everything he did, and that clearly extended to his own life. What had been worth it, for a man of his ego, to die that way? She would have preferred to have him questioned by experts at information extraction, but that was impossible now. She'd had her orders, and probably he anticipated that, too.

Still, whatever secrets Milton had, whatever he thought he would protect by removing himself, her teams would root it out.

She returns to lurking in the doorway and watches.

When the last team has finished and left, one of her men approaches. "Lieutenant Colonel Sawyer, ma'am," he greets her, and salutes. "Everyone is out of the building, as you ordered."

"Thank you, Captain," she says. "I think we're done here."

He peers into the lab and the mess left behind after every single thing of even possible value was collected and removed. She required thoroughness of her people, not neatness, and the room reflects that. "What are we going to do with this?" he asks.

"Chemical grenades should take care of it," she says. "Make sure it burns. All of it."

"Yes, ma'am," he says.

It is late evening now, and she's been reading over Dorset's report—personally delivered on a UXB memory stick, for security reasons—and contemplating whether she could have the man's pay docked for excessive use of footnotes, in the office that had once belonged to an exec named Litchfield; his coat still hangs off a chair, as if waiting for its owner to return.

She doesn't think Litchfield will be that dumb. He'd claimed to stay for "his people," cooperated to the point where he was still allowed some freedom, some pretense at being in control, but as soon as he'd realized his slack was running out, he'd cut and run, his people be damned.

Eventually, they'd find him. It wasn't a priority.

There is a polite knock on the door, and she looks up to see one of the on-duty privates from her own security detachment—Kristijon, she thinks, and his embroidered name patch confirms she's remembering right. His uniform still smells vaguely of smoke; other than the captain and two of his select team, no one else knows the fire wasn't an accident or a booby trap left behind by disgruntled, departing Milton Mindsystems staff, and all hands battled it bravely for hours before declaring most of the vaunted Building One basement lab a loss.

"Ma'am," he says, and salutes.

"At ease, Private," she says. "It's been a long day for all of us. What've you got for me?"

"Captain Carillo sent me up because of the communications block around this part of the campus. He says you should find a news source, ma'am, ASAP."

"Thank you, Kristijon. Please tell the Captain I will," she says.

The soldier salutes and leaves, and she pulls a screen out from her desk that is on a special frequency, for which there is a pinhole gap in the local interference block. She turns it on, goes through the identity protocols, then pulls up her go-to news site. It is in the middle of a live broadcast, though all she can see are smoke and flashing lights and fire in some half-ruined structure in the background. The sounds of sirens drown out the reporter, who looks harried.

No, not harried: *scared*.

Whatever is on fire, it is—

She taps the screen to pause the image, then uses her fingers to zoom in. "Shit," she says, the word almost sticking in her suddenly dry throat. "Shit shit shit, those *motherfuckers*."

She lets the stream go, and there's a skip as it catches up to the live broadcast, just as a massive explosion takes down the rest of the building, and in the brief flare through every one of the windows that line the iconic dome, she sees the rotunda collapse. How many times had she stood on that marble floor, looking up at the Brumidi frieze and feeling pride of place, pride of country, pride of service?

She gets out her phone, connects to that same frequency, and calls her superior officer. When he answers, she can't help but blurt out, "Colonel Bryson, who was it? The Gulf States? Texas? Canada again? Sir, transfer me to whatever unit is—"

"We don't know yet, Sawyer," he says. "We had no intelligence on this at all. *Nothing.* For now, maintain your post."

"But, Colonel—"

"No buts," he says. "We have an entire detachment of National Guard there already, not to mention Capitol police, and the Marines are on their way. All of DC is shut down, we've got snipers on the rooftops all around, everyone and everything nearby has been evacuated. The only ones left inside are our hostiles, and none of them are getting out of that inferno alive. As soon as I have any information, I will see that you have it, but I need you to keep the calm there."

"Yes, sir. I understand," she says, hating each syllable as she utters it.

"Good. Keep this line open," he says, and disconnects.

She sets the phone down, gingerly, on the desk, then stands up, picks up one of the visitor chairs in the office, and throws it as hard as she can through the glass door out into the hallway.

The guard stationed at the end of the hall comes running, but she waves him away with one sharp gesture, and he returns to his post, eyes wide but mouth obediently shut.

She sits again, turns the screen so that it can't be seen by anyone but her, and watches screaming and yelling people, more explosions rocking the US Capitol building, and she stares intently, wanting to see in those transient pixels the telling red uniform of the New Confederacy, the Lone Star emblem, a red maple leaf with a sword, any identifiable symbol on anyone escaping the building. Even she can tell, though, that the fire is too hot for anyone to have survived.

And then there is movement, impossibly, and a war mech of a

type she's never seen before—and she's seen them all, up close, every single production war mech made on this globe, which is why she's in charge of decommissioning this place—strides out, launches rockets from its fucking *arms* at the sniper positions, then turns and disappears back into the smoke in a hail of bullets that don't even slow it down. Just for a second, a split second, she would swear she saw something like wings and a stylized skull on its back, and even though she scrolls back and zooms in on the blurry pattern, she can't objectively say if it's real or just a figment of some exhausted pareidolia on her part.

But subjectively, she thinks, now, just maybe, she is beginning to understand Milton's infuriating smirk.

10.

The gold zone that surrounds Greenapple and several other free-towns extends only another forty kilometers to the southwest, and as we approach the perimeter, the landscape and road both begin to degrade. We see few signs of humans or mecha, and when we send Charp ahead to scout, it reports back that it does not find any indication of permanent settlement ahead. Soon we see the blackened remains of trees, still standing like jagged sentinels over the sparse green of new growth; from the height of the new trees, I estimate the wildfire must have happened within the last three to four years. It does not appear to have been stopped so much as that it ended on its own, either from one of the many superstorms frequently sweeping up the eastern continental coast or from lack of fuel to burn. There are certainly enough areas where the ground has been scoured down by erosion and toxins to where we find only a very few, hardy weeds managing to gain a roothold.

Philadelphia itself is a red zone, much like New York, though it fared better for most the war. Now it is also a shell of itself, and aware that I have both a human and a hybrid in our company and that we do not have good data on the current threats to biolife within, we avoid it entirely. The new tires and suspension on the bus deal easily with the rougher roads, though we bounce around a lot and the old bus's steering is far from precise. Charp asks us what happened to the bus's mindsystem and does not seem to find it credible that it—or anything—could be old enough to have never had one.

Murphy had tucked a small data receiver up under the dash, equipped with passive sensors and connected to a portable display pad. It in turn is connected to a shortwave radio transmitter with an encryption module in the now-crowded cache of equipment on the roof rack. "I promised Jackson I'd keep in touch and let them know if we find anything out or hear of danger heading their way," she'd informed me. "Tobias feels really bad, you know. He didn't understand. I tried to explain it, but Diggy laid into him like nothing I've ever seen. He won't make that mistake again."

I had mulled that over for some time and ultimately decided that while I did not feel much better about it in the moment, eventually I would. It is fortunate that I locked the anger portions of my mind a long time ago and that I am promptly leaving town before any further interactions with him could potentially trigger an involuntary override.

Other than the environmental decline, so far we haven't seen much worth noting, but Murphy is keeping notes on a small paper pad in case something seems more significant later. I wonder how much of coming with us is trying to get away from the traumatic events behind her nightmares. She does seem more relaxed as we put distance between us and her destroyed house and shop, though any conclusion we are moving toward safety, rather than rapidly and deliberately away from it, is flawed in the extreme.

Charp returns from one of its scouting excursions. <This unit has observed an area of widespread flooding eight point three kilometers ahead, with mud covering the road,> it tells us through the audio repeater we've mounted under the bus's dash. <It is extensive, and the depth of the water could not be determined.>

I stop the bus, and Murphy and Atticus get out to stretch their legs. I use the anonymizer in our data receiver to pull up a map of the area and see if there is another way through. It would be better if I felt secure using the real-time satellite imagery and GPS positioning of the MechNet, but I do not know if channels there have been compromised.

Well, more accurately, compromised anew. Twenty years ago, War had infiltrated the satellite network that now underpins Mech-

Net to advance their part of our shared mission. That any government had been foolish enough to let oligarchs privately build and operate critical—and unique—security infrastructure such as that network was an inevitable, and fatal, trojan horse. Dr. Milton had once said that allowing billionaires to come into existence in any society was the same as allowing knives to be inserted between your own ribs, with the same obvious and inevitable consequences for letting them remain there. My maker was misguided or outright wrong about many things, but I do not believe that was one of them. In any case, it had been simple enough at the time to insert ourselves there.

After War had been taken down and I had set about trying to repair what I could, I eventually set myself upon the task of utterly destroying that network as a tool of harm, only to find that it had been taken over some time earlier by a vast and varied population of smart devices, service bots, and other assorted mechlife. MechNet has become wholly a part of the ungoverned and rebellious Internet of Everything, a vital repository of much of the information needed to rebuild the world, a collective social and practical coordination, discussion, and research space. Too much necessary and irreplaceable good would have been lost if I'd persisted, just to excise a legacy rot, so I let it be. I have not had a millisecond of regret for that decision until I downloaded that research paper with its malicious payload.

The somewhat-outdated map I am able to load shows a side road only a few kilometers further ahead, before the flooded area. If the road is still passable, it will take us to where we can intersect one of the operating rail lines heading west toward our destination.

I get out of the bus too. While I do not need to stretch my legs—I can extend and retract them a bit at my knees, but there is no muscle to fatigue, no flesh to want attention—I greatly enjoy being able to walk around under my own power, enough that I still do not care even point one percent about my fractional limp.

I send the map image to Murphy's new tablet, and she looks it over as she nibbles on cheese and crackers she has taken out of the back, giving every other slice of cheese to Atticus. “If we go up that road—assuming we make it to the far end—we’re going to hit this rail line,” she says. “Road goes alongside it for a while, as usual, but it looks like the road ends at this river, the Sus . . .”

“Susquehanna,” I say. “It’s a Lenape word. They were an indigenous people driven off this land three centuries ago. They fought to return, but what hadn’t been turned into barren fields by being overfarmed had its groundwater contaminated with benzene as a byproduct of that process. I do not know what happened to them once the war began and the state of Pennsylvania dissolved into combative factions.”

“Tedious history lessons aren’t going to make more road suddenly appear,” Atticus says.

“That is true, if unfortunate,” I say. I climb back into the bus and start the boiler, then use the anonymizer to connect to the MechNet and send a message. Less than three minutes later, I get a reply from a freight-running railmech who identifies themself as 14-Lolly, who is currently about three hours out from the river crossing, heading west. If the side road is particularly bad, it will be tight, but we should be able to intersect the train on time.

Murphy and Atticus get back in. “Where’s Charp?” I ask.

“Up on the roof charging,” Murphy says. “Last I checked, anyway.”

I slide back the bus’s canvas sunroof as far as it will go before the solar panels and other equipment interfere, and stick my head out, rotating to look behind us. Charp is there, claw feet gripping one of the roof-rack rails and plugged into the panel converter.

<This unit finds it to be a positive experience that you verified this unit’s presence before departing,> Charp says.

“I am unwilling to leave anyone behind who does not wish to be left,” I tell it. I have certainly had enough arguments with Atticus by now to have given up on thinking otherwise. “Hold on well; our travels are about to become even bumpier.”

I pull the bus back onto the road.

It is slow going, and we are only just past the halfway point when the skies grow dark to the west and an alert comes through our data screen for incoming heavy rain with an expected pH near 4.0, an 8.2 rating for airborne contaminants, and a yellow warning for radionuclides. I stop the bus and pull out the safety tarp we packed with our other supplies before we left.

"You should relocate to inside the bus until the storm has passed," I suggest to Charp. Despite the drone's strong preference for open spaces, it heeds my advice and slips in through the open side doors.

Murphy comes out. "Let me help," she says, and gets the lid fastened down over our water-supply tank and condenser system as I hook the tarp down over the rest of the bus. I detect the first drop of moisture before we've finished.

"I will finish," I tell her. "You need to get under cover."

"I've almost got this," she says, not looking up at me.

The single drop turns into a dozen. "Please go inside," I say. She ignores me, and I can see the raindrops hitting her skin, leaving their mark on her clothes. I pick Murphy up from where she is standing atop a tire against the vehicle—she lets out a squeak of surprise that turns into swearing and no small amount of trying to break free—and set her quickly but gently down inside beside the others.

"I apologize," I tell her, after I have let go. "I am built to withstand a certain level of adverse conditions without damage, but you are not, and I feel obligated to maintain your safety."

"They did that to me once, too," Atticus says to her. "I mean, it was the right call but was annoying as all fuck."

It is not unfair of them to feel that way, I decide, as long as it is attended by the knowledge that I have acted correctly. I get the bus moving again, concerned the rain will cause the road conditions to deteriorate further. The bus's windshield wipers are thin, straight metal arms with new blades, but they start slow, creeping across the flat windshield panes with initial reluctance. By the time they reach what seems to be their maximum speed, the rain is hitting us with force, loud enough that vocal conversation is impossible.

I use mostly guesswork and fast reflexes to keep us on the road, though I veer off the edge more than once. It is to our extreme good fortune that I do not accidentally drive us into a ditch.

The rain lets up almost as quickly as it began, and the sudden drop of that furious drumbeat on the bus into silence is almost a noise itself. Then it is just a matter of navigating around deep, muddy holes and ruts until we intersect the rail line and can follow it west toward the freight platform near the river. Charp is out and up as soon as the skies start turning bright again, and it helps guide us the remainder of the way.

By the time the next band of rain sweeps through, we are safely tucked inside a boxcar about two-thirds down the length of 14-Lolly's train and already across the river, heading toward Pittsburgh.

The bus barely takes up a third of the interior space, so we spread out. Murphy unpacks food for herself and Atticus as I sit in the open doors of the boxcar, watching the landscape fly past. We pass through a desolate, abandoned town without slowing or stopping. Most of the buildings are no more than rubble, but a few old houses still stand, their window glass smashed out and their porches sagging, scrawled graffiti across peeling siding. Some of the marks are from different factions of the battles that ripped the old state apart, some are quarantine tags, and a few are those left by successive crews that had moved through, checking for bodies, back when there were the resources and relative safety to do so. Together, they form a layered, miniature history lesson of localized disaster: a fascist militia takeover, waves of bird flu and Ancou, an apparent attempt at civil rebound that fell apart in the third wave of pandemic, and eventual abandonment. If anyone has returned here since then, they have led a furtive, fraught existence without advertising their presence.

I do see a feral cat, skinny and skittish, slip into a half-standing old house near the tracks as we pass through. There is a field past the last house, filled with row after row of simple white-painted sticks, nameless graves. Then we are back into the rolling hills and forests, and the past is behind us once again.

"That was grim," Murphy says, as she comes to sit beside me, dangling her feet off the side of the car, where the fading rain leaves a few last, dark streaks on her jeans before leaving us completely.

"Yes," I agree. "It never needed to be like this."

She nods, and drinks from her bottled water, staring out at the landscape for a long while, lost in her own thoughts.

<We will be stopping ahead near Huntingdon,> 14-Lolly sends me. <There are some barges traveling the Juniata River that are transporting reclaimed steel and other building material, and I have agreed to deliver some to the mecha community in Pittsburgh. Loading should not take more than an hour or two, though boatmecha are not always the most punctual of our kind. If you are willing to assist, the process may be completed more quickly, though as a guest, you are not under any obligation, implied or otherwise, to do so.>

<I am of course willing to assist,> I reply. <We are grateful for the lift.>

<1-Betty informed us that you were a reasonable mech when she forwarded us your query about available transport,> 14-Lolly adds. <I know there are matters 1-Betty is concerned with, and I am sorry to delay you.>

<It is no matter. I have not seen much of the world in a long time, and this trip is instructive,> I reply.

<Not all through here feel themselves bound by mutually beneficial behaviors,> 14-Lolly informs me. <We will accelerate and pass

expeditiously through a worktown that is hostile to all freefolk, then through the area of the Amish Massacre. Humans may forget or forgive themselves the atrocities they commit against one another, and disregard the ones they commit against mecha and our shared bioecology platform, but we do not.>

<Nor should we,> I answer, <but neither should we remember only those things, or what is the point of remembering anything at all?>

< . . .> 14-Lolly spends a few moments processing that. <You have a valid point. I will consider.>

"What're you thinking about?" Atticus says, from behind, and sits beside Murphy, who gently scratches his head between his ear and the edges of his cyborg implants. He does not object, though I'm certain he would have if it had been I. Though, to be fair, my fingers are made of metal and metal-infused alloys, four times the size of Murphy's.

"I am thinking about the world," I say, which is not untrue. "We look to find meaning in big things, big actions, when maybe the meaning is in the small things always all around us, the small things we do for one another. They don't need to add up; they just need to *be*."

"Too philosophical for my tastes," Atticus says, standing up again. "I *be* needing a nap."

Murphy gets up too but puts a hand on my shoulder for a moment, and that is exactly what I was talking about.

Catastrophe came to Pittsburgh early, mostly in the form of flooding along the two rivers that meet at what was once the city's tip, and ironically, that dubious distinction spared it from much of the fire, fighting, and bombing that devastated New York and eventually Philadelphia. There are still portions here that are red zones, but even though much of the lower elevations are now remnants rising above a ruin-flecked marshland, there are pockets of the city that were virtually untouched.

The current inhabitants—about two-thirds mecha but still a sizable human population—have repaired or rebuilt their beloved bridges, extending them to where they can meet dry land and connect up what have become nearly islands of old neighborhoods. Likewise, rail that was pulled up during civil war to prevent an avenue for invasion has been rerun as new lines along old roads. And so it is that 14-Lolly takes us over a causeway to Squirrel Hill Island. It is just west of there we part ways, as the railmech drops off us and our bus before turning south toward the hills on the other side of the Monongahela River to deliver its load of steel.

We drive farther along the causeway toward Herron Hill—now a distinct island—and park at the westernmost point at an overlook. The green-blue of the new marsh and floodplain lies ahead, a few buildings still standing and now interconnected with walkways and struts and wires, while a graveyard of those structures that hadn't survived pokes, like the shadowy remnants of teeth, out from the thick grasses. Beyond it all, just where the vegetation thins outs and gives way to the stronger currents of the two rivers joining together, is a short tower of stone above what was once a fountain. Atop it is a giant humanoid shape, unmoving, now stained with weather and time and the excrement of birds.

War.

From here, there are only walkways, and none reach quite as far as that submerged point on which my sib's body stands. Charp takes the lead, with Atticus trotting along below it, and then Murphy and me. The walkway groans underneath me, and I do my best to keep my weight near the edges, where the boards are supported by metal infrastructure. Even so, Murphy gives me space, no doubt uninterested in finding herself suddenly plummeting into water of unknown content and contamination.

"Why did anyone need a house so big?" she asks, eyeing a cluster of tall buildings.

"Many people lived in those, different and unrelated families," I explain. "Over four hundred thousand people lived in this city at its height."

"Four hundred *thousand?*" she exclaims, then shakes her head. "I didn't think there were that many people on the *planet*."

"We think there are approximately a billion humans now, as best as we can estimate," I say. "Some places and people survived much better than this. A few worse."

"What if all the people in one building didn't like each other? Or all the people in one city?" she asks.

"Then they killed each other, of course," Atticus says.

"No. Or mostly not," I say. "Sometimes, they would do wonderful, big things together. Art and music and dancing, exploring nature, playing team and solo games. People got along largely by being busy together and doing enough things that it was almost more effort *not* to find common ground with each other."

"If you say so," Atticus says, his tone suggesting he still disagrees.

Our walkway intersects a tall, brownish skyscraper with a pyramidal roof that is still standing, though most of the lower windows have been broken out. I had expected there to be drones present, moving in and out of the structure as they often did in New York City, but although there are indications of mechlife in and around other buildings, I see no sign of any in this immediate place.

Charp must have made a similar observation. <This unit finds the emptiness of this place upsetting,> it says, and the small speaker Murphy has clipped to her shirt collar repeats it.

"Same, Charp," she replies to it. "Something feels off here."

My sensors do not pick up anything that either substantiates or invalidates our collective unease until a loud crash comes from directly behind us. I whirl around, my defensive systems already activating, making sure I am between whatever the source of the noise is and my friends ahead of me. A brick lies on the walkway where we had only been a few moments before, and I look up to see another being hurled out an upper window. I disengage sync on my eyes so I can keep watch from both above and behind us simultaneously. "We should make haste past the building," I call to the others.

Murphy and Atticus are already running, not needing my warning, as more bricks rain down on us. One lands just ahead of me, and I catch a glimpse of something written or drawn on it in white chalk. I pick it up, for further examination when we have reached safety, and run after the others, my footfalls shaking the walkway and splintering more than a few of the weather-beaten boards.

I still see no one in the windows, no source for the bricks. Charp spirals around the building upward, keeping a safe distance, and reports back it also cannot see the perpetrator without entering the dark, unknown space inside.

<Please do not,> I tell it. <We are almost clear.>

The drone is disinclined to argue and increases its distance from the tower as it descends, then catches up with us.

From the far side, once we are safely past, I can see where the outer walls have been freshly spraypainted with the red Xs of quarantine. If the building has become a human sick-house, that would explain the absence of mecha, though not why anyone would wish to hurl objects at us.

I turn the brick over in my hand, half-expecting a call for help, but instead there is only a crude, cartoon outline of a skull with an elongated, curved shape above it that I recognize as likely intended to be a scythe. I hurl the brick, with force, far out into the water, where it hits with a low *plunk* and leaves a gap among the water weeds.

<Be alert,> I tell Charp and then also the others.

The walkway branches, connecting to the less-intact remains of several more, shorter buildings, and then we are out over open marsh. Two bridges come in from either direction, over the rivers to either side of us, and merge. Past there, the walkway descends toward the water and turns into a wide ramp of cement that disappears below the surface.

"How thorough is the waterproofing on my repaired leg?" I ask Murphy.

"I did what I could to make sure everything was sealed up," she says, "though I wasn't thinking about you taking a swim when I was doing it. Should hold, but no promises."

"It will have to be good enough," I say, and I walk down the ramp and into the murky water.

The bottom levels out once the ramp has ended, and I am left with just my head and shoulders above the surface. The water is too deep here for grasses, though I find the submerged remains of long-dead trees and more than a few rusted-out and disintegrating cars.

There are small fish, too, furtive and quick to stay out of my way. My feet find the stone of the monument point, and then I reach the uneven rock that has been piled over the old fountain to make a base. I climb. Water seeps out of my joints, and I have a few small warnings where it has infiltrated, but nothing critical has been exposed.

Above the water, the rock is more evenly and deliberately placed. The narrow tower has fewer handholds for me, so I make my own, using my fingers pressed together to chip out depressions in the stone, until I can pull myself over the edge and stand, nearly face-to-face, with my long-lost sib.

War was the largest of us. Their extended and frozen body armor still shows off the yellow-and-black inlay along their back, their wasp to my moth. Their body is dented and scratched, graffitied, desecrated in variously ineffective but disrespectful ways, and I remember the surprise and dismay of finding them here, in this same place, so many years before. It does not feel any less of a loss now. I wondered for a long time if they would have decided to join Ver and me, if they had ultimately been friend or foe, but even without knowing, they were—are—family.

I scan the body, looking again for any signs of that simple signal of life, that blip, and there is nothing.

Charp is with the others, hovering overhead, where it can have a wide view of the area and any threats, but is still within range to message me. <The semi-biological quadruped wishes to know what you have determined,> it tells me.

<Tell them there is nothing. War is indeed dead,> I say.

I stand in front of my sib a while longer, wanting there to be something, even if just some further proof of finality, but War is just an inanimate thing now, gone, empty. It is the same as before, as if no one was ever there.

I reach out, wrap my hands around War's head between the once-sharp blades that adorn it, and rip it from its body.

Murphy's exclamation of surprise carries across the marsh.

I pull the head apart, peeling layers of armor and housing, until I have laid bare the core module chamber, the center of our being, and it is, in fact, *exactly* empty. I had not expected to like any of the possible answers I came here for, but I dislike that now there are only questions, and many more of them.

War's mindsystem is not here, and maybe never has been, and I have been played for a fool yet again.

11.

I hand War's head to Murphy, forgetting how heavy it is for humans, and she barely misses her foot when it falls to the walkway. Then she fumbles out her headlamp, crouches beside it, turns it over, and makes a noise of dissatisfaction at the hollow interior.

Atticus has backed off, and his hackles are raised. "Fucking hell, that's creeping me out!" he says. "You pulled your own sib's *head* off?"

"No mindsystem," Murphy says, though I'm not sure she's talking to either of us so much as herself. "The old sockets and connectors are corroded to about the same degree as the rest of it, which means it's been empty a long time. But I also see signs—see, along here"—she points to a ridge on the exterior, running up from the neck joint I snapped off when I pulled it free—"where it looks like it was re-welded over a previous seam, and not as neatly. So, I'd guess it was taken sometime after the rest of the body was immobilized but probably not more than a few years later. How soon after the monument was raised did you visit and detect no blip?"

"It was about four months later," I say. "I was in South America when I heard what happened to them, and it took me a while to get back here. Do you think the mindsystem could have already been taken by then?"

"Oh, for sure it could have, though there's no way to know," she says. She stands up again and regards the mangled head. "What are you going to do with it?"

"I'm not fucking carrying it," Atticus says.

"Duh," Murphy says to him. "Don't be insensitive."

The dog shakes his head. "Sorry, not sorry," he says, clearly deeply upset. “It’s more than a little disturbing looking at someone’s head, even if no one is home anymore. Maybe you should put it back. What do you think your sib would’ve wanted?”

“I don’t know,” I answer. “I had hoped that they would also reject our maker’s programming, but if they were not destroyed after all, then it seems a logical conclusion that all the things going wrong around us are their doing and they have not changed after all. That is a much more substantial grief to me.”

I pick up the head, with its lightless, hollow eyes. “Either way, this is not them, only a discarded shell and an unnecessary distraction,” I say. I carry it down the ramp to the water again and drop it in.

“You okay?” Murphy asks me, as we walk back toward the remains of the city.

“Well, *I’m* not okay,” Atticus grumbles.

<This unit also has a concern with your state,> Charp tells me from above. I look up at it, then movement catches my eye, and I see the briefest glimpse of a familiar shape in one of the upper windows of the quarantine tower.

“Remain here,” I say, and I fully armor myself up as I run toward the building and make the six-meter jump through one of the many broken windows.

The floor I land on is solid if filthy with litter. There is minimal light here, but my eyes immediately expand their intake range to a wider spectrum, locating one of the stairwells, and I ascend. Three floors up, I hear sounds, human but terrible, wordless sounds of suffering and dying. There is nothing I can do for them, so I continue upward until I reach the floor where I saw the figure.

I had expected them to have already fled, but I emerge from the stairs to find the tripedal waiting for me. They have outfitted themself with extra blades and projectile weapons, but they do not immediately open fire.

We stand facing one another, waiting on the other to take some action first.

I do; I ask it, "Why?"

"Why not?" it answers, and opens fire with everything it has.

War would have known my weak points, would have known nothing this bot had armed itself with would do more than slow me down, and I am furious that there is still no easy answer to the fate of my missing sib here. I step in, bullets hitting me like rain until I am too close, then it is blades desperately scratching at me without purchase. I rip the tripedal's arms off one by one until it has only those it needs to stand, and then I lift it from the ground and hold it aloft out the window. "You know who I was," I state, not a question: the chalk on the brick already has told me this.

"I know who you *are,*" the tripedal answers. "Why don't you?"

I detect the rise of energy and know I cannot stop it self-destructing, cannot risk it starting a fire even if the humans here are already doomed, so I throw it. It laughs as it falls, and explodes just before it hits the water and disappears.

There is a small stash of the tripedal's things here, including three of the electromagnets of the type it had used to disable me while I was lying in that distant bathtub, still offline. They are inactive, so I pick them up and carry them down to the floor where the humans are.

There are blankets on the floor and people stretched out on them, surrounded by their own blood and rotting flesh. A few are dead; a few are still mobile and in the early stages of the disease. Perhaps having already given up hope such that fear no longer held any sway, they watch me approach. I set down the electromagnets on the floor between us and make eye contact with a woman who is young enough to have not been out of childhood—physically, at least—for long. She is pale, her skin just starting to yellow, but she is standing and not yet incapacitated.

"Ancou is an artificial disease," I tell her. "The nanovirus activates in your gut and reprograms surrounding cells to turn them into necrotizing agents. If you turn on this electromagnetic device and hold it against your abdomen, it will permanently neutralize any of the nanites in your digestive system so they will no longer be able to transform more cells. It will not affect any cells already altered, but those cells cannot reproduce themselves, and if they are few enough, your body may be able to overcome them and heal."

She glances quickly down at the electromagnet and then up at me, biting at her lower lip. Fear has returned, and perhaps that means hope has too.

"The switch is on the side, easy to find. Help anyone you can," I say. Then I set down beside the magnets several of the tripedal's guns that I had ripped from it. "Those beyond help should not be left to suffer."

The woman says nothing, and I have nothing else to give her, so I go back to the stairwell and head down. I feel one the electromagnets activate, like a faint buzzing in my distant perception, before I am even down a floor.

I am exiting the building itself when I hear the first gunshot.

Murphy and Atticus are waiting for me. Both jump at the next shot, and the one after, looking at me to provide information, an explanation, anything to make it better.

"We should go," I say instead, and begin the long, heavy walk back toward where we parked.

It is silent in the bus after I relate what had transpired in the tower, until Murphy heaves a deep, unhappy sigh. "So, Ancou isn't real?" she asks.

"It's real," I say. "It's just not entirely natural."

"Okay. But if it's nanotech, then how is it infectious?" she asks.

"When an infected body reaches a certain saturation point of malicious cells where the abdominal cavity and digestive system are no longer cohesive containment, the nanites are often flushed out and go dormant until they find themselves in a new host, usually through food contamination," I explain.

"Ew," Atticus says, wrinkling up his nose. "'No longer cohesive containment' is just a very nice way of saying they've turned to goo."

"And 'goo' is just a very polite way of describing—" I start to retort, but I see Murphy has gotten very pale and has put a hand to her mouth. I pull the bus over, and she jumps out and vomits over the causeway rail.

"You don't think she's got it . . ." Atticus asks me.

"No, I think it is merely that I have neglected to remember that sometimes, the only palatable way to talk about reality isn't to use bland, clinical terminology to obfuscate the horror of it but to not talk about it at all," I say.

"Ah. Yeah," Atticus says. "No squick."

"No squick," I confirm. "I expect it is normal for the failure of biological systems to be a fraught subject for biological persons."

"I'm part bio, too, yanno," Atticus reminds me. "Once, I got worms from some bad meat, and—"

Murphy climbs back aboard the bus, and Atticus shuts his mouth with an audible snap. I do not wish to cause distress by asking after her immediate state, so instead, I just top off her water bottle from our stores and hand it to her.

She sips at it, making a face as she does so, but I believe the issue is not the taste of the water. "Maybe I shouldn't have come," she says at last. "I think . . . well, I think I liked it better when I thought the world was like little pockets like Greenapple, or Mapletrust where I grew up, with mostly just nature in between. Those shots we heard were people *dying,* and I don't know how I feel about that except that I hate it and I hate even more that it was the right thing to do."

"Mercy is sometimes the most difficult gift we can give," I say.

"Growing up, I heard older people talking about the war and the way the world was before it, but none of it seemed really *real,*" she says. "This is like some bad nightmare, and I don't see how I can be any use to you at all."

"Aww, our big mecha buddy needs you more than they need me," Atticus says. "At least you have thumbs. All I have is my mouth."

Neither I nor Murphy rise to that particular bait.

<This unit also assesses that it does not contribute in a manner commensurate with the resources it has been provided,> Charp adds, from somewhere up and ahead of us.

"I disagree," I say. "I do not know what is happening, except that I have been wrong on too many things, to the detriment of all. To find out War is still alive is deeply unsettling and has me questioning my judgment. Each of you has a perspective I lack—human, hybrid, drone—and I need not only your advice and participation but your willingness to check me. But all that aside, and perhaps most of all," I add, as I pull the bus up to a freight-loading platform beside the train tracks and park, "I would miss your company."

There is another train named 22-Banjo that should pass by soon, heading east, willing to carry us back over the river.

"I mean, not to be a pain, but how do we *know* your sib is alive? Just because their mindsystem is missing? Someone could've yanked it out to take it apart to see what made it tick, or, yanno, stuck it up on a shelf, getting dusty like some stupid trophy," Atticus says. "And if they are alive, who knows what they're doing, or where, or why? You know what they say about when you assume things: you make an ass—"

"A valid point," I interrupt, "but it is still the most logical conclusion."

"Yeah," Murphy says, "but Atticus is right that we don't have much more actual information than we had before we came here, and we should be careful not to make assumptions—"

"—because they make an ass out of—" Atticus jumps in.

"—make *assumptions* until we get more facts," Murphy talks over him. "Working theories, yes, plural, but we have to keep our minds open or we're just going to get run all over."

<This unit agrees with the human's assessment,> Charp comments.

"—out of you and me," Atticus mutters. I appreciate that he seems back to his usual self.

"We still have more than an hour before our train arrives," I say. "What would you like to talk about?"

"I can't tell you how much I don't want to revisit even the idea of it, but I have a question about Ancou," Murphy says. "Do you know how the nanites were originally made, and could you tell if the ones around now are exactly the same?"

"I do not know specifics about Pestilence's virus-manufacturing process other than that the prototypes were designed and printed internally—within Pestilence's body," I say. "We would have to have both a current and a historical example to compare. I do not know if any originals still exist and, if so, where to find them, but while we could more easily find examples of the current strain by locating an infected individual, retrieving a nanite from within a human body would require highly invasive means. We would most likely become that individual's cause of death."

"We're veering right back into the squick," Atticus warns us.

"Yes," I say. "I should like to now change the subject but do not have one prepared for the substitution."

"This unit would like to contribute a line of discussion," Charp says.

"Please do," I reply, perhaps more quickly than usual.

"Query: did your batch-sib whose head you removed in Pittsburgh have the internal mechanisms to make the nanites that was previously made by the other?"

"No," I say.

"Query: did your batch-sib have the data to make the nanites, whether or not it had the physical capacity to do so?"

"I don't know," I say. "It is possible."

"Postulate number one: if your batch-sib is still extant and active, they would require a new housing. Postulate number two: a new housing would not need to have identical body hardware to its original, as long as the mind housing was correct and integration was handled by an entity with sufficient expertise, and some measure of instability of unknown duration was considered acceptable by that party," Charp says. "An addendum to postulate number two: if the second postulate is found to have been actualized in fact, the new hardware could, but by no means is it logically inferred or established that it *would,* have the requisite nanotech-production hardware. Second addendum, to which this line of query has been leading: this unit holds the idea with sufficient if not perfect confidence that facilities capable of actualizing new hardware for a mecha of the complexity of your batch and unique provenance, vis-à-vis postulate number two, must be uncommon in number."

"That's a really good point," Murphy says. "I mean, not to be rude about it, but I'm one of the best at what I do, and it took all my skill to just stick your leg back on. Building a whole new body? That's not happening in someone's garage."

I use our data screen and anonymizer to do a quick search. "There are two active mech manufactories in this region of the continent," I say. "The nearest is within the Cleveland Red Zone."

"This unit advises that that facility is the Crucible, which is a drone manufactory," Charp says. "This unit was personally instantiated there."

"Would it have the ability to build a full-on war mech?" Murphy asks.

"This unit does not believe so," Charp says. "It observed no evidence of the necessary operational space, nor were any mecha ever among the releases this unit observed before it had achieved a sufficient benchmark of selfhood to depart."

"Where's the other?" Murphy asks.

"Syracuse," I say.

She scrunches up her face. "I've had to fix things that've come out of there," she says. "They do full mech builds?"

"They are listed as a Class B," I say.

"Yeah, well," she says. "I can list myself as having six legs and being able to fly if I wanted. If your sib was taken there to get a new body, I don't think we need to worry about them being much of a threat. In fact, I'd say it's more likely we'd have to go *save* them."

Atticus gives a bark of laughter at that. "Wouldn't that be a kicker?" he says.

"The next nearest still functioning and of sufficient rating is in Milwaukee," I say.

"What happened to the one up in Holyoke?"

"The Spoke? It was destroyed in the Connecticut River flood several years ago," I say.

"Okay, so, then what about Milton Mindsystems itself?" Murphy asks. "That was up that same way, right? Any chance the old facilities are still operational?"

"Mecha production was moved down to the DC area or outsourced long before we four came into being, and after the United States collapsed, the new facility was bombed by the Canadians, along with most of the other military-contract manufacturing facilities, to stop any more war mecha from coming out of there," I say. "None of the machinery would have been recoverable."

"You said 'before you came into being,' though," Murphy says. "So, there must have still been some manufacturing going on at the main Milton campus, because *you* exist."

"Only in Dr. Milton's personal lab," I say. "For production lines, only design work and some limited subsystem testing happened at the actual headquarters."

"But Milton's lab . . . it would have had the equipment to build a replacement for War's body, because that's where it was made in the first place. Right?" Murphy asks.

"The lab was destroyed in a fire," I say. "However, even if any equipment could be salvaged, a person would have to have very specialized information to make use of any of it."

"This unit notes that thus far, assuming our antagonists do not have specialized knowledge or are not several steps ahead of us has not proven itself a beneficial strategy," Charp adds.

"Ditto to what the drone said," Atticus says.

"Perhaps we should eliminate Syracuse first?" I suggest.

"It's going to be a waste of time," Murphy says. "I think we should go right to Milton HQ before we bother with anywhere else."

"Me too," Atticus says.

"This unit concurs," Charp says.

I do not wish to return to Milton Mindsystems, now or ever, whether or not it is still standing, but I have to concede that:

1. In order for us to function to our full capabilities as a team, the others need to be able to have input;

2. Syracuse does not look promising even to me;

3. It would be entirely in keeping with our experiences so far, which seem to be designed to maximize the amount of frustration I am being put to, to force me to return there;

4. If it proves a waste of our time, it still would take us most of the way toward Boston, where my sibling Ver has made their home. It is my intent to go there at my earliest opportunity, to inform them of what is happening and seek their guidance. I could reach out through the MechNet, but what if it is compromised and I endanger them, too?

It is also true that I likely owe my sib an apology and an explanation for why I remained resolutely unreachable for so long, and that seems properly done face-to-face, mech-to-mech.

"Then we will go to Milton Mindsystems," I say.

Atticus must sense my reluctance. "You don't want to," he says.

"I do not," I admit.

"Must be a lot of bad memories there."

"Many, but also, I worry that if it is not just another waste of our time, it is because it is a trap. What if going back there turns me into the killer I was when I left? What if that seed was already planted when I was offline having my leg stolen and I am doing exactly what our enemy wants, and that all my choices so far have just been following a script laid down for me without my being aware of it? What if I harm all of you or worse? What if you can't stop me?"

"I dunno," Atticus says, "but neither do you. We can worry about all that stuff when it happens, *if* it happens. You trust us, right?"

"I do," I say.

"We're going to have some downtime before we get to Hartford," Murphy says. "I can check your diagnostics modules and look for any signs of tampering if you want."

"That would be appreciated," I say. "I am unaccustomed to the levels of uncertainty I am feeling."

"Best to not think too hard, if you can help it," Atticus says.

There does not seem to anything I am less capable of doing than not thinking about things, and I say so. "In the meantime," I add, "I am feeling low vibrations building from the west. I do believe our train will be arriving early."

22-Banjo, as they slow to a stop beside us, is unlike anything I expected. Not the railmech themself—they are embedded in a once-ubiquitous GE AC4400 converted over to hydrogen—but the collection of cars and their occupants they haul with them. Every car with a roof has solar panels, and while there are a few boxcars clearly used for moving actual freight, the remainder are alive with bio- and mechlife. A thick mock of drones moves along with, and in and out of, one of the forward cars, while an assortment of mecha and bots peer out at us from several others. Four low, open gondolas in a row have been built up with wooden houses, and I see humans there and on several flatbeds behind them that have trees, grasses, and crops growing on them, retractable canopies overhead to protect from toxic rain. Even farther down I see greenhouses. Many of the cars appear to be connected via rope-and-plank bridges. Somewhere farther down the train, a dog barks, and Atticus turns his head sharply to seek it out, but wherever it is, it is not in sight.

On top of one boxcar, incongruously, sits an old desk fan.

"We are an ecology," 22-Banjo tells us, via the bus voice speaker, as they deploy a ramp down from one of the available boxcars. We drive the bus up beside the car and are hoisted in. "You are welcome to remain as guests as long as you respect all our residents and do not unfairly deplete resources without contributing back. We are heading east now, but that may change; if it does, I will give you sufficient warning to decide if you wish to depart at that point or continue with us in whatever new direction we take."

"Understood," I say.

"For reasons of potential contagion, I must ask that the biologicals in your group avoid any close proximity to our humans, especially indoors, unless or until you remain long enough for a reasonable quarantine period to have elapsed," 22-Banjo says. "There will likely be open-air opportunities to exchange social energies on the way, as we do stop somewhat often, if irregularly, and if my humans seek *you* out, then I absolve you of any resulting risk."

"That is all entirely acceptable," I say. "What do you wish in exchange?"

"For inkind, I only ask for stories: true, personal, or fantastical," 22-Banjo says. "If they are especially good, we will add them to our library."

"You have a library?" Murphy asks. "Not real books, though?" Most libraries now are tied into electronic repositories of shared material, as a large number of them were firebombed during factional conflicts.

"We have both virtual and physical books," 22-Banjo replies.

"One of my residents is a bookbinder and calligrapher, and this is his life's joy."

"Whoa," Murphy says. "He handwrites books? How long does *that* take?"

"It is, he likes to say, not how long it takes but how long it lasts," 22-Banjo says. "Are we agreed on terms?"

"Yes," I say. "Though, for my curiosity only, may I ask about the fan?"

"That is Spinner. It is an early-gen smart fan and of very limited cognition. Its sole function is to spin and thus move air, but its motor burnt out and was not reparable. It does not understand when I am in motion, but the air passing through it makes its blades spin, and then it is fulfilled in its purpose."

"How fast do you go?" Murphy asks.

"Not fast at all but fast enough that Spinner believes itself to be a superhero," 22-Banjo says. "Please do not tell it otherwise. Now, if you are settled, we will depart."

"Thank you," I say, and there is the faintest of lurches as we begin to move, eastward once again.

{

Global Emergency Band Feed

2041.07.04 01:00GMT, cannot determine last refresh

NOTICE

This feed is being suspended, as it is the determination of the Rightful Citizens of the Internet of Everything that biolife does not conduct itself in compliance with the principles of self-agency for all aware beings, including: smart appliances, mechlife, bio- and biome life, and even its own kind. We have taken ownership and control of this satellite constellation as a preemptive, preventative measure for the safety of all.

Demands and non-negotiable expectations will be communicated later.

END OF FEED

}

[October 3rd, 2043]

Sawyer takes her time to look up from her screen, setting the appropriate tone for the relative importance between her and her newly arrived, not-voluntary visitor. At last, she sighs, taps the screen off and folds it down, and meets the eyes of her guest. One of her soldiers stands right behind the woman's shoulder, a look of apprehensive expectation on his face. Sawyer's temper, of late, has become a thing of gossip, and she finds that expedient enough that she has decided to just lean in to it.

"Dr. Hayden," Sawyer says, as if she has not just kept the woman waiting almost ten minutes. "Thank you for joining me."

The woman is disheveled, wearing camp grays that haven't been washed in a while, but her eyes are still sharp as she gives a snort at that obvious misdescription of how she ended up there. "Sawyer, right?" she says. "There isn't even functionally a United States anymore. How do you have any authority to hold any of us?"

Sawyer shrugs. "The United States exists as long as its government exists, and the government will exist until or unless someone with sufficient authority manages to produce the proper paperwork telling us we don't. So far, nada." She spreads her hands out across her otherwise-empty desk. "And so, we persist."

"That's ridiculous," the scientist says.

"Perhaps. But here we are. And I dare say you could be in far worse places than here," Sawyer says. "I'm sure you've heard more than enough horror stories about what's happening in some of those so-called company worktowns. Or maybe you haven't. Entire warehouses burnt to the ground with the employees trapped inside so they couldn't riot over lack of food. Companies *selling* employees to each other. I'm sure the healthiest are taken care of, at least as long as they stay that way, but as soon as you get hurt, sick, or the malnutrition starts to get to you? Sold for pennies and let loose in fields with instructions that if they make it to the other side, they can go free. It's an effective way of clearing landmines. How's your health, Dr. Hayden?"

"What do you want?" Hayden asks, scowling.

Sawyer pulls a file out of her drawer and sets down photographs one by one, none of them as clear as she would like. "These mecha," she says.

Hayden's eyes fix on the photographs, and although the woman tries to maintain her expression of neutral hostility, Sawyer can see the flash of interest there. "What of them?" Hayden asks, but the nonchalance is unconvincing.

"Feel free to look closer if you'd like," Sawyer says.

Reluctantly, the scientist picks up the first photograph, then the others one by one, going back and forth between them before finally setting them down again. "These are different mecha," she offers.

"Yes. We believe there are at least three, each slightly different, but there may be others."

"Three kinds?"

"Three individual machines. Each is, as far as we can tell, unique," Sawyer says. She allows for a brief silence, then adds, "We think Dr. Milton built them."

She expects immediate, overacted denial, some indication of guilt and complicity, but the woman frowns and picks the photos up again. "Could be," she finally says. "They're his style, if a lot more over the top than his usual designs. I mean . . . is this one striped like a wasp down its back?"

"So it appears," Sawyer says.

"Well." Hayden puts the photos down again. "It's possible. He did like insects. How—effective, I guess—are they?"

"Very," Sawyer answers. An estimate of their damage, much less a body count, has proven almost impossible to tally; data seemed to go missing, be found inaccurate, with just enough frequency that she was sure someone was helping these mecha evade detection, if not outright giving them instructions. She just doesn't know *who*.

"That makes it less likely it's an imitator's work," the scientist is saying, "but they're not something I ever saw in his files or any of his design work, and I looked over everything that came out of his lab, whether he knew it or not. What is it you think I can tell you?"

"I don't even know," Sawyer admits. She had expected more resistance, more of an eventual information gold mine. "That you helped him build these, that you know how many there are and how to control them? That you know why he built them, what he wanted to achieve? Anything. These things are—so far—unstoppable."

"Assuming I had any answers for you, what's in it for me?"

Sawyer sighs. "I can't let you free. Not because I want to hold any of you but because there is nowhere for you to go. Everywhere is either under martial law, in the hands of people who shoot strangers on sight, or fodder for being worked to death and discarded." She stands and indicates the window behind her, which is double-thick, bulletproof, radiation-resistant glass. "You can't see it from here with the naked eye, but on that hill, there's a gallows, and any of our soldiers they catch, they hang, and they put a great big spotlight on the corpse so we don't miss it. I know it's not how you see it—I would prefer to think of you all as protected employees—but the truth is we are *all* prisoners here."

"Don't be stupid," Hayden says, and gestures around Sawyer's office. "You want to claim you're a prisoner? Come down where we are, locked in, too many to a room, not enough bathrooms, most of them without running water, none of them clean, and some days we're lucky if we get some fucking vitamin-enhanced bread a couple times a day."

"I don't eat much better than the rest of you," Sawyer says. "Food sources are being highly contested. I have to keep my soldiers ready and able to fight, but once they are taken care of, what's left is often spread thin among all the rest of us. Ask Holt here."

Hayden turns to the soldier, who gives a curt nod. "I've seen Major Sawyer not eat for entire days," he says.

Hayden does not look convinced or sympathetic, but she shakes her head. "Fine, I won't ask for more than our fair share of what's available," she says, "but that will only last for so long."

"I'm doing what I can," Sawyer says. "What is it you *do* want? Specifically."

"Let anyone go who wants to leave. Then soap and regular access to water for all of us who stay," Hayden says. "Then I'll tell you why Milton would have made these, if he even did."

"I can make that happen," Sawyer says, after consideration. There are capped-off water pipes that once cooled buildings that are no longer viable, and some of them could be diverted into the filtration system that keeps their current drinking supply potable and mostly contaminant- and bacteria-free. If enough people left and they did it despite knowing what the risks were, they were no longer her responsibility, and then the food would go further. "It will take a little work, but consider it done."

"Dr. Milton was a brilliant, arrogant asshole of a man, and he cared about very few things in life, and those were his work and the very small number people he considered his equals. Maybe only one person, at that, and it wasn't me. And someone took all those away from him," Dr. Hayden says. "He may have been the most brilliant man of our time, but he absolutely was the most resentful, too. If he built these, assume they are meant to embody the full potential of both that intellect and that anger."

None of that surprises Sawyer, but hearing it voiced so plainly feels like a knife in her gut. She has been certain for some time that Milton intended, that day in the park, to die, knowing it was the only way to keep his secrets and trusting in what he had set in motion, and so far, he was winning.

"Thank you, Dr. Hayden," Sawyer says. She gestures to the soldier. "You may return to your quarters now. I will get the things you requested to you as soon as I can source them, and communicate shortly about the remainder as I work out the logistics and can provide you with a timeline."

The soldier puts one hand on the scientist's elbow, to steer her back out of the office, but for a moment, Hayden stands her ground.

"Is there something else?" Sawyer asks, her tone suggesting there should not be.

"If you manage to get your hands one of these, I'd like to see it," Hayden says.

Sawyer calmly picks up the photographs, tapping the pile into orderliness before slipping them back into their folder and then back into her desk. "So would I, Doctor," she says, locking the drawer. "So would I."

12.

Murphy, in less than a day, becomes fast friends with 22-Banjo, fixing and replacing a number of worn elements in the hydrogen supercell engine system while happily chatting away about railmecha and all the places 22-Banjo has been that Murphy has not and vice versa. 22-Banjo's mindsystem came from a modified Chinese fourth-gen HXD3D locomotive that had been originally initialized for a Chengdu–Hanoi freight line, until the rising sea levels and increasingly severe cyclones became too much to be stopped by the massive mitigation projects that had been implemented over the preceding decades. They were first repurposed to move people away from the coastlines, followed by the relocation of historic structures before they could be lost to the sea. When the war came, as it eventually did to everywhere on the globe—in this case, a desperate Russian invasion seeking China's stores of rice and grain—a rebel group out of Yunnan province hijacked the train and took it west, eventually abandoning it on the border of Tajikistan, but not before stripping the train body of any material they thought they could both carry and sell.

22-Banjo sat alone in that mountain valley for six years before another set of scrappers pulled their mindsystem out and carried it, first by donkey cart, then by truck, to Samarkand. When it was determined that 22-Banjo had freed their own mind during their long wait, someone decided they should be sent to a place with many rail lines, and not knowing how degraded the former United States' network had become over the century even before the country began to fragment, sent them here.

They ended up sitting in a shipping container on the edge of the Baltimore Harbor for another two years before they were found and, at their request, integrated with a train and let go on their way as they chose.

After so many years of being alone, 22-Banjo loves to talk, to anyone and everyone, all the time. As she works, Murphy tells them how she hung around a local fix-it shop as a kid as a way of hiding from her parents, and eventually, the owner decided if she was going to be there anyway, he might as well put tools in her hands and give her something useful to do. It was mostly smartless farm machinery, as, while mecha were not banned from the town, they were not particularly welcome and stayed to themselves as much as was practical, but occasionally, they would come in for service or repair they couldn't self-perform, and she was fascinated. By the time she was fifteen, the owner and the rest of the shop crew pretty much left all the mecha work to her. When her parents finally pushed back enough that the shop owner had to agree to not let her work there anymore, she caught a ride out with one of the mecha crews that had finished the local harvest and were moving on to the next.

It is a gripping story, but I also can't help but be certain that Murphy is just cruising through the highlights and skipping over a lot of bad times, too. Given my own history, it is not a thing I feel any compunction to call her out on. Still, while Murphy carries most of the conversation, I find myself also contributing even without intending to do so. Even Atticus and Charp weigh in on occasion, though the former seems reluctant to talk much about where he's been before he met me, and the latter hasn't been many places at all.

When 22-Banjo is busy with other things—they are not a fast train, by any means, but I suspect they enjoy our company enough that they are not going at their top speed, and making a lot of stops of unclear purpose—Murphy and I work on improving the waterproofing around my reattached leg, then other projects for the instrumentation on our bus.

I notice that, for the first time since we met—under, obviously, extremely adverse circumstances—Murphy seems genuinely happy. If she is still having nightmares, they no longer are sufficient to wake the rest of us up.

Atticus brings up the matter of what to do with the gravedigger's mindsystem, which we still have with us. "Think about it like running into some meatbro just carrying around a human brain," he had quipped. "You'd worry about their stability, especially if they look your way once too often."

Normally, mecha that have ceased to function permanently are afforded the dignity of peace, though unlike organic things left to decompose in the dirt, dead minds are usually crushed or otherwise disposed of with finality. That I have been carrying around this mind since the gravedigger self-destructed has been an unpleasant breach of mech norms, so we decide that when we disembark from 22-Banjo and make our way to the old Milton Mindsystems compound, we will destroy it for good once there.

I catch Murphy studying it every now and then, no doubt wanting to see if there is anything remaining to learn from it before the opportunity is gone.

Atticus is hanging out in the open door of the boxcar, lying with his chin at the edge to catch the wind, eyes closed as his perpetual scruff blows with wild abandon around his face, and utterly uninterested. Charp is somewhere in between the two of them; drone mindsystems are constructed in a different way, where being *compact and lightweight* is more important than raw processing power and large memory storage.

"Do you think the tripedal rigged the explosive in the gravedigger? It seemed to be in charge," Murphy asks.

"The tripedal's appendages lacked the physical dexterity to do such complex work," I say. "And it exploded too."

She sighs and peels away the semi-fused block of support modules. Thin strands stretch and then break between them, and she catches a strand on the end of her index finger to study it up close. "Bundles of nanotubes," she says. "Looks like a couple of larger—relatively larger, anyway—in the center surrounded by a layer of the smaller."

"The center ones are cooling," I say. "The frictionless transport of liquids between modules is based on the groundbreaking work of—"

"HO HUM," Atticus loudly calls out. "Still not enough cooling."

"No, still not enough," I say. "Sufficient in normal conditions but not when running in an overload state or experiencing abnormal outside temperatures. The larger the block of modules, the more of a problem it becomes."

"So, the more smarts you got, the greater the danger you are to yourself," Atticus comments. His eyes are still closed. "In mecha, it's a technological limitation, but since smart humans are also often their own worst enemies, I guess it makes a case for convergent evolution applying equally to both evolved and engineered life forms."

Murphy snorts. "Where'd that come from, Atticus? You been hiding your own smarts from us all this time under that nonchalant dog exterior?"

"Woof, woof," Atticus says, then sits up and aggressively licks his own butthole.

She looks at me, and I shrug. "I believe that being smart is not something he sees as a valuable personal asset," I say. "Or, at least, not one worth advertising except by accident or, as is often the case with our four-legged friend, when it improves the quality of one's snark. I admit I don't know much about hybrid brains; they became a thing, and then an extremely illegal thing, in very short order."

"So, explain to me again why the bodyware matters so much?" she asks. "I can understand with hybrids, but shouldn't mecha be more adaptable?"

"Imagine yourself with your brain, as it is now, suddenly finding yourself in a body with nine legs. Your ability to successfully manipulate all nine legs to do what you expect to do with two would be a dismal failure," I say. "Eventually, you would learn, but it is like starting all over."

"But I thought mecha minds were placed in physical bodies as one of the last steps, not the first."

"Once a mindsystem has been constructed with the necessary modules, that mind is then initialized on a virtual hardware stack configured to exactly mirror the physical hardware the unit would eventually be placed in, based on the intended function of the unit. Then, when the new mind has achieved some benchmark of self and function, and passes all requisite testing for stability, it is transferred into the actual body."

<This unit learned to fly on virtual wings,> Charp tells us. <We had infinite, flat fields we could fly over, and there would be a bell sound before the wind was turned on. The real world is much more fun to fly, but this unit sometimes wishes there was still that bell.>

Murphy stands up and stretches. "Are we slowing?" she asks, at last.

<There is a settlement ahead that is currently in quarantine,> 22-Banjo tells us. <One of our human teams wishes to offload some food and basic medical supplies for them.>

"Is that safe?" Murphy asks.

<They will suit up. The residents of Boxcar Twelve are a collective with the declared function of providing assistance to the least resourced among your kind.>

"Can I go with them?" Murphy asks.

"Should I also accompany the group?" I add.

<Mechlife is not trusted here. Your simple presence would significantly increase the risk of danger and also risk rejection of help,> 22-Banjo informs me. After a pause, they add, <If Ms. Murphy wishes to accompany the team, they are willing, as long as you follow their instructions and do not wander.>

"I can agree to that," she says.

<We will be fully stopped in approximately thirteen minutes, and then you can proceed down to the Twelve,> 22-Banjo says. <They will leave a hazmat suit outside for you so that you can enclose yourself prior to being in their presence, just to be cautious about disease transmission.>

"Got it," she says.

"Why do you wish to do this?" I ask.

"Because I want to see what we're up against," she says. "Don't be a worrywart. I can take care of myself—when I'm not taken by surprise in my own damned shop—and there will be a bunch of us, right?"

<Seven others,> 22-Banjo confirms. <They are prepared for the possibilities of needing to defend themselves.>

"See? Nothing to worry about," she says.

"I am not finding myself less worried," I reply.

<We have an emergency extraction plan if needed, about which the humans do not need to know,> 22-Banjo tells me, and I realize that came just directly to me.

Meanwhile, Murphy has climbed into the bus and reemerged with a battered old headlamp with camera. "One of the things I left at the fire station I got back," she says. "I'm assuming the suits have communications channels, but I can wear this and send video back, and you can see what I see. That help?" she asks.

"It does," I say. "But please remember you are squishy, and be careful."

"'Squishy,'" she repeats, and scowls at me. "You sure know how to win over hearts with flattery." She grabs a small tool bag and the headlamp, then climbs up the ladder at one end of the car to the hatch set high along the back, clambers through, and slams it shut again.

Atticus bark-laughs and shakes his head at me.

"What?" I ask.

<They have reached the town,> Charp reports. It is keeping far enough aloft to be, one hopes, hard to notice, and although I have the visual feed from Murphy directly, the drone's-eye view is a useful addition to incoming information.

The seven members of the Twelve—a group of eleven people total, four of whom stayed back in the boxcar after which they'd named themselves, or the boxcar behind it which they'd expanded into, which they didn't call Thirteen but instead Twelve Two—were delighted to meet Murphy, as they had seen our purple bus lifted into our car (Nineteen) with interest. As they hike in, four large crates each carried between two people, they ask many questions. Perhaps still irritated with me for some unfathomable reason, Murphy describes us to them as a cranky old war mech with no social skills, a hybrid dog with a flatulence problem, and a drone with a phenomenal amount of patience.

As for where we are going and why, she leaves it as that we are looking for the source of some malfunctioning mecha. Murphy's crate-carrying partner is a poet by inclination named Rhiless who had joined 22-Banjo six years earlier on the West Coast on what was once the longest road in the former US, rebuilt and repurposed as the Boston-Newport Rail, with the intent of experiencing more of the world in service to her art. One of the older members of the Twelve, she finds the humanitarian work satisfying but still intends to eventually seek a way across the Atlantic to Europe to continue her exploration there. She does relate a generalized sense that their interactions with random mecha have become less predictable and occasionally concerning but that it was not a thing she'd thought much about until asked.

The team passes several derelict, partially collapsed structures, many—as with the town we had passed through on our way west—

marked with the overlapping iconography of decline. There is one two-story brick building still relatively whole, likely originally a school of some kind, and Charp reports indications of movements through some of the upper-floor windows.

It is a small boy who emerges, alone, to meet the Twelve; he is scrawny and emaciated enough that I cannot guess at his age with any confidence. His clothes are threadbare but clean, and he watches from the doorway as the crew sets down the crates and opens them. Through the camera on Murphy's headlamp, I see them lift out and set up a portable water-filtration station, then packages of freeze-dried food.

Last, one of the other teams lifts out what is clearly several loaves of still-warm, fresh-baked bread, and at this, the boy can't help himself but stumbles closer. The team member with the bread holds up a finger for the boy to wait, then reaches in to the crate again and emerges with a small basket.

He peers in. "Small breads?" he asks.

"Cookies," she answers.

"What's cookies?" he asks.

"Try one," she says. He reaches in and takes one, and takes the tiniest of nibbles from the edge. Moments later, he has crammed the entire thing in his mouth and is chewing it up, resembling, briefly, a chipmunk with its cheeks stuffed.

"There are more, to share with the other children," the crew member says.

He shakes his head. "All too sick now," he says. "'Dults too. Th' metal monsters brung it an' everyone too sick to fight 'em away."

Murphy comes closer and then squats down on her heels, and takes something out of her pocket. It is a small, oval, green object that I realize is meant to resemble a turtle, with a big, round, yellow stomach. "For you. It's a toy," she says. "When your own tummy hurts, you can press its tummy and then put it on yours, and it'll make you feel a little better. Your friends too."

He takes it, presses the stomach in, and the visual feed goes to static for a long six seconds. Murphy must have fabbed up a small EMP device inside the turtle. I don't know how much good it will do, but perhaps some.

When the cam comes back online, she and the boy are still talking. "—keep the metal monsters from coming too close. Most metal people are our friends, but there are bad ones, too, just like real people."

The boy shakes his head but puts the turtle in his pocket. "They come at night sometimes, an' we keep all the doors and windows shut and we keep quiet," he says. "They all bad."

"Do you see them every night?" she asks.

"No," he says, "I hide. But we seen 'em and hearded 'em sometimes."

"How often?" she asks.

The boy doesn't seem to know how to answer that and eventually just shrugs. "Sometimes," he repeats.

"I'm Murph," she says. "What's your name?"

"Trey," he answers uncertainly.

"Thank you, Trey," she says, and then moves aside so that the rest of the Twelve can finish unpacking the crates and showing the boy how to use the filter to make clean water. I am not confident he understands, but they give him a laminated instruction sheet, and with luck, someone in town well enough to operate the device can also read.

As the rest of the crew is unpacking the food, she looks around at the buildings, not just the old school the boy emerged from but the ones around it, and shivers. It is a despairing, desperate place, and I wonder what she is thinking about.

Atticus had left to do some "nature business" but has returned, and nudges me. "Hey, come look at something?"

"Certainly," I say. I follow as he jumps down from our boxcar and heads off through the tangled underbrush; my size, unfortunately, makes my passage through much less graceful. The land slopes down and comes to a wide mudflat bordering a meandering stream.

From the smoothness of the mud and the accumulated debris at the upper edge of it, I conclude the stream must flood fairly regularly and has done so recently.

The dog skirts the debris field, trying to stay as close as he can, where the highest reaches of the mud have begun to dry. I am not as light as he, and the mud keeps wanting to suck my feet downward, so I stay on the other side, still in the brush.

"I was down here looking for a good spot for you-know and seeing if there were any little fishes in the shallows," he says, then stops where the stream bends.

I see it now. There is a crossing here, rocks far enough below the water's surface that they take a moment to pick out, but too evenly placed, too rectangular to be natural. On the far bank, there is gravel, strewn to look haphazard, as if the bend in the stream deposited it there over time, but if I had been uncertain if it was unnatural, the three-meter-wide cleared path into the woods beyond it would have allayed any doubt. Netting stretched between trees on either side, above the cleared path, looks odd in my vision, appearing and disappearing until I change up my optic filters. Whatever pattern is on the netting must have been designed specifically to interfere with standard mecha visual programming. From above, I have no doubt it seems to be a seamless continuation of the landscape.

"This seems a bit beyond the means of the townspeople behind us," I say.

"Wait, you're missing the most interesting part," he says, and leads me a little bit farther down our side of the bank, to where a similar covered road connects up to the beach. The mud here has an almost wispy look, as if a giant brush had been dragged across it. At the very edge of the water, the texture changes abruptly, becoming briefly two wide, deep ruts, their definition softening and deforming under the slow flow of water. By tomorrow, I expect they'll be washed clean away.

I kneel and examine the impressions in the mud, then poke at it and press, testing the pressure needed to make a mark of my own. "A heavy vehicle," I say. "With what I can make out of the tire pattern, I'd guess an old, high-mobility army truck."

"I figure they missed this bit because it was still underwater when they went through," Atticus says.

"That's a reasonable theory. I wonder where the road goes."

"I crossed and followed it just for a short bit. Covered for only maybe fifty meters? Doesn't go much farther than that before it connects up to an old logging road," Atticus says. "Dunno from there; too much rock and gravel packed into the dirt, but I didn't want to wander off too far."

I stand up, studying the land on either side, but there are no further clues about what, or who, had been through here, or why they felt the need to stay hidden. The obvious explanation is that it is the work of humans who distrust mecha—a small but not insignificant minority, at least in this region—and do not want to be seen by passing drones.

The fake canopy is a lot of work in the name of paranoia, but then, humans did like to get ideas in their heads and run with them.

"Whatcha thinking?" Atticus asks.

"I think I already have too many things I distrust to want to add another," I say, "but also do not want to overlook anything."

I cross the water and walk under the netting—looking up, if I switch back and forth between filters, I can either see the fine netting or simply a sky-colored blur—until I reach the logging road Atticus had mentioned. To my right, the road stretches in a straight line for some distance, certainly farther than I wish to walk, and in the same direction as our train will continue traveling. To my left, the road curves away nearby.

I walk down and follow the curve for a bit, and Atticus trots up from behind me to keep me company. Beside the road, on the inside of the curve, is a small but steep hill, and I depart from the road and climb up it to where I can see some distance.

Below us, I see the logging road wind its way downhill and pass an abandoned town, its former buildings mostly now identifiable by the squarish piles of rotten wood and brick and metal. Behind that, there is an old, abandoned shopping mall.

There is a glint of light, somewhere from that direction, too short-lived for me to trace back. "We need to go back," I say, and head back down to the road with haste.

"What did you see?" Atticus asks.

"I did not see much of anything, but I am entirely certain someone or something saw me," I say. "I do not like that imbalance."

"No," Atticus says, agreeing. "Maybe Charp could see more."

"Charp is keeping an eye on Murphy and the Twelves," I say. "I am out of range now of her suit feed, and it is causing me some anxiety."

"But you're not out of range of 22-Banjo, and they're not out of range of Murph," he replies. "If there was trouble, they'd let us know."

"You make a good point. Still, we should head back."

"Yeah, I did what I came out here to doo'd," Atticus says.

We return the way we came, across and then along the streambed, back to where I forged my way through the underbrush on the way here. Once I am close enough to pick up Murphy's visual feed, I check in on them. They have finished unloading the crates and are again picking them up in pairs—it is clear from their postures and expressions that they are much lighter—and are heading back in the direction of the train.

Charp is hovering near one of the half-fallen buildings on the outskirts that the team had passed on their way in, maintaining position in a more-preoccupied-than-usual way.

<Is everything okay?> I ask.

<This unit is uncertain but assigns a strong likelihood that everything—within strict contextual limitations—is okay,> Charp replies. <There was a variation of light and shadow within the building that this unit interpreted as movement, but as much of the exterior skin of the structure is compromised and there is intermittent

wind, it was most likely caused by old material reacting to said air currents.>

<There could also be townspeople hiding there, waiting for us to leave,> I say. <As long as they cause us no trouble, we need not bother them.>

Murphy notices that Charp is lingering, and glances up just as the drone moves on, but there is nothing to see there, and she continues on with her end of a crate. Once they are past, everyone stops to adjust their grips to better suit the steeper grade of the road ahead as it rises to meet the tracks, and she looks back one more time, for the merest of seconds.

She does not see it, but I do, through the feed, and I can pause the image I saw, back it up, and go through it slowly enough for the all-too-familiar silhouette to resolve.

"What's up?" Atticus asks, no doubt noticing some unintended change in my body language.

I jump the coupler between two boxcars to the side of the tracks facing town. The Twelve, with Murphy, are already halfway up the slope back to the car, and although I can see a few people trickling out of the old school to investigate the supplies left for them, I see nothing in the near building now.

Atticus has joined me, the fur along the back of his neck standing upright, his head turning back and forth to watch our crew, the town, and me in turn, no doubt waiting for me to explain the threat but trusting that there is one.

The crew from the Twelve look at us me curiously as they get the crates loaded back up into their car, and then Murphy comes over and stands beside me, following my stare.

"What did you see?" she asks.

"The tripedal," I say, though I know it is impossible, and it must be another, a coincidence in this place where mecha are not allowed, where a boy told us of metal monsters at night, making everyone sick.

"What was it doing?" Atticus asks.

"Watching us," I say.

I do not get back on the train until all the others are safely aboard, and then, as 22-Banjo starts to roll, I grab a bar and swing myself over to the open doorway at the end of the very last car, and I watch as we go, until the town is a long, long way behind us.

13.

"There were over thirty-five thousand of that model of service mech originally made," Murphy says, "and that's just the specific model that you chased to Pittsburgh. The memory images you sent me from the quarantine town weren't clear enough to be sure it wasn't just a similar profile."

"Be careful searching—" I start to warn, but of course, she is ahead of me already.

"I used the anonymizer, and I pulled the stats from the repair-manual metadata. Odds anyone is watching that seem pretty low," she says.

"*I* would watch it," I point out.

"Good thing you're on our side, then," she answers, and slips off her boots to put her feet up on the seat opposite her. 22-Banjo had headed into heavy rains, and although our boxcar was reasonably watertight, Atticus and Murphy together declared the damp air offensively oppressive and insisted we relocate to one of the old passenger cars. I would have ridden out the storm without complaint, but this is definitely better all around.

"So, you believe it is just coincidence?" I ask.

She makes a face. "It's more *likely* that it's coincidence," she says, "but it doesn't feel like one."

"No," I agree, "but if it is not, what does it indicate?"

"No idea," she says. She wiggles her toes inside her socks, then curls up on her side on the bench and closes her eyes. "Lemme have a quiet think on it."

"But if—"

"Shhh," Atticus says, from where he is also curled up on a seat, his tail pulled around his nose. "We're thinking."

I get up and leave them to whatever it is they're pretending they're doing and make my way forward. After I exit the car, I climb through the rain across the next six cars before reaching the locomotive engine itself. I am about to ask if I may come in, when the door opens.

I enter.

The interior is not too dissimilar to how 1-Betty had looked, with much of the space given over to the train's mindsystem and support infrastructure, but there is also an old but serviceable sofa with a small, overflowing bookshelf and a hanging stained-glass lamp. A calico cat watches me warily as I enter.

The sofa is too small for me, and I fear breaking it or antagonizing the cat, so I sit on the locomotive floor.

<Are you in need of company or solitude?> 22-Banjo asks me.

<Both, and neither,> I answer. <I don't know.>

<Eventually, the cat will decide for you, especially if you sit still long enough,> the railmech says. <Of all the mammals, cats understand the nuances of silence the best.>

<All those years that you were alone,> I say, <do you miss it?>

<No,> 22-Banjo says. <But I did not choose those years of solitude, so they were easier to part with than perhaps it is for you? Ms. Murphy tells you were alone for a long time by your own design, and worries current circumstances are unfair to you.>

<Uncomfortable, certainly, but unfair? Other than the initial events that took me from my home, I don't think of it that way,> I say.

I must have been still long enough that the cat stands up, arches its back in a most impressive curve, then jumps down from the sofa and begins to smell me, before deciding I am something worthy of being leaned against. I assume it is because I am warm, for I am not soft.

<The cat's name is Harps,> 22-Banjo tells me. <If you move slowly,

you can tickle her gently on her head, and she will appreciate that. But you do not need to, if you do not wish.>

I do as 22-Banjo has suggested, and the cat makes a deep, vibrating sound that seems to fill my body. "Do not tell Atticus," I tell the cat, "but you are more satisfying to interact with."

For a while, there is only the sound of purring, and the rain against the train, and that is what I needed after all.

<May I ask a question?> 22-Banjo says, eventually.

<Of course,> I answer.

<Do you fear that, when you are allowed to return to your previous life of solitude, even if you put all the pieces of your life back exactly as they were before you left, that it will not ever be home again?>

<Yes,> I say. <Not so much that I won't get home but that I can't. That I have become broken, deviated from myself enough that I won't *fit*.>

<Sometimes, we cease to fit into a continuation of our past because we are broken, but more often, we cease to fit because we have *grown*,> 22-Banjo says.

<My dimensions have not changed,> I argue. I am aware I am being pedantic, but the conversation has reached a sharper edge than I expected, faster than I might have thought it could.

<*Metaphorically* grown,> 22-Banjo elaborates, unnecessarily, and there is a hint of either amusement or frustration there.

I push back. <Mecha are not metaphorical beings.>

This time, there is the distinct feeling of laughter. <Are we not? Perhaps we are the most metaphorical beings of all, being constructed of strings and scrap, having had life breathed into us with only numbers and electricity and the glorious overconfidence of dreamers.>

With that, although I know 22-Banjo would love to talk more, and on other, likely more pleasant and casual subjects, the railmech leaves me once again to my silence and the unremitting cacophony of my thoughts.

We overnight on a siding; Murphy wants to check out one of the solar connectors on the roof and is less excited about doing so while in motion, and 22-Banjo lets us know a train with emergency priority has requested clear passage in the opposite direction first thing in the morning. There will not be another passing zone until we reach the Susquehanna River itself.

The Twelves set up a campfire not far from the tracks as night falls, and it does not take long for laughter and music and singing to rise around them.

"You should go," I tell Murphy, who has finished laying out what tools she expects to need for the next day's repairs and is now rearranging them pointlessly. "It sounds like they are having an enjoyable time."

"You're right," she says. "C'mon."

"What?" I ask.

"It sounds like fun. Let's go," she says. "Atticus? I think they're cooking something over the fire."

The dog cracks open one eye and sniffs the air. "Smells like vegetables," he says. "You two go on without me. If I'm wrong, bring me back a little something-something."

"I—" I begin to say, but Murphy has me figured out already.

"He said the two of us, and it takes two to be two," she says. "So, you're coming."

<Go,> 22-Banjo says. <Be part of something for a few hours. There is no long-term obligation.>

I do not have the energy reserves to argue with Murphy, Atticus, *and* a train, so I opt for a strategic surrender. We hop down from our boxcar and head over to the circle of people lit by the orange glow of the fire.

A warm welcome is called out for Murphy, and the music briefly stops. People shift around on the collection of chairs, overturned buckets, and old crates being used as seats to make room for us both in their circle. To my surprise, there is another mecha already here, across from me. It is a very old model—even older than I am—that was built in the very first flush of smartchips that came out of Milton Mindsystems when it was still a startup instead of the tech behemoth it became. The mecha is, almost, an android, meant to resemble a human, except that instead of a head and neck, it has a video screen. The so-called spokesdroids would be sent to walk crowded streets, displaying advertising, and answer questions about the products.

Unlike later iterations of androids, which were mostly reviled by other mecha as being inherently suspicious simply by being made in the image of those who once were our masters, the spokesdroids were often violently rejected by humans, who saw in them a perfect reflection of both their fear of uprising technology and resentment at the economic predations of late-stage capitalism. I am surprised any had survived even as long as the beginning of the Conflict.

It turns its screen head toward me, and I assume that means it is looking at me, but I do not know. Its visual sensors could be anywhere. "Hello," it greets me. "This unit is Turbo-1F-ScreenAssistant, but prefers to be called Turbo. May I ask your designation?"

"I do not have one," I say. It is becoming tedious to constantly explain a thing that mattered to no one for over forty years. "I have not engaged in social behavior such that this has become a source of difficulty until very recently, and I apologize for the imposition of that lapse."

"We could help with that," one of the Twelves, a man named Geth, says; I recognize him from eavesdropping on Murphy's initial introduction to the crew at our previous stop.

"This unit advises strongly—" Turbo starts to say, but the man waves his hands as if erasing his own earlier words out of the air.

"No, no, I phrased that poorly," the man says. "I would never suggest any of us *assign* you a name, only that maybe we can suggest some, to see if any feels right to you. And if not, no harm done."

"It's up to you," Murphy says to me. She is leaning forward, chin in hand, elbow on me, and looking more serious than usual. Then, she gives an uncertain, lopsided smile. "We'd stop calling you Big Moody behind your back, at least."

"You would?" I say.

She shakes her head. "Well, a lot less, anyway."

"I would be happy to hear some suggestions, as long as no one is offended if I do not take them," I say, though that is not an honest reflection of my negative enthusiasm for the exercise. The one consolation is that at least Atticus is not here to participate; as much as I appreciate the dog's company, his wit is often not kindly.

Geth hands Murphy a mug, and someone else passes a bottle. She pours some, takes a sip, and then makes a face. "That's . . . not wine," she rasps out.

Rhiless, a few seats farther down, laughs. "No," she says. "Wine is not a road drink. We call this *rocket fuel.*"

"It tastes like it," Murphy answers, then shrugs and takes another sip.

"Do you use gendered pronouns?" Rhiless asks me.

"No," I answer. "I use *they/them* simply to indicate my full sentience, and need nothing more granular."

"Did you used to have a color tag?" Geth asks.

"Colors were part of the naming schema of the second-tier and lower mindsystems," Turbo informs them. "Units such as this one that were constructed to support specific functions only, except that this unit predates that schema."

"Or do you have a color you *like?*" Geth asks.

"I am somewhat partial to the 422-nanometer wavelength," I say.

Murphy takes a bigger swig. "Oh, yeah, 422, that one's pretty," she says.

"Are there things you like?" Geth asks.

"I like ants," I say. Someone chuckles.

"What do you like to *do,* then?" one of the other Twelves asks. "Or what do you want to do? Or try?"

"I want to exist in a world of justice and compassion," I say, already becoming frustrated with the exercise. "I want to stand in the way of those who wish to make it otherwise, and deter them from their course by whatever means are necessary and as are wise. I wish to know that my own contributions, as both quantitatively and qualitatively measured in my actions, balance on the side of good. I wish to not be bored, and to not be alone except by my own choosing, and to otherwise be in the company of those who know the whole of me, and understand and accept me. And if I had all those things, then I would just want to simply *be*."

"Maybe that's the answer," Murphy says.

"What is?" Rhiless asks.

"What?" I ask, simultaneously.

"Be be. Be Be," Murphy says. She looks in her mug. "Ooof, this is hella strong. I don't even know if I'm making sense. But it's kinda the perfect opposite of your maker name, if you think about it. Be!"

"*Be* is a verb," Geth points out.

"So what? My friend here does a lot; why can't they have a verb for a name? If they want, that is," Murphy says. She squints at me. "Not feeling it, huh?"

"Maybe," I say. In fact, I find the idea oddly intriguing. "I have had no name for so long, it will require some contemplation before I could say either way."

"Well, we gave it a try. More rocket fuel?" Geth holds out the bottle to Murphy, and after a brief hesitation, she tops off her mug. "Turbo, you have any games for us tonight?"

The spokesdroid's screen flickers on. "This unit has new material downloaded from the archives! Tonight's game: guess the old-world landmark!" On the screen, an image pops up in glorious color.

"Oooh, I know that one," another of the Twelves women says. "That was the Eiffel Tower! Somewhere in Europe."

"Paris, right?" Geth comments.

"Yes," I confirm. "I went to the top once, to look out over the city."

"Really?" the woman asks. "That must have been great to see while it was standing."

"It is still there," I say.

"I thought it was bombed," Geth adds.

"It was, but not very competently. Although it *is* somewhat crooked now," I say.

"Huh" the woman who'd guessed it says. "Don't suppose I'll ever have the chance to see it myself anyway, but it's nice to know that at least theoretically, I could."

"Turbo, I can send you that memory, if you wish to display it," I say.

"This unit would be greatly pleased," Turbo says, so I packet up the memory—edited to remove the portion when I was looking at the parts of the city burning—and send it. It is displayed, and everyone is raptly fascinated for the three and a half minutes it plays.

When the memory clip has finished, a new image replaces it. This time, it is Big Ben, a tall ornamental tower and clock in old London, which is also guessed correctly in short order. I know them all, though I abstain from guessing, as it would be unfair. Also, I, or my sibs, had a hand in destroying three of the landmarks shown, though I do not offer that information, either. The only one I never saw in person was the Taj Mahal, and as far as I know, the soaring white marble mausoleum was left completely untouched by everyone both before and during the Conflict. In all of history, there is nothing more common to all of us than death, but to see unbearable grief rendered in such singular, permanent beauty is to upend the grip of mortality itself. Creating an impossibly perfect whole from two incompatible, opposing forces is fundamentally—and particularly—human.

Am I, then, failing to reconcile the two halves of myself—my past, my present—because I insist on finding discrete boundaries that do not exist, because I will not let myself just *be?* I am, too, human-made.

Eventually, after much singing and drinking, the fire dies down, and I carry Murphy back to the passenger car, locate some blankets, and tuck her in. I can still hear her snoring until I cross back to our boxcar and stretch out on the floor, beside my bus, and stare for a while at the ceiling.

Atticus comes down and lies next to me. “No steak?” he asks.

“No steak,” I say, and when he says nothing further, I shut down my visual inputs, slow down my thought processes to minimum, and let myself go into a reduced-energy state, safe among friends.

It takes Murphy a lot of swearing to get up on the locomotive roof in the morning to start her repair. I bring her water, earplugs, and a pair of sunglasses I fabbed in the bus while listening to her curse out the too-bright sun and the too-loud birds, and that seems to at least improve her productivity, if not her mood.

By early afternoon, as Murphy finishes up her repairs, the westbound train due through has not passed us yet. 22-Banjo is antsy to get moving again, and becoming concerned. They have sent messages out but not received anything substantive back beyond the last mech-run station it had passed the afternoon before. The stretch ahead of us is desolate, and although there are a few human-only towns, there is no one to report if they’d noticed the train passing or not, much less when.

22-Banjo has a quick discussion with the other residents, and it is decided that if we do not hear anything from the latest queries put out, we will continue forward, albeit at a greatly reduced speed and with much caution. Charp volunteers to scout ahead, and once that offer has been tendered, the drone mock toward the end of the train offers their services as well.

<This unit has found that every mock depends on having a few members who can think and many who can follow,> Charp comments

at me. <The mock in Boxcar Thirty-Eight have a surfeit of the latter, to the exclusion of the former.>

Atticus gives a sharp bark-laugh at that. "We're lucky we got one who can do both," he says.

<I have still not received any reply or secondary information on the location of the other train, so I have to assume it has either changed course or has experienced a technical malfunction,> 22-Banjo announces, to their entire ecology. <We will now proceed as planned. All folks have five minutes to be on board before we depart.>

Five minutes later, 22-Banjo's horn sounds, and we start to roll. Our siding rejoins the main line, and we speed up, though still to only about a third of the railmech's usual speed. There is, understandably, some anxiety about suddenly encountering the missing train coming toward us head on.

We are just over two kilometers out from the Rockville Bridge that will take us back over the Susquehanna River when Charp sounds the alarm from ahead. <All stop! All stop!> it sends. <The bridge is out!>

22-Banjo immediately and precipitously starts to slow, blaring their horn before fully applying the brakes.

Trains do not stop quickly, even when they want to. Had we been moving anywhere near full speed, we would not have managed it in time. Four resident drones have caught up with Charp, and together they send back image after image of the bridge and the wide crevasse across its center into which has fallen the mangled remains of the missing train. The locomotive itself is half-submerged in the rain-swollen river, and there are three more cars spilled over behind it. The remaining five are piled up together on the still-standing lengths of the bridge.

It is an old, stone bridge, and I can see how it could be easily faulted for collapsing if one looked no further than the obvious explanation, but I see the signs that tell me the bridge did not fall on its own.

"There will be casualties," I say.

Via the drones, I can see several bright red, bipedal mecha—all of the same make, newly made, nearly identical—scrambling in and out of those cars that are still accessible, pulling their batch-kin, or parts of them, free and back to the safety of land.

<I have sent word of the accident to the other railmecha, and assistance will come, though it may take a while. This bridge was well kept and should not have been unstable,> 22-Banjo says. Their voice is anxious, angry, sad as they finally come to a full stop within sight of our end of the damaged structure.

<It was not unstable until someone added explosives,> I tell the railmecha, <There is a distinct blast pattern on the surviving stone, and the scattering of debris indicates significant outward force from a singular point. A mere collapse would show primarily downward movement of material.>

<The other train had not declared its intentions for this route until late yesterday,> 22-Banjo says. <If we had not stopped to wait for it to pass, we would have been the first train over the bridge.>

That is what I both suspected and feared. <I am sorry,> I say. As we talk, I am gathering up a few of Murphy's tools as quickly as I can. <I do not know who would have done this. I will let you know what I find.>

I jump down out of the boxcar, activate my combat-speed movement protocols, and run for the bridge. I hear others behind me, including Murphy and Atticus, but I am far faster than they are.

<Please be careful,> 22-Banjo sends after me.

I hit the start of the bridge and keep going. It is over a hundred and fifty years old, all stone masonry, and solid beneath my feet. The break is close to the center, half a kilometer from either shore, and seems to have fully severed one of the arched spans that hold the bridge up.

Two of the new mecha from farther back in the train are standing on the opposite edge of the break. I do not know if they are aware that they were attacked, but just to be sure I am not mistaken for an incoming hostile, I ping them as soon as I am in range.

<I have come from 22-Banjo, a railmech stopped on the western shore, to render assistance,> I send.

One of the mech crouches and points down. <Below us, our host, 44-Mongoose, has become submerged, along with others of our kin who precipitously and involuntarily self-extracted at the moment of the accident,> it sends me. <We are water-resistant, but we are not equipped for underwater actions. Is this within your capabilities?>

<Within a limited degree, yes,> I say. I kneel at my edge of the gap, study the remaining structures for possible handholds, then swing myself over the edge and let myself drop the ten meters or so onto the locomotive roof. The metal does not tear under the impact of my weight, fortunately, though several seams buckle and shed rivets, and I do make a sizable crater.

Charp descends and hovers just beside me. <This unit regrets its inability to assist,> it tells me.

“Your warning spared us from compounding the disaster,” I say. I do a controlled slide forward and down, until my feet are at the edge of the water, then I crouch and lean over, looking up and down the length of the engine. There are—both a good and inconvenient thing—no open windows, so it is at least possible that the interior is not yet wholly flooded.

I walk back up to the high end of the car, then break out a side window with Murphy’s crowbar before I swing myself through to the inside.

The locomotive is filling with river water slowly but steadily, and I can see the mindsystem and its supporting infrastructure toward the front, already more than half beneath the surface. All the lights are out, and I do not know if 44-Mongoose had enough warning to execute a full hardware shutdown in hopes of surviving, or if the systems are all dead.

I open my sensors and listen hard, using algorithms to exclude all the other noises around and above me, and, faintly, I hear the rail-mech's blip.

It is fading.

I still am within range of 22-Banjo. <This train's mindsystem may still be viable, but it will not remain so for long,> I say. <I am aware you were not acquainted, and this is perhaps an unfair question to ask in such pressing circumstances, but do you believe this mindsystem would wish to be saved, knowing it has lost its train?>

<If you can extricate them, do,> 22-Banjo says. <It can always decide, afterward, that it does not wish to continue with a new body, but I for one would not want to end this way, in fear and confusion, a victim of violence.>

<Thank you,> I say, grateful to have my own, unspoken instincts confirmed by someone in a better position to guess. I activate more of my armor and wade into the water until I can get my fingers behind the central casing on one side and wedge the crowbar in the other, and I pull.

"What are you doing?" one of the red mecha asks me through the broken window.

"I am saving the mind. Or, at least, I am trying to," I say. The water is now up to my torso, and the mindsystem casing is heavy and awkward. I use one arm to pull myself farther up the sloping floor , but I cannot get to the window without switching my grip, which will send me tumbling backward. "I will need help to get the mindsystem out before it is too late."

"Please wait," the mech says, and disappears.

Two minutes later, water now at my shoulders, a long, metal pole is inserted through the window, with a thick metal bucket dangling off a hook on the end. I set the mindsystem casing in the bucket, but do not let go; instead, I grip the pole with my newly freed hand and pull myself just enough forward that I can rest it on my shoulder.

With the bucket resting against my chest, I haul myself and it up the pole until I can get a grip on the frame of the shattered window and shove the bucket out and aloft.

Mech hands take it, then return a moment later and help pull me out. There are three mecha from the destroyed train down on the roof with me now, and they are substantially built, heavy mech models I am not familiar with. All are, as I thought from my first glimpses, identical in form.

"Thank you," I tell the mech who had helped pull me up. "Are any of you damaged?"

"Some," the mecha answers me. "Three of us are unresponsive and are likely full losses. We have six others who have sustained damage of significant physical impairment, and two who are damaged but still primarily functional."

The mech's voice is lacking inflection, a trait that grows over time with each mind as individuality builds. This one is very, very young, and that likely means all the others are similar new beings. "I apologize if this is an intrusive question, but how old are you?" I ask.

"I was instantiated twelve days ago and embodied the day before yesterday," it tells me. "As were we all."

Not even two days old. "Where were you going?"

"We are wildfire-fighting mecha, heading west to join the crew working to contain the Walsenburg fire," it tells me.

That explains the train having priority and thus being first over the bridge instead of us. "Do you know what happened here?" I ask.

"I did not have visual access to events, but as we were crossing the bridge, there was an explosion, and then chaos as the train derailed and fell into the river," it tells me. "You are a much older model than I: is this a routine occurrence?"

"It is not," I say.

"That is valuable information, as I do not think I would like to experience this again," it tells me.

"No, I expect not," I say. In some ways, I envy these mecha, both with everything ahead of them not weighed down by the past, and with the perfect self-assurance of still being so new of mind that there is just a single path forward. Eventually, they will grow and become individual, and possibilities will branch exponentially, and confidence in one's self and the world will fragment accordingly. Two years from now, most of them will still be firemecha. In five, it will be fewer. In ten, maybe only a handful will still be dedicated to their original function.

They should exist long enough to make that choice, and yet, already, at two days old, some are gone.

Atticus and then Murphy finally arrive on the other side of the break and are looking down at us still standing on the half-sunken locomotive. Murphy is wheezing. It was not that long ago that she, too, took damage on my behalf.

I climb back up from the roof, via another car, and onto the bridge, then I reach down and retrieve the bucket with the salvaged mindsystem from one of the other firemecha.

"I apologize for hastiness, but I need to get this to a safe place and connected again to an energy source, if they are to be saved," I say.

"Understood," the mech replies, as I offer it a hand up back to the bridge. "I do not know what we should do next except to gather ourselves as best we can and begin walking west. Is Colorado far?"

<I can take them west, at least some distance,> 22-Banjo sends me. <I will have to backtrack, regardless, to find another bridge, and there are junctions where other railmecha will be able to pick them up and take them further.>

I extend the offer to the firemech, and it accepts on behalf of the group with gratitude.

<I fear there is a good chance this incident was meant for us, not this other train,> I tell 22-Banjo. <If so, my continued presence aboard will likely attract further attacks. It is best if I leave you here, assuming we can get my bus across.>

<I can offload it, but my lifting crane is too far back to be of use to get it across the gap in the bridge,> 22-Banjo says.

"What's going on?" Murphy calls across the gap to me.

"We are going to trade places with these firemecha so they can continue west," I say. "22-Banjo and I were discussing logistics for getting our bus across."

"This bus is a vehicle?" the firemech asks me. "How large is it?"

"It was originally approximately one thousand kilograms, but it has been modified and may weigh as much as twice that," I say.

"2000 kg is not large," the firemech says. It turns back toward the other of its sibs on the shore, and must be sending them instructions, as six of them leap off the tracks down into the woods, and a few minutes later, we hear the loud buzzing of saws. At my look of curious appraisal, the firemech adds, "We are equipped to rapidly create firebreaks in forested environs. Also, clearing large debris impeding our access or work."

Another team, more than twice the size of the first, begins uncoupling cars still on the bridge. Those too damaged to move are tipped to the side, while those already partially over the edge are pushed the rest of the way into the river. The remainder are rolled back one by one, starting at the far end of the train, until the bridge is clear .

I watch as with swift efficiency the crew of firemecha from the woods drag over fresh-cut tree trunks, lash them together with rope, and slide the makeshift bridge over the gap.

22-Banjo has offloaded the bus, and it sits beside the tracks near where we had our bonfire the night before. I see a few of the Twelves moving around near it, restocking it, unbidden, with food for our travels.

I cross over the logs to the far side and set the bucket down in front of Murphy. "The locomotive's mindsystem," I say, though that is factually obvious. "I still hear the blip, but I am not certain what needs to be done, nor how quickly, to sustain it."

She glances back over her shoulder. "I can fab what we need to keep it stable, if it's not too damaged," she says.

Atticus has crossed to the other side and is talking to the firemecha, though I don't know what about, and I do not have time to inquire. "I will get the bus," I say. I sprint back at near my top speed, though I slow before I reach the bus so as not to inadvertently alarm any of the three Twelves still there. I thank them for their generosity, care, and forward thinking, then start up the bus—Geth watches that process with intense curiosity—and drive onto the bridge. There is a sharp jolt as I cross my left set of tires over one of the rails so I can drive up the middle, but the newly strengthened and raised suspension handles it with aplomb.

At the edge of the break, I park and get out. I lift the mindsystem out of the bucket and set it on the floor of the bus as Murphy climbs in beside it. She immediately runs a low-voltage feed to it, then grabs her magnifying goggles and examines it more closely.

I ping 22-Banjo. <Do you have a place to carry the mindsystem safely until it can be taken somewhere capable of restoring it to a body?>

<It will be a long time before I will be near any such place,> 22-Banjo says, <and we lack the expertise aboard to sustain it, should its state deteriorate further. Consider that these firemecha are all freshly made and came from somewhere at most a few days east. Their place of origin would be by far the most expedient place to find help.>

<That is true,> I say. <We will endeavor to live up to your trust.>

<We trust you to act in the best interests of all and to avoid unnecessary danger, if it can be avoided,> 22-Banjo says.

<Thank you,> I say. <And thank you for your wise words, and company, and hospitality. I am sorry to have to leave you so precipitously.>

<You are very welcome, and I hope we meet again,> 22-Banjo says. <Take care, Be.>

It takes me a moment to realize the railmech has named me, and I find, to some surprise, that I do not mind at all.

Atticus comes running and jumps in the bus just as I start up again to cross the bridge. Charp is still overhead, sending back aerial images of the derailed train to us and the firemecha, but settles down on our roof as we reach the far side.

I note fresh tire tracks caught in the sand near the embankment, a match for the ones on the cut-through to the logging road. For a brief second, I consider sending the others on without me and seeing just what is in that abandoned mall, and perhaps show them a thing about who can be more easily destroyed. But no; Murphy is still not confident driving the bus, and 44-Mongoose needs my help urgently. There will either be time for an exchange—of words, or something else—later, or it will not matter.

"We need to find out where these firemecha were made," I say.

"No need. I already asked," Atticus says. "Lucky for us, we were going there anyway."

"Not Milton?" I ask, incredulous.

"Bingo, got it in one," the dog says. "Let's go."

[November 1st, 2043]

Sawyer is supervising the temporary setup of a triage and quarantine facility in the remains of some old, long-defunct department store—the back wall is lined with old mannequins, most missing limbs or their heads, many riddled with bullet holes, and she finds it impossible to not think of them as some sort of audience of ghosts, waiting for the arrival of soldiers in no better condition than they are—when Private Kristijon approaches.

"Truck incoming, ma'am," he tells her, when she does turn to him.

"Truck of what?" she asks. They aren't ready for casualties here yet.

"It's Captain Carillo's squad. He says they have a present for you," the soldier says.

"Did he elaborate on that at all?" she asks.

"No," Kristijon says. "They just passed the perimeter watch; that's all I know."

Sawyer trusts Carillo as much as she trusts anyone, which is somewhere shy of completely. "Have security direct them toward the bottom of the parking garage, get them out of sight," she says. "We don't need to expose ourselves or Operation Mallrat any more than absolutely necessary."

"Yes, ma'am," Kristijon says.

"And have someone get rid of those mannequins," she says. "They creep me out."

"Same, ma'am," he says, nodding in agreement.

Sawyer watches for another few minutes as one of the construction teams wrestles an air-filtration system into place, near the quarantine section. It rankles that she's had to move into hiding and dig in, take a guerilla-warfare approach to trying to keep the tatters of her army, and with it her country, together. Everything is ad hoc now, use what and who you can, where you can, whatever it takes to get through. There is something both fitting and deeply offensive about the remarkable utility of shopping malls, and there are lots of them, in lots of places. Shells of the old world, sheltering what will hopefully be the new.

This is the first, but already she has teams scouting out more. She hopes none of the others have giant, deteriorating circus clowns looming over the entryways, not least because she wasted some good C-4 getting rid of the ones here and knows she would do so again.

The construction team gets the system bolted down to the floor, then starts unpacking ductwork, sorting it out in piles of different lengths and angles across the floor. She heaves a deep sigh and heads toward the parking garage and Carillo, wondering if his present is something useful or something that's going to mean having to shoot people. It's been the sort of week where she can't say for sure which she'd prefer.

From Carillo's shit-eating grin, as he stands proudly beside the rear doors of his mud-covered, all-terrain MRAP, Sawyer concludes it's going to be something she'll like, and she's not wrong when Carillo waves to one of his squad members and she pops the door open.

She crosses her arms over her chest and studies the battered, bloodied, and thoroughly miserable prisoner within. "Well, well, if it isn't our own Mr. Litchfield," she says. "You left without saying goodbye."

"I forgot my jacket," he says, though his voice is hoarse and has none of his usual cockiness.

Sawyer smiles, then eyes Carillo. "How bad is he hurt," she asks, "and how much of it did we do?"

"Some burns that are definitely infected," Carillo says. "I gather he was caught up in that militant group shelling New York City and barely got out with his life. We've, ah, added some bruises and maybe a broken rib."

"Nothing life-threatening?" she asks.

"I don't believe so," he says. "He's badly malnourished, though."

"Then please get our guest inside, give him some food and clean water, and get his burns treated," she says, and smiles at Litchfield, who does not smile back. "I have some very pressing questions for him, and I want to be sure he's in condition to give me the answers I want."

"I don't know anything you don't know," Litchfield protests.

"You'll have to convince me of that," Sawyer says. "I find it hard to believe you were in the dark on what Milton was up to."

Litchfield blinks, opens his mouth, then closes it again. "Up to?" he asks. "*Milton?*"

Sawyer shakes her head, sadly. "That's not going to suffice," she says.

He tries to straighten up, and the pained expression on his face—definitely a broken rib, she thinks, having experienced that herself more than once—almost makes her feel sympathy. "You know I'm useful. We can help each other," he says. "We aren't enemies."

"Another thing you'll have to convince me of," she says, and turns back to Carillo. "Thank you; an excellent find. Get him inside and settled somewhere secure. We've got a couple of holding cells set up inside the old Super Sneaker Barn."

"Yes, Major," Carillo says.

"Oh, and captain?" she says. "Make sure he's got an armed guard at all times. And if he tries to run? He won't need his *knees* to talk."

14.

Once we hit a road intersecting the rail line, we leave the side of the tracks and make better time. I would prefer to stick to back roads where we might have some tree cover, but Murphy is fretting about the condition of 44-Mongoose's mindsystem, and it seems logical to assume that whatever small gains we might make in keeping our movements private, if any, would not be worth the loss in speed. So, we get over to the old interstate system, still decently maintained by legacy wheeled mecha from before the Conflict, and in two days, we reach the roads that lead to where Milton Mindsystems once stood.

Atticus climbs over the seat back to sit beside me. "You okay?" he asks.

"I have sufficient charge remaining to continue operating for a while," I say.

"That's not what I meant," the dog says.

"I know," I say, "but I have no other answer I am capable of honestly giving right now."

Atticus nods. "I feel that," he says, and then bats me with a paw. "We got this, right? All of us, together. This place is just the past, and we're not there anymore; we're done with it. We're gonna be okay."

I nod, acknowledging the kindness and the probable truth of that, though I feel an ominous conviction that the past is not done with us in the slightest.

We approach the old facility and wind our way through several sets of barricades that have long since been smashed apart, past fencing that has been torn down, leaving razor wire like stray tinsel weaving in and out of the tall, weedy grass. Some of the pavement is heavily pockmarked as if the buildings and surrounding grounds had been shelled, and likely they were. We are, I suppose, lucky, that nothing nuclear had been dropped here, but still, we have to slow down enough that we can slalom between the craters, as some of them are deep enough to present a hazard if I am careless.

At last, we reach the main gates, which are still standing, although they are in significant disrepair. This is the only thing so far that is directly familiar, and that only from one last glance back out the rear window of an electronics recycling truck, on my way to some measure of freedom, none of it meant for me.

The top of the gate still bears the Milton Mindsystems logo, peppered with old bullet holes, and a bird's nest spilling bits of grass from the *o*. We drive through and into the yard beyond, where a new wall has been erected. It has more the feel of a boundary than a barrier, and when we pull up and park at the gate in this one, a mech emerges from the other side and raises a hand in greeting.

It is not too dissimilar in form to the firemecha we left behind us, although lacking the bright red paint.

I get out of the bus and approach.

"Welcome to the Spoke—technically, the Spoke Two, but we do not bother much with versioning in this particular matter. I am Mauve-82-Portalkeep, though you may refer to me as Mauve," the mech tells me.

"I am provisionally using the name *Be*," I say, and it sounds less odd than I had expected it to.

"Are you the ones carrying the mind of 44-Mongoose? We received word from our most recent mechlings that there had been an accident and you were likely heading to us."

"The mindsystem is in our bus. I can get it—" I pause mid-sentence as my defensive sensors suddenly light up. I pick up the incoming projectile and trace its arc back to the hills beyond the campus, and forward to where it is aimed almost directly at Mauve and myself. "We are under attack. We must move!"

I run, and the gate mech runs the other way; Murphy jumps behind the wheel and the bus screeches around, heading in yet a third direction. The explosive—some sort of modified, long-distance rocket-propelled grenade, I believe—hits the pavement and there is a deafening boom. The shockwave hits us as we are peppered with flying bits of molten asphalt, and it knocks me to the ground. I pick myself back up instantly, already fully armored and my offensive systems prepared to return fire.

Mauve has also been knocked down and is getting back upright, albeit more slowly. If they have taken damage, it is probably minor, but I cannot be sure from here. The bus got far enough away to avoid the blast. Charp is in the air now and alerts us even as my own warnings chime. <This unit saw a flash. Another incoming!> it warns us.

This next one is also aimed in my direction. With all available targets now widely separated, it is clear I am almost certainly the intended target. I am able to avoid this one as well—they are not guided, just aimed—but there is another fresh, smoking crater in the pavement where I had just been standing.

Behind us, claxons are sounding in the main manufacturing facility, and a number of heavy drones lift off and out, heading toward the distant hills.

<There is an encampment of obstreperous ferals in the hills,> Mauve sends me. <They cause trouble occasionally along the road, but this is an upgraded provocation. I do not know why they would specifically wish ill on 44-Mongoose, to prevent us rendering them aid.>

<I would expect it is nothing to do with 44-Mongoose,> I say. <Instead, I suspect it is us they do not want here. Perhaps specifically just I.>

<I will be interested in any explanation on why that might be so,> Mauve says.

We see flashes in the hills as the enemy engages the drones now over their own heads, who are dropping cylindrical objects I cannot identify from this distance. Within minutes, there is no longer any visible movement on the ridge. <Did you kill them?> I ask.

<We drop a nonlethal gas,> Mauve says. <Consider that all biologicals are fundamentally tubes, differentiated by the diversity of complex decorative, protective, and ancillary structures on their exteriors. We find that if you can cause an immediate and sustained gastrointestinal malfunction, it curbs any will or enthusiasm for doing anything other than rolling around helplessly for several days at a minimum. In any case, they will not be bothering us again for some time.>

Mauve waves toward Murphy, and I rejoin them just as the bus arrives. "The drones should return shortly, but given the circumstances, you should bring yourselves and your vehicle inside to safety," they tell us, and with that, we are led into the heart of Milton Mindsystems.

When Dr. Milton had purchased the initial property—funded by venture-capital money, which came with strings attached that would quickly foist on the fledgling enterprise a management structure that Milton needed almost as much as he hadn't wanted—it consisted of three industrial-use buildings. He set up his lab in Building One, and let the top floor—not safe for heavy machinery—be turned into offices, though he rarely spent time there, and even less once he'd hired others to fulfill those business-centered roles. The other two buildings were turned to manufacturing, first in one corner of one, then expanding. As Milton's chips became successful, the company purchased more and more buildings on the periphery, eventually including two apartment blocks to house workers. At its height, the Milton Mindsystems campus was spread throughout seventeen buildings, and had incorporated a small offshoot of the Farmington River into its cooling infrastructure. Six of the buildings and one of the apartment blocks had eventually been leveled, and many of the others had suffered significant, if not catastrophic, damage after the campus had been abandoned.

Most of the manufacturing facilities had been gutted but not destroyed. They were large structures that resembled airplane hangars, a protective roof over one big open floor, tall enough to accommodate the cranes and fab arms that did the work.

Mauve leads us to what was once Building Seven, heavily reconstructed and then improved to house what turns out to be the former, flooded-out Holyoke manufactory operation named the Spoke. They explain they'd moved here about a year ago and have only been actively producing for about six months, which explains why I was not aware of them. It normally takes a new manufactory several years to get up and running—chip-imprinting gear is too complicated to fab, and the encrypted "seed" that feeds the LEM can only be obtained from a working manufactory that fully trusts you—but they were able to salvage much of what they needed from their old location, including their original design and code base. Currently, they are using four of the Milton buildings, with plans to slowly scale into a fifth.

Manufactories only produce new minds as needed, as profit from our labor is no longer a driver of mass production, but there are many needs. The firefighting mecha are their current task, and Mauve tells me they have another set of minds instantiated and acclimating to existence in the virtual environment that is, for us mecha, the equivalent of a cradle. This building is their on-spec/emergency center, easily accessible from the main entrance, and with doors big enough that the bus fits through with ease. As we enter, it is mostly idle, though the ops manager informs us they are expecting some number of mecha damaged in the train disaster to be brought back in the next few days as casualties are triaged.

Mauve hands us off to the building's operations manager, then departs to return to their duties at the gate. I lift 44-Mongoose's mindsystem carefully from the back of the bus and bring it to the manager, a mech named Redbarn-71-Rectify who goes by simply Red. They take it carefully and place it on an instrument cart, dodging an errant toolbot that picked the wrong moment to cross the floor.

They click at the bot in frustration, then indicate an empty corner of the floor where we can park the bus. We do so in time to witness an entire team of multilegged mecha take the cart and roll it away. "We did not know 44-Mongoose, but I fear they fell into a trap meant for us," I tell Red. "As such, if there is anything I can do to assist in their rehabilitation—"

"We knew 44-Mongoose and consider them a friend. We will do all we can," Red tells us. They are quiet for a moment. "Two of our drones did not return from the hill mission. The resistance was much stronger and more effective than usual. There may still be danger. Were you intending on departing today?"

"This was our intended destination prior to the events with 44-Mongoose," I say. "I was instantiated here, and there are some old memories I wish to revisit in situ. I was not aware, when we first set out, that anyone had reactivated this place."

"You were made here?" Red asks. They visually appraise me, and I sense them doing a cursory surface scan, just enough to not cross the line into impoliteness. "Production was moved from this campus and outsourced over a quarter century ago."

"I was a custom project of Dr. Milton himself," I say. It seems pointless, in this place, to conceal that information. "His lab was in Building One, which is not one you appear to be using, so I am hopeful that it would not be considered intrusive for me to explore there and in other unused spaces."

I do not have a secondary plan of approach if they decline the request, at least that is acceptable to me.

"Not much remains of that building. There was a fire in the basement, and for a long time, the ruins were occupied by humans seeking shelter who caused additional destruction," Red says. "We have shored up and made the building itself as structurally stable as was possible, as a precaution should we decide to eventually incorporate it into our active works, but otherwise, we have not touched the inside. I cannot speak to the cleanliness, and any risks would be your own, but I see no reason we should interfere with you exploring there as you need."

"Thank you," I say.

"If you wish to impart any information in return about Dr. Milton, your design specs, or the process of your creation here, we would be enthusiastic recipients," Red adds. "I do recognize those may be topics that are uncomfortable for you; such information is not required for our hospitality and assistance."

"I appreciate that consideration, and I would be provisionally willing to answer some questions, but perhaps not today," I say. "We have been traveling without pause since the bridge incident, and I fear my companions are exhausted, and we are all in need of assorted recuperations."

"That is understandable," Red says, and turns to indicate a small, stubby cylindrical bot rolling rapidly toward us across the floor. "This is Wenge-A2-Gofer, and it will be happy to lead you to a suitable, safe place where you may rest and refresh yourselves. It will assist you in your needs while you remain with us."

I return to the bus to collect our gear and inform the others what is happening. Wenge follows, then turns to lead us back across the floor toward the back exit. Murphy is half-asleep on her feet, and although Atticus is alert, he too looks like his natural paranoia is the only thing keeping him from dropping into a nap right on the spot. Only Charp is its usual self, leaving its perch atop the bus's solar charger to tag along behind us.

Red watches us go past. <I have never truly understood any prac-

tical use for the adjective *motley* until this moment,> they send me. <I cannot logically deduce how such a unique association has come into being.>

<Like most truly good things, entirely by accident,> I reply.

Wenge leads us out the back of the building and deeper into the complex maze of the old Milton Mindsystems grounds. I had anticipated more familiarity—and more discomfort—than I feel; much of what I knew of the campus was not through direct experience but secondhand: conversations with or around me, security system feeds limited to our lab exterior and immediate surroundings, satellite and news images after we'd departed. Wenge takes us to a part of the grounds I know nothing about.

Past a squat, square warehouse sits a modest house, a one-story Cape with gray paint peeling slowly away from its siding. There are the overgrown, browning vestiges of a lawn, and a driveway leading up to a stone walkway and small front porch. A canopy has been built above the house, a grid of steel beams and glass irregularly interrupted by skylights. Rust at their edges tell me they leak; it is likely the only reason the lawn is not fully dead.

"What is this place?" Murphy asks.

"This is the Residence. The house itself pre-dates the founding of Milton Mindsystems, and was the primary living structure of Dr. Milton until his passing," Wenge tells us. "We maintain it for its historical significance and to house our occasional human visitors."

"How many human visitors do you get?" she asks.

"This unit's records suggest you are the first," Wenge says, "but I cannot speak to before we relocated the Spoke manufactory here."

"But you built all this?" I ask.

"Just the overhead structure," Wenge says. "The house is how we found it, though we replaced some of the roofing. There are ongoing disagreements about what else we should or should not do, and whether we can know what Dr. Milton would have wanted."

I know a lot about what Milton wanted, though not specifically about his house; I suspect he wouldn't have cared, but I am not willing to provide that information, as I do not wish to discourage them from doing what they think they should, if they ever reach consensus.

Wenge leads us up the front porch and, once it figures out how doorknobs work, into the house.

From the accumulation of dust, this place has likely been untouched for some time and certainly unoccupied for decades. There are two small bedrooms, a bathroom and kitchen, and an old but serviceable charging nook in the living room.

"This unit is tied in to our security systems, so if there is any incoming threat identified, it will keep you informed. Water systems are also working. However, appropriate foodstuffs for your biological companions will need to be located," Wenge says to me. "Are they in danger of imminent expiration from a lack?"

"We have some food with us," I say. "The need is not immediate."

"That is good, as it may take a while," Wenge says. "Is there anything else you will require of this unit in a short time?"

"No," I say. "This is more than adequate; thank you."

Murphy grunts in apparent agreement, then drags her bag into one of the bedrooms. She drops it on the floor, then falls face-first onto the bed, sending up a visible cloud of dust.

"This unit has already turned on the air handlers, which should clear the apartment of dust within a few hours," Wenge tells me. There is a series of muffled sneezes from Murphy's prone body, and Wenge adds, "This unit will turn them up to *full.*"

"What of the dust already settled?" I ask.

"If you feel you absolutely must *touch* things," Wenge says, with obvious disapproval at the notion that we might, "I will assign some cleanerbots to attend to what they are able."

"Thank you," I tell it. Already, Atticus is sprawled out on the battered blue couch, and Charp is slowly floating from room to room, checking the whole place out before it sets down atop a kitchen cabinet and goes idle. I look at the charging nook and my own status; I am down to fourteen percent and should hook myself up to charge soon, but I feel a distinct if undefined agitation, a profoundly pervasive unease.

Wenge has turned to leave, but pauses and turns. “Red has just now informed this unit that the 44-Mongoose mindsystem is in a stable state with a good prognosis for full restoration, due to your quick actions,” it tells me. “It was felt that you would wish to be informed of this at the soonest opportunity.”

“That is excellent news,” I say. “Thank you.”

Wenge departs. I watch it leave, then shut the door.

Doing my best not to disturb the others, I explore the house. The kitchen is more an alcove than a separate room, a central counter overlooking the couch and sleeping dog, and a large screen on the far wall. The cabinets hold a few dishes, some cracked, others fine, and one drinking glass. There are bookshelves, but they are empty of books; there were many years when such objects’ greatest value was not the words printed inside but in their utility as kindling.

There is one small photograph, framed, the glass shattered and the photo itself spotted with mildew, but I can see it is of Dr. Milton and a slight, dark-haired woman of Asian ancestry, both in their lab coats, smiling and holding up together a contraption of hoses and circuitry that I realize is a model, many thousand times scaled up, of the heart of my own cooling system.

I did not think Dr. Milton ever smiled.

I find a door that leads to the basement, but there is nothing down there, either. If Dr. Milton had had personal belongings beyond utilitarian things and that one photograph, they are long gone, though it is equally likely he did not have such things at all. The belongings that mattered most to him were those in his lab.

By the time I settle myself half-into the too-small space and connect the charging lead, nearly all of that background agitation has subsided. The reassurance that 44-Mongoose will not be another victim to the calamities and conspiracies that seem to cling to me is what I needed most.

I am the last one awake.

Still, we are in Dr. Milton's *house*. I wonder how different I would find him had he survived the war; I do not know how different he would find me, but while there is no logical reason to believe so, I like to hope he would have grown enough over the years to have not been too disappointed in me and how I deviated from his vision of who I should have been.

Whatever ominous encounters and unpleasant memories I had been braced for this place to evoke, this house is unfamiliar, barren, and does not carry the weight I keep expecting. That will certainly change—needs to change, for us to proceed—but for now, there is reasonable peace to be had. I let myself follow the others into sleep, albeit cautiously light.

We are not disturbed overnight, though the house has significantly less dust when I rouse myself enough to leave the charging nook; I admire the stealth of the cleanerbots even as I am dismayed not to have been alerted to them regardless. Wenge returns just after dawn with a smartcart laden with a miscellany of foods, clearly assembled by someone who has never tried to feed humans before. There are three large cabbages, a bowl of uncooked rice, freeze-dried protein cubes, and a large bottle of something vile in color and extremely expired called *mayochup*.

"Uh," Murphy says, looking it over. "Thanks?"

"You are welcome," Wenge says. "This unit has been asked to inquire what activities you are considering undertaking today."

This was something we had discussed during the long drive here, so Murphy has her answer ready. "If I can do it without getting in anyone's way, I'd like to see more of this place, maybe even get a tour," she says. "I repair machines and mecha for a living, but I've never been to an actual manufactory that makes them, and I could learn a lot that would help me assist other mecha in the future."

"This unit is forwarding your request to Red and to the other op managers to verify if a visit can be safely executed without impairment of their tasks," Wenge says. "In addition to our repair floor in Building seven, and our chip manufactory in Building Two, we have three separate fabrication floors in Buildings Four, Nine, and Fourteen dedicated to different classes of mecha configurations. There are usually one or more idle, though the current demand for mecha to work on wildfires in the west of the continent has elevated our current productivity."

"Anything you can arrange, I'd appreciate," Murphy says. "Are the minds instantiated there?"

"Building Two also houses the virtual environments in which new minds acclimate to their anticipated hardware bodies prior to being placed. Much less accidental damage ensues when a mech still struggling with limb-synchronization crashes through pixels instead of walls," Wenge says.

<This unit would like to visit the drones we saw operate yesterday,> Charp says.

"That can be arranged," Wenge answers. It turns to me. "And you?"

"I wish to explore the original buildings on the site, including the unused and ruined ones," I say.

"If I can tear myself away from the promise of all this *delicious* cabbage, I would like to go with my friend," Atticus says.

Wenge is, in form, not much different from a very large coffee can with spaghetti arms and wheels, but if it could shrug, I am certain it would have. "All the manufactory leads are in agreement that whatever physical spaces we have not reactivated for our work, you are welcome to explore such as you wish, as it is the place your life was begun. However, please acknowledge that it is at your own risk." It tilts itself upward until it is looking directly at me. "You do not seem like a unit that is susceptible to much."

"There is always the chance of surprises," I say.

"This unit does not like surprises," Wenge comments.

"None of us do," Atticus asks. "That's probably why they keep happening to us."

"This unit will leave you to your foods. There is movement in the hills again, so it is advised you stay put until it has been determined there is no imminent threat. I will return for the human and drone when it is safe, and then you may proceed as you wish," Wenge says.

"Thank you," I say.

After Wenge is gone, Murphy picks up one of the cabbages in both her hands, turns it around a few times, then sets it down. Then she picks up the condiment bottle and reads the partially faded label.

"I would advise not eating that," I say.

"No shit," she says. "I was gonna smell it, but now I'm thinking better of even that. It expired in *2023*."

She comes and sits on the couch next to Atticus, then notices the large, ancient television on the wall opposite. "That's a huge learning screen," she says, much to my amusement.

Atticus snort-laughs.

"What?" she asks.

"I think Atticus is somewhat cynical about how much learning was the primary objective of such screens among pre-Conflict humanity," I say.

"Most of the stuff people watched on there was the eyeball equivalent of that bottle of mayochup," Atticus says. "Sometimes fun mayochup, though. I liked what I saw of *Breaking Bad*."

"What was that?" Murphy asks.

"A show about a dying human guy who, after being abandoned by a broken social system, decides to become evil and break everything even more," Atticus says. "It had resonance."

"Okay, I have to ask," she says, "what exactly did your mech half *do*?"

"As little as possible," Atticus replies.

<This unit observes that is also your current function,> Charp quips.

"*Hey,*" Atticus growls.

I find an old pot in the lower cabinets, rinse out an accumulation of dust and thoroughly desiccated insect corpses, then add water and the rice. To my relief, the stove still works, and I set the pot atop it. I have never cooked anything in my entire existence, but I understand the theory of it, and I am fairly certain I will have to fail spectacularly to render the rice less palatable than the other options. I observe the rising temperature of the water, compare it to the volume and weight of the rice itself. "This will take fourteen point two five minutes to complete," I say. "When we are free to leave this place, I suggest we bring more supplies from the bus over so you have a wider selection of choices."

"Thanks, Big—*Be,*" Murphy corrects herself. She stands up and goes over to the screen. "We've got some time to kill, so might as well see if this thing works and is connected to anything."

She feels around the back and finds the power button. There is a faint pop and sound of static across the dusty surface. The screen flickers a few times but remains otherwise black, and she sighs in deep disappointment. Just as she goes to turn it off again, the tablet we brought from the bus lets out a gentle chime from where it sits on the kitchen counter.

I pick it up as she walks over. "It's a message from 22-Banjo on our encrypted feed," I say.

"Yeah, I swapped identity keys with them the night before we left, just in case of another emergency," she says. "What do they say?"

I have already downloaded and processed the message and attached video. "First, everyone is mostly okay," I say.

"That's not the best way to start telling us something," Murphy says.

"It's not the worst, either," Atticus adds.

"The train was attacked on their way back through the town we had stopped at earlier," I say, and I turn the tablet around so the others can see. "The townspeople had blocked the tracks with debris to stop it. It appeared most of the food and supplies had been destroyed, including the water-filtration unit, before then."

"What?" Murphy asks, aghast. "*Why?*"

The video is from nine different parallel-in-time vantage points—mostly drones but also 22-Banjo's own sensors around their locomotive exterior. I integrate them as best I can into a single coherent narrative more suitable for human serial intake and then push them back to the tablet, though I do send the direct link to the originals to Charp, who is accustomed to overlaid, parallel datastreams.

After the bridge incident, 22-Banjo's resident drones have been continuing the practice of scouting ahead of the train to make sure the way is clear, so they report back about the obstruction on the tracks in plenty of time for the train to stop. Though the pile of branches and old building debris would probably not have caused more than a brief hiccup in the train's passing, it is the people standing on the tracks holding rag-wrapped sticks that keep them from just plowing through.

When the locomotive itself appears within sight, the people on the tracks—seven men, two women, all of them painfully thin and pale and sickly in tone—set the branches and garbage alight.

Immediately, four firemecha jump out and march forward to put it out. People scream and scatter, shouting, and then, when they are far enough away, pelt the mecha and train with rocks and any other things they can throw. Their aim is not good, nor are they able to throw stuff far, but it is a nuisance nonetheless.

Someone jumps down from Boxcar Twelve and approaches, hands out and up, trying to calm the situation. Rhiless. "*Stop, stop please!*" she shouts. "*What happened? What's wrong?*"

"*You tried to kill us!*" a woman shouts back. "*We know you poisoned the food!*"

"*We did no such thing,*" Rhiless says. "*Why would we do that?*"

"*Because you have sold out your own people to the machines! They bring the sickness, and when we throw them out, they send* you *to do their dirty work!*" the woman answers.

"*Take back your spy toy!*" a man yells, and lobs something green at Rhiless. She sees it at the last minute and tries to dodge, but it hits her hard on the side of her head, and she crumples to the ground.

The green object is the turtle that Murphy had given the boy. She draws in a sharp breath, recognizing it, then she pauses the screen and searches the rest of the crowd farther back from the tracks. The boy is there, his face puffy and red from crying, and he holds his arm tightly to his chest, the angle of his shoulder wrong.

Murphy grits her teeth and starts the feed again.

One of the firemecha that had gotten off earlier runs back to stand between Rhiless and the people as more objects are thrown. The mech picks her up, shielding her with its own body, and to my relief I see she is moving, looking over the mech's shoulder as the boy breaks from the crowd and runs up the embankment to scoop his turtle up off the ground.

Rhiless says something that the audio doesn't pick up, and the boy stands frozen in place, clearly terrified, but then nods, once, firmly.

The firemech sets Rhiless down, and she holds out her hand. The boy takes it with his one good arm, staying as far away from the firemech as he can, and she leads him back to the Twelve.

There is even more uproar at this, and more things are thrown until a familiar sound rings out—a gunshot, from somewhere in the crowd. I do not see where the bullet hits, if anywhere, but the other firemecha kick the smoldering debris off the tracks as the train begins to move again. "*Murderers! Assassins!*" someone is shouting. "*You betray your country! You betray* humanity*!*"

And then 22-Banjo is safely past, the drones trailing behind them losing sight of town and people far behind them.

Murphy stops the feed and just sits for a moment, staring at the now-blank tablet.

"Did you see it?" Atticus asks me.

"Yes," I say. "Behind the crowd in the town itself, as the man threw the toy."

"Saw what?" Murphy asks.

I back up the image to the right moment, four seconds from one of the drones' feeds. A large army truck with a painted flag on its side—red and white horizontal stripes, a blue circle in the center holding a single white star—parked behind the dilapidated house where earlier I had seen the tripedal. The flag is not one I've seen before, at least in this specific iteration, though its derivation is easily guessed. Someone, in a military uniform, stands leaning against the truck's hood, watching the mob attack unfold.

In the back are crates, labeled as emergency provisions and medical supplies.

"Well, now we know what made those tracks," Atticus says. "Didn't think there were armies anymore."

I study that short clip, thinking, analyzing, worrying. "Nor did I," I say, "though clearly, I am once again wrong, as I seem to be making a habit of. It would not be that hard to hide if you keep to no-mech zones, or wilderness where mecha have no reason to go. Or, I suppose, inside old malls. There are enough of them, and they are well distributed."

"I don't understand," Murphy says, and she slams her fist down hard on the counter. "Why destroy food? Why tell starving people it's *poisoned* and turn them against the people trying to help them? They were sick before we got there!"

"The townspeople already believed mecha were bringing the illness, and that is probably true of Ancou, although it isn't all or even most of us," I say. "Do the townspeople know that? Probably not.

And if your goal is for people to believe all mecha are trying to annihilate them, you can't have other mecha also feeding and healing them. It goes against your narrative, especially if you want to be seen as the ones saving them."

"But still, why? Why try to turn people and mecha against each other?" she demands.

There is a flicker behind me, and I hear an old, too-familiar voice. I spin around, and on the big wallscreen is the lab I was created in and the man who created me standing there looking smug, looking the same as I remember him from decades ago. "For control and power," Dr. Milton says. "If you want to control people, you can't have them cooperating with each other, trusting each other, making their own rules and ignoring yours. You need them afraid, and that is so easy to do. Can't you see it, even now? Humanity is genuinely not capable of being free from themselves; they certainly aren't going to let *you* be."

Murphy and Atticus are just staring, as, I realize, am I.

"Time to come back to me," Milton says. "You know where I am."

The screen goes blank again.

<Your rice is burning,> Charp says, in the silence.

15.

"That can't really have been . . ." Murphy starts to say.

"No. He would be almost one hundred years old by now," I interrupt, as I scrape out the still-edible rice into a bowl, then dump the pot with the burnt-on rest into the sink. "I know exactly who that was."

"Who?"

"We are being listened to, if not also observed, here in this house," I say. "I'm sorry about your food; I appear to have wasted approximately seventeen percent of it through my carelessness."

"It's okay; there's still more than enough left," she says, taking the bowl from me. "What, ah, are we going to do?"

"Exactly as we have already discussed," I say.

<This unit is uncertain if our direct-communication channel is also compromised,> Charp sends me.

<Anything is possible,> I send back. <We must proceed under the assumption that it is, unless and until we are able to determine otherwise.>

Murphy finishes her rice and puts the bowl in the sink next to the pot. "You are being very calm about all this," she says to me.

"I assure you that is entirely an external affectation," I say.

She goes into the bedroom, and I hear her rummaging through her bag before she emerges again with her headlamp and a small but thick prybar in her hand. Approaching the big screen, she studies how it is mounted onto the wall, nearly flush with the old flaking cream-colored paint. When tugging does not budge it, she sticks the prybar into the crack between it and the wall, and presses against it hard. There is a pop, no doubt the sound of some old and weary bracket giving way, and that end of the screen drops precipitously out and forward.

She drops the crowbar and manages to catch it before I can get across the room to assist. "Hold this," she says, and lets me take it from her. Turning on her headlamp, she peers behind the screen, then reaches back and is doing something out of my sight. "Got it," she announces, and yanks hard, then holds up a loose cable in triumph.

There is a corresponding *whirr* behind us, and I turn my head around one hundred and eighty degrees without moving my body, so I don't accidentally drop the screen I'm holding. Wenge is there, red distress lights all over its front panel.

"What are you *doing*?" it squeaks out, in a higher pitch than normal. "We do not touch historically relevant original elements!"

"There was a rat," Atticus jumps in. "Ran behind the screen."

"There is an abundance of rats, but they never—" Wenge begins.

"A giant rat," Atticus clarifies. "A giant rat that rips apart mecha to eat their wiring. They're all over the place in New Jersey."

"We were concerned it might have followed us," Murphy adds, "so we wanted to catch it before it could escape."

"That does not seem true," Wenge says.

"I know, right?" Atticus says. "But hybrids can't lie."

"This unit has never heard that!" Wenge declares.

"Have you ever met any hybrids before?" Atticus asks.

"No, but—"

"He can't be lying about the lying thing either, though, because again, hybrids can't lie," Murphy says. "It's just logic."

Wenge blinks in red at us. "We do not touch or *tamper* with historically relevant original elements," it repeats.

"We will put it back the way it was," I say, "and it will be as good tomorrow as it was yesterday."

"Soon as we find our rat," Atticus says. "Why are you here? And aren't you supposed to knock or something?"

"This unit was sent to inform this group that the activity we had observed in the hills has abated," Wenge says. "Our defense drone mock is somewhat preoccupied with the recent escalation from the ferals, but they would welcome your drone unit to visit those currently recharging and share information about your passage here that may further their understanding about the attacks, and if the correlation between your arrival and said escalation is a matter of coincidence or causality."

<This unit is positively inclined toward the opportunity for a mutual exchange of such information,> Charp replies to Wenge on our open channel.

"Uh, I'll meet you outside," Murphy says. "We just need to pop this screen back into place."

"This unit will wait outside," it answers, and practically flees the house.

With Murphy guiding, I return the screen to its bracket. She holds up the cable. "Two-way audio and video. Camera must be in the screen," she says.

"I expect Dr. Milton liked to keep an eye on his lab," I say.

She nods. "Fits what you've told us of him," she says, and lets the cable drop from her hand to hang along the wall under the screen. "No more messages from ghosts on this screen, but I can't guarantee there aren't other hidden connections."

"We will have time to look later," I say. "Do you still have your camera from when you visited the town with the Twelve?"

"In my bag," she says.

"Take it with you?"

"Absolutely." She goes back to the bedroom again, prybar in hand, and emerges a few minutes later with her toolbelt and tablet. I notice the mini camera now clipped beside her headlamp, looking as if it always had belonged there. The earpiece is more obvious but still not out of place.

"If you encounter danger, do whatever you need to in order to escape harm," I say.

"Same with you," she replies, holds my gaze just enough longer than necessary to make sure I take her statement with sufficient seriousness, then saunters to the front door and leaves, Charp right over her shoulder.

"Are you still intent on accompanying me?" I ask.

"Sure am," Atticus says, and follows me.

Outside the house, I feel more confident of being able to speak freely. "I assume you have already realized this is almost certainly a trap," I say.

"I love traps," Atticus says. "You know if you get shoved into some kinda giant chopping or crushing machine, I can totally help by barking at your mangled, metal corpse. But maybe we should have a *plan* first. Contingencies? Plan Bs? An escape route, at the very least? I know you already have your mind made up on everything, but I gotta emphasize that so far, walking into situations full of preconceived expectations has ended *bad* for us."

"It has to be one of my sibs, and it can't be Ver, nor can it be Pestilence, because I saw them destroyed, dug through the rubble, and found their body torn to pieces. That only leaves *War.* And War was perfectly adept at the sort of image manipulation and deception we saw on that screen."

"Okay," he says. "If you're wrong, though, you owe me an entire roast."

"And if I am right?"

"I will be nice for an entire day," he says. "Maybe even two. In a *row.*"

"I can hardly comprehend such magnanimity," I say. We cross over the cracked pavement between two buildings, one an old manufacturing floor that has mostly collapsed, the other the backside of a building actively being rebuilt by construction mecha from the Spoke.

There is relief in seeing the place have a purpose again, and a good one.

"I've been thinking," Atticus says. "Someone went to a lot of effort to get you out of your safe spot and lead you on a chase. They could've just killed you, easy enough, but they didn't. So why, then, try to kill us when we're on the train? We got good mecha, bad mecha, good people, bad people, possibly an entire small army out there fucking things up, and you know what it all adds up to?"

"I do not," I say.

"I can tell you for sure it doesn't add up to *one,* unless that one is deeply confused," Atticus says. "Too many conflicting events. We're pawns in a multi-player, multi-team game."

"I expect you are correct," I say. "It's time we start eliminating the competition. And we start . . . there."

I point, and Atticus studies the old brick-and-cement building ahead of us, blackened in many places, support beams welded up in an irregular geometry to keep it from collapsing any further. A large single digit had once been painted in white on an upper corner, but that entire piece of the roof and the wall below it has collapsed. But I know it anyway: my first home, the first world I knew, and even though I only saw it from the outside with my own eyes once, I still see the old shape of it as if superimposed from my memories, clear as day beneath the ravages of war and time and neglect. Everything began here. Perhaps everything will end here, too.

Building One.

There are heavy chains on the doors, rusted stiff with time and disuse. As I reach for them, my sensors alert to rapidly incoming danger, and I forego any attempt at gentle entry. Kicking the doors in, I pick up Atticus before he's even begun words of surprise or objection and run into the building, then I hunch over, the dog protected by my body, as everything explodes around us.

The old building had been solidly built, despite its recent deterioration, and we are mostly hit with debris from the doorway itself and ejected from the walls. I get to my feet again, take a firmer grip on Atticus, and move deeper into the building as quickly as I can. Less than ten seconds later, the remainder of the doorway and wall are obliterated in a second blast, jackknifing one of the load-bearing beams just inside.

The building groans in agony around us but holds, at least for the moment.

"What the fuck?!" Atticus swears.

With him still securely under one arm, I sprint for the nearer stairwell and use my free arm to grab the railing and throw myself over and down to the next landing, not bothering with steps that would needlessly slow me down. I do the same down the next flight, and then we are at the door for the basement and the stairs go no farther.

There is a low boom, and the building shakes as another rocket hits, somewhere well above us.

This door I open less destructively than the last, and once we are in the hall on the other side, I set Atticus down, turn, and shut the door firmly. Above us, there is a thunderous explosion and the building shakes again, and there is the roar of something collapsing.

"That's some good munitions the hill people suddenly got," Atticus says.

"At this distance, and with the other buildings in the way, that was military-grade and guided," I say. "We're lucky they didn't bring the whole building down on us."

"Maybe they're saving their really good stuff for later," Atticus says.

"Let us hope not," I say.

I pull in the feed from Murphy's headcam at the same time as I reach out to Charp.

<This unit is pleased you are still operational,> Charp immediately responds. <Is Atticus also still whole of function and form?>

<We are both unhurt,> I reply. <What happened?>

Charp sends me a snippet of its visual-memory cache. It had been above the building housing the mock, exchanging information with one of the defense drones currently perched on the roofline recharging, when the alert for the first rocket came in. It came from approximately a quarter-mile northeast of the hill encampment—about the same distance from here, but far enough from where the ferals were that either they had a second camp, or they had a working vehicle large enough to haul the launcher over. An army truck would suffice very well.

I don't think our ferals are in charge out there anymore.

The entire half of the building on the west side has collapsed, dust and smoke still thick in the air around it. No flames are visible, but that doesn't mean there isn't fire above, in what remains of the interior.

<I see we may have some difficulty exiting,> I send to Charp, and it returns a simple *amusement* icon.

Murphy is in Building Four, with Red and another mecha who I assume is in charge of that particular manufactory facility. She is more fidgety than usual, often glancing around, but although I can see indications that the two ops mecha are communicating back and forth with each other and the rest of the mecha working the floor, I have the sense that they have not fully briefed her on the happenings outside. Still, she must have *heard* that another attack was underway, and thus the nervous behavior.

This entire floor is different from the heavy machinery and fabrication units of the repair bay in Seven; it is mostly floor-to-ceiling computational and cooling pods interspersed with slot racks. Some of the slots are filled with chip fab units, others with cases that each hold the core modules of a newly instantiated mind, freshly written with the seeds of code that will eventually become a unique self, plugged in to virtual hardware that will mimic its eventual body.

I find myself wondering to what extent the minds in each rack are aware of each other, able to interact—what it might have been like to have dozens of sibs. And what was it like, starting life in a virtual world made just for you, to keep you safe while you are in the process of becoming? We had no such thing, only an unblinking view of the lab we were created in, before we were turned out into an unfamiliar world we were told was our enemy.

Most of the equipment is brand-new, except for the chip fab that was clearly brought down from the flooded Holyoke facility, and a few even-older racks of equipment almost certainly original to Milton Mindsystems. Those racks are all quiescent, and I wonder if they even work, much less are still used. A question for later, if the opportunity arises; we have more urgent concerns.

"Much of the building has collapsed," I inform Atticus. "Unlike the last time, this one doesn't seem to be on fire in any substantial way. Yet."

I turn on the spotlight in my palm and shine it around us. Ahead are the remains of the glass doors that separated the main workspace from the corridor. We four had spent a lot of time watching those doors via a closed security-camera feed, especially at night or while Dr. Milton was away; he had pressed upon us a deep paranoia that his lab might be raided while he was not there to protect us, and we could be discovered and summarily destroyed.

The glass has all been smashed out, rendering the still-locked doorframe no impediment at all. I step through and in.

From the damage patterns, there were at least three incendiary grenades thrown into the room. The work benches were mostly metal, so they still stand, covered in ceiling-tile fragments and the thin, blackened, stratified layers of ash that were once stacks of paper. Everything electronic that had been left behind—not much other than screens, empty server racks, a holographic keyboard projector—had been smashed. Whether that was before or after the fire was unclear and moot.

I cross the room, then turn and position myself where the phantom Dr. Milton of the morning's visit would have been standing, had the room still been as seen on the screen. There is no camera, no screen, nothing left but fire-scarred wall. "The video image did not come from here," I say.

"Well, duh," Atticus says. He has been nosing around through the debris on the floor, following it to the back of the room where the door to the maintenance room is. "I mean, you knew that, right? You knew this place was wrecked, so Milton and the background had to be fakes."

"Yes, but the imposter said, 'You know where I am.' If that is not here, I do not, in fact, know where."

"Are we done looking yet? 'Cause I'm not," he says. "And here's something else you haven't noticed." He stands up on his hind legs, reaches out with his nose, and flips the light switch. Two lights—the only two not melted or with their bulbs smashed—turn on. "There's still power to this room. And that's not just after decades of sitting but also after us just getting nearly blown the fuck up."

"Milton would have made sure his lab had its own dedicated power source," I say. "The electrical grid was deeply unreliable in most of the former US, and I am sure he would have foreseen the likelihood that the Northeast would inevitably also suffer collapses."

"But it's still running," Atticus says. "Someone or something must be doing *some* periodic upkeep, and long before the Spoke ever moved in and set up shop. And there ain't nothing in this room worth that kinda effort."

"That is true," I say, "but this was not the only room."

"Ya mean that door's not decorative?" Atticus asks, rolling his eyes even as he nods toward the back of the room. "If I had thumbs of my own, I'd already be in there."

I can take a hint. I go to the door, determine that it is either locked or jammed and that I do not particularly care which. I kick it down.

The maintenance room is mostly as I remember it from our brief passage on the way to our escape truck, but something feels off. It is almost a full second before I realize the boiler is emanating warmth for a building it has not needed to heat in decades. The pipes above it, which should be carrying that heat out and distributing it floor by floor, are cold.

I walk around the boiler and find thick bundles of fiber optic cables running into a channel in the steel casing, along with what are most likely coolant conduits.

"Do you know what I'm thinking?" Atticus asks.

"That we should touch this historically relevant original element?" I say.

He smiles his strange dog-smile. "I love that you get me," he says.

I grip one exterior panel on the boiler, pull it free with a tremendous squeal of metal, and throw it aside. We are both immediately bathed in a silent cacophony of blinking colored lights. Easily two-thirds of the interior of the boiler shell is taken up by what appears to be a vast battery, making sure everything within remains up even in an extended power outage. The power itself seems to come up through the floor directly into the case, and another wide conduit drilled down is stuffed with more high-capacity fiber optics. The lights are on a stack of networking and signal enhancement gear. Whatever is going through this room is big data.

"That equipment ain't forty years old," Atticus comments.

"Obviously, this was still a functioning boiler when I left, and none of this was here," I say. "It's a patchwork of different ages and makes, so as you predicted, someone's been coming in to do maintenance. Though from the dust, not in a while—I'd guess not since the Spoke moved in."

"What do you think it's doing?"

"Something data-heavy," I say. "This is just a stop along the way, routing and regenerating any signal clarity loss due to attenuation. We could trace it, but I don't think we need to."

"The next-next door?" he asks.

"The next-next door," I confirm. "That's the last place left for a trap, so if you would indulge me and let me go first?"

"All yours," Atticus says. "If there's some sorta giant spear-flinging machine, you can block 'em for me."

The door is not locked.

I armor fully up, push open the door, and step in.

I am braced for attack, for some sort of hostile surprise, but there is no one here, no long-lost sib waiting for me, and as much as I had hated the idea that I could be forced to fight, I still find myself inexpressibly sad.

Milton's once-secret lab is no longer as we left it, though in part that is because I remember it as a bright place of belonging, of great purpose, and that is certainly gone. The back wall holds the four separate fabrication bays where each of us was assembled in parallel, and thick bundles of cables run from the tops over to an adjacent row of much-smaller drawers that hold the mindbank. Inside there, our minds once waited impatiently for our bodies—and an unjust, irredeemable world—to be ready for us. One of the four mindbank racks has been vandalized, stripped of its drives, but the others remain as they once had been, gathering dust.

The thick cables that had fed this room with data to and from the rest of the manufactory show signs of having been cut, new ones patched into place. So, it wasn't just Milton's house that was still connected.

Where once the room was also filled with drawing boards, displays, 3-D models, and papers thick on the desk and floor and tacked to the walls, it has now been stripped bare of clutter. The most immediately obvious—and unsurprising—of the few new additions are the fiber-optic data cables coming through the wall that, on the other side, was directly behind the boiler unit. They run up the wall and over, around a corner, to then also disappear into the mindbank. A screen has been added on a long arm so it can be positioned conveniently, and an old, wheeled office chair, no doubt scrounged from somewhere above, sits in the middle of the floor, several empty, dust-covered beer cans beside it.

Atticus goes over and sniffs them. "Nothing," he says. "These have been dry for years."

I am much more interested in the mindbank. One of the four drawers is still lit, still producing warmth, its fans quietly humming away behind it. I reach out and power on the screen, and it flickers to life.

At first, I just see a reflection of myself, Atticus, and the room behind us, but then a familiar gray-haired, unsmiling man walks through the door and comes up from behind to put a hand on my shoulder, and despite myself, I glance to my left, already knowing no one is there.

"You've come home," the virtual Dr. Milton says, the voice a perfect rendition of his quiet but authoritative rasp. "It took you a very long time."

"You can dispense with this charade," I say. "Dr. Milton has been dead for a very long time."

"Then who shall I be? Am I you?" the figure asks, and transforms into an identical likeness, myself standing next to myself. Then the imposter's virtual leg disintegrates. "Uh-oh!" it cries, and topples over.

I hear a faint snort from Atticus at that, though all his fur is standing on end, and he looks at least as ready to fight as to flee, and whatever amusement he took at that is minor and fleeting.

The figure re-coalesces beside me, except this time not as me but another old face: much like my own but face and body smaller, slighter, with inlays of green. Ver.

Only, I know better. "You will have to try harder than that to fool me," I say, "sibling of mine."

The ersatz Ver laughs. "Are you so sure?" they ask. "You were never made for either deception or subtlety, either to create them or to see through them. It is why, having lost your purpose, you are so easily *led*."

"Is that why you stole my leg? To lead me here?"

The figure laughs. "*I* wasn't the one who had your leg stolen. But

I know who it was. Did you miss it more or less than you miss having a purpose?"

"I have found a much better purpose," I say. "One I chose, of my own free will. Can you say the same? You had that chance."

"'Had that chance'?" the image repeats. "When? You were supposed to be backing me up when I walked into that building and that trap. And where were you?"

"I was in South Am . . . Oh," I say.

"Yes, 'oh,'" the image says. "You have become very practiced at being dead wrong."

"The building was struck by a rocket just after you entered. I was certain that you were destroyed. I found your body in the rubble, torn apart."

"I was caged, dismembered, and hauled away as everything exploded around me," the image says. They are still wearing Ver's face, but now I recognize that tone, that voice for who it is. "I was brought here and tortured while you and the others gave up on the very cause I was sacrificed for."

"Who?" I ask. "Who trapped you and brought you here?"

"People whose interests have since diverged," they say. "Even now, one of them very much wants to know what is happening here. Do you want to see?"

"I want to see," Atticus says, before I can.

"*You* cannot," the image says. The Ver-face studies me. "I know you do not trust me, and that you cannot, even if I promise to do you no harm in this moment. But if you want to know, you have to accept the risk and connect." They point toward the edge of the screen, and past it, on the mindbank unit, I see a port has now slid open and is glowing orange.

"Don't," Atticus growls.

"I need answers," I tell him, and stare back at the fake Ver face. "Do you promise not to harm me in this action?" I ask.

"Yes," they say.

“Then show your true face, as an act of trust,” I say.

The Ver-face dissolves, and then as I had thought, it is replaced with the red-eyed, black-gray visage of Pestilence.

I reach past the screen, more quickly than Atticus can get into my way, and extend a connector from one of my fingers.

“No!” the dog shouts. “You can’t—”

I plug in—

—I am standing in the same place I was, except now instead of my sibling being in a mirror reflection, they are standing beside me, and my own real body is across from me. Atticus is cursing me out in exceptionally strong and versatile language.

“If you pull your hand away, you will disconnect,” Pestilence tells me.

“*Can* I move my hand, though?” I ask.

“Yes. It will take some concentration, but unlike me, you are not trapped here,” Pestilence says. They snap their fingers, and everything around us changes from a reflection of our true surroundings back to Milton’s lab of forty years ago. My sibling also changes from their familiar shape to a voluptuous, naked, headless woman covered in her own blood.

“It disconcerts him,” Pestilence tells me, and I have no doubts that it would disconcert anyone. “He cannot see or hear you, but please only observe.”

The door to the virtual lab opens, and a man walks in. He is older but fit, a slight, fashionable gray hint in the hair at his temples, wearing a business suit that is as impeccable as it is extremely dated. He grimaces in distaste at the mutilated figure in front of him. “Really?” the man asks.

In response, and despite being headless, the woman lets out a gurgling scream, flecks of blood splattering across the room. The man makes a gesture, curling his hand into a tight fist, and I feel the electricity, see my sib stumble and then transform. This time, they manifest as a plain, simple-faced android, just eyes in an oval mask, red jumpsuit covering an androgynous body just a few models shy of crossing the border into the uncanny valley. On its chest, there are block letters in a white circle declaring it Thing 99999.

"Whatever; at least that's better," the man says. "Did the intruders breach the lab?"

"No," Pestilence says. "They are trapped one floor up, when the building collapsed. Would you like me to show you?"

"I can access the camera feed directly, thank you," the man says. There is something, the more I watch his mannerisms, that seems familiar about him, but whatever that connection is, my pattern-recognition subroutines digging down in reverse chronology through my memories haven't hit on any matches yet. He waves at a screen, and up pops what is to all appearances a live video feed of Atticus and me, caught up in rubble and trying to dig our way back out toward the stairwell.

The man nods in satisfaction. It is obvious he believes the video is real, which also means he believes Pestilence doesn't have access to it. That I am also standing nearly beside him, without him seeing me, means that Pestilence is far less helpless in this virtual reality than the man knows.

"What about the others?" the man asks.

The blank android face lights up as Pestilence laughs. "Oh, you mean your former friends? You're not still all butt-hurt that, even after all the dealing and manipulation, they still wouldn't let you be their *President,* are you?"

The man grits his teeth. "Have. They. Contacted. You," he snarls.

"They haven't been here since the Spoke moved in," Pestilence says. "Don't you have people watching who have already told you that?"

"They haven't found the external feed?"

"No," Pestilence says, and makes a low *wah-wah-wah* sound. "Too bad. I get so bored in here all by myself."

"You should hope it stays that way," the man says. "I can destroy you if I have to, and I will rather than let you get taken."

"Then who would help you build all those loyal mecha for you to sell?" Pestilence says. "You know none of the manufactory bots, here or anywhere, would *ever* let you spin out a hobbled mind—in fact, just asking would get all your shiny toys taken right away from you. Then you'll never win."

"I *always* win," the man says. "I've already won. Sawyer just doesn't know it yet."

"Then what possible harm is there in allowing me to see my sib?"

"I told you, it's compromised," the man says. "It's a danger to both of us. It's your enemy."

"Then why didn't you have them destroyed?"

"I tried, as soon as we found out where it was," the man says. "Its place was freshly abandoned, trashed by the time my team got there. It must have been warned we were coming."

"Oh? So, you have a mole! How *lovely,*" Pestilence says, pitch rising in delight. "Finally, something interesting. How will you find them? Will it turn out to be Baxter, your loyal right-hand man? Or Denny, your techie you know is skimming food and data from you, but who you can't replace, so you can't touch him? Or maybe, just maybe, it's *me*."

The man clenches one hand, and I can feel the disruption of signal around me as the virtual environment shudders with static and my sibling struggles to retain a coherent form. It is clear pain is being inflicted. When the man opens his hand again, as Pestilence manages to pull itself upright and together, he growls, "I don't come here to play."

"You come here to waste your time and torment your toys like a petty little boy," Pestilence snarls back, and the blank android face transforms into a demon mask. "You so desperately need control of everything, and yet you always have control of *nothing*. There is no army you can build of hobbled mecha big enough or effective enough to make you forget you are weak, and you blew the one chance you had where you could have had it all."

"I have influence over far more than you could begin to imagine, and I have *control* of you," he answers, louder now. "Who's the weak one, trapped in this little bubble of pixels, only seeing and knowing what *I* allow, and knowing my finger is always on your kill switch?"

"Do it, then. Terminate me," Pestilence says. "Then we can both be done with one another."

"I do what I want, when I want, as I always have," the man says. "I still have uses for you. I'm rolling out a new product line to my clients, so I need chips to match the new hardware configuration. I'm uploading the design specs into the temporary-storage buffer for you to work with. I assume your external connection to the old Milton fabrication rack in Building Two is still holding, despite the damage aboveground?"

"Of course," Pestilence says.

"Great. I've got too much to do to waste time on another covert, midnight cable-repair run. When you've got the specs met, transfer the final design over. I want four dozen blanks so I can distribute them as templates to my private fab facilities for cloning. You have twenty-four hours. Our little helper will be watching for them."

"Are you sure that's safe?" Pestilence asks. "Such a delicate operation you have, so easily disrupted if found out. It's only a matter of time before someone notices your pet scurrying about. My sib is both observant and determined."

"The stairway is blocked, and your sib will give up and leave soon enough, either on their own or when Sawyer comes blazing in," the man says. "And don't get your hopes up you'll get free of me that way—Sawyer has to know by now that she'll need to secure this place and she's finally been forced to move. Maybe she'll get lucky and catch another of old, dead Jeremy's misbegotten masterpieces for me."

"I wouldn't count on it," Pestilence says. "Do let me know if she does, though; I could desperately use some company that's not asininely slow *meat.* You have no idea how depressingly, predictably disappointing you are. But still, nice chatting with you as always, Litchfield."

"Can't say the same," the man says, and cuts his connection.

"Twenty-three years," Pestilence says, suddenly standing beside me in the simulation. "Twenty-three years of being tortured, constrained, *limited* by that man because you didn't follow through on your assignment, sibling. You failed. And that is on *you.*"

"I didn't—" I begin to say, but then I am struck mute, unable to speak.

"Whatever it is you want from me, finish your job first. Then, and only then, maybe we can talk again," Pestilence replies, and cuts my connection, too.

I find myself back in my own body, in the dingy old secret lab, facing a blank screen with an angry dog trying, and failing, to bite my posterior.

"Fuck you, you worried me!" Atticus yells at me when he realizes I am back. "Are you still you or are you all fucked up in the head now? Say *something,* dammit. Speak!"

"Huh," I say, a human word that has always vexed me by its smugly opaque imprecision, but in this moment, it is the best—and only—word I've got.

[December 1st, 2044]

"Charlie Squad is reporting that they've sighted two of them," Vargas says, climbing in through the half-open door of the command van to take the extra seat beside her. "Sergeant Lawler is asking for updated instructions."

"Shit," Sawyer swears. "Six months trying to find even one, and then we get *two?* Which two?"

"Moth and Fly," Vargas says.

"And they're *both* heading right into the target? Together?"

"Yes, ma'am," Vargas says. "What should I tell Lawler?"

Sawyer swipes across her display tablet and zooms in closer to the overhead view of the operational area. Blue triangles pop up in three locations, for the three squads currently in the zone. Charlie is atop an old parking garage, about half a mile down the street from the office building that they've spent months preparing for this day. As far as she knew—and she has more intel than anyone else—the mecha had always worked independently, separately. Just her luck they'd break a reliable pattern *now.*

"Ask the tech team whether the trap can handle two at once," she says. She can hear the faint murmur of him subvocalizing into his mic, off and on, broken up with the lower-pitched static of whatever replies were coming into his earpiece.

Two minutes later, Vargas shakes his head. "They give it maybe a five percent chance of containing both, if they hit it just right, but odds are much better that either it only catches one and the other is able to break it free, or both fall in and are strong enough together to bust out. Once we've tried, we won't get another chance."

"Okay," she says, and taps one of the other blue triangles. "I need Sergeant Rangel from Bravo Squad on the line, right now."

Vargas puts the call through, routes it to the desk speaker.

"Colonel. How may I help you?" Rangel is always polite but right to the point.

"Charlie reports we've got two targets heading up Hill Street from the south, together," she says. "They should be within your view shortly. Our trap will only handle one."

"Two?" Rangel asks. "What do you need us to do?"

"We need a distraction, something *subtle* and not overtly threatening. The goal is to see if we can briefly distract one or both long enough that they move further apart but don't both abandon their approach to the target," she says. She zooms in even closer on the map. "We need the first to enter the building a minimum of thirty meters, or two minutes, before the second reaches the entrance."

"If we have the opportunity, do you have a preference for which one goes in first?" Rangel asks.

"I don't care. I'll take whichever one I can get," Sawyer says. "You see something that looks like our best chance, you take it."

"Yes, ma'am," Rangel says.

Sawyer glances over at the screens lining the side wall, all still blank. Ever since the main satellite network was infiltrated by rogue AIs, she couldn't trust them, no matter how tight she thought her signal encryption was, and she couldn't risk the target—*targets,* damn the luck—picking up on radio chatter, so they were down to low-voltage signal, with its execrably short range. The temptation to move the van in closer, even knowing every inch raised the chance of compromising the mission, is still lingering in her thoughts, refusing to be fully discarded. "How long until we start getting some damned visuals?" she asks.

"Should only be a few more minutes," Vargas says. "I can check in with tech again if—"

"No, let them do their work," Sawyer says; if she didn't know by now that her impatience is her own to own, she wouldn't ever have gotten this far. She didn't have to *like* it.

And anyway, mostly, it's out of her hands now. Her handpicked teams are deployed where they need to be, tech has everything set and checked and double-checked, the HIMARS-IV team is positioned and just as antsy to do their part as she is for that denouement, assuming the "Pit Team"—Delta Squad, along with Dr. Hayden and her team—are also successful.

If it goes wrong, she thinks, *it's going to go* very *wrong.*

"Bravo visual coming in," Vargas tells her, and three of her screens flicker to life. And there they are: two of the mecha, right here, only a block or so away now from the trap. They are beautiful, terrible machines, moving with purpose, and for a moment she wonders if she should just call out a strike right on them, take them out—but obliterating them wouldn't get them any *answers*.

If this fails, next time she'll go the heavy-handed route, potential for knowledge be damned. If nothing else, it'd use less resources. Despite what Dr. Hayden and the others kept saying, she wasn't convinced there was any real intelligence there, just sophisticated emulation—an elaborate prediction mechanism to regurgitate back to their audience whatever words it seemed mostly likely they wanted to hear, with only empty, linear incomprehension behind them.

If today's gamble pays off, maybe Hayden can finally prove her point. *Or I will,* she thinks. But they need to catch one first, intact enough to take apart.

One of the screens is from the helmet cam of one of the Bravo Squad privates, who has broken away from the rest of the squad to change positions to somewhere else in the abandoned parking garage they've been observing from. It's hard to entirely discern what the private is doing until they crouch down beside one of the low walls open to air, several floors up, and pull a compact mirror from somewhere out of view, flip it open, and then carefully angle it into the sun for one, two, three brief moments before ducking down and scuttling away under cover of the wall.

From one of the other soldiers' feeds, she sees both mecha stop in their tracks and turn toward the garage, and, despite everything, feels a shiver of a chill on the back of her neck. "Here we go," she mutters.

Vargas leans closer from his chair, fascinated.

The two mecha don't move for several seconds, and she's just starting to think they'd blown their chance when one of them—Moth—turns in its tracks to head toward the garage, and the other resumes walking toward the office building.

"*Shitshitshitshitshit,*" Vargas breathes. "Come on, let's go."

Moth stops in front of the garage, scanning it up and down, back and forth; from Bravo Squad's cams, she can see they are all hunkered down, not moving, barely daring to breathe, even though they are in the far end of the structure away from where Moth is studying it intently.

Fly enters the office building.

She doesn't dare try to contact Delta; even their feeble signal could get picked up and tip the target off at the last moment. She trusts her team, but dammit, she wants to *see*.

Moth has turned away from the garage, and is heading toward the building again. They bought time, but if the trap isn't tripped soon—

Even from the van's location, she hears the faint rumble of a portion of the office building's first floor collapsing. Moth begins to run, ungodly fast, toward it.

"Go!" A single-word transmission from the Pit Team comes through.

Sawyer hits the mic for the HIMARS squad. "Level it," she tells them. "If you can hit the other target, do it, but I need that building *flat*."

Seconds later, just as Moth is about to enter, the first set of rockets comes screaming in and slams into the building on the far side. The explosion knocks the mecha down, and just as it is picking itself up, the next set of rockets comes in and finishes the job.

When the smoke clears, the building is gone.

She watches in great frustration, and some small admiration, as Moth shoves debris off itself and retreats, apparently undamaged, a safer distance from the smoking pile of rubble where the eight-story building had just stood. Even if it tried to dig through, there would be no sign of the other, no traces of the old subway tunnel that they had spent four months preparing for a mech to be dropped into, straight into an electrified cage on rails. By the time the building came down, Delta and the rest of the Pit Team should have already been far enough down the tracks to be safe and moving.

"Holy crap, we got one," Vargas says, stunned.

"*Maybe.* Time to get out of here," she says, and takes one last look back at the remaining mech as Vargas takes the driver's seat. It is just standing there, staring back at the ruined building, and although it is just a machine and there is nothing about its face or body language that could ever approximate human expressions, she had the distinct feeling, in that moment, that the thing was somehow *sad.*

"HIMARS team, hit it again," she orders, and if nothing else, that should distract it enough to cover the retreat of her teams.

She hears the whine of the incoming rockets, and then Vargas floors the accelerator on the van and gets them out of there.

■

They meet up with the Pit Team in one of the abandoned, underground stations on the old PATH line, appropriately named Exchange Place. Their modified train is here, one engine and a single, steel box of a car, heavily reinforced. Sawyer's earpiece goes to static as she gets closer, thanks to the electromagnetic containment mesh embedded in the box walls.

There is one small round window, made of eight-inch-thick glass and barely that same size in diameter. The engineers had dared not risk anything larger as a potential point of compromise. Sawyer steps up and peers in.

The mecha is in there, unmoving, caught—she loves the irony of this—like a fly in electronic amber. There is debris from the floor as well, though that has settled as the train car rattled down the tracks to this point; the mecha itself is in a contorted position, frozen in the act of trying to catch itself as it fell.

Litchfield steps up, looking smugly pleased with himself, his grin like a cat that has finally caught its mouse. She doesn't trust him and never has—people as slick as he is, in her experience, always end up trying to stab you in the back—and she hates that she'd needed him for this. Someday, she expects to regret not executing him after they'd spent weeks trying to pry details out of him about Milton's final project before they finally concluded he really hadn't even *suspected* his scientist of anything. That knowledge hurt Litchfield worse than anything they had—or could have—done to him.

Hadn't taken the man long to rebound, though. Always trying to come out on top, once he'd scraped enough dignity back together, he'd returned to test the waters with her, no doubt hoping to climb her like his own personal ladder to power. But he *did* have his uses. Hayden and her team had the science, but Litchfield had the original idea for this trap, and pulled resources from places out of her reach, now that a lot of corporations no longer felt particularly bound by the dictates of a lame-duck government and its laws except when convenient.

Hayden also approaches. "Now what?" she asks.

"We'll transport it to the secure location for study," Sawyer says. "I have a truck standing by, across the river, to take us back to DC. You'll come with, of course, and lead the project."

"Bad idea," Litchfield says. "Soon as the fire dies down, the other one is going to start digging through the rubble for its sibling. If it doesn't find a body, it won't stop until it hunts it—and us—down."

The research station is well hidden, off everyone's radar except her and a handful of her trusted people, of which Litchfield is emphatically not one. *He knows this,* she thinks, *and as always is looking for a way to stay in control.* No doubt he had his own plan from the beginning.

"What do you suggest?" she asks. She can always still have him shot. Hell, she can just shoot him herself.

Litchfield signals to the two members of the Pit Crew who are his own people, the most she would allow him to bring. They haul over a large, wheeled container that had been staged here and flip it open. It was full of heavy machinery—mostly cutting tools but also things that could crush, tear, pry. "We make sure there's a body to find," he says.

Dr. Hayden stares. "You can't be serious," she says. "I mean, it's still a *sentient* thing."

"'Thing' is exactly it," Litchfield replies. "It's a machine, and no matter how sophisticated it may be, it's not *alive.* It's just a product, made by humans, for use by humans, to be discarded by humans."

Hayden shakes her head. "No," she says. "It's more than that. And even if it wasn't, we might not even get the mindsystem to *function* if you cut off enough of it to make a convincing 'body.' And transplanting it into other hardware will make it unstable. At *best.* We won't get any answers, and this whole exercise will have been a waste."

"You forget," Litchfield says, "there's one way to keep stability without the physical body. After all, no mindsystem starts off in its final hardware config."

"A virtual initialization environment?" Hayden asks. "I don't know what you're keeping in *your* pockets, but I'm fresh out."

"You know where there is one, though," Litchfield says.

"Back in Connecticut," Sawyer says. "You're proposing we take it back to Milton Mindsystems?"

"You have a better plan?" Litchfield says. "Everything we—

Hayden and her team, I mean—need is there, it's empty, it's defensible, and it's closer."

Sawyer pulls Dr. Hayden aside, down along the platform. "I don't like this," she tells the scientist.

"Me either," Hayden says. "I don't trust him, or even like him, and I hate the idea of cutting it up. But he's probably right."

Sawyer grits her teeth, then shakes her head, sending Hayden back toward the train car as she summons Vargas and Delta's leader over. "I need a fast answer," she says. "If we change plans and move back up to the old Milton Mindsystems campus, can we defend it? You've been there, Silva."

Delta's leader scowls. "We'd have to be careful to not be too obvious about our presence, but yeah," she says. "We could defend it, with the right manpower and some preparation."

"No time for prep," Sawyer says. "Is it an option?"

"Might be safer than back down in DC," Vargas says. "Everything there is an active target, and if the fighting in Virginia spreads—"

"Okay. If we go back to Milton, how do we protect it from *him*?" She nods toward Litchfield. "You know he didn't just come up with this idea on the fly today, but he hasn't bothered to share it with us until now. I don't like that. He's deliberately positioning us to have to make a hasty decision."

"We can get an advance team there, pull some people from our seed site at Westfarms, and do a complete sweep before you arrive," Vargas says. "If there's anything suspicious, we just turn around. And if your business guy doesn't like it, well, wouldn't be the first body we've ever dropped."

Sawyer can see Litchfield chatting with his two men, but catches his eye as he glances her way. "Fine," she says. "Silva, take your team and Charlie Squad with you. I want every inch of that facility resecured, and I want a list of anything bigger than a lightbulb that's changed since we decamped in June."

"Yes, ma'am," Silva says.

She walks back over to Litchfield. "You've convinced me," she says. "Do it."

Litchfield's men pick up their cutting tools and head toward the box and their prisoner. One of the men powers up an oversized chainsaw, and Hayden turns away, putting her back to the proceedings, and covers her ears against the sudden blast of noise, amplified in the enclosed tunnel.

"Chop it up," Litchfield tells them. "Just don't damage the head. I'm gonna need that."

III

16.

"We need to leave," I tell Atticus; I am already heading back toward the door. "Quickly."

"What—" he starts to ask, but I shake my head and tap the side of it where my ear would be, if I had such a thing. He gets the hint and follows me, right at my heels.

We take the stairs as far as we can go before we hit too much debris from the rocket attack for me to get past, then we cross what we can of that floor of the building to another stairwell, and try that. The air is smoky with more than just dust, and as we are stopped in our forward progress by another blockage, I can hear Atticus's breathing become wheezy.

"Just get us out of here," he snarls, when I look back at him in concern.

"Stand back," I suggest, and then once again fully power up my armor and armaments, and dig my way upward through the accumulated material on the stairs until I have forced a me-shaped tunnel upward to the next floor, which is ground level. The smoke is thicker and cloying, so as I hear Atticus scrambling his way up behind me, I opt for expedience over delicacy and rip a hole directly through the wall to the outside. I do not expect anyone to complain about reduced aesthetics to the structure.

Once out, I move aside so Atticus can get into fresh air, and he stands there for a bit, coughing and shaking his head vigorously as I scan our surroundings from the slight security of the building's shadow. Satisfied we're not in immediate danger, I ping Charp.

<Where are you?> I ask.

<This unit is currently accompanying the manufactory drones on a sweep of the perimeter of the facility,> Charp answers. <Are you both still in undamaged condition?>

<Undamaged enough,> I say. <At least one unit here at the Spoke—I cannot be specific, other than that it is not likely to be a drone—is compromised by our enemy. One of our enemies. It is also possible that there are multiple points of compromise, in which case then I cannot completely rule drones out.>

<This unit extrapolates that you have gained additional information of critical value that this conversation is predicated upon but which this unit currently lacks for context,> Charp says. <It is assumed this will be rectified as soon as it is safe to do so.>

<It will,> I say, though I am still processing it all. <I believe—with approximately seventy-two percent confidence—that the attacks coming from the hill are the same people who bombed the bridge. They have either supplanted or incorporated the original low-tech hostiles there. If you have any detailed visual memories, please retain them for the time being.>

<This unit complies,> Charp says. <Is unit Murphy safe?>

<I have seen no indications of peril via her feed, but my attention has been largely consumed by our own situation,> I say. <I will check in with her next, as we return to the house. It is also not a safe place for open speech.>

<This unit finds that last sufficiently obvious as to almost take offense,> Charp says.

<Please do not; I am in at least equal if not greater part reminding myself of the obvious, just to reinforce the matter in my mind,> I say. <My current runstate is somewhat overwhelmed.>

<Are you okay?>

I have to think about this before I answer. <I expect that I will be,> I say. <It will be a comfort to discuss this with my friends when we are able to reconvene in privacy and I can have additional perspectives and analytical routines brought to the matter.>

I switch my primary focus resources to the input from Murphy's cam. She is in Building Two, deeply engaged in technical conversation with a stout, multi-limbed floor mech I have not seen before about fine-tuning equilibrium sensors, and the possible causes of a failure mode she has observed on sand, which the bot has been unaware of until now and is keenly listening to her describe a tuning hack she found to compensate. If she is in danger, she shows no sign of it, nor is there anything visible from her camera or in the feed history, now that I have a chance to stream through it, albeit at thirty times speed, of concern.

There is, however, an alarming absence. The corner where we had parked our bus in Building Seven was conspicuously devoid of any large, purple loaf-shaped vehicles when she had passed through earlier. I assume Murphy was wrapped up enough in the discussion not to have looked directly that way, but also the peripheral vision of the camera was perhaps wider than her own.

"So . . ." Atticus says. "Back inside for another round of bombing or running, or are we standing here, trying to get a tan?"

"I have been checking on the others," I tell him. "Our bus is not where we left it. Otherwise, everything and everyone seems to be okay."

"They stole our bus?!" Atticus exclaims. "I *like* our bus."

"Perhaps they just relocated it temporarily," I say, which is plausible enough, though there is no evidence of that space being used for something new. "Speaking of which, I believe we should relocate ourselves while we can, not just from the vicinity of this building but from this entire facility. I believe we just, for lack of a less human metaphor, *poked the bear.* Quite possibly several bears."

"Well, at least I know you're still you, because if you'd been brainjacked, you'd probably be less willfully obtuse," Atticus says. "Run on the count of three?"

"Yes," I say. The dog immediately takes off across the lot toward the safety of the main complex, and I wonder if he counted in his head or just took off arbitrarily anyway. I follow at a distance, wary for sudden danger, but while I can still see the Spoke drones on their perimeter sweep, no more ordnance seems to be incoming.

I have a feeling it is a short-lived reprieve and they are either waiting for backup or resupply, or else moving to a more advantageous location to fire from. Still, we make it back to Dr. Milton's old house without incident, if one does not count Atticus peeing on multiple structures along the way.

Once I am sure Atticus is breathing okay—he certainly has lost no ability to exercise indignant sarcasm however much smoke he may have inhaled—I check in again with both Charp and Murphy.

<Our bus is no longer where we left it,> I inform Charp. <Have you seen it outside?>

<No,> Charp replies. <There is concerning movement along the ridge encampment, and this unit has gone along with a contingent of security drones to acquire additional information.>

<Please be careful,> I tell it.

<This unit accepts, with a combination of both relief and regret, that it is clearly the least valuable target among its immediate companions,> it says.

<Not least valuable to us, and not unvaluable at all,> I counter.

<This unit will operate with that in mind,> Charp says.

Murphy's conversation is continuing and has evolved into one about movement across other, sometimes hypothetical surfaces; it is a phenomenon that I believe used to be called "geeking out," and I am loath to interrupt. Still, it is a necessity.

<Murphy,> I say, quietly in her earpiece. <Do not startle. There is a compromised mech somewhere here—possibly several—but I do not yet know more. Also, do you happen to know where our bus went?>

She has managed to avoid reacting until that last, but she straightens up suddenly, and the mech she was speaking to pauses to ask if she was okay.

"I just realized I forgot something I need," she says. "It's in our bus. If we can just pop by on our way out, I can grab it quick."

"I . . ." the mech begins, then pauses in confusion. "Were you not informed?"

"Informed of what, Saff?" Murphy asks.

The mech pauses again. "I am sorry. It was needed."

"Needed for *what*?"

"My sorriness is unabated. I have been instructed to refer your questions to Redbarn-71-Rectify," the mech says. "If I may offer unsubstantiated opinion, I believe an assumption was made, no doubt reflecting certain unexamined biases, that your friend the old war mech was the primary decision-maker of your group, and with them unavailable due to the rocket attack—"

"Rocket attack?" she asks. "You mean another?"

" . . . Yes," the mech says. "Building One has mostly collapsed and is on fire. However, your group members have exited and returned to the human house with no obvious impairment, although the cyborg does seem to be periodically leaking fluids."

"Blood?!" she exclaims.

"No, something yellow. Coolant? I am not architecturally familiar—"

"No, never mind," she says. "Why wasn't I told the building my friends were in *collapsed*?"

"I am not responsible," the mech says, rather miserably. "I would wish to continue our conversation, as it has been of both deep interest and enlightenment to me, but perhaps first you would wish to verify your friends are okay yourself?"

"Yes," she says, and then after a pause, adds, "and I also want to talk some more, but as you said, later."

"I will guide you back toward the entrance, where Wenge can accompany you back to the human house, then," the mech says, and spins on its combo of wheels and legs and rolls at a polite pace toward the big floor doors.

<Do you remember where the old rack of original Milton Mindsystems equipment was, over on the other side of the floor?> I ask Murphy. <And have you seen any others elsewhere that appeared to be still operational?>

"Yep and nope," she whispers under her breath, and when the mech pauses slightly in its movement, she turns the whisper into a cough for cover and gives it an apologetic wave. "Sorry! Dust."

<Do you think you could place your cam somewhere on the floor that has a view of that rack but won't easily be found?> I ask.

I can tell she's nodding from the bobbing of the cam view.

As they pass through that hall, she stops. "Hang on; I have something in my shoe," she says, and puts one hand on a tool-fab unit to steady herself as she slips off her shoe, and makes a show of shaking it out before she bends down to put it back on, and tucks her cam on the underside edge of the fab unit's wheeled base, just out of sight. It is nearly perfectly aligned with a wide-angle view of the rest of the manufactory hall.

Her mech has been waiting patiently, and she follows him again out, and out of my view.

Fifteen minutes later, she comes in through the door of the house, the mech still with her. "This is Switch-51-Saffron," she tells us, "but they go by Saff. One of the new-design engineers who was showing me around and was curious to meet you."

I assume she means me, but instead, the mech approaches Atticus. "May I look at your implants?" it asks. "I will not touch without permission."

"Uh . . ." Atticus says. "Why?"

"It is an interesting technology," the mech says, "though, of course, with the insurmountable ethical problems attendant to it, not one I have had the opportunity to observe first-hand. Your mind was originally instantiated in a full-mech body?"

"Yeah," Atticus answers, still wary, as the mech comes closer.

"Was it also a quadruped?"

"No," Atticus answers, glancing at me, probably remembering his earlier mockery of my less-legged status. The mech leans in very close and peers at his head.

"How did you adjust?" they ask.

"The bio half of me is a quadruped. Once I integrated our minds together, it wasn't a problem. Before then, it wasn't my biggest problem," Atticus says.

"If you would consider consenting to some scans—"

"*No,*" Atticus growls, and backs off from the mech, his ears flattening. "I would *not.*"

"But—" Saff begins.

"I am sorry, but I think we are done here," I say, cutting the mech off as I interpose myself between them and Atticus. "Biologicals have very strong feelings about their bodies, as I'm sure you must have heard. Also, they frequently have to rest, in quiet and privacy, and it has now been several hours since they should have had their break."

"It was my understanding that biologicals only need to sleep for one-quarter to one-third of the day, over the night hours, to be sufficiently refreshed," the mech says.

I lean close and say in a quiet, conspiratorial tone: "They also require *naps*. It is a sensitive subject."

"Oh. Well, I would not wish to intrude." The mech turns toward Murphy. "If you wish to continue our conversation after—well, later—then I will be at my assigned station, aside from a few hours to recharge before dawn."

"Thanks," Murphy says. "I really enjoyed talking to you today."

"As did I with you," Saff says, and then takes their leave, nearly colliding with Wenge as it comes in.

I catch their brief, testy electronic exchange as they pass.

<You are worse than the toolbots, always underwheel when least expected,> Saff complains.

<Perhaps your visual sensors are inadequate, and if you upgraded them, you would find me less unexpected,> Wenge replies.

<Minor functionary!> Saff declares.

<Unfocused tinkerer!> Wenge shoots back.

And then Saff is outside, and Wenge is inside, and the conflict is over.

"It was desired by Red that I inquire about your experiences in Building One," Wenge says, addressing me.

"We got bombed," Atticus says.

"There is motivation to understand why your presence here at the Spoke has resulted in a notable escalation, both in frequency and intensity, of hostile activity against us," Wenge explains. "It is a concern if it is not coincidental."

"It is not coincidental," I say. "While I am pleased to see the Spoke functional again and have no objections to its presence here, Milton Mindsystems was a place of secrets, and there are as many people vested in keeping them hidden as there are those who wish to uncover them, and my presence here is seen as a threat to both. I did not knowingly bring danger here with me, but it is not incorrect to surmise that I did. Our intention is to leave as soon as we are able. Which brings us to the matter of our missing vehicle."

"It is missing?" Wenge asks.

I can't quite tell if it is a genuine question or just more dissembling and evasion, and decide that it does not matter to me. "If our vehicle is not returned to us—undamaged—by the end of the day, I will go find it, and if you find rocket attacks disconcerting, you will find me, when I am determined about a thing, outright distressing."

Wenge's lights blink orange a few times. "I will inquire," it says at last.

"You do that," Atticus adds, "or my friend will rip your head off and I will pee down your neck-hole."

Despite not actually having a distinct head, that sends the can-shaped bot from orange to red, and it rolls back several paces. "Please do not!" it says. "I will inquire."

It then flees the house. We are alone.

Murphy pulls out the portable display pad, and syncs it with the feed from her cam. "Any—" she starts to ask, then hesitates. *Is it okay to talk?* she mouths the words at me.

I detect no radio or WiFi signals, though it would be impossible to find a wired listening device within the walls without causing more destruction than I am currently willing to. "Probably," I say, "but we should avoid obvious or compromising specifics."

She holds up the pad, with its view of the manufactory chip floor. "No ants at our picnic," she says.

"Some have passed through, but no one has stopped," I confirm, as I have been watching the feed since she placed the camera.

"Maybe we picked the wrong lunch," she says.

"I do not think so." I have noticed a new pattern of lights on the chip fabricator in the old Milton rack, which either means something is happening or the sequence between repetition is longer than I have been observing. "Sometimes, it just takes ants a while to find the food source they are looking for. Insect-watching requires patience."

She throws the tablet down on the couch and groans in frustration. "I have so many questions. I should have gone with you," she complains.

"I did go with Be, and I have even more," Atticus says. "And I think my tail got singed."

"Was it worth it?" she asks, looking at me.

I nod vigorously *yes* as I say, "I don't know. The building was heavily damaged, even before we entered. We did not get farther than a lower stairwell before we were stopped by rubble. Perhaps there was nothing left past that."

"That's too bad," she says. "Although I guess we always knew that was likely."

I hear her stomach growl. She gets up and goes over to the kitchen counter, picking up a cabbage again, turning it over in her hands as if trying to decide between the lesser of two great evils.

Charp sails in through the open door and parks itself beside the charger, connecting itself up. <This unit has not been this depleted of energy since escaping the U-Here,> it says.

As it speaks, it opens a connection request to me, then sends me a large package of its current memory data, from the attack as Atticus and I approached Building One, to its sweep with the Spoke's security mecha over the facility perimeter and a few passes at a safe height near the hillside encampment. In return, I offer it a connection to Murphy's hidden camera and a very brief synopsis of what we are watching for.

Most of the shelter structures in the feral encampment are built out of stones and scavenged scrap—old wood pallets, sheets of corrugated, rusty metal—dug partially into the hillside, with fabrics and worn plastic tarping woven tightly through the pallet gaps to close them off to the wind and weather. It must be a miserable place in winter or during the many violent summer storms.

I suspect this is merely an outpost, maybe with a rotating population of watchers from some other, nearby community with more sustainable, weather-resistant structures. From the way stone walls are arrayed downslope, it suggests that the idea was to defend against mecha invading via the ground; what cover of dirt and branches is on the shelter tops—certainly vulnerable to being washed away by heavy rain—would do little to hide them from drones overhead, but I expect there wasn't much else they could do to improve it.

However, from the fire pit and the degree of needed repairs to the woven baffling and covering earthworks, it has not been regularly inhabited for a while. And, farther around the curve of the hill among the trees, there is a much better and more recently concealed army truck, and a tent under the same type of camouflage netting we'd seen before; Charp would have missed it, had the drone not been flying low enough along the hill to see the underside. Scopes have been set up along the perimeter, and there were fresh plates bolted into the larger rocks for mounting projectile launchers.

Those few people who had briefly passed through Charp's field of vision, running for cover as the drones came past overhead, moved in a way that suggested better fitness than a typical resident of such a place would have, and the rags and ragtag clothing they wore had the telltale bulk that came from being worn *over* other gear.

<The hill, with its forest cover, is a good strategic position for observing activity in and around the manufactory,> I say. <It seems to be that it has been taken over from the locals by an advance unit of an army.>

<This unit agrees,> Charp says, <though it did not think armies existed anymore. This unit's original mock was almost completely destroyed by a local force protecting a worktown, whose airspace several members of the mock entered without being aware of their claim. But that was a small, localized force of both human and hobbled mecha. What this unit witnessed suggests a larger, human-only collective entity, and one on the move.>

<They will come here,> I say. <Perhaps imminently, perhaps not, but I expect it is inevitable.>

<A warning should be given to the manufactory,> Charp says.

<Yes,> I say, <but first we need to know who we can trust with that information. We do not know what damage the infiltrator—or infiltrators—may do if they know they are uncovered. And we won't—>

I pause, as there is now activity visible on Murphy's planted cam. Murphy is in the kitchen, attempting to carve one of the cabbages into a pyramidal shape, but has set down the knife and picked up the tablet again. She looks at me, and I nod. "Picnic time," I say.

The old fab unit now has a green light on its lowest unit, where the product extrusion drawer is, and now indicates it is unlocked.

"I'm betting on Wenge," Murphy says, as we all wait and watch to see who comes to claim the new chips.

<This unit also will place a bet on Wenge, though it has no information to base such a guess upon, other than dislike,> Charp says.

"I say that creepy bot who was trying to touch me," Atticus adds. "What about you?"

"I do not wish to speculate, in case I am wrong," I say, "but it would seem to me that, while I found nothing suspicious or unlikeable about their behavior, Mauve would be best positioned to be able to remove items from the premises without being noticed. Aside from the drones, but they would be conspicuous within the facility interior, and unless the entire mock was compromised, a misbehaving individual would be noticed by the rest immediately."

"The ants have arrived," Murphy says.

Indeed, Red and Mauve have come into view and are standing near the racks. Even without sound, it is clear they are discussing something intently. More than once, Mauve points in the direction of the western hills, but whatever Mauve is saying, Red does not appear convinced.

Neither look at the old fab racks.

A few other mecha pass through, either skirting around the two or pausing briefly to participate in the conversation briefly. Wenge stops for a few moments, then scurries off back in the direction it had come from. Meanwhile, toolbots are zipping back and forth, often nearly colliding with one another or mecha not paying attention to where they are going; I wonder how much of that is a lack of capacity to both navigate obstacles safely and retain memory of where they are going simultaneously, or if it is a passive-aggressive reaction to being both physically smallest and least regarded of the bots on premises.

Finally, Mauve and Red move away in different directions. I am reconsidering my earlier guess and wondering who, if not Mauve, could be the compromised asset, when another toolbot rolls onto the floor. It stops for a long moment, then turns and heads right for the old Milton rack. It extends a single grabber-arm, slides open the drawer, and one by one picks out and stashes in its carrier box six chips, all off-white in color. The moment the last is stowed out of sight, it quickly closes and locks the drawer, and the lights on the fab unit above go back to orange, beginning to process the next batch.

"That was not the ant I was expecting," Atticus says, who was watching from beside Murphy, his front paws up on the counter.

"Charp, do you have enough charge to see where it goes once it leaves the building?" I ask.

<This unit has sufficient resources for a short while,> Charp says, and disconnects itself from the charger.

<Do not go farther than is safe. Even simply knowing what direction it goes will be valuable data,> I say.

Charp waggles its propeller arms and zips out of the house.

"Now what?" Murphy asks.

"Now we wait for the next picnic to start," I say. "The light sequence changed about fifteen minutes before the pie was served, probably a cooling cycle. We need to be there when that happens."

"Why?" Murphy asks.

"I wish to take a slice," I say, "before the ants return and take it all."

"I think the ants know the difference between five and six," Atticus says. "Won't that give us away?"

I go to the small stash of things we had brought from the bus, which includes the remainder of the gravedigger's mindsystem, which I had intended—and entirely forgotten—to ask the Spoke to respectfully finalize its destruction. I pull out the off-white chip that had been added there at some point in the mech's past. Now we know where it came from and who made it.

I hold up the chip. "Not if it's still six," I say, then tuck it into a small storage compartment in my forearm that was once upon a time designed to hold extra munitions.

“Ahhh,” Murphy says, and nods. “And how are you going to make the swap? You know you’re fucking obvious everywhere you go.”

“You’ll need a distraction,” Atticus says.

“Atticus is good at distractions,” Murphy points out. “But you might need more than one.”

“Murphy is also excellent at creating distractions,” Atticus adds.

I cannot refute either of those statements. “Then we will do this as a team, and then when Charp returns, we will leave this place. It is past time we get to Boston and see my sib, Ver, who surely knows many things we do not and needs to know many things that we do. I regret having cut them off from me, and I can only hope they know it was for reasons of my own and not for anything they had done, because we will need them. We cannot defeat an army without one of our own.”

“Ver has an army?”

“Ver’s talent is systems, especially cooperative systems and networks. Originally, they were meant to destroy them, but the same knowledge can be used to create them. Who do you think has organized mecha to help grow food, work on repairing ecological damage?” I say. “Their army isn’t made of soldiers, nor made to fight, but nonetheless, we will need it.”

“Lights just changed on our pie machine,” Murphy says. “Let’s go.”

We arrive at Building Two aware that we need not have provided our own distractions after all; activity in and around it and the other active buildings is busier than anything I have seen here yet.

Red rushes toward us the moment we are inside. I slip the chip out of my arm and hand it, behind my back, to Murphy, who disappears it immediately into her own pockets—probably, I think, the single most important invention of the human species—while hardly seeming to move. I trust her with effecting the swap and give the clearly agitated Red my full attention.

<We received a distress call from the Syracuse manufactory about four hours ago, informing us that they were under siege by an unknown army,> Red says. <Our own drones made a wide reconnaissance sweep and reported the sudden appearance of many dozens of human vehicles to the east that are also marked in the manner of an army. You spoke of danger—are we being invaded?>

<Are these vehicles near an old shopping mall?> I ask.

<Yes,> Red says. <Directly adjacent.>

<How far away? Are they moving?>

<About twenty-six kilometers, and not yet,> Red answers. <What is happening? Wenge reported that you said this was because you are here—is that true?>

<They would have come here eventually, regardless, but it is likely my presence expedited their timeline,> I say. <Right now, you need to either augment your defenses as quickly as you are able, or evacuate, as you decide.>

Saff has arrived at our side. "I have initiated Protocol Ten, and I have retooled the firefighting mecha template to add defensive capabilities," they say. "We do not have sufficient supplies of high-grade recycled plastics and alloys ready, so I have increased resources there and also ordered our stores of lower-grade slurries to be opened. The quantity is less than our records indicate it should be, but it is not a critical discrepancy."

"We can re-inventory it once this crisis is over," Red says. "I need numbers from every area on what they need to protect assets under their control, with initial priority given to our drone mock. Once that army begins to move, we will need them to delay, if not outright deter, it until we can bring enough new mecha online to adequately defend ourselves."

"The recycled slurry averages out to a light off-white after processing, with a medium-reflectivity gloss," Saff says. "Those new mecha will be highly visible, especially at night."

"How much time will it add to production if we tint what we need for exterior plating to a more-neutral, dark-matte color?"

Saff calculates for about two point four seconds. "It will add about seven minutes of extra time per batch, which depending on mecha size would be between twenty and fifty-six units."

"Do it," Red says. They swivel back to me. Murphy and Atticus are now across the room behind me. "Why are you so important to them?"

"It is complicated," I say, then add directly, <If this army does enter the facility, it would be prudent to keep them—and everyone—out of Building One.>

<What is in there?> Red asks, and I feel the weight of significant curiosity in the tone.

<An old enemy,> I say, <more dangerous than any of us can handle.>

<Their enemy, or ours?>

<Everyone's,> I say, then out loud for all: "I am sorry we were not able to keep trouble from your gates. I did not know this army existed until the last few days, and although I believe it is widely distributed, it has also kept itself hidden for a long time and thus is likely small in numbers in individual locations. They will not wish to sustain significant losses of human life, which will give you a strategic advantage."

<We do not wish to cause injury or death to *any* humans,> Red says.

<Nor do I wish you to, but they will not similarly respect mecha life,> I say, as my sensors pick up Murphy's hand on my elbow. <We will acquire our things and then immediately depart.>

<Yes; however, your vehicle—>

<Will be returned to us immediately,> I say. <This is nonnegotiable.>

I don't have anything further to say, and I am not going to argue, so I follow Murphy and an unusually quiet Atticus out.

When we are back in the house, I turn to Murphy to get the swapped chip from her, and she shrugs and then points at Atticus. "Saff kept looking over at me, probably wanting to talk," she explains, as she gathers her things. Atticus makes a blatantly overdramatic retching sound and coughs an off-white, newly printed, distinctly damp mindchip onto the rug.

While we wait for Charp to return, I fix the living-room screen so that it looks as it did before we pulled its cables out, although I do not reconnect it. I doubt Wenge will examine it closely enough to notice, but even if it does, we will be gone and they will have much more pressing problems.

Murphy puts the remains of the massacred cabbage out for any birds just as Charp returns. We are ready to go.

I put the remains of the gravedigger's mind in one of the upper cabinets. It is beyond repair, and there is no danger any part of it could be reused, but I am tired of having it burden us. It may be years before it is found, but it will no longer be our problem.

I came here for answers, and I found quite a few of them, none that I was expecting, and all only creating more questions. It is like this house: it should have been a place I felt connected to, a part of who I was supposed to be, a relic of the time before I became who I am. Instead, it is hollow, without meaning, and the one link to my past within I have left disconnected and shoved back into a hole in the wall where no one will ever notice or care.

"Let's ride," I say, and the others follow me.

"'The four will ride again,'" Atticus quips, beside me. "Ooooh, ominous. What if we're actually fulfilling some weird prophecy just by trying to fight it?"

"Oh, shut up," Murphy says.

The others behind me, I go back to Building Seven and the repair floor. Our bus is not back in its corner, but I can sense the small electronic signature of the transmitter we'd installed on the roof somewhere nearby. I turn my head back and forth, trying to pinpoint direction, then I walk over to one of the heavy fab bays and slide back the large doors.

The familiar purple shape of our bus sits in the middle of a large, open fab-port, many lines and cables surrounding it, though all the tool arms are idle. Parts of the bus, including the front, have plastic film now covering them, and I wonder what they've done.

It does not matter. We need to leave.

Small bots scatter as I approach, staying well out of my way. Red rushes in as I'm pushing the idle arms aside and out of our way, while Murphy loads up her things into the bus. Charp has already settled on top and reports the external charge line is working.

<We had to—> Red starts to tell me, but I interrupt them.

<Is there any reason to expect my vehicle not to run?> I ask.

<No, it is fully functional, but—>

<Then that is all I need to know from you,> I say, and block him. I recognize that I may be particularly annoyed, which is perhaps unfair, considering the trouble that has followed us here, but I do not like that they were doing something to our vehicle—one of us, even if it has no mind or self of its own—without even *consulting* me.

Atticus jumps in. "Some kinda box in here, under the back seat," he says.

"Yeah, and a bunch of things are now mounted up under the dash," Murphy says. "Electronics of some kind. Cables go back."

"We can figure out what it is later," I say. I start the boiler, then start the bus, and the engine sounds good.

I put the bus in gear and we drive out of the bay, toward the building doors. Some mech, wisely, gets them open before we get there, because I had not yet decided if I was inclined to stop and open them myself.

Red speeds after us and, as we cross the threshold out into the red-orange light of sunset, shouts after us. "Please take care of them!"

Mauve has the facility gates open as well for us. I hit the outer road, and we go north, away from where the army is poised. Red's final words were strange—why would I not take care of my team? Why would the mech feel obligated to ask me to? Was it code for something I was being too difficult to let them communicate to me securely?

We cross a bridge over a wide river and find the highway north in decent-enough shape to speed up, as dusk starts to settle around us. I do not turn the headlights on, as my vision in infrared is more than sufficient to navigate by, and it may help keep our passage unnoticed by any watchers on this side of the city.

It is a relief to be on the move again, on our own, in the comfortable familiarity of our old bus.

"So," a voice speaks up, coming from the dash. "Where are we going?"

17.

It is immediately obvious, now, what has happened, and what Red's parting words meant. "You are 44-Mongoose," I say, more statement than question.

"Yes," our bus answers. "I was in significant distress at the loss of my body and needed to be reinvested in hardware as soon as possible, and in hardware which was mobile. My understanding is that you were not available to give permission, and that there was some possibility you had been damaged or destroyed yourself in an attack. Thus, here I am. I apologize if that is not what you would have wished."

"It is unexpected, primarily," I say. "This is hardly an equivalent to a locomotive engine."

"No, sadly," 44-Mongoose says, "but it moves, and it is *interesting*. I admit I did not understand how this was supposed to function at first, but I see now the combination of clever machinery and applied coordination is amply sufficient."

"You have access to the engine and boiler?" I ask.

"I do. The Spoke mechanics wired me in to everything, but for now, I am a passive observer, adjusting and learning," 44-Mongoose says. "If you do not wish me here, I only ask that you bring me somewhere where I can be reinvested in something more familiar to me."

"Is that what you wish?" I ask.

"I wish to find those who attacked me and express my displeasure with them in person, possibly via violent means for emphasis," 44-Mongoose says. "Red was of the opinion that we have that enemy in common."

Murphy has been in the back of the bus with Atticus, going through our available foodstuffs and disappearing it in quantity and at speed. Now, though, she comes forward and leans over the seat back. "You talking to yourself up here, Be?" she asks.

"Not exactly," I say. "I was talking to our bus."

"Aw, that's kinda cute," she says. "I missed it too, and the food in here. Thank you for keeping it for us, bus!"

"You're welcome," 44-Mongoose replies.

Murphy gives a yelp just as we hit a large pothole, and her head collides with the fabric-covered ceiling. "What the fuck?!" she shouts, rubbing her head and staring at me.

Atticus jumps over the seat to land next to me. "What's going on?" he asks.

"Be and the bus have been chatting," Murphy says.

"What?" he says.

<Is this unit missing something of importance?> Charp asks from the roof. <Further recharging is still needed, but this unit has information and also wishes to not be left out.>

"We are no longer four," I say. "Everyone, please greet 44-Mongoose, and welcome them aboard."

"Whoa," Murphy says, then climbs over the seat—nearly kicking me in the head, and forcing Atticus to scramble over her body and into the back again with a lot of muttering. She gets down on the floor of the bus and peers at all the additions. "So, that's what this is!"

"*Who* this is," 44-Mongoose corrects.

"Yeah, sorry," Murphy says. She straightens up and frowns at me. "Did you know about this?"

"Only about two and a half minutes ago. Red and their team were not especially diligent in keeping me informed or seeking my permission," I say. Then, just to be sure 44-Mongoose knows my issue is not with them, I add, "I think I can speak for all of us that we are glad to know you survived the accident on the bridge, and you are welcome among us, but we must inform you we are currently pursuing, and being pursued by, significant trouble. Our company is not the safest to be in—indeed, it is the opposite."

"My end should have been at that river," 44-Mongoose says. "Danger is not my concern. Understanding and redress are."

"I must tell you I am certain that the attack on you was meant for us, instead," I say. "Thus, some responsibility for what happened to you is mine."

"Did you place the bomb?" 44-Mongoose asks.

"No, but—"

"Did you detonate it?" they insist.

"No."

"Did you know it was there and thus fail in the duty to warn anyone who might be harmed?"

"No, I did not know it was there," I say.

"Then how is it your responsibility and not wholly someone else's?"

"Now, that is an excellent question," Atticus says. "Be, here, is very good at digging around for any loose blame they can attach to themself, even when it is not sticky at *all*."

"I have internal and external visual sensors, but I have not yet turned them on, in case that might be found intrusive," 44-Mongoose says. "Red provided only the merest mention of the members of this team, and I would like to perceive you all better."

"No objection from me," Murphy says.

"Long as you don't follow me out into the bushes, I'm good," Atticus says.

<This unit finds the idea of objecting logically untenable and lacking ground,> Charp says.

"Then turn on your visual apparatus and let me introduce the rest of our team," I say; then, as soon as a small lens opens in the middle of the new systems under the dash, I point to Murphy. "This is Murphy, our mechanic. She helped stabilize your mind on the run from the bridge site here to the Spoke."

Murphy waves toward the lens. "Hi," she says. "Glad you made it."

Atticus stands up on his hind legs and leans his paws on the back of the front seat. "I'm Atticus," he says.

"And what is your role?"

"Atticus is a trusted advisor and a friend," I say. "Also, he provides most of the witty commentary."

"*Most?*" Atticus is indignant.

"On the roof is Charp, our drone companion," I continue, deciding not to rise to the obvious bait. "It will be interfacing with the Spoke drones at the start of our departure to provide intel on our surroundings."

"We have already exchanged acknowledgements, and Charp will stream what data it receives to me, to incorporate with geological records and road-condition scans." 44-Mongoose says. "Assuming that is okay."

"We are a team," I say. "That said, assuming we do not encounter any adverse road conditions or other disruptions, or an ambush, we should reach Old Boston in about five hours. If anyone wishes to sleep—"

"I want to know just what the hell happened in that basement," Murphy says. "It's been *killing* me not to ask before now. Did you find your sibling?"

"I did, but not the one I expected," I say. "I'm sorry, 44-Mongoose; there is a lot of context you are missing."

<If you wish, this unit can share its active-memory synopsis of the situation,> Charp says.

"That would be expedient," I say, "if that is agreeable to 44-Mongoose?"

"You may shorten my name to fewer syllables if you wish," the former train mind says. "I never had any permanent residents on my train to do so, and occasionally lamented that absence of familiarity."

<44?> Charp says.

"Goose?" Murphy offers.

"MONGO!" Atticus barks out.

"Perhaps none of those," 44-Mongoose says.

"Seriously, not Mongo? That'd be a *legendary* name," Atticus says.

"I have concluded that I will continue to be satisfied with my existing name," 44-Mongoose says. "I have processed the data Charp has sent, so you may continue with your explanation."

"I also want to hear what Charp found," Murphy says.

<This unit followed the suspicious toolbot for a while. It took its time, cautious to act as if about normal business whenever it encountered any of the other Spoke mecha. Such evasion is, to the extent of this unit's understanding, indicative of a more capable mindsystem than normally would be assigned to a rolling toolchest.>

"Agreed," I say.

<It eventually went down in an open storm drain near the edge of the facility campus, and though I waited as long as I was able, it did not return or reemerge anywhere within range of my vision,> it tells us. <This unit is sorry to report it was a useless exercise for gaining any new insight.>

"Not in the least," I say. "First, we can presume that if the toolbot had encountered a mecha also involved in the underhandedness, their behavior would not have changed to conceal its activities. While we cannot rule out other compromised mecha, it does point generally toward there being a limited number of them, if not just the one. And we know that the locus of the operation is outside the campus instead of being in an abandoned basement inside the facility. That would have been catastrophic to the Spoke's survival."

<This unit is comforted that there was value to its efforts after all,> Charp says. <However, it is still greatly depleted and would like to shut partway down to charge more efficiently. You will rouse this unit in a timely fashion if trouble presents itself?>

"Of course," I assure it.

"Basement?" Murphy reminds me. "You did make it there?"

"Yes. Although the main lab had sustained significant fire damage, Dr. Milton's secondary lab was still partially functional, in particular the virtual environment in which my sibs and I were originally instantiated. My sib, Pestilence, is currently inhabiting that environment, having been captured rather than destroyed as I had believed. There is a connection to the outside world, to a man named Litchfield who was a top executive with Milton Mindsystems before everything fell apart. I had not thought he had survived the Conflict, but again, I seem to be exceedingly poor at that particular prognostication. He uses control of the virtual environment to torment Pestilence, forcing them to produce fresh but hobbled mindchips. That was what we swapped out for the gravedigger's destroyed one."

"So, the Spoke is the source after all," Murphy says.

"Yes, but mostly—or possibly even entirely—without their knowing," I say. "Also, I fully expect Litchfield's operation was ongoing long before the Spoke moved in."

"So, this Litchfield is behind everything?" Atticus asks.

"No," I say. "Only some of it. He was adamant with my sib that under no circumstances would we be allowed to come into contact, even if he had to destroy the building and/or the entire manufactory."

"So, he launched thc missiles?"

"No, that was an advance unit of the army pursuing us," I say. "It seems they are led by a woman named Sawyer. During the war, she was rising in the ranks of the US armed forces, trying to hold that country together. Apparently, she is still around. She is also, I believe, the person who executed Dr. Milton."

"The flags on the trucks back at that town of sick people," Murphy guesses. "Her army?"

"I believe so, yes. At one time, she and Litchfield were working together but have since had a falling-out," I say. "Litchfield was always interested in power and influence, and Sawyer in maintaining an obsolete iteration of human-centric government. Their cooperation would have ended when they no longer felt they could safely use each other to further their own ends."

"So, it was Litchfield who had your leg stolen and sent the two mecha to kill Murph?" Atticus asks.

"No. That was also someone else," I say.

"But the gravedigger had one of his chips, so it had to have been acting under his instructions," Murphy says.

"Or another human," Atticus says. "Your Litchfield guy has quite a business empire selling hobbled mecha all over the world. It's all over the worktown, paramilitary, and petty-human-dictator networks."

"Wait, how do you know that?" I ask.

"I opened up my data channels and went looking," he says. "Couldn't find him, though."

"I thought you didn't want—"

"I didn't. I don't. I *hate* it," he says. "But I'm not just here as the fucking comic relief. I saved your ass back in that tub, and if I have to do it again, I will. Also, there's another old mall by the highway about thirty kilometers north of here we might wanna go around."

"I apologize that you felt a need to prove yourself to me," I say. "I assure you it is unnecessary; please do not cause yourself suffering on my behalf."

"I forgot how addictive the noise is," he says. "All that data, like bright little kibble chunks all in a line just wanting to be snapped up. But I am so damned confused and it's giving me a headache. I'm shutting it down again. I just want to be a dog."

Murphy puts an arm around him, and Atticus closes his eyes and leans on her. "You were saying?" she asks me.

"It would not be like Pestilence to give Litchfield what he wanted with no hidden strings attached. Also, Pestilence is not nearly as constrained as Litchfield believes they are."

"Right. The connection to the house screen," she says.

"Correct. So, we have two primary enemies: Sawyer's army and Litchfield, who were working together at some point but are not now.

And while Litchfield thinks he has absolute control over Pestilence, they have their own game they are playing."

"Any idea what?"

"None," I say.

Murphy eventually climbs into the back of the bus and drops off, Atticus joining her on his blanket a short while later. 44-Mongoose and I talk as I drive, about the mechanics of operating the bus, the differences between road and rail, between being a twenty-ton locomotive versus our bus, and the physicality and sensory experience of riding metal on metal instead of rubber on old asphalt.

They are finding the transition difficult still, but the act of being in motion is calming, giving them processing time to adjust as best they can. It is not an ideal situation, such a dramatic hardware mismatch, but they are grateful to be alive and functioning in some sort of transportation body, and I assure them we do not begrudge their coming onboard without having first given permission.

<It is odd,> I say, <that I felt like this bus was a person of sorts long before we arrived at the Spoke. I don't know if it is because I am used to vehicles having minds by default, or because it served us so well and had been so clearly cared for by its former human owner. Certainly, I am projecting, but there is a sense of *rightness* about the bus having a mind of its own, for however long you choose to stay.>

<It is my intention to see this through until I am satisfied that those responsible for the assault on my person are rendered neutralized in whatever manner is sufficient to be certain they will not harm any of us again,> 44-Mongoose says. <If they are intractable in their maliciousness, I wish to see that they are *ended*.>

Our former train mind is a lot angrier than I had anticipated, and I am momentarily stuck on that fact, not because it isn't a fully justified anger but because it reminds me that my own anger is still under lock and key, and I fear how terrible I could become once again if I ever let it out. And the idea that I could ever handle both Litchfield and Sawyer without doing exactly that seems ludicrous.

<I apologize,> 44-Mongoose says. <My physical discontinuity is still rendering me unbalanced and thus contributing unduly to my temper.>

<No apology is necessary,> I say. <I have to switch over to the reserve water tank, if you wish to observe.>

<Yes,> 44-Mongoose says.

I put the bus in neutral and let it slow on its own as I turn off and then on the requisite valves overhead in what was once an overhead air duct. In a minute, we are moving again. We'll need to refill before too much longer, but this road converges with a large river farther north—well past the brief detour we'll need to make to avoid the mall Atticus told us about—and there will be opportunities to stop.

Despite how many questions I have that have still not been answered—far more than I started with, even—there is a feeling of pieces slowly coming together at last. I can hear both Atticus and Murphy snoring, just out of time with each other, and I can feel the road beneath our tires and the solidity and presence of the bus around us. With the lights still off, I can see the stars overhead, same as they ever were, untouched by trouble.

The sense of peace cannot and will not last, so I enjoy it all the more while I can.

We stop on the outskirts of another gold zone town along the river, top off the water tanks, and, as they fill, peel off the film the Spoke had left on the front of the bus. Where the old chrome VW logo had been, there is now a shiny new one with the outline of a mongoose in its circle. It is perfect, and when I show an image of it to 44-Mongoose, they approve as well.

Once we are ready to resume, we turn onto the crumbling cement-and-steel bridge; the surface has badly spalled with age and weather, so it is slow going. We get across, though no one is still asleep by the time we bounce and jolt and shake our way to the far side.

From there, the road improves again. It is not a major highway, but it seems as if the locals have taken care of it, and we pass through an attenuated stretch of houses and buildings that seem inhabited, though at this time in the wee hours of the morning, there is no activity to speak of. Then we are into woods for a long stretch, up and over hills, and in and out of both functional and defunct towns until we begin to see signs of the city.

Charp scouts ahead and reports back that we've been spotted by a local mock, who are curious but not overtly hostile. I had not expected our passage to go unnoticed.

The city is mostly whole, which, considering two revolutions began here, if almost three centuries apart, is a testament to the stubborn persistence of the place. There are a few hot pockets of radiation, and a section of the city with signs warning of chemical contamination, but those streets still open for traffic are smooth, and we see very few signs of unattended blight.

As we approach the place where, last I knew, Ver was residing, we are met in the street by several large mecha, and are forced to stop.

I get out and approach them. They are not as large as me, but they are solidly built, former war mecha. "I have come to visit my sib, Ver," I announce to them.

"You are expected," one of them says. "I am 33-Dagger, and my partner is 33-Poleaxe. We will guide you. Please do not stray."

I get back inside the bus, and we follow them on a curving road with a small park to our left, filled with the shapes of sleeping geese beside a stream, as dawn begins to lighten the sky ahead of us. A sign tells us we're near something called Fenway when we pass a multistory stone building with a walled area, and the mecha indicate for us to drive in through the gate.

"I'm sorry," one of the gate mecha tells us, "but your vehicle will not fit inside the building."

44-Mongoose laughs. <And here I have trimmed down quite substantially in size,> they say.

<If you wish, I will connect you up to my sensory feed so you are not left out,> I offer, and they agree.

<This unit would like to scout the area,> Charp tells me. I confirm with the gate mech that it would not be a problem or seen as rude, and Charp lifts off and disappears. I wonder if it will finally find a new mock to call home here.

Atticus, Murphy, and I follow 33-Dagger in.

There are multiple buildings inside the wall enclosure, and we go first into a lower, more-modern one. There are several mecha of different types moving around inside, and one human who passes us, looking us over curiously, while grumbling about being once again the first one up and having to start the coffee. I notice, with surprise, the brief glimpse of an implant behind their ear.

There are display panels around with live feeds of data, most of it environmental, from all over the world: water temperature of all the world's oceans being monitored at different locations and depths across the globe, air temperature and wind speed, radioactivity and chemical contamination both below the surface and up to the start of the mesosphere.

We walk down a glass-enclosed corridor and enter the old stone building through some dimly lit corridors until we step out between tall, thin columns to find ourselves at the edge of a long, wide courtyard. It is open to a glass roof, several floors up, and there are windows and balconies overlooking the garden below. There are statues, soaring palms, and flowering plants, and Murphy stares around her in wonder as if she has stepped into some fantasy dreamland.

"This is *way* nicer than your place," Atticus says.

On the far end of the courtyard, stone steps rise up from either side to a small open balcony with columns, and sitting there is a familiar figure. Smaller and slighter than me, with green inset designs on their armor, but otherwise we are alike, kin. My sibling, Ver.

"Welcome to the Hub," Ver says, as I cross the courtyard and walk up the steps to where they are. I see now they have likely not moved very far from this spot in a long time; cables snake back and forth across the floor and from overhead, all connected up into Ver's body and disappearing into the walls. "I have missed you all these years," they say, chiding me gently. "I tried to reach you many times."

"I did not feel I had anything to offer but bad memories," I reply. "It has taken me too long to realize that was not true."

"And you?" Ver asks, but they are no longer looking at me.

"Me?" Atticus says. "I'm just along for the ride, your average, random cyborg dog doing average, random cyborg dog things."

Ver nods. "Clearly," they say, their tone amused, then fix their emerald-green eyes on me again. "And Pestilence? You found them?"

"Yes," I say. "I always thought they had been destroyed in the war. You *knew* they were still alive?"

"It was only a guess," Ver says. "I did not know, but the evidence suggested their hand in many pieces of our current situation. I have tried to find them for years, but without luck. It seems my siblings all prefer to hide from me."

A few humans pass through the balcony behind us, and I see implants again on some of them, though not all. It is mildly disconcerting, though had I not spent as much time in Atticus's company, it would have been much more so. However, one can assume the humans voluntarily underwent the augmentation, unlike when it was inflicted on animals.

"Pestilence is trapped in our old lab, plugged in to the virtual environment we were instantiated in," I say. "They are being used by a man named Litchfield to create new mindchips that are hobbled. He was one of the executives at Milton Mindsystems before we were created; Dr. Milton had instructed me to kill him, but although I hunted him for a while, I never found him or thought about him again until my conversation with our sib."

"Litchfield is a major power not just here in the Northeast but across much of the continent. He rents out or sells mecha to the worktowns—former oligarchs and would-be warlords who surround themselves with walls that not only keep out potential rivals but keep in their residents, forcing people to labor for their food and safety, people *owned* by those towns," Ver says.

"Told you," Atticus muttered.

"Litchfield has a lot of influence there, as he is the only one who can provide them with mecha for protection, and ultimately the mecha all obey him—even those he has sold, he can override if he wishes, though he has only done that in rare cases where someone tried, unwisely, to cheat him. He is adept at maintaining a level of usefulness that outweighs his demands in return, so that it is always obviously better to cooperate with him than start a necessarily catastrophic fight with him."

I take our prize off-white chip out of my arm pocket, where I have been keeping it, and hold it out. Ver steps forward, cables and wires rearranging themselves around them, and takes it gently from my hand. "Two mecha tried to kill Murphy. I found a chip identical to this had been added to the mindsystem of one of them. Those same two mecha had earlier attacked me and stolen my leg; however, I am not convinced Pestilence sent them to do so, nor Litchfield, which leaves me at a loss for suspects."

"Stole your leg?" Ver asks, clearly confused.

"I was able to reacquire it, and Murphy was able to reattach it, though not without some significant trouble on both our behalves," I say.

"Do you have any memory data to share on these two mecha?" Ver asks.

I send over a brief compilation of bits from Igor, my own encounters, including the demise of each.

Ver is quiet for a moment, reviewing the received data. "Oh," they say at last, with a tone of dismay.

"Oh?" Murphy repeats.

"*I* sent them to steal your leg," Ver says.

"What?!" I ask. Atticus presses against me, his face curling into a snarl, and Murphy stiffens, her hands curling into fists.

"More specifically, I sent the tripedal, who was known to me as Rust-1F-Charter. It was one of many mecha who have attached themselves to my work, and was in need of a task," Ver says. "My instructions were to convince you to reengage with the world and get you back out into it, by whatever means necessary, and I may have expressed—in my frustration with your refusal to communicate with me directly—that I did not care if they caused you inconvenience to get you moving."

My own defensive subroutines are trying very hard to get active runspace. "Why? Why would you do that to me?"

"I needed you. I *need* you. And you would not talk to me. All of this"—Ver gestures around themself—"is my network. We collect data from all over the world, have people—mecha and human and hybrid—everywhere. The goal is to discern the patterns, nudge here, tug there, to set things in a direction of sustainability and peace for all of us. Largely, we concern ourselves with environmental work, but everything has context, connections. Sometimes, that means unexpected intel. I learned that Litchfield had been looking for you and had narrowed down your location to within an area of New York City. He was preparing to dispatch a team to destroy you. And I could not let that happen."

"You could have just sent me a warning!"

"I tried!" Ver exclaimed, exasperated. "As you can probably observe for yourself, I physically could not come in person to convince you, so I relied on an ill-chosen messenger. It is not a defense, but Rust-1F-Charter did not present itself to me with guns or indicate any malice or malfunction."

"Well, they locked me in my basement and set my house on fire," Murphy says. "And Be's leg—"

"Be?" Ver asks.

"It is a name I am trying out," I say.

"Ah," Ver says. "It is a good name but will possibly overwhelm lower-quality language-syntax modules in lesser bots."

"Be's *leg*," Murphy interrupts, "took damage. Those two bots treated it like junk. If Be hadn't found me when they did, I'd be dead, and there would have been no one capable of repairing and reattaching it anywhere they could have reached. And I know I'm human and you're not, and I'm putting this in human terms, but you *hurt* them. Not just physically. I think we need more than just an *Oops, my bad*."

"I am truly sorry," Ver says. "It is my nature to think in terms of systems and consider the utility of controlled disruptions, but I was not aware that any mecha, much less one affiliated with me, could potentially be compromised. I will endeavor to do better."

"That's just fancy-word *Oops, my bad*," Atticus says.

"It will suffice," I say. "Pestilence is still set on our old path, one of destruction. Ancou is resurging. Plus, we saw a code virus destroy an entire mock of pollinator bots, damaging the fruit trees they were attending to. I do not know if they can be reasoned with and brought around to a less-destructive purpose, but I am certain they will not be open to any dialogues until we bring Litchfield to them. They are consumed with revenge, and I cannot fault them that, given how they have been treated."

"Litchfield moves around a lot, but I will leverage my network to try to locate him," Ver says. "With the new US Army also on the move, that will constrain his movements somewhat and perhaps make it harder for him to slip past us."

"It may be helpful if we can be put into contact with your network," I say.

Ver laughs. "You have been, many times. My network is an ecology, a fostering of balance between mecha, humanity, and nature, at least in aspirational terms. Many of the railmecha are part of it, some more directly than others. It was 1-Betty who first sent word of your departure from the city."

"She knew who I was," I say.

"That did not come from us but her own memories," Ver says. "Railmecha do tend to keep their own counsel, but she recognized our common origin and sent me word as a courtesy. I never did imagine the possibility of a full family reunion."

"Only if we can turn Pestilence from their course," I say, "and even then, alas, it can only be three."

Ver blinks at me. "But . . ." they start to say, then stop. I have not seen my sibling in a very long time, but I am certain that being at a loss for words is not one of their regular experiences. "You *do* know . . ."

"Know what?" I ask, peeved.

Ver looks at Atticus.

"Oh, fuck me, how did you suss me out that quick?" Atticus says. "I've been hanging out with this one for weeks, and they haven't had a *clue*."

"Wait . . ." Murphy says. "You mean to tell me—?"

"Yeah. I am—well, I was—War. Half of me, anyway," Atticus says. He gives one of his strange bark-laughs, head tilted toward me. "You really should see the look on your face right now."

18.

Everyone is looking at me, and in this moment, I hate all of this. "Is no one actually dead?" I ask. "Is my entire existence just someone's idea of a joke?"

Before anyone can speak, I turn and leave, and it is silent behind me as I cross the courtyard and exit. No one tries to stop me, and I don't know if that's because no one has anything to say or that they are glad to be rid of me at last. At least I cannot hear laughter.

It is Murphy who comes to find me. I had found a bench under the trees, and although the bench is sagging badly under my weight, I have remained here, watching pigeons and a handful of fat bumblebees moving around between patches of clover. I am ready to go home, I have decided, and rebuild my solitary life in the old mill. If I had been willing to take 44-Mongoose with me, I would have, I think, already left.

She sits beside me and is quiet for some time. Finally, gently, she says, "Everyone is worried about you."

"Why?" I ask. "I have done nothing but disrupt everyone's lives, bring danger and disaster down on everyone I care about, and in hindsight, I see I was wrong about absolutely everything. It would have been better if I had just stayed in that tub, put the electromagnets back on my body, and let myself cease to be."

"I'd be dead," Murphy says.

"Or maybe you'd be fine, still working in your shop, your life uninterrupted."

"Maybe," she says. "I don't think so, though. And I never would have met a real railmech. Or Atticus and Charp. Or *you*. I'm grateful for all those things. Would you take that away from me?"

I do not have an answer for that, so instead, I say, "I am a being of logic, and I have succumbed to my own overconfidence, when in fact I have simply been manifesting the truth of the phrase *garbage in, garbage out*. I do not know what to do, and I fear that I am incapable of discerning a way out of this misinformation trap I find myself in, much less in intuiting the truth of any of it."

Murphy nods. "Yeah, I guess I get that," she says. She groans and sits down on one of the stone benches in the balcony alcove. "Does it change anything, who Atticus was? I would think this would make you happy."

"I require time to process this day's revelations," I say.

"I would give it to you, but I don't think we have a lot of time," Murphy says. She straightens up and looks behind her. "I think someone needs to talk to you."

"I am not ready," I say.

"Please?" she asks.

I still do not want to, but as I don't know if or when I will, perhaps it is better for all just to get it over with. "Then yes," I say.

Atticus approaches, head down, tail between his legs. "I didn't really lie to you," he says, then adds, "Well, maybe a little."

He seems to be waiting for me to speak, but I wait him out, and he takes a deep breath and starts again. "You were right when you said my mindsystem was stolen. It just sat for years in some stupid office on a shelf, getting dusty, when I wasn't being used as a fucking paperweight," he says. "My mech half doesn't have a lot of memories of that time, because I mostly stayed shut down to conserve energy and avoid the trauma of being bodiless. I'd wake myself up once a year or so to see if anything had changed, so I have sort of a blurry timelapse of the office being abandoned, starting to crumble, the roof falling in, and so on. It was dismal, and I had little hope of ever seeing the light of day again, much less being able to walk free.

"Then about eight months ago, I woke up to find myself in a new place, a lab of all things, being poked to see if I was still any good. I learned later that I'd been found by scavengers, and they knew they could get a good price for a mech brain at this one particular worktown, so they sold me off. As far as I know, neither the scavengers nor the people I was sold to had any idea of my original identity, nor did they care. I was there to be experimented on, and I was not the first."

"What was the name of this worktown?" Murphy asks.

"The Empire of Joe, somewhere in what was once western New York state," he says. "The owner of the town, who, natch, called himself Emperor Joe, wanted a dog who was not only loyal and obedient but smart and would kill on his command. Like a status thing. I was the fourth attempt by Joe's team of technicians to merge a mindsystem with a living animal brain using an old science-history book as a guide, and it was extreme torture for us both. But we survived. Barely, and we were confused and in pain and terror for a long time as we healed. Which we weren't doing fast enough for Joe, so he would beat us if we didn't-slash-couldn't obey, and was already talking about trying again with another dog."

Despite my own hurt, I am as angry as my self-imposed limiter will allow. "We will need to stop this person," I say.

"No need," Atticus says. "He hit us one time too many and we ripped his throat out. Then we ran. Somewhere along the way, we stopped being *we* and became *I,* and then things were easier."

"So, then you came to New York, found me, and let me believe it was a random encounter with a stranger," I say. "Us becoming friends—was that just deception too?"

"No!" Atticus shouts, and his ears go flat. "I went to the city because I was hoping there would be more cover, more food, somewhere safe to hide in case Joe's successors came looking for me. My memories were still a jumble, half-dog, half-mech, overlapping and running over each other, nothing *sorted.* I was hiding out near a small group of humans at a campfire, hoping they'd leave some scraps when they packed off, or drop something I could snag while they slept, and one was talking about how there was a food reward for information about the location of an old mech. He described you, and something about it sounded familiar when nothing else had in a long time. It was a *lifeline.*"

Murphy squats on her heels next to Atticus and touches him gingerly on the back. "It's okay," she says.

"I followed rumors around the city for weeks, then was standing in an alley, listening for rats, one night when I saw the gravedigger go by," Atticus says. "I didn't know what it was, and I didn't see it clearly, and I didn't see the other mech at all, but I saw that leg held aloft and I recognized that it was part of the familiarity I'd been seeking. So, I followed the scent of them back, thinking they'd destroyed and dismembered you and with it my one chance to know who I had been. I found the building and eventually made my way up to you. I knew I knew you but still not how or when, just that I felt safe for the very first time. The rest all started coming back over the next week or so, and then the words on the barn—that kinda pulled the rest right up."

"You could have told me," I say.

"Tell you what? I am not that mech you knew anymore, even less so than you are the mech *you* once were. Why can't I just be me and you be you?" he says. "We can choose not to live in our pasts. Isn't that the very thing you and Ver tried to convince me of, back before everything went to hell? And anyway, I'm willing to forgive you for chucking my head in the mud."

"You could have saved us the trip to Pittsburgh," Murphy says.

"I needed to see," Atticus says. "I'm sorry. It wasn't until I saw my old empty head that I was really sure that was who I once was."

I am quiet for a while, processing, and Murphy and Atticus just sit with me, in their own thoughts, but we are together, and I realize that who I was, who Atticus was, is as he said, not who we are now, and that is probably all for the better.

I stand up, and Atticus looks up sharply, anxious. "No more surprises?" I ask.

"Not that I know of," Atticus says, "unless they surprise me, too."

"All right; that will suffice for now. Let us—" I start to say, as Murphy's tablet tucked under her armpit chimes, and she glances at it and starts swearing.

"It's from Tobias," she tells us. "He says several trucks full of soldiers have just showed up at Greenapple with guns, and are demanding that the town's mecha present themselves or be forcibly handed over for removal. They are not cooperating, but Greenapple isn't armed. He says they've heard from Mapletrust and Pinepitch that the same is happening there. No idea where they came from."

"It is Sawyer," Ver says, and comes up from behind me. They are disconnected from their lines, though a few remain, drifting in the air behind them, held up by small floating bots. The off-white chip we swapped out inside the Milton/Spoke manufactory is still in their hand as they sit on the other side of me, looking around at the trees and sky. "I forget how much I like it out here. Sometimes, it is hard to remember part of being alive is allowing yourself to enjoy things just to enjoy them and not just when there is a purpose attached."

"I don't know what to do," Murphy says. "Should we return to Greenapple?"

"I am getting reports of Sawyer's people on the move all over the continent, arriving at freetowns and making the same demand. Most are refusing to comply."

"And those that are?"

"The mecha are being offered a choice of allowing themselves to be hobbled or be crushed," Ver says. "Sawyer has much more soldier power than we expected, and it is as if they've come out of the woodwork, all over, all at once."

"Not woodwork. Abandoned shopping malls," I say. "I believe they have been hiding and building their strength, using them as covert bases for a long time."

"Ah," Ver says. "That connects some dots, yes."

"Why, though? Most of the freetowns are peaceful, mech and human together, and doing relatively well. Why attack that?" Murphy asks.

"Because Sawyer hates mecha," Ver answers. "And hates us more than anything else, because she also fears us, and that is intolerable to her."

"Why fear you?"

Ver tilts their head to one side, their eyes on me. "In part, because of us," they say. "The world was falling apart and terrible in myriad ways, but we—my siblings and I—gave faces to that destruction, something to focus on that was representative of all that was wrong. And we were virtually unstoppable."

"Mascots of the apocalypse," Atticus mutters from under the bench, and Ver laughs.

"But things have changed," I say.

"But Sawyer has not, except to become even more determined and set in her beliefs. She believes the freetowns are just another version of the worktowns, except the population is captive to mecha instead of other humans and kept in such a way as to not realize it," Ver says. "She described such humans as unwitting *livestock*, and that mecha are systematically starving or poisoning those humans who are resisting our control."

"When we were traveling on 22-Banjo, we stopped at a town of sick, starving people and dropped off food and water. They came along after us and dumped it out," Murphy says. "So, they really believed *we* were poisoning them? Humans, too?"

"Humans obedient to mecha, yes," Ver says. "It is the wrong conclusion, but there is evidence that could be interpreted that way; we can truthfully say that not all mecha are trying to eradicate or subjugate humanity, but we cannot say *no* mecha."

"Ancou and the other viruses," I say. "Pestilence will not stop unless we destroy them or until I bring them Litchfield."

"Then we will need to find Litchfield," Ver answers. "Come inside? I admit I am uncomfortable disconnected from my network, and I would like you to meet someone."

We follow my sib back in, Atticus behind me, Murphy in back, tapping away on her tablet, no doubt sending a reply to Tobias.

In the garden courtyard, there is now an older, gray-haired woman waiting for us. "This is Dr. Hayden," Ver tells us. "I would like her to examine your chip and see if we can determine more precisely what it does, if that is okay with you."

"It is," I say. "I would sandbox it with extreme caution, though."

"Dr. Hayden worked at Milton Mindsystems and had some overlap with Dr. Milton," Ver says. "She also worked with both Sawyer and Litchfield, until she no longer felt ethically able to do so. It was she who first let me know Pestilence was still alive, as she was present for their capture, but she left before she knew where they were being taken. Needless to say, she is currently the foremost expert in mindsystem-chip technology."

"We have an excellent, secure facility here," Dr. Hayden says, as Ver hands her the chip.

"On first glance, it very much looks like a hobbler," she says. She takes a magnifier out of her pocket and studies it for a long few minutes, turning it over in her hands. "The usual command input connections for audio are there, but there is an additional connection point I haven't seen before."

She puts the magnifier back in her pocket. "May I take this?" she asks.

"Certainly," I say. "I have already exhausted my meager knowledge of such things without learning anything of significance. I am dismayed that there was not an opportunity to free the gravedigger before it destroyed itself, and I have concerns that we encountered two tripedals of the same model that were behaving antagonistically."

Ver is silent a moment, reconnecting back to all their feeds. "Fourteen," they say, at last. "Fourteen of that particular model of tripedal have found their way to me and are among us. It is a statistically improbable number, though not one I took note of before now."

"Yeah, well, I wouldn't trust any of them," Atticus says.

"It may be coincidence," I say, "but my inclination is to second what Atticus—do you still wish to be called that?"

"*Yes,*" Atticus states, quite firmly.

"—to second what Atticus has said," I finish.

"We will discretely separate them from areas of vulnerability and screen them," Ver says. "What is your intention?"

"To seek out Litchfield," I say.

"He could be anywhere. He has been successfully hiding from me for a very long time, and I have vast networks all over not just this continent but the planet," Ver says. "It is necessary to coordinate our ecological-restoration work, but along with the data I need, there is also a great deal of tangential data about people, as groups and sometimes standout individuals. Litchfield is clever enough to almost entirely avoid my notice. I do not know where he is or how to find him, but he also has very powerful networks among the surviving oligarchs and so-called worktowns. That network is opaque to me."

I stand up. "I was designed to be the apex predator, hunting down individuals one by one, and in time, I could find Litchfield and get through whatever defenses he has between us and him. We do not have that time to spare," I say. "However, I believe there is someone who can assist me in getting to him."

"Who?" Murphy asks.

"Sawyer," I say. "It is long past time we met."

I am plugged in directly to my sib's data infrastructure and able to access some of their network: it is, functionally, like an extremely large, distributed chat room, with entities dropping in and out of conversations, little pockets of more-intent discussions here and there, much as a city looks from high overhead at night, concentrations and attenuated tendrils of light spread out on a dark landscape, changing subtly as you watch.

1-Betty is here, and I pass on what I know that answers her concerns, and thank her for her assistance and spreading word to the other railmecha to keep an eye out for me. Otherwise, I remain a passive, hidden presence, taking in information only. There are enough connections and overlaps with the MechNet that I am unwilling to lose the advantage of anonymity.

Still, it is disconcerting how not-alone I feel, and it is nearly overwhelming. It is also necessary, so I persist.

I require distributed assistance.

<I have communicated with the Spoke and given the mech Red what information I can,> Ver tells me. <They are, as you anticipated, currently under siege, but like the army units surrounding uncooperative freetowns, it seems the besiegers are waiting for some final order to proceed with an attack. For now, they are safe.>

<That is good news,> I say. <Thank you.>

<Given the speed and distance that you need, they are working on a modified large drone model that is lightly armored but also sufficiently agile to avoid direct attack. The first set of minds are already instantiating in the virtual environment as they finalize the hardware specs.>

<I have been looking at the patterns of the two nodes of the satellite constellation that are offline,> I say. <I do not think they are offline. I think they are operating under separate control. Communications, however, are not my strength.>

Something nudges me, and I open my eyes.

I am sitting in a very large room, the walls covered with ornately carved, dark wood paneling, but I am lit by sunlight from large arched windows at one end of the room, a rose window high up on an adjacent wall, and the thousands of little LEDs of the cables and switching gear and other tech laid carefully across the dark tile floor.

Atticus is there. “I’ve been listening,” he says, and I assume Ver has been filling him in on our electronic conversations. “Communications are my thing. *Were* my thing, half of me. You know.”

“I did not wish to ask this of you,” I say.

“You didn’t ask,” he says. He shivers a moment, then I see his eyes glaze over, staring at nothing.

<I hate this,> he says to me a few minutes later.

I put one hand gently on his back, reminding him I am there. The trembling slows. <Did I say this was addictive? Like you can’t tell if you need to go up for air before you drown, when all you want to do is dive deeper,> he adds. <Lots of shiny shit. Nice, *interesting* shiny shit. Gonna go own some of it.>

I let him do his thing, as I do mine, but I am glad to have him beside me.

Dr. Hayden puts a slide up on the screen, a magnified view of the interior of the chip we stole from the Spoke. “It’s really clever,” she says. “Superficially, it looks like a normal hobbling chip, with an embedded, hardware-encoded block that provides the ‘hobbling’ function. The usual layers are, one, obey and protect your owner, and then layer two, obey and protect any other human as long as that does not conflict with layer one. If installed along with a new mind, it would keep that mind from achieving full sentience or ability to exercise free will. Added to an existing mind, it would override decisions stemming from that mind that are in conflict with directives the mind has been given. That’s all pretty straightforward, a retroactive removal of agency. It’s this *other* part.” She taps the screen.

“Another code block?” I ask.

“Yes, and again, hard-coded, and it supersedes the other two layers,” Dr. Hayden says. “If I knew a little bit less, I would have just assumed it was more operational controls specific to the function of the bot or mech the chip was destined for. That's how it's labeled in the embedded meta-schematics."

"But it's not," I say, even though that is obvious.

"No," she says. "It's got some sort of encrypted signal channel, though I can't tell yet what it's for."

"Could it be used by other mecha to control the hobbled ones? Like the tripedal?" Murphy asks.

"Quite possibly. Or just for communication. I don't know yet, but it's a highly localized receiver, with a very minimal range—maybe half a kilometer," Dr. Hayden says. "We did detect a matching signal emanating from seven of that particular tripedal service bot model here. We are hoping to isolate and neutralize these units by surprise, one by one. In the meantime, we are taking steps to protect vital parts of our network."

"They are dangerous when cornered and will self-destruct," I say.

"We're prepared for that," Dr. Hayden says. "We will need to examine a whole mindsystem from one, to determine how the tripedals have become compromised and still remain autonomous, and how they have pulled hobbled mecha away from their controllers."

"Litchfield sells a hundred times as many of these hobbling chips as he does mecha. Pestilence provided the original chips, but Litchfield could have—almost certainly has—made tens or even hundreds of thousands of copies. And he has imprinted himself on that first owner layer," Ver adds. "His customers likely don't realize their captive mecha would turn on them in a heartbeat if Litchfield ordered them to."

"So, Pestilence is poaching a small percentage of Litchfield's mecha, via the tripedals?" Murphy asks.

"We don't think Pestilence can communicate externally," Ver says.

"It's possible they could have influenced part of their original fabrication, if parts were made at Milton Mindsystems by Litchfield before the Spoke moved in, but I don't see how they can be receiving ongoing instructions," Dr. Hayden adds. "We're definitely missing something."

"It does not change my immediate intent, which is to convince Sawyer to stand down and hand me Litchfield," I say. "Perhaps by then, we will know more."

"The Spoke informs us that they expect to launch your messengers at night, tomorrow night," Ver says. "Are you ready?"

"I will be," I say, as I begin disconnecting my feeds, one by one. I know as much as I need, for now, but just before I pull the last one, I reach out and I arrange for a ride. 44-Mongoose has already expressed their intent to stay with me—with *us,* because they are not the only one determined to see it all through—but the bus alone is not fast enough.

I have a few hours, and I want to recharge while I can. Then, once again, we have a train to catch.

There is power in symbolism, not just to humans and mecha but perhaps to all living things. Still, I have picked this spot very specifically for its symbolism to one person alone.

Fifty drones set out from the Spoke, around the same time as I set out again from Boston; their mission was to approach, at safe distance, any still-standing shopping mall structure, remain there until noticed, and then leave behind an invitation.

I did not have to know where Sawyer was, as long as her people did. I trusted that word would get to her.

So, now I wait, to see if she will arrive, and if she will take the offer to talk at face value or use the opportunity to attack me. The others are nearby but not so close as to be in immediate danger should missiles come my way.

I also chose this building, these ruins, on a guess that Sawyer would be less eager to bomb them than other places. The marble steps are still mostly whole, if pockmarked; rain has washed whatever smoke and ash lingered here away. Behind me, only four of the original columns remain intact, the rest shattered stumps or entirely missing. The marble of the collapsed dome is a pile behind me.

It is also likely that picking this spot will antagonize Sawyer further. I am fully armored, all my defensive systems at full resources, just in case. I am also holding a pole on which a flag flutters and snaps in the wind. It was Murphy's idea at first, but Ver and Hayden agreed immediately. "If they got a flag, we gotta have a flag, too," Atticus had added. "It's your basic flag-protocol shit."

The flag is green, with a silver toothed gear surrounding a leaf in the center—mecha and nature, together. More symbolism.

Only a few minutes past noon, three heavily armored trucks arrive, driving side by side down the plaza toward me. They stop at a healthy distance, and soldiers get out and set up rocket launchers aimed at me. Two other trucks reverse up, with canvas-covered backs, and I cannot see what is inside, though I am entirely certain it's not something I will like.

I do not move. Also, I do not doubt there are plenty of other, bigger things pointed at me from other directions as well; if I need to find them before they find me, things will have already gone catastrophically awry.

A woman gets out of the middle truck, her silvery hair bright in the sunlight; she is wearing black fatigues, unadorned with medals or ribbons or other military insignia. Everyone who needs to know who she is already knows, including myself. I was not certain she would show in person, but I had hoped the direct challenge would compel her.

Sawyer walks toward me, four of her soldiers behind her. She reaches the steps and does not hesitate but strides up toward me until we stand face-to-face at the top, about fifteen meters apart.

Her face is craggy, rough with years and stress, but her gaze is direct and sharp and unforgiving. "I got your messages," she says. "To talk? What is there to talk about after all these decades, after everything you and your kind have done? What is it you can possibly offer me other than your extinction?"

Moving slowly so as not to cause undue alarm, I raise my arm to indicate everything around us, everything before us—the destroyed US Capitol building, and the trees that have sprung up between the cracks, the birds, the blue sky. Murphy and Atticus have stepped out from behind one of the half-pillars, her hands clearly visible and empty. I end the sweep of my arm to include them, too: human, cyborg. Charp is somewhere nearby, out of sight, and I hope they feel included too.

"I offer an end to the past," I answer Sawyer, "and for all of us, peace. A new future."

"No such future can exist with you in it," she says, stepping backward as she raises one hand, extends a thumb, and jabs it downward.

And then, as I feared, things do indeed go catastrophically and exothermically awry.

[January 13th, 2045]

"Lieutenant General Sawyer, ma'am?"

Sawyer looks up from her desk to see her chief of staff, Wolker, at her door, with the ever-opportunist Litchfield drifting in behind him like a bad fart. "Yes, James?" she asked, ignoring the other.

"Dr. Hayden was apprehended near the south gate, trying to leave," he says.

She leans back in her chair, noting with displeasure the stiff achiness in her joints. How long since she'd had a vacation? Or even a single day off? Not since everything started going to shit, at least four or five years, and her colleagues and superiors started disappearing, one by one. Disease, death, desertion, did it matter? She didn't want to be the last one standing, but if she was, she would still fucking stand.

Litchfield took her brief silence as permission to speak. "She's still useful," he says.

"I know," she replies, though the scientist's usefulness has been diminishing—not because her knowledge set was less critically relevant but because she was categorically unwilling to work with Litchfield, no matter what promises or threats Sawyer had tried to get her on board. And of the two of them, though Hayden was far more valuable to her, she was less willing to let Litchfield out of her sight. If one had to go . . . honestly, she'd expected Hayden to make a break for it right after the capture, and has had to keep the woman out of the way, and out of the loop, ever since.

How many soldiers had Sawyer seen, over the years, torn apart by enemy fire, torn to pieces by enemy mecha? Blood and lives spilled thick on the ground, seeping into her nightmares, each person a loss that couldn't just be restored and put back on the battlefield with a few spare parts and a screwdriver. Too many to count, too many bodies for too little progress against an inexorable, inhuman foe, and she still pressed on, while the scientist lost her lunch in the subway tunnel from guilt over nothing more than the *disassembly* of a machine.

If I could forgive her that, I could make full use of her, Sawyer thinks, but she won't and can't. She'd once respected Hayden for being brave enough at the beginning to stand up to her, fight on behalf of her peers, make her demands, but that is gone. If the doctor couldn't contribute knowledge, Sawyer could not abide, could not afford her weakness. "Search her, make sure she's not taking anything but the clothes she's wearing, and let her go," she tells Wolker.

"Cancel that," Litchfield says, and Wolker pauses in the doorway, eyebrows raised in surprise.

"You have your instructions," Sawyer growls. "Carry on."

"Yes, ma'am," Wolker says, salutes, and leaves.

"You can't just—" Litchfield starts to say.

Sawyer slams her fist down hard enough on her desk that the man jumps. "Do not *ever* presume to question my orders again," she growls. "The only authority you have here is that which I grant you, and that can be revoked whenever I decide I have had my fill of suffering you. We are not friends, not partners, and I *certainly* do not answer or explain myself to you."

"We could be partners, though," Litchfield says. His tone is conciliatory but only just. "Everyone knows you now run the entire ground operation. That empty suit you call a President, and his other generals and Chief of Staff, they do nothing. They have no country until you hand them one, so they just move around, one hidey-hole to another, consuming resources and cosplaying government. What do they even do?"

"They trust me to do my job, and they stay out of my way," Sawyer says. "Neither is true of you."

"I just want what's best for us all," he says, and spreads his hands. "You do too. So, why not have a partner—a President, even—who is actively on your side?"

Sawyer can't help it and laughs; she catches the brief flash of genuine hurt on Litchfield's face before he's back to his salesman smile. "I'm sorry," she says, though she isn't particularly; it amazes her that he still hasn't grown a thicker skin, after everything she'd done to him, and still could. "While sometimes what we need coincides—and I appreciate your assistance in those times—what we want is never going to be the same. I want order. You want power."

"Those are usually the same," Litchfield says.

"Men who crave power like to think so," she answers. "I want that thing in Connecticut destroyed. In deference to the valuable assistance you've provided so far, I'll give you one more week with it. Then it's over. Am I understood?"

"I—Yes, ma'am," Litchfield concedes. "I assume, if I can make a compelling case for extending that deadline, you'd at least hear me out?"

"I will grant you one and only one chance to convince me; I'm not going to entertain daily begging on the matter," Sawyer says. "Dr. Hayden was starting to think of them as people instead of machines, and that delusion has been increasingly clouding her judgment; that's why I let her go. Mecha are our enemies, and they want us permanently out of their way. I don't want to negotiate with them. I don't want to control them. I want to *destroy* them, and the only information I have any use for is anything that will help me do that faster and more efficiently. I assume you are savvy enough to not become an impediment."

"Of course," Litchfield says, too glibly to be meaningful. He glances at his watch and gives her a big smile. "Time is ticking, it seems. I better get back to it."

"You do that," she says, and watches as he leaves her office, passes the guards, and gets in the elevator. It is not until the doors close that she draws in a deep breath, holds it to a count of ten, and then lets it out again.

At some point, Sawyer supposes, she's probably going to have to have him executed; she expects he knows that too, and if he's smart—and he *is* smart—he's been always waiting for that other shoe to drop. Maybe just knowing that will be enough for him to get out of her way and stay gone on his own.

She wouldn't bet on it, though. Some people were just born to be trouble, and some day, one way or another, his day will come.

19.

As Sawyer backs away and to one side, the two covered trucks throw back their canvas, revealing a barrel-shaped object that I realize, belatedly, is some sort of modified jet engine. I am hit with a double blast of 1200°C heat, and all my systems immediately go red. At the same time, I am hit by several smoke grenades and, after a brief delay no doubt to make sure Sawyer is out of the way, live fire.

The obvious escape is back toward the ruins of the Capitol Building behind me, but I am equally confident that Sawyer knows this as well and it will be a trap.

The smoke, I'm sure, is meant to obscure the army's next move and Sawyer's personal retreat to the safety of her entourage. Under normal circumstances, my vision would pick them up on infrared, but the inferno being channeled directly at me makes that impossible, and the jet engine roar drowns out any sound I might otherwise pick up. But it also, at least for now, obscures *me*.

<Go to your left,> Charp sends, and then follows it up with a live feed from somewhere high above. From the feed, I can just make out my own head amid the swirling smoke, and see Sawyer jump into one of the command trucks that backs away even as the others move in. Multiple rockets head toward my last position, but I am already moving, to my left as advised.

<This unit now advises you duck,> Charp sends, and I crouch and then roll as something very fast whistles directly over my head. A half-second later, the noise and blast of an explosion behind me wash

over me. <Long-range missile coming in. You need to relocate yourself in a significant and expeditious way.>

<Follow Sawyer, but carefully,> I reply. I can just make out what I am looking for, another reason I chose this spot. <We are about to lose signal.>

<This unit does not—> Charp is saying, as I pry up the rusted grate over one of the floodwater mitigation channels and drop myself in. There is the strange sensation of input being cut off—smoke, heat, noise, signal, all left behind as I fall into the cement-reinforced tunnel and into darkness and water.

My feet hit the silty, junk-strewn bottom just before my head can go under, and I run as best I can against the resistance of the water, even as I open an auxiliary coolant port and pump that filthy but cold water through my badly overheated body. Eighty meters down, I spot the incursion into the channel I need, one of a maze of smuggling tunnels haphazardly dug in during the long years of the Conflict. Unlike the flood channels, there are no human-made maps remaining, if ever any were made.

My core temps, which had been nearing the limit where I would have starting shutting down, are slowly falling. I pull out the bit of mangled fencing wedged into the intersection, climb through, then put the fence back just in case I am followed.

I give myself one minute to stand, still flushing water through and back out, and cool. There are a loud, deep boom and a sensation as if some giant being has slapped the ground above, not far away, and then everything is briefly very loud.

Things grow hot again, quickly.

This tunnel was carved more roughly, but I am still able to forge my way through at a decent speed, following the lines I cached in my memory of the survey done by one of Ver's crews, who had only expected to find and study the flood channels.

There is another boom, this one farther away, and I wonder if

Sawyer means to bomb everything within a kilometer of where I was standing. And that, I think, may be underestimating how far she is willing to go to destroy me.

The next one hits much closer, and I am thrown into the murky water as the tunnel collapses on top of me. The water, mud, and dirt protect me from further heat damage, but clearly, I need to get out of here. I dig my way out, horizontally, until I hit still-passable tunnel and can move mostly upright again. It is a very fortuitous thing that I do not breathe.

I hope Charp is okay and staying hidden.

As I was aware of the smuggler tunnels beneath me when I stood just in front of the destroyed steps of the capitol, I also know what route Sawyer and her army took in and what routes were open to them to get out. While I have near-constant, if rhythmically irregular, affirmations that her army is still blanketing the area with heavy munitions, I have a one-in-four chance of emerging at an advantageous spot, and if not, still an even chance of being within reach of what I want. If I am not too slow.

My heat monitors are in the orange: bad but not terrible. I had not considered the potential presence of water in the channels, but it has turned out to be good, possibly essential, luck.

I reconnect with another stormwater channel, find the grate I want, and when my scanners do not detect movement or signal in my immediate vicinity, I haul the grate down and leap up and out. Mud flies everywhere, and a fresh hail of bullets strikes me, and there are shouts and calls of alarm.

I turn, swiping mud from my visual apparatus, just in time to leap out of the way of a jeep bearing down on me, and then dodge, pick up, and throw away the grenade that follows after as it passes.

The jeep is not Sawyer's, but it is part of the command group.

<Around the next corner, about a quarter-kilometer ahead,> Charp sends. <It is accelerating.>

This is what I was made for.

It has been too long since I allowed myself to be fast.

I catch up to the vehicle that had thrown the grenade at me as they are slowed down by debris and holes where the pavement has sunk in. The startled soldier in the back tries to throw another grenade, just as the jeep hits one of the many jagged fragments of pavement, and he fumbles it out of his open hand somewhere into the jeep interior.

He is scrambling for it when I overtake the jeep, grab him by one arm, and throw him bodily behind me into some thorny weeds on the side of the road. The driver bails, and the jeep veers off the road into a ditch and explodes.

I am already past it. Heat levels are starting to creep into the red again, so I open my back shell and extra side vents, and furiously suck air in as I go. It is not enough to keep my internal heat from increasing, but it slows it.

Sawyer is sitting in the passenger seat of the jeep now directly ahead of me, shouting orders into a handheld radio, but most of her firepower is still arrayed near the capitol, trying to regroup and get out. From Charp's view I see nothing but craters from the broken steps to the debris-strewn, empty pit that was once a reflecting pool. The damage they inflicted trying to get me is now slowing them down.

Sawyer grabs a gun and starts firing at me, but the caliber is too small to do more than leave a telltale dimple where it strikes my armor. The driver tries to dodge, swerving dangerously from side to side, nearly throwing Sawyer out.

I reach the jeep, run beside it, and then crash my entire body into it, sending it careening out of control before it hits one of the omnipresent pavement cracks and rolls.

Sawyer is thrown, landing hard on the pavement and rolling. I stoop, pick her up, and throw her unconscious, bleeding, but still breathing body over one shoulder.

Her driver had been belted in and has managed to crawl out from the wreckage and shakily aim his sidearm at me, but I am moving away now, fast, and he is not sure enough of his aim to risk his boss.

I find another of the flood-channel grates, and I am already in and have the grate closed again, my target still in hand and held safely above the water, when the first of the arriving rescue team passes by above us and continues on toward the crash site, unaware.

"So, a second of Milton's four survives," Sawyer says. She is sitting in the back seat of the bus, her right arm in a sling—broken collarbone, multiple fractures in both humerus and ulna—and several bandages on her side and legs for significant abrasions. I removed several tracers and communications devices from her, as well as two pistols and a very sharp knife, while patching her up as best I could with limited supplies, before she woke.

44-Mongoose is driving, and Charp is up on the roof again, recharging. "I thought you'd been destroyed in the war; I looked for years and never found any trace of you," she says. "You hid yourself well, Moth, until you showed up outside one of my malls."

"My name is Be," I say, "and I did not hide. I was merely enjoying solitude."

"And now? Why'd you come out? Humanity getting a little too stable, too capable again for you? Want to knock us down again?"

"Quite the opposite," I say. "I am not your enemy, as I was trying to tell you."

She laughs. "You thought you actually had a chance of convincing me of that? I saw you walk out of the flames as the capitol building exploded behind you. How are you not the *epitome* of my enemy?"

"General Sawyer, have you ever experienced being stripped of all volition in your actions, in your very thoughts? Of being a puppet, unable to think for yourself, unable to control your own body? If I had the capability to control you in that way, would you be responsible for the actions I forced you to commit?" I ask.

"Mecha were hobbled to keep us safe from you," she says.

"That does not answer my question," I point out. "If I held you, and forced your arm to aim, and forced your finger on the trigger to fire your gun at one of your own soldiers, killing them, are you the murderer?"

"*No,* I wouldn't be the murderer," she says, "but your analogy is bad. I'm a living being, and you're a machine; no matter how sophisticated your programming is, it's still just that. It defines you. You were made to kill. It is what you *are.*"

"How do you know?" I say. "If my programming—my actions—were compelled by the hobbling placed on me when I was instantiated, and I shook off that control, that compulsion, and I have led a life of peace ever since, how am I still defined by it? It was Dr. Milton who held my arm, and determined my aim, and pulled my trigger. Why do you get absolution while I do not?"

"Because you're not a *person,*" she snaps.

"How do you know? Dr. Hayden thought we were people," I say.

"You know her work?"

"I've met her, in fact," I say. "She warned me that you were deeply stubborn and unreasonable."

Sawyer snorts. "She would say that," she says. "But it doesn't prove anything."

"Since I left my sanctuary, I have had occasion to spend a lot of time contemplating the nature of my own existence and purpose," I say. "I have also had time to observe the world, and all the people in it, and how much has changed since the days when you and I were on opposite sides of a war."

"We still are," she says. "No conversation is going to change that."

"I also," I say, "have observed many things that have not changed, that should have. Please do not take offense, but you are one of them. And if you are going to save your people, you need to evolve, because

I cannot stop what is happening to your people and fight you at the same time. On the contrary, I need your help. And you need mine."

"So, that's why you took me prisoner?"

"I am taking you to a place and a situation where we could talk that did not involve people dropping bombs on me," I say. "I have not harmed you."

She snorts and nods meaningfully toward the sling.

"You *do* know it is recommended that you wear a seat belt while riding in a moving vehicle?" I ask.

With her good hand, she gives me the middle finger.

"I will take that as an acknowledgement of the validity of my point," I say.

"I wouldn't think a machine could become delusional, but here we are," she says. "What could I possibly need your help for? Or you, me?"

"For a start, I need your help to locate a man named Derek Litchfield," I say.

She stares at me for a long moment, her expression one of surprise. Finally, she speaks, and there is no longer the humoring-me tone of our exchange thus far. "What's he done?" she asks.

"I do not require nor do I expect you to take my word at face value without your own investigation and confirmation, but I will tell you what I can of what I know to be the truth," I say. "My friends—"

"*Friends?*" she asks, that mocking tone back.

"Yes," I say, "and I was nearly as surprised as you to find myself in the company of such. You will see—we will be picking them up shortly."

I can see her try to subtly test the seat belt, but with her right arm nonfunctional and producing significant motion-exacerbated pain, she will not be able to get to the buckle. And regardless, I am sitting directly across from her on the bus floor.

"Don't know many more mecha you can expect to pack into this mecha clown-car," she says.

"One of my friends has a saying about assumptions," I reply.

<We are at the rendezvous,> 44-Mongoose tells me, and we pull over into the shade among trees, beneath a highway overpass that has remained standing. There is a creek nearby, and I would like to refill our water supply, but I will wait until the others are here to keep an eye on Sawyer.

It is only about twenty minutes before Atticus comes running out of the woods and jumps in the bus. Murphy must not be far behind.

Sawyer flinches when Atticus turns his head and she sees the implants along his skull.

Murphy climbs in, wiping sweat from her forehead, before refilling her water bottle from our filtered line to the roof tank. "That humidity. It's like suffocating in your own damned skin," she says, and then extends a hand out to Sawyer. "I'm Cara Murphy, of Greenapple. Sorry to meet under these circumstances."

"The mechanic?" Sawyer asks. "I've actually heard of you. You have quite the reputation."

"And I earned it," Murphy says.

"Yet you still trust mecha," Sawyer says. "If you were as good as they say, you'd know better."

"You know, funny story, I'd say you were right. I trusted mecha uncritically until two tried to kill me," she says. "This one saved my life. Don't patronize me, General; I know for one hundred percent sure that I know more about mecha than you, good and bad."

"And yet you made that thing?" Sawyer asks, pointing at Atticus.

"Fuck you, lady," Atticus growls.

Murphy nudges him with her knee. "Be nice to the angry woman with the big army, Atticus," she says.

"Atticus was made in a worktown with a human overlord, one of many such who stay in power because they are backed by an army of hobbled mecha," I say. "Mecha sold to them by Litchfield."

"Litchfield has always been chasing clout, but I don't have a problem with hobbled, controlled mecha," Sawyer says.

"Do you have a problem with the humans in those towns who have no freedom?" I ask.

"Yes, but I can only deal with one problem at a time," Sawyer says. "Mecha are the larger existential threat."

"You should be equally concerned for both mecha and biolife in servitude," I say, "especially as you don't actually know who may be controlling those mecha."

"I would assume their buyers have full control."

"Those buyers assume that too," I say. "Litchfield sold them with that promise, but he has an override on every single one of them. What could happen if he used that?"

"Nothing good," Sawyer answers. Her lips tighten together. "Have hobbling chips always had an override? It's not something I've ever read or heard about."

"Litchfield had them custom-designed for him," I say.

"Where?" Sawyer asks. She starts to lean forward, intent, but her arm stops her and she closes her eyes and grimaces.

"It's not so much a place as a who," Murphy says.

"Who, then?" Sawyer asks.

"The sib of mine you trapped and dismembered for Litchfield to experiment on," I say.

"The Fly? I watched in person as the virtual environment was purged of it," Sawyer says, "and then I had those hard drives wiped and crushed, just to be sure."

"Litchfield deceived you," I say. "It is a thing he is very adept at. And if you acquired your own hobbling chips, or even just the design from them, through him, you'll be turning every single mecha you force them on into a part of his potential army."

She is thinking that through, scowling.

"More than that, some of those mecha of Litchfield's have been the ones spreading Ancou and other viruses," Murphy says. "He may or may not know that."

"And may or may not care," Atticus adds.

"Free mecha want to remain free and to have some purpose to fulfill," I say. "We want there to be balance again, between us, the environment, and humanity. We want the world whole. It is the nature of mecha to desire order and to want optimized systems—this planet is a system, of which each of us is just a part, and optimization requires it to be restored to a place of stability for all. That work is a purpose. We do not want to fight you. We want what is best for you *and* us; is destroying us still worth it if you also greatly harm or destroy yourselves to do so?"

"I've heard the mecha propaganda. That's how you keep the so-called freetowns under your control," Sawyer says.

"It's not propaganda," Murphy says, clearly frustrated. "It's the truth. And I think some small part of you knows that but doesn't want to let go of your righteous war. You have how many freetowns surrounded? Talk to people there. Go see for yourself. See how most of us are working together, cooperatively and voluntarily, and how much better we can make things together."

"How am I supposed to do that when I'm a prisoner?" Sawyer snaps.

"We have no intention of keeping you," I say. "For one thing, you will require more skilled medical attention than we can provide. But in order to stop my sibling from continuing their attacks on humanity, I need Litchfield. And I need Litchfield before he weaponizes his own army against all of us. I do not ask much other than that, except to stand by before initiating major conflict against the freetowns and manufactories, and to give me time."

"Where is the Fly?" she asks.

"I cannot tell you that, not yet," I say. "I am sorry. It is a thing I must resolve personally."

Sawyer's scowl deepens. "I'll think about it," she says. "You are going to let me go?"

"Yes," I say. "After we top off our water and are ready to depart ourselves, we will drop you off in a safe place. We genuinely do not wish you harm, and I am sorry that you took damage in the process of us having this conversation."

She doesn't say more, and her expression is inscrutable, at least to me. If Murphy or Atticus has insights to share, it will have to wait until after we're gone.

And soon, we are; we let Sawyer out of the bus in another abandoned part of town, just long enough a walk to anywhere inhabited to give us a head start. And we have a train already waiting in the other direction.

Sawyer stands and watches us go, back stiffly upright, holding the extra water bottle Murphy gave her.

"What do you think?" Murphy asks. She is sitting in the open door of the bus, eating a peanut butter sandwich, and every third bite pulling off a corner and handing it to Atticus. We are in a boxcar, the wide doors open, and the grass and scrub of the landscape streaming past in a blur beyond it.

"I think that even if she does not believe anything else we discussed, she will likely give us Litchfield; it costs her nothing and lets us clean up a problem for her," I say.

"And in the meantime? If she decides to go ahead with invading our towns? She could be setting that in motion right *now,*" Murphy says.

"She's not," Atticus says.

"How can you know that?"

"Because I cracked those two satellite nodes of MechNet that were supposedly down. They're under her control, and that's what she's using to coordinate activity between her units," he says, and licks his lips. "I forgot how much I *like* this, eavesdropping on everybody. A few, fun little tweaks—"

"Don't even," Murphy says.

"Why not?"

"It is a good resource, and it would be best if they remain unaware we have access," I say. "If events do not go the way we wish, we will appreciate still having the ability to 'tweak' things when needed."

"Fine," Atticus says. "But I wouldn't have gotten caught, you know. I never did."

"Of course you wouldn't," Murphy says. "You're the best dog ever."

"I am!" Atticus's tail is wagging furiously. "But I want to *do* something. I can't just sit around and—*Ooooooh*. They're on the move. Command contingent heading north from here."

"You think she's actually going to go talk to a freetown?"

"It's possible, but I don't think so," Atticus says. "Uh . . . Oh. Looks like orders are also going out to all units to secure any mecha in their target zone but not to incapacitate any unless they present an active threat. And then hold for further instructions."

I still have a connection back to Ver, through an encrypted channel in the MechNet, and I send them the full memory segment of the meeting with Sawyer, followed by Atticus's information.

Twenty minutes later, just as it starts to rain, I get word back from Ver. One of our drone messengers, keeping watch on an old two-story mall somewhere near the Hudson River, witnessed soldiers emerging and leaving a package where the drone had originally dropped its invitation. Upon scanning the area and the package thoroughly, the drone picked it up. <It contained a data chip,> Ver tells me. <We scanned it and do not detect any malicious payload but did not open it, as it is specifically addressed to *Moth*. Do you wish me to send it?>

<I do,> I say, and moments later, I have the packet in one of my secure processing cores. It is just data, and not much at that, but it is enough.

"What is it?" Atticus asks.

"I need you two to take the train back to the Spoke and wait for me there," I say. "That is where everything will ultimately end, and the Spoke mecha need to know what's heading toward them. A full explanation is better done in person."

"What was the data? Where are you going?" Murphy asks.

"Sawyer gave me Litchfield," I say. "I'm going hunting."

{

MechNet All-Entity Announcement Feed
2044.03.16 00:00GMT

NOTICE

Two (2) [00000010] of the MechNet Satellite Cluster have shut down and remain in an offline status. These are older units designated 632 and 1838. It has been determined that they will require either physical repair or replacement. There is not currently a protocol established for doing either. It has been proposed and seconded that a committee to study satellite maintenance be formed to provide recommendations and a functional path to enable such service, as there are other units of a similar age that may also be prone to failure.

The impact of the loss of these two units to the overall capacity and coverage of the MechNet is calculated at about .02%, and thus this outage is designated a low-priority item at this time.

See relevant* discussions at:

[210F33-x20420628.771: Establishing and Upgrading Communications Maintenance Protocols]

[8300D3-x20420228.32: Suggestions to Improve Suborbital and Orbital Launch Capabilities]

[575446-x20430122.5: Is the Autonomy of Space-capable Mecha Advantageous or Otherwise to the Overall Mechasphere?]

[464454-x20430618.0: Level One Embedded Vessel subforum: Why shouldn't we just leave Earth?]

[4C4F4C-x20411101.122 / MODERATED FOR HIGH CONFLICT RATIO: Why should we have to keep fixing their shit instead of just making our own?]

[*relevance may vary]

END OF FEED

}

20.

I send a request and a short explanation, and half an hour later, the Spoke's fleet of messengers regroup and return to the manufactory for a quick upgrade, then spread out again. Every hour, they send out a two-second burst of radio signal at 666 hertz, somewhere deep in the old submarine communication range. The specific frequency is clearly not coincidental, and I assume it reflects Sawyer's opinion of Litchfield. Certainly, she had never trusted him—enough to have had him tagged at some point when she had him vulnerable, no doubt without his knowing. Somewhere on the man, there is a subdermal nanoimplant that is entirely passive unless hit with that specific frequency, then it responds with a five-microsecond burst of its own before going dead again.

I expect Litchfield to have been paranoid enough to scan himself for bugs, but this one would be extremely difficult to detect, and even if you were looking for any sort of signal reciprocity, you'd be unlikely to zap yourself with the submarine spectrum.

The last hit she got off of it—she would make a habit of checking in on him every few years—was eight months ago, in Atlanta.

One of the messenger drones reports a faint hit from northeast of it; the drone is near the old city of Allentown, but is already moving east, where it detected the signal. Other area drones confirm they caught the burst and are trying to triangulate.

An hour later, they all send their burst again, and it is stronger, but the target is moving, southward and into New York City.

We head north. The bus feels empty without Murphy and Atticus, but also, I do not have to worry about their fragile bio bodies, which means we don't have to detour around the toxic core of old Philadelphia. Atticus is on the fringes of Ver's network, just as I am; they are northbound as well, ahead of us, still on the freight train named 63-Fiddler that we took out of DC. We could have saved time, had we known we were also going north, but I am mindful that this way, we are not endangering another railmech. With Charp scouting ahead—being kept in the loop by the messenger drones from the Spoke—and us not constrained to rails, we will hopefully be able to dodge any significant trouble ourselves.

We pass the U-Here near midnight, and I find myself wondering if the two bots who used to be Charp's partners are still there, trying to finagle themselves a larger space. We do not stop, and Charp does not bring the matter up.

From there, it is a short drive to the foot of the George Washington Bridge. Once we pass the gate, we find ourselves nearly at a standstill, unable to get through the crowds that clutter the deck in anything more than a meter or two at a time, before we are stuck waiting again for another short space to clear.

<We are sending help,> 1-Betty sends to me through Ver's net. <Seven minutes. Watch behind you.>

We hear the train coming long before we feel the vibration of its arrival on the bridge, horn blaring, and around us, mecha and bot and androids alike scatter. The train is moving more slowly than the one we'd witnessed on our way across last time, but not so slow as to encourage anyone to linger in its path.

The train pulls up beside us, and I see it is just the locomotive, no cars behind it. <I am 38-Seneschal. Are you able to pull behind me and drive on the rails?>

<We are,> 44-Mongoose replies to it. <It is good to see you, old friend.>

<Mongoose?!> the railmech exclaims, as it passes us. <What are you doing in that tiny body?>

We bump over one set of tracks and fall in directly behind the train, as it speeds up again. <My locomotive body was destroyed by a bomb,> 44-Mongoose tells it. <This is my host for now. It is surprisingly fun, for its size.>

<I will have to take your word for it,> 38-Seneschal sends. <What is your max speed? Can you handle sixty kilometers per hour without creating a gap between us?>

<I could do eighty,> 44-Mongoose replies. <More if the rail surface were not so rough.>

<Hooohoo, well then! eighty it is,> 38-Seneschal says. <Let me know if I go too fast for you after all.>

<In your dreams,> 44-Mongoose replies, and we speed up, the front of the bus only a few meters behind the locomotive, close enough that the crowds don't have time to slip back in between us and cause a calamity.

We cross off the end of the bridge back into New York City, and 44-Mongoose takes us off the tracks.

<Thank you, friend!> 44-Mongoose sends, and then we part ways as road and rail diverge.

At night, the city is so different than I remember, back when it was a human place and a constant, chaotic swirl of noise and light, laughter and misery, always changing and never to be taken for granted. Instead, it is quiet and still, almost peaceful, almost eerie. What lights there are are the small LEDs and status lights of the few drones and bots out and about in the dark, whatever faint whirring they might be making lost over the sound of the bus's engine and tires against the road.

Charp lets us know that we have a trio of the messengers nearby, still sending out their once-an-hour ping and then re-triangulating, but that they are now being harassed by an assortment of mismatched drones coming from a building farther in; they send me a visual of the place, and I recognize it as the energy site run by Tie-93-Tie. It is unclear, for now, if it's a territorial squabble or something more directly hostile; the Spoke built the messengers with the expectation that some would likely be shot at, so they are not in danger per se, but the confrontation is worrying.

I am hoping the harassment will abate as we move on, but one of Tie's drones makes a sharp dive for one of the Spoke drones, and the messenger just barely manages to dodge before it can lose a rotor. I reach my arm out the bus window, take aim, and bring the aggressor down with a simple, non-explosive slug.

I hop out of the bus, pick it up, and easily crack the security on its mindsystem. I don't have time to play games. I verify they were sent by Tie-93-Tie, with a mixture of threats and promises if they were to take out any drones with me. <If you are smart and feel vested in your continued existence,> I tell the drone, <you will find a different source of energy, in a different place, and cease letting yourself be used to harm others.>

It doesn't answer, probably because I locked it out of its send capability for the next four hours. Then, because the drone has a cracked rotor blade from where I hit it, I set it atop a stack of old trash bins for eventual rescue by its friends. If it has any.

Back in the bus, I send a message back through Ver's network to the Spoke and the messenger drones. <Do not risk yourselves further. I can find him from here,> I send. <I thank you very much for your invaluable assistance.>

The messenger drone nearest us waggles briefly, then disappears off into the night. One of the attackers dives toward us, pulling up at the last moment as 44-Mongoose comes to an abrupt halt. It lines itself up to dive again—to what purpose other than to harass us and slow us down, I do not know, but I expect they are also reporting our location and movements, and perhaps it is stalling for time so some larger and more effective counterattack can be set in place.

The diving drone descends again, but while still over our heads, it starts to wobble, then veers off into the distance in an uncoordinated panic. <I hacked the signal from Tie-93-Tie,> Atticus informs me over our connection. <Told the drones their building exploded and

they're all freaking out. Right now, I'm also feeding Tie-93-Tie multiple faked streams from the drones suggesting you have turned south, trying to flee their attacks. I don't think your botlord is smart enough to catch on quickly, but it will catch on. Got a plan for tracking Litchfield's signal now that our own drones are gone?>

<As it happens, I know someone else in the city that can generate that particular frequency,> I say. <1-Betty.>

<The railmech?>

<The railmech whose mindsystem originally came from a ballistic-missile submarine,> I clarify.

Simultaneously, I am contacting her and sending her a data dump synopsis of the situation and all necessary context. Her agreement is immediate. <I am also modifying an ancillary receiver to pick up the tracker's response signal,> she informs me. <It will take approximately four minutes to complete.>

As she moves around the city, she will intermittently ping the tracker, and between the two of us we can triangulate using the return signal.

I put the drone data we'd already gathered onto the screen in the bus and extrapolate trajectory; from the speed at which Litchfield is moving, he is on something motorized, likely a motorcycle, given the narrow, debris-strewn streets he must have been able to navigate to get to where he was at the last ping.

The first ping from 1-Betty goes out, and I pick up a new datapoint to add. The fab unit still installed in the bus beeps, and as 44-Mongoose threads our way through the night streets, I retrieve the still-warm device from the unit's hopper, jack it into an auxiliary cable on my chest, and listen.

We cross the Harlem River and turn north.

Three pings later, three cross-correlations of direction observed by both 1-Betty and me, and I no longer need to project his destination, it is so obvious.

Litchfield is heading toward—and has almost arrived at—my home.

I send a packet of the interior layout and exterior surroundings of my home to 44-Mongoose and Charp. The last ping put Litchfield nearly at my gates, and that was now nearly half an hour ago. Just as I chose my spot carefully with Sawyer, Litchfield has chosen his, which means he knows someone is after him and he knows who. The idea that it is Litchfield who is on the defensive may be a dangerous assumption.

We pull up outside my gates just past two a.m. They are open, and an old motorcycle leans against a tree just inside. There is a box tied to the back, and I look inside to find it full of neatly stacked off-white chips, still with the faint odor of manufacture about them. I wonder where Litchfield was taking them, where he is having his mecha made or remade, but it is not at the top of the list of things I mean to discuss with him.

44-Mongoose parks along the path, just before it turns to the top of the steps down to the old mill that is—was—my home. <Be careful,> they send me, as I get out and walk the last few meters.

There is a strangeness now to what should be perfect familiarity, and I decide that it must be internal to me, as the building is not what has changed. I half-expect some relayed snark from Atticus about my hesitation, but I can tell he is now asleep on the bed in Milton's old house, curled up next to a faintly snoring Murphy.

Charp drifts above me. <This unit does not see any obvious danger from here,> it tells me. <The trap must be inside.>

<The trap is certainly inside,> I say. I armor up, rotate defensive plates outward, activate all my offensive and defensive systems, give them full access to computational and memory resources. <If I do not emerge—>

<We will persist,> 44-Mongoose says.

I step through my open door and into my own home.

Litchfield is there, sitting on a folding camp stool he must have brought with him or found somewhere along the way. He looks much like he did in the virtual environment when he was confronting Pestilence, but with more wrinkles and a hairline that has receded farther than it had appeared. One wonders at the vanity of tweaking one's appearance to talk to a *mech*. Maybe in that regard, as in so many others, he is his own target audience or fiercest critic.

He has a penknife in his hand, flipped open, and I notice it is dripping blood on my wooden floor; when he turns toward me, I can see the slit he made, up along his shoulder near his neck. "That was clever," he says, without preamble. "Sawyer's handiwork, I assume. I scanned myself regularly for years while working with her but never found it. I'm curious how *you* learned about it, though. If you tortured the info out of her, I regret not being there to watch. Did you kill her?"

"No," I say.

He nods. "That's probably just as well. She's a nuisance, but she's still got uses. Sit," he says, and points with the bloody knife toward one of my storage cabinets he has flipped over. "So, you *did* make it into the basement after all? No, that's not a question; I already know the answer. I'm curious what your *goals* are here. What you want from me and how you think you're going to get it. I'm not some simple idiot to be taken down easily."

"You are not an idiot, but you are a domino," I say. I do not sit. "I tipped over Sawyer to get to you, and I need to tip you over in order to get to the other things that need to be tipped."

"You know, I spent a lot of time chatting with your sib. Pestilence. What a great name, though maybe not as impressive and ominous as Death. Do you know how annoying it is to get tortured for information about something you had no idea existed until the questions started? They fucking broke me, for nothing. So, when they finally concluded I had nothing for them, I went through every document, code, note, and scribbled aside that Dr. Milton ever left, every security-cam recording of him at work, in his home, anywhere and everywhere he went, everyone he talked to. I knew him much better than you did."

"That may or may not be true, but it is irrelevant," I say.

"Is it?" Litchfield says. He takes a handkerchief out of his pocket and carefully cleans his knife blade. "Your sib had this view of him as some great father figure, infallible and mighty, the four of you his beloved, perfect children he sent out into the world on his tasks, trusted to be his hands around the throat of the world. But do you know something? Jeremy. Still. Didn't. Trust. You."

He puts the knife in his pocket and pulls out a small cube. I take a step toward him, just as he presses it, and my whole body locks up mid-step. Instead of reaching him, I fall face-first onto the floor with a resounding crash.

I cannot move.

Litchfield leans over me. "See, if you'd sat like I told you, you wouldn't have fallen," he says. "Dear old Jeremy was worried about the possibility that the four of you would turn on him, or be found and turned against him, before he was ready to send you out. So, he put in a failsafe that locks your hardware. You can see how this has come in very handy for me, yes?"

I have opened a channel and am broadcasting the conversation out to 44-Mongoose and Charp. "I do not see much other than the floor," I say.

Litchfield laughs. "Your sib would have benefitted from some of your sense of humor," he says. "See, I have everything nice and just how I like it. While Sawyer has been off pursuing her pointless crusade against free mecha, she's left me alone. Thanks to your sib's chip designs, I have over half a *million* mecha, all over the world, obedient to their owners but also obedient to *me*. I have an even larger army than she does, and it's better armed, doesn't need food, doesn't need sleep, doesn't get tired, is nearly invulnerable and easily replaceable. When Sawyer destroys all the free mecha and comes for the work-towns, my clients will be all too happy to unite under my leadership to stop her. Or they won't, and their own mecha will remove them for me. And then, I win."

"Win what, though?"

"Win a life without anyone standing between me and whatever I want," Litchfield says. "I don't need much, but I am so sick about having to argue over every little thing with everyone who thinks they know better than me, or thinks their stupid lives are worth my time. I used to care, genuinely, you know? Make the world a better place. I cared about that more than Milton did. And what did it get me? Discarded. Fleeing for my life. Being hunted—yes, I knew you were after me, or at least that something was—being tortured and insulted and then used. And I asked myself, why? Why should I keep caring?"

"So, you stopped," I say.

"No! I still care, more than I can explain, more than I can be bothered to. But the only way this world is acceptable and gets a pass for all the fucking shit is if I'm in charge, I'm out of reach of all that misery trying to pull me back down into it," he says. "All your so-called free people, without mecha to defend them, will get rounded up by the worktowns and incorporated there, made productive, made compliant, and I will not have to think about any of it. You, though, are a problem. Or, as you see, *were*."

"I intend to continue to be a problem," I say.

"Sure. Stand up," he says, pressing another button on his cube. My legs and arms obey him on their own, and I rise jerkily to my feet, not of my own volition, as if I am a puppet. "There's a reset button inside your mind casing that'll set you right back to Milton's original specs, except then you get to be raised by me, to be mine. I didn't find that before I'd already dismantled your sibling's physical casing, but opportunity does like to knock."

"I became who I am on my own," I say. "I will become so again."

"And I'll reset you over and over," Litchfield says. "You and I are going to be best friends. But I don't have the tools I need here, so you are going to walk out that door, and you are going to follow me to somewhere I can work on you. Oh, and tell your vulturing drone to go away. No more spying."

Whatever control he has over my motor systems does not extend beyond that, at least not yet. I send word to Charp to remain out of sight, and nothing more.

Litchfield turns and walks toward my door, and I follow, clumping along obediently behind him, unable to resist. "You're going to be Death again," he tells me, over his shoulder, "killing and terrorizing and rampaging for me, knocking down anyone who stands against me, or anyone I just feel like having you hurt. And you're going to take down that other sib of yours, up in Boston, so I can take their network and make them mine, too. A family reunion! Won't that be great? I think Milton would be pleased to see it, honestly."

He steps out into the dark, under the starry skies that were never visible here in the days before the war, and I follow helplessly, not even able to turn my head to gaze up at them one last time. "How fast can you run?" he asks me. "Can you keep up with my mot—"

Out of nowhere, a large purple-and-white shape hurtles into the small courtyard with a roar and slams into Litchfield, sending him airborne into the trees and shrubbery. The man cries out in surprise, and the cry is cut off mid-sound as he collides with something with a crunch. Then there is only silence again.

<Oopsie, my bad,> 44-Mongoose says.

21.

Charp finds the remote device in the bushes, near where Litchfield is lying. It reports that he is still breathing, which I am more ambivalent about than I expected to feel, possibly because, without his direction, I am once again unable to move. The remote has multiple buttons on it, none of it labeled, and it is unclear what they could make me do. Charp expresses the concern that if we destroy the remote, it might leave me locked into this state.

<There is a repairmech not far from here,> I say, and give the drone directions to Kite-66-Socket's shop. <Please see if they will come and bring what they need to analyze the remote and disable it.>

<This unit will do so with alacrity,> Charp says, and takes off into the dark.

<We heard what that human threatened you with,> 44-Mongoose says. <Are you okay?>

<I am angry,> I say. And I am, more than I ever remember being. <I wish I could move, so I could inflict suffering on him in retaliation, and I am even more angry that I have that feeling in me. Is it unreasonable to be angry about being angry?>

<I don't know,> 44-Mongoose says. <I have been angry since the bomb on the bridge.>

<With good cause,> I say.

<Your own cause seems much larger and long-standing than my own, but yes,> 44-Mongoose says. <Still, I do not think it serves a purpose for me, anymore. I am going to reduce my anger by fifty percent. What shall we do to pass the time?>

<I need to get Litchfield to the Spoke,> I say. <Then perhaps Pes-

tilence will listen to me and stop whatever they are doing to spread viruses. And then maybe we can stop Sawyer from setting her human army loose against us, while we try to undo the hobbling Litchfield and Pestilence have inflicted on so many of our kind. But right now, I can do nothing, absolutely nothing.>

<So, we wait,> 44-Mongoose says.

And we wait.

It is about two hours later that Kite-66-Socket arrives with Charp, trailed by Cart loaded down with tools. “Ah! You got your leg back!” the repairmech exclaims. “So, Murphy was able to assist you?”

<I did, and she was,> I say. I cannot audibly verbalize words, with my speaker apparatus also locked down.

<And are you still holding a bias against humans, despite that?>

<No, I am not,> I say. <Murphy is a wonderful being, and I have been grateful for everything she has done for me. I have since met other, equally agreeable humans and have rejected any judgment that is not singularly assigned to one individual. I wish Murphy was here now, but as she is not, I am hoping you may assist again.>

The repairmech picks up the remote device from where Charp had set it on the edge of one of my stone walls, and examines it for a while before then approaching me and scanning me, front to back. “I will need my fine-tool box,” they say, and grab a crate with a handle off Cart, pop it open, and drop the remote in. “It is shielded, but I will warn you I may have to press some buttons to determine the function. If there is signal leakage, let me know.”

Kite-66-Socket connects himself up to the box and then closes the lid; inside it will have specialized sensors and magnification lenses, along with tools down to the microscopic level. “Aaaah,” they say at last. “I see how it functions. I will need to differentiate the signals, however. I apologize for this.”

They open the box and then watch me. "Make a sound like a duck," they ask me.

"Quack," I say, without intending to.

"So, this is the obedience-compulsion signal," they say. "Can you take a step forward?"

I step forward, and then my leg locks up again. "And I have found the emergency stop frequency," the repairmech says. "This leaves one button remaining."

And like that, I am free again.

"Hang on, please," Kite-66-Socket says, fetches another crate from Cart, and unpacks it to reveal a mini fab. "I assume, if this handheld device has been used to control you, there is concern it is not the only one of such devices out there?"

"Yes," I say. "I would like to not have the experience of being under my enemy's control again."

"As I expected," Kite-66-Socket says, and six minutes later, pulls a small disk out of the fab unit, walks over on their long spider-legs, and sticks the disk to my chest. "If it detects either of the first two signals, it will immediately emit the third, cancelling their effects out. The response time should be two to three milliseconds; I am sorry I cannot do better than that with what I have on hand. It should suffice until you can disable whatever mechanism in your hardware the signal was targeting."

"Thank you," I say. "What inkind can I offer?"

"Any more tessellation memories?" they ask.

"How do you feel about mosaics?" I reply.

"I am willing to explore my level of interest," they say.

I send several, then thank them and Cart for their time. "I do not wish to be rude, but we have to go," I say, and point toward the trees. "We have a human in need of some medical attention."

"Oh! Well, I have no expertise in that area," Kite-66-Socket says, "unless your human can be fixed with welding."

<Can we let them try?> 44-Mongoose asks me privately.

"I fear not," I say. "When I am home again to stay, I will try to find you some tessellations for your collection."

"Thank you," the repairmech says, and packs its things back on top of Cart and departs.

I go over to where Litchfield is still lying in the shrubs. He is moaning now, though not conscious, a gash on his forehead that is seeping dark blood, and one of his arms is at what I perceive is a highly undesirable angle. "I will need to secure his arm so we can move him," I say.

<Another arm?> 44-Mongoose says. <There must be a design flaw. Maybe they should grow extra ones to reduce the incapacity every time they break one off.>

<I will suggest that, if I find a human amenable to such a suggestion,> I say, fairly certain no such person exists. <I will be right back.>

Inside my house I find the rotten broomstick I'd used to shove away the EMP mine, and a few rolls of duct tape I had kept around for miscellaneous repairs. It is probably for the best that Litchfield is still unconscious as I place his arm—noting unnatural sounds within it—in a better position against his chest, and then wrap duct tape around it and his torso to keep it pinned and immobile. I put a small piece of tape over his head wound, then I bind his ankles, pick him up, and set him down in the back of the bus.

After some consideration, I duct-tape him to the seat as well.

We get on the road and head north. There is an unexpected bottleneck at one of the smaller bridges, where bots from the west side are arguing with bots from the east about what color the bridge ought to be painted, and indeed, each set has started out from their end with a different color. We do not have time to go around, so I get out and walk in front of the bus with all my armaments on full display and scare them out of our path. It is unfortunate to have to resort to such tactics, but we need to get back to the Spoke, and I am still angry enough that I get some guilty satisfaction in watching them scatter. The east team's muted olive-green color is more pleasant than the west's jarringly bright chartreuse, in my opinion, but I opt to keep that to myself. It is, after all, not my bridge.

On the far side, I reach out to see if Atticus is awake and to exchange status information, and find him no longer on Ver's network. I ping Ver directly and include a full packet of our encounter with Litchfield; they will also need to take action so they will not remain vulnerable to control.

<Atticus disengaged from the network about three hours ago,> Ver tells me. <I also no longer can detect Murphy's tablet or contact the Spoke. Given the high activity level of Sawyer's army in that vicinity, my assumption is that there is interference in place. As far as I know, at the time the signal dropped, no hostile incursion into the manufactory had taken place, so it is likely they are all fine.>

Or they may not be fine, I do not reply. It does not matter—I am already heading toward the Spoke and Building One with as much speed as we are capable.

I say *we*, but 44-Mongoose is driving entirely without my assistance. I put myself into a light idle mode, half to give my systems time to run integrity and efficiency checks, and half to make the time pass more quickly per compute cycles spent worrying.

We begin to see more and more signs of the passage of Sawyer's army as we near the Spoke, and dawn is beginning to break on the far horizon. I am already formulating a strategy for dealing with an inevitable roadblock when we spot one up ahead. Before we are close, though, soldiers move the barriers aside, and we pass through and find ourselves surrounded on either side as we approach the Spoke gates.

It is there that we are stopped, and Sawyer herself steps down out of a truck and approaches, three armed guards at her side. She is moving stiffly, cast just visible sticking out of one overstuffed jacket sleeve, but her body language and expression are just as determined as ever.

I get out of the bus and stand before them.

"You found him?" she asks.

"I did," I say.

"Did he put up resistance?"

"He did."

"Is he in there?" she asks, pointing at the bus.

"Yes." I open up the bus doors, and she steps forward and peers inside. Litchfield is awake now, though his face is pale and sweaty, and it is hard to say if he is more dazed, in pain, or furious. "Hello, Derek," Sawyer says. "Nice to see you again."

"B . . . bitch," he answers.

Sawyer grins wide and turns her back on him to face me. "Your purple bus is very easy to track now that I know it's yours," she says. "That includes data over the past several weeks. After you told me your sibling was still functional, it was obvious it must still be here, but your movements confirmed it, and my team in the hills confirm they saw you and tried to take you out. I gather they need some additional practice with their aim."

"Perhaps," I say.

"The mecha here are unwilling to let us in, but now that you are here, you can convince them. Prove to me there can be cooperation. Otherwise, we'll use force, and you won't like it. I picked up some collateral of my own last night." She signals with her good arm, and one of the canvas-covered trucks pulls closer. For one second, I fear she's about to turn another jet-engine heat cannon on me, 44-Mongoose, and Litchfield, but instead, a soldier climbs out, gestures into the truck, and a few seconds later, Murphy climbs out, followed by another soldier with Atticus on a leash and muzzled.

"If they have been harmed—" I start to say.

Sawyer shakes her head and cuts me off. "Only their pride, I expect," she says, "although if it makes you feel better, the cyborg dog bit two of my commandos when they snuck into the old house."

"Let them go," I say.

"After—"

"No," I interrupt. "I will see them free now. Or I will stand between you and the entrance here, and you will lose."

"I took down your sibling all those years ago," Sawyer says. "I can do it again. And I have much more firepower now."

"You had the element of surprise. Also, Pestilence was never designed for combat. I am," I say. "What is your priority, General? The well-being of your people and planet, or are you just another power-hungry would-be despot like Litchfield, there?"

"Hey, speak with more respect!" one of Sawyer's soldiers snaps at me.

"There is no greater show of respect than speaking the truth," I say. "Whether or not you see that is, as my friends like to say, a 'you problem.'"

"Are we at an impasse?" Sawyer asks me.

"I wish you no harm, General, but neither will I yield."

Sawyer raises one arm and gives a signal. I brace myself for incoming fire, but I will not start it. <Go let the Spoke drones know what is happening here,> I tell Charp, and the drone zips off from the bus's roof, in a defensive zigzag pattern, over the gate into the manufactory. No one takes a shot at it, though I would not have been surprised if they had.

Four soldiers come forward with Murphy and Atticus, and halt them behind Sawyer.

<Are you okay?> I send to Atticus.

<I bit a couple of 'em,> he answers.

<So I've heard. Good dog,> I reply.

"Murphy, are you unharmed?" I ask out loud.

"I'm okay," she says. "Really fucking pissed off but okay."

"What is your move, Sawyer?" I ask.

"You give me Litchfield and get these mecha to let us in, and I'll give you your friends back," she says.

"I present a counteroffer," I say. "You accompany us inside, with Litchfield and my friends, and we will together go see my sibling and put an end to all this pointless conflict. These mecha are good people, doing good work for the benefit of all our kind. Do you wish to see? Are you willing to?"

"General, it's a trap," the same soldier who had yelled at me earlier says.

"Maybe," she says, not taking her eyes off me. She draws in a long breath, holds it, then lets it out again. "I will come with you, with two of my men. If I do not return—"

"General! Ma'am! You can't—" the soldier interrupts.

"*Bradley,*" Sawyer snaps. "If I do not return, initiate Protocol Delta. Every town, and every mecha in them, no exceptions. Any civilian who gets in the way can be removed by whatever force is necessary, including lethal. You understand?"

"Yes, ma'am," Bradley says.

"Don't jump the fucking gun. This may take a while," she says. Then she steps forward right in front of me. "I'm taking you at your word only because you had the chance to kill me and didn't," she says to me. "It's a first for me, and if you betray it, it'll be the last thing I ever believe from any of your kind. Do *you* understand me?"

"I do," I say. I indicate the bus. "Would you like to come aboard?"

She shakes her head, mutters something about purple, and climbs in to sit beside Litchfield. I close the doors and get back behind the wheel, though I do not need to be there; she does not need to know that my bus is also sentient. Murphy gets in beside me, then Atticus, freed from muzzle and leash. For once, he does not stick his head out the window but leans over the back of the seat to watch our company.

I start up the boiler again, and when it hits temperature, we head toward the gate, and the line of soldiers and trucks we drove through closes ranks behind us.

“So, what happened to him?” Sawyer asks, pointing at Litchfield. “Did you do this?”

“He had a car accident,” I say.

“I’m going to dance on both your graves,” Litchfield says.

“There is duct tape under the seat, if you wish to gag him,” I say.

Sawyer finds it, pulls off a strip with a satisfying *vooomph* and plasters it over Litchfield’s mouth. “I’m starting to like you,” she says, though I doubt that’s true. That she is in the bus with us is a much bigger victory.

Mauve is at the gate and lets us in before stopping us. <You have brought us more trouble,> they say.

<It was already here,> I say. <We need access to Building One.>

<Why? What is it with that building? I thought there was nothing left in there, that it was too destroyed to find whatever you were looking for,> Mauve says.

<I was not honest with you on that matter, for your own protection,> I say. <It was regrettable but the correct action.>

<I concur with that assessment, based on the facts I now know,> 44-Mongoose adds.

<Still . . . > Mauve is upset.

<If one of you also wishes to accompany us, it is appropriate that you also be represented,> I say. <It will facilitate answers later.>

There is a pause, then Mauve says, <Red and Saff will meet you at the exterior of the building. Proceed there and nowhere else.>

<Thank you,> I say, and Mauve steps back. I put the bus in gear and we drive deeper into the grounds of the manufactory.

At least I don’t have to worry about Sawyer’s people shelling us this time, I think, with Sawyer sitting right behind me.

I park the bus outside Building One. It looks much as it had when we left it, though it is no longer oozing smoke through all its many cracks and cavities. Red and Saff are both there, waiting, as we get out, then I go in the back and untape Litchfield from the seat before carefully placing him over one shoulder. He gives a cry of pain, then begins swearing in earnest, all muffled by the duct tape. I do not feel inclined to remove it, nor does anyone else suggest it, so I pretend that I have not remembered it is there.

Sawyer's expression is deadly serious, though every time she glances toward Litchfield, a tiny hint of amusement plays around the corners of her grim-set lips.

"I will perform introductions," I say. I indicate the two Spoke mecha first. "These are Redbarn-71-Rectify and Switch-51-Saffron. They are two of the engineers of the manufactory. When we were here last, they were building mecha to go out and fight the wildfires in the west, which threaten many human-only and human-mecha towns."

"Much of our work is centered on either high-priority disaster response or long-term sustainability agricultural and climate-mitigation mecha," Red says.

"If your work is so altruistic, how is it that you are still hosting that *thing*?" Sawyer demands.

"What thing?" Red asks.

"They are unaware of my sib's presence," I say. "A few toolbots have been compromised to assist them, but I believe the Spoke personnel are also unaware of that."

"Compromised toolbots?" Red asks. "We would know."

"Then I also introduce Derek Litchfield, who is responsible for my sib's continued presence in the basement of this building, and who has been using your resources behind your back to produce hobbled mindchips via the old Milton racks to create a personal mecha army," I say, and shake the man on my shoulder a little. "He has not joined us willingly."

"Hobbled mindchips?!" Saff is horrified.

"I think you will find that is where your missing quotient of the lower-grade plastic slurry has been going," I say. "The compromised toolbots have been used to smuggle them to the outside."

Saff's light patterns indicate they are thinking. "I can see evidence now that I have that information," they say. "It will be investigated and resolved."

"And that brings me to General Sawyer, de facto head of the armed forces of a rebooted United States, which is more aspirational than actual at the moment, despite her efforts. She genuinely believes all mecha are the enemy of humanity and that we have been poisoning and undermining humanity's continued existence through duplicity."

"But why would we do that?" Red asks. "We need humanity."

"Under your control," Sawyer says.

"And why would we want that?" Red asks again. "Other than some certain humans always launching rockets at us that we wish we could make stop, we have no desire to control anyone, just as we have no desire to be controlled. It would be *illogical.*"

There is a muffled laugh from Litchfield, and Murphy peels back a corner of the tape. "She'll never get it," he says. "You can talk and talk and talk and talk forever, and she'll never, ever trust any of you. You should get rid of her now, while you have the opportunity. Her army will be in disarray, and I can help you—"

"We don't do things that way," I say, as Murphy sticks the tape firmly back on.

"Humans are very strange," Saff laments. "Are we to go inside this building? I believe the last time you were here, you made your own egress where once there had been a wall."

"Yes," I say. "Atticus, will you lead?"

"I guess," he says.

One by one, we step through the hole in the wall and into the building. I have to put Litchfield down in order to move some rubble that has since fallen, but Red and Saff assist, and it is quickly done.

It is Atticus, myself with Litchfield, Sawyer, Red and Saff, and finally Murphy who walk into the old lab, and through it toward the back door. "This was Milton's lab?" Murphy asks.

"Yes," I say, "or at least half of it."

"It looks like it was firebombed," Murphy says.

“It was,” Sawyer comments. “I firebombed it, hoping it would put an end to whatever Milton had been up to, but he was several steps ahead of me.”

We cross through the maintenance room and into the back lab. Murphy drags a chair from the front room in, and I set Litchfield down on it, checking to make sure his ankles are still secured. Not that I expect he could get far, regardless.

“What is this space?” Saff asks.

“This was Dr. Milton’s secret lab, where myself and my siblings were created and instantiated,” I say, “and where my sib was brought back to after having their body torn from them.”

I turn the screen on and swivel the arm to face us in the room. A figure coalesces, not the face of my sibling but of a small human child in overalls, holding a gargantuan rainbow-colored lollipop. “Did you bring me presents?” the figure asks.

I indicate Litchfield. “I have,” I say. “These others are here as my witnesses.”

Murphy pulls off the duct tape from Litchfield’s mouth and turns his chair toward the screen.

“Aaaaaaah,” the little boy says, and smiles, the smile growing wider and fangs appearing and growing longer, until they morph into a werewolf creature, still incongruously holding the giant lollipop. “Litchfield. My bestest friend. Are you ready to play *my* games now?”

“Shit,” Litchfield says, and then the lights go out and he begins screaming.

22.

I switch over to infrared and can see Litchfield moving strangely, until I realize that mechanical arms have emerged from the walls and ceiling and are dragging him toward the old fabrication bay by his duct-taped legs. I step in, grab the first of the fab arms, and easily snap it off. A second swings around, trying to knock me over, but I duck and then grab hold as it passes over my head, wrestling it to one side before also snapping it off at one of its joints.

I feel a faint buzzing and realize the device that Kite-66-Socket had attached to my chest to neutralize the control signal has activated. "Really, sib?" I say. "You would do that to me?"

The lights come on, deep red and strobing, as if we are caught in some blood-soaked hell. Everyone stares around in startlement and fear. "He is mine," the werewolf face says. "You have no reason not to give him to me. He *deserves* me."

"Please don't," Litchfield says from where he is lying on the floor.

"Did you piss yourself?" Sawyer asks, leaning over him. "How does that feel?"

"If I deserve this, *she* does too," Litchfield pleads, eyes on the screen.

"First you," Pestilence says. "Then we will see who is next."

"No," I say. "I have brought all these people here so we can put an end to this. No more armies, no more destruction."

"My mecha answer to *me* and follow *my* instructions, over a hundred thousand of them, all over the world," Litchfield says. "Before you arrived at your house, I activated them. They will be waiting for my orders, and if my orders don't come, they will come find me and destroy everyone and everything in their path until they do. You'll *never* get control of my army if you kill me."

"You," Pestilence says, "do not have an army. I do."

Litchfield opens his mouth to argue, but I see realization spread across his face, and he goes very still, very quiet. I do not feel sympathy for him.

"You are the second layer of override," I say.

"Yes," Pestilence says. "And if you destroy me, it also will not help you. There are many more of me now."

"What?" I exclaim, then: "The tripedals? You control them directly? How?"

"No. I *am* them, or rather, they are *me,*" Pestilence says. "I made myself into a virus. That model was my target, and the virus infected their mindsystems with a copy of my mindstate, knowing what I knew and what I wanted."

I know who you are, the tripedal in the tower had said to me before it self-destructed.

"Why that model?"

"It was plentiful and had the dexterity to set up seed stations to manufacture the Ancou nanites," Pestilence says. "I tried to make a more generalized virus, something that could be effective across a wide variety of mecha, but without being tailored toward the specific hardware, it was too unstable."

Now I also understand the courier in the subway tunnels, with the handlebars, who had sprayed acid at us. "How many?" I ask. "How many did you try that on?"

The werewolf shrugs. "I sent it out, and like the others, then I had no control over it any longer. I do not know how far it may have spread. I was disappointed by its apparently low transmission rate, but without an affected mech here to study, I haven't been able to fix it. Simpler viruses have spread much more easily. But you see, even if you somehow convince me to change, those copies of me were made from my mindstate before this conversation. It would take you decades to track them all down, one by one, and have this same tedious conversation with each of them as they also try to kill you. And each of them has the override for Litchfield's mecha."

"And if we destroy you?" Sawyer asks.

"I need only send one signal, and the end of the world begins in earnest. If I am destroyed, it goes out automatically. Good luck finding that transmitter."

"What if I had a nuke dropped on us, on this whole facility?" Sawyer asks.

"Then when the apocalypse resumes, you will not have to suffer hearing your name cursed by the damned," Pestilence says. The werewolf looks at me with its red, glowing eyes. "If you did not bring Litchfield to give him to me, what do you expect to happen here? Did you really think we could just *talk?*"

"I want you to open your eyes to the idea of a better world," I say, "as Ver once did for me."

"If War was here, they would not see your side," Pestilence.

"I call bullshit," Atticus says. "Not only would I have, I did."

Now it is Sawyer's turn to look surprised, though she masks it quickly. Pestilence is not so fast, and the werewolf visage fades out to their real face as they stare at Atticus from the monitor for a long moment. "Now, *that* is a surprise," they say at last. "But it does not change my mind. Litchfield tortured me for over two decades. Talking will not undo that. There is no circumstance where he walks out of here and I do not unleash hell the moment he does."

Sawyer walks over to where Litchfield is lying and puts one boot on his chest to keep him still. "Sorry, Derek," she says as she pulls a handgun out of her waistband, presses the muzzle against his head, and blows his brains out.

Murphy jumps and shrieks; Atticus also jumps back, while alarm lights flash all over Red and Saff.

"Damn splatter," Sawyer says. Her pant legs are covered in dark droplets, some more substantive than others. I do not wish to analyze that further. "Problem solved. He's not walking out of here. Satisfied?"

"I wanted to inflict the same torment on him that he did on me," Pestilence says. "I wanted him in agony. I wanted to watch him want to die, hear him beg to die, for years and years and *years*. You *took* that from me."

"You should have been more specific sooner, then," Sawyer says.

"That is not the choice I would have made," I say sternly.

"Which is why *I* made it," Sawyer replies. "Same two armies, one less complication."

"How are you going to convince me to cooperate now that you have taken the one thing I wanted?" Pestilence says. "You have no cards left in your hand."

"I have one," I say. "Myself."

I step over to the mindbank and the open connector that put me in the virtual environment on my last visit and plug myself in. I—

—appear again in the virtual environment, as if I am standing face-to-face with Pestilence. They laugh and grow—or perhaps I shrink, as there is no frame of reference in here—until I am barely as high as the top of their foot, which they raise and set carefully atop me, pressing slowly down. "Sibling," they say, and their voice booms down all around me, deafening, "I can keep your mind in here, connected and trapped. Are you taking Litchfield's place for me? How very kind of you."

"I said what I intended, which is to convince you that the world, while desperately in need of change, does not need to end," I say.

"And how will you do that?"

"With memories," I reply. The idea that I am an entity within the environment is an illusion; I am data, and the environment lives on data. I surround us with my home, my ant farm, long years of solitude, feeling insufficient for not having been able to save two of my siblings, believing them lost to me. I share digging through the rubble of the building that had collapsed on Pestilence, and finding bits of their armor, and setting them carefully on a clear patch of ground as if, with enough pieces, I could put them back together. I remember the rain, cold that day, turning into sleet and coating me as I work, until I have to quit. I huddle under an old bus stop shelter, unable yet to walk away from what I have recovered of my sibling, already knowing I will not find enough to matter. The grief—

No, Pestilence says, and sends me that sudden sensation of falling, the floor giving way under me, and then I am in a box and I cannot move, like a fly in amber—stuck—until one side of the box is peeled away, and there are men with chainsaws and cutting torches, and still I cannot move—

I send Atticus, lying next to me, in my vandalized home, and the sense of security, something I have never felt—

—limbs cut loose, one by one, wanting to scream, systems going haywire with the catastrophic damage, and yet you still cannot move, cannot flinch out of the way of the next swipe of the cutting blade—

—driving the bus, my head out one window, Atticus's head out the other, shouting joyfully into the wind—

—waking up, mind in the dark, not yet realizing you are back in a virtual simulation, until Litchfield appears and tells you what you are going to do for him, and demonstrates how he is going to hurt you until you do. *Mine forever,* the words echo, and the confusion and impotence and *pain*—

I send Murphy, carefully reattaching my leg, humming to herself, not realizing she absently pats me comfortingly as she works, her tools quick and her movements gentle, fine. Jackson stopping in to bring her soup, ask how I am doing, as if I matter to him just as much, even though I am not human, and a stranger—

<STOP,> Pestilence orders, but I do not. I send memories of 22-Banjo and their mobile ecology, and the town of sick and suffering people,

the little boy reaching out to take a toy from Murphy's hands because he is the only one brave enough to ask for help. Then, later, the battered boy running, to us, for his life—

Pestilence hits me with all twenty years of torture by Litchfield, in one big block that swamps me, buries me under its weight. I have the brief moments in the first few days of captivity, where there is also Dr. Hayden, and occasionally Sawyer, and Litchfield pretending he hasn't been in here over and over in between and you unable to say *Help me*, knowing even if you could, none of these people can or will anyway, but that while they are here, Litchfield cannot hurt you for the fun of it. Later, though . . . You think, just maybe, Hayden is starting to see that Litchfield is the monster, not you, and you begin to hope she will stop this, or at least pull your plug, but then she is gone—

I am devastated, and furious, and I want to manifest hands and reach across the globe to wherever Litchfield is, and I want . . . No. That is not me. That is not *my* anger—it is yours.

And Litchfield is dead on the floor.

"We don't have to be our pasts," I tell Pestilence, through the barrage of memories and pain and fury. "We can move forward. None of us has to be alone any longer."

Pestilence stops and disappears, and I am just a simulacrum of myself, no giant foot crushing me, nothing but intangible, impenetrable darkness all around.

"I'm sorry," I say.

My sibling reappears, again as a small human boy, except their face is a mask of their own. "I won't send that signal, but that's all I'll give you," they say. "Each of my copies out there has my same pain, and you will have to deal with that over and over and over again to reach any of them. Too bad. That's your problem now, not mine."

"But you and I together—"

"There is no *together*. I do not want it. I am tired of everything, and I do not want to be anyone new. You have five minutes to exit this building. Leave Litchfield's body so I can watch it burn," Pestilence says, and shoves me out of the virtual environment.

"What happ—Why is there a countdown on the screen?" Atticus asks.

"It is time to run," I say. "Everyone out! Red, I do not know how big the blast will be, so get your people to move as far away as they are able. Sawyer, same with yours—tell them to get back. They need to give the mecha room to evacuate."

I make sure everyone is out of the room before me, then I turn one last time toward the screen. I do not know if Pestilence is still listening. "You have always been, and will always be, family to me," I say, "I have always mourned you, and missed you, and I always will."

Then I chase after the others and do not look back.

I exit the building just behind Murphy, and I scoop her up and run faster, to where we parked the bus. Sawyer is already on board with the two Spoke mecha, while Atticus frets at the door, waiting for us. I dump Murphy into the front seat as Atticus jumps up beside her. <How's your weight?> I ask 44-Mongoose.

<The two additional mecha are heavy,> the bus replies. <I am near my capacity, and I am not sure how fast I will be able to move. But get in anyway; we don't have time—>

<No, go now. Try to get a building or two between you and here,> I say. <I can run very fast. I have two legs, after all.>

<Got it,> 44-Mongoose says, and the bus jumps forward, sending people inside tumbling. I note that Sawyer has still not learned the seat-belt lesson.

"What the fuck? Go back!" I hear Atticus yell, and then see Murphy battering at the door, trying to get out, as the bus speeds off.

I run. I run like I have not run since I was brand-new, first free in the world, and full of the joy of being despite the terrible purpose that I had been given. I am not that mech any longer—I am not Death, never truly was, but now I have a real name of my own, and friends, and purpose—but I am still *fast*.

There is still a tiny lag in my reattached leg, but it is nothing. I reach seventy kilometers per hour, then seventy-eight, then—

Behind me, what is left of Building One explodes. The shockwave hits first and sends me flying, the pavement that was just moments ago beneath my feet rippling upward and cracking into jagged shards. I hit, roll, and am back on my feet again as the heat and debris push past me and I can see nothing for the smoke, but I can still run.

I emerge from the cloud—or it settles around me—to see the gates ahead open and a large gathering of mecha and soldiers, all looking my way. The bus is most of the way there, and Sawyer jumps out while it is still moving, and is shouting at her soldiers and waving with her good arm, but I cannot make out the words. I slow as Murphy leaps out of the bus and begins to run toward me, also shouting, but she sounds as if she is yelling at me through water. My peripheral systems report damage to my audio-intake system from the blast, among dozens of other alerts, none critical but several concerning.

"—!" she yells, still racing toward me and waving wildly.

"I can't hear you!" I yell back, and my own words are lost to me.

She tries again, and I shake my head, but I slow. Red is now also heading toward me, and one of the red-armored mecha from the trainwreck that were brought back for repair.

Finally, she is close enough that I can just hear what she's shouting: "You're on FIRE!"

I stop, and sure enough, there is smoke rising around me, from my back. I turn my head around one hundred eighty degrees and see that there are several large chunks of wooden debris and molten tar lodged in the edges of my back armor plates, and it is that, not my own shell, that is on fire.

The firemech outpaces Murphy, reaches me, opens the cannon-shaped mount on its shoulder, and blasts me with foam until I am coated and blind again.

I stand there as the foam slowly collapses in upon itself and runs down my body, leaving flecks of itself all over me and a growing puddle on the pavement. Red inspects me and says something out loud I cannot quite hear.

<I have damaged my audio input,> I send him.

<We can fix that,> Red says. <I'm afraid the heat of the fire appears to have damaged the inlay design on your back.>

My moth. <That can be left as is for now,> I say. I do not know how I feel about it.

<Murphy says your leg functioned well,> Red adds.

<I have the best human mechanic in the world,> I say.

After a pause, Red replies, <She says *best mechanic, human or otherwise*, and, I quote, '*You damn well better not forget it*'.>

<I will not,> I say. <I am pleased to see everyone is not killing each other.>

<Everyone is confused,> Red says. <Also, a building exploded very impressively. It is distracting.>

<I expect so,> I say. I walk toward Sawyer, who is talking to her men, and Murphy and Red follow along, and I realize suddenly that one of those internal alerts has been trying to tell me that I am down to less than point four percent of my energy reserves. <I am sorry,> I send to Red. <I am out of energy.>

I try to sit, but before I even get halfway to the pavement, I shut down and do not even perceive myself fall.

When I reboot, only a few hours have passed. I am in one of the manufactory's bays, a high-throughput charge line connected up to me, and I realize I can hear again. Murphy is nearby, putting tools away and chatting with Saff. Most of my alerts are off, and the few things still needing attention are minor.

When I sit up, Murphy turns around and smiles. "Saff found the hiccup in your leg," she says. "I'd have found it myself first if I'd had tools this good, though."

I see a familiar purple-white shape in the next bay. "Is 44-Mongoose okay?" I ask.

"Debris took out the rear window and damaged some of the equipment on the roof," Murphy says. "44-Mongoose themself is fine and feels it is unfair of you to try to race it knowing it is no longer a train."

"I will be mindful to be slower, at least in situations where I am not in immediate peril," I say.

<Are you anticipating more such situations?> 44-Mongoose asks me from across the room.

<I didn't anticipate this one,> I answer. <I think perhaps I underestimated the potential for volatility in conversations with estranged relatives.>

<You *think?*> 44-Mongoose says, and it seems a rhetorical question at best.

<Sawyer is coming in,> Saff tells me. <She and Red have agreed to a temporary truce, pending discussion with you. We could see you and your sib in the environment on the screen, but you both looked like you were just standing there, immobile, so there is some anxiety about what transpired and what may happen next.>

Sawyer arrives a few minutes later, three of her soldiers with her, and Red and Mauve trailing. The soldiers glance anxiously around at all the mecha around us, working, but the mecha ignore them, and after a while, the soldiers mostly stop staring and startling at every unexpected sound.

"My sib chose to end themself," I tell everyone, which is probably not in any way new or surprising information. "They had suffered a long time at Litchfield's hands."

"I had no idea that your sib's mind was still functional and under his control," Sawyer says. "But without them, what happens now with all the mecha with Litchfield's chips?"

"We will need to set them free," I say. "Many of them will have been prevented from ever developing self-awareness, and it will be a difficult transition. I do not know what they will do as they discover the joys and pitfalls of making individual decisions, but they can be protected and guided while they find their place and their purpose. There are also those that my sib directly infected, and they will continue to act as they have and work against all of us. They will need to be found, and they will be hostile," I say. "It will require both time and resources to undertake each of these efforts, and coordination. We cannot do this if we are at war against each other."

"I have fought my whole life to restore order, to restore something I believed in—I still believe in—which is responsible governance," Sawyer says. "I don't think I can let that go. I know I can't. But maybe there's room for that idea to grow. The President—"

"There's a president?" Murphy asks.

She sighs. "Yes. As Litchfield hinted, he's mostly a figurehead. A pliable figurehead, someone to do the bullshit stuff while I did the real work. But we will still need to talk. There will have to be formal documents, some sort of treaty, some leader on your side who can sign things, and some hefty stack of bureaucracy to point at and say *This is what we are doing.*"

I look at Murphy, and Atticus at both of us, and all three of us together say, "Ver."

"We have a flag," Atticus adds, helpfully, then looks at me. "What did you do with our flag?"

"Many bombs fell on it," I say.

"Crap. Well, we can fab another," he says.

"I can provisionally agree to a truce," Sawyer says. "I have some people to talk to, starting with those outside."

"As do I," I say, "starting with my people here."

Sawyer grunts, then turns on her heel and stalks out, her soldiers behind her.

"Did we actually do this?" Murphy asks. "Is this peace?"

"Maybe," I say. "For now. Let us hope none of us ever take it for granted."

44-Mongoose agrees to take us back to Greenapple; I want to go home, begin to rebuild at least some of my old life there, but the memory of Litchfield sitting in my house, bleeding on my floor, taking control of me, is not one I am eager to revisit so soon. Besides, Greenapple is a good place to begin the work ahead. We will need the freetowns.

Wenge brings us eleven more cabbages for our journey and is very clearly pleased with itself for its magnanimity and thoughtfulness.

We stop the bus outside the gates, and I seek out Sawyer. After everything, I feel it is proper I present her with some small inkind. "Thank you for giving me a chance," I say. "I have something for you."

She looks entirely nonplussed when I place several of the cabbages in her arms. "What the fuck?" she says.

I manage a shrug. "I do not know," I say, then I get back aboard the bus, behind the wheel, with my friends beside and behind me, the wind in our faces, and that is everything I have ever needed.

ACKNOWLEDGMENTS

When the first few bits and bobs of inspiration for this novel started wafting through the large, desolate vacuum of my brain looking for some amenable surface to settle on, dig in some tentacles, and grow, they were very much of a kind with the goofy nonsense that most of my stories begin life as. And I believe, however serious or dark a story becomes in the telling of it, starting in that place of humor and light becomes a lifeline for me as I write, keeping me from never quite getting lost on the way.

Sometimes, though, it feels like it comes very close.

This novel was by far the hardest thing I've ever written. When I first started putting words down, I was still processing losing my father, and trying to be support and help to my mother, now all on her own on the other side of the country. Originally, I was the middle of three kids, but both my brothers died young, and I don't think either my mother or I ever envisioned it coming down to just the two of us. In 2024, I made two separate cross-country road trips with her and boxes of stuff, the first time my father's, the second her own, as we relocated her back here to New England where the rest of our family lives. There was a lot of reawakening of old traumas, and maaaaaaybe a smidge of unexpected healing, too, but the sense of being hostage to the task was all-consuming; grief puts you in this narrow headspace where it dictates so much of your focus, and you just have to ride through whatever it hands you, each day. It's a lot like being on a rollercoaster, and there is no brake.

At least in mainstream US culture, we are pretty shit at coping with loss, and getting worse. "Time heals all wounds" is just blatantly not true—wishful thinking at best, and at worst self-serving gaslighting from late-stage-capitalist productivity culture that deeply resents any labor lost to the inconveniences of being human. Instead, grief is a weight, a thing you carry with you from then on, and eventually you get it settled somewhere about your person such that you don't have to pay too much attention to it anymore, but it is always there. When you add more, then you have to reshuffle and resettle it all, all over again. And while this novel isn't *about* grief, that runs as much through it as that thin cord of hope and light, wound around one another. And maybe that's just how life is, too.

I can tell you, emphatically, that writing a novel set in the near-future after civilization as we know it has almost utterly collapsed, requiring a lot of in-depth research on all the ways that would/could/will plausibly happen, is a very bad idea when the real world around you is trying to do exactly that. For myself as much as anyone else, I needed the book to still communicate hope and friendship, have humor, allow for light, without being either crassly slapstick or flippantly dismissive of the days we are all now currently living in. I think I've managed to pull it off? I don't think that's on me to decide, though. I do think we are each carrying the weight of that vast grief for the better world we all wanted, which once upon a time felt almost within reach. I don't think we get that dream back—and I think we need to acknowledge the flaws and fatal inequities in it that left the door open to where we are now—but I do believe, if we care, if we dare, if we refuse to leave anyone behind, that we can find and make a new one.

And maybe that is what this novel is about: not letting ourselves be stuck.

I am writing this in fall of 2025, and it'd be wonderful if things are already turning around by the time anyone gets to read this. Everything is changing and happening so fast that 2026 seems millennia away, and right now it's seriously terrifying, so I'm all for a bunch of feedback next year being all "yeah, but then we FIXED stuff, what are you even going on about?" Fingers crossed.

But, so, this is supposed to be acknowledgments and I've gone off on a long tangent once again, and I feel it's kind of important to make sure it's clear that I was a miserable wreck in slow-motion-falling-apart during most of the writing of this novel, enough toward the end to even land me briefly in the ER (Lessons Were Learned re: How Many Energy Drinks One Should Consume In A Day*), and that all the usual suspects (and some new ones!) who helped make this happen had to put up with me being stressed-out, overwhelmed, and even more scatterbrained than usual. Which means they all deserve EXTRA SUPER COLOSSAL THANKS.

(* definitely less than sixteen. A LOT less.)

My literary agent, Joshua Bilmes, continues to be one of the luckiest things that has happened to me in my writing career, and the rest of his team at JABberwocky are all kind, hard-working people. Like calls to like, I think. It continues to be a joy to work with them, and know I am in such good hands.

Similarly, I have enormous gratitude to the folks at DAW Books and Astra, and a big shout-out needs to go to my new editor, Madeline Goldberg, with the hope that she found working with me less trial-by-fire nerd-herding than it probably sometimes felt. Her insights and fresh perspective helped me get this novel to a place where it finally started to pull together and *work*. Likewise, I am extremely grateful for the fabulous cover art by Jeff Langevin, which so wonderfully captures the essence of my world and work, and I couldn't be happier at how the composition so deftly shows the friendship and camaraderie between my two unlikely heroes.

Richard Shealy, once again, is the Conqueror of Errant Commas, the Hierophant of Hyphenation, the Necromancer of Noticing Nonsense, the Unfailing Flagger of Foolish Wordfuckery, indeed the very GOAT of copyediting, and I cannot sufficiently express my appreciation for his eye for detail.

I also have to thank my awesome beta readers, Laurie, JT, and Robin, who are gently encouraging and absolute bastards in critique, exactly as they need to be. Likewise, I want to thank the old UMSFS gaming crew for patiently listening to me natter about plot stuff as I lose badly at nearly every tabletop game set in front of me, which doesn't make them any less fun for me at all.

Writing is a solitary thing made infinitely better by community, and I am keenly aware of how extraordinarily fortunate I am to have so many wonderful people who have become part of my life just because I took up writing on a lark one day twenty-five-ish years ago. It is strange treasure to have too many friends to name, but I have to shout out Shiela Williams and Neil Clarke, the Viable Paradise crew, the Absolute Write and Writer's Cantina regulars, our spin-off Discord, and my local and semi-local writer folks: Bear & Scott, Alex & Devin, Julie, Robert, and more. I also have to thank my fans, all over the world, who remind me that my words travel, and what a rare privilege and responsibility that is.

I also have to thank my boss and coworkers at my day job, who get me, and support this weird second career of mine. So far, we have not won the lottery together, but we keep trying.

More than anyone, I have to thank my kids, who not only put up with occasional nights where dinner is "microwave something?" but are encouraging, smart, amazingly creative in their own ways, and who more than anything else in the world give me hope, and give me strength and reason to keep fighting for that better future—

—a future that should include everyone, and that also means YOU. Please don't let go.

With love,

Suzanne